THE TIGRAN CHRONICLES: THE RESCUES

M. W. DENDLER

Serenity Mountain Publishing

Published by Serenity Mountain Publishing

Midland, Michigan

The Tigran Chronicles: The Rescues

©2025 by Meg Welch Dendler

All rights reserved.

www.megdendler.com

First Edition

ISBN: 979-8990827776

Cover design by Sweet N' Spicy Designs.

Interior design by Serenity Mountain Publishing.

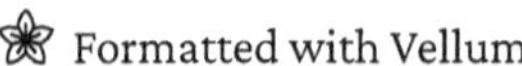 Formatted with Vellum

1

MAY 2178

Taliya sat motionless on the edge of the bed, barely breathing. Footsteps shuffled on the bamboo floorboards of the hallway. Her tail involuntarily swept across the bedspread, but being still no longer mattered. They were just outside the door. She sighed, trying not to dig her claws into the bedding because she'd only have to mend the punctures later.

"I can smell you out there," she whispered.

"No you can't," a kit's voice from the hallway responded. "You just heard our feets."

"Jai, I can smell you too."

The kits giggled, and muffled padding down the hallway indicated the twins had headed back to their rooms. Maybe they would stay there. *Why is this a drama every damn night?* Hiding in the bedroom hadn't helped.

"You are part tiger, you demons," she grumbled after them. "You should love to sleep."

More giggles echoed down the hallway.

Kano shifted in the bed next to her. "What's wrong?"

"Nothing. Sorry." She kissed him on the forehead. "Go back to sleep."

After three weeks away in Missouri—assisting with recovery from a Category 6 tornado that leveled three towns—she hoped he'd catch up on some rest. Then be ready for private time with her before the rest of the house woke up.

Assuming she ever got them all to sleep in the first place.

When she peeked out the bedroom door, there was no sign of the roaming twins. That was progress.

Heading into the living room, Taliya began her presleep round of the house. Gathering random plates and cups, she set them in the big metal sink and wiped down the bamboo counters. From the big window there, she checked out her parents' cottage, about thirty yards across an open lawn. Grammy Shreya and Grampa Jai had been by for dinner that night to welcome Kano home. Now their log cabin was dark.

Dilating her eyes to see better across the yard, she spotted the Belgian Malinois guard dogs resting peacefully near the chicken coop. If anything made it through the security system around the compound, Cairo and Elektra would know immediately. Their noses were at least as capable as a tigran's.

One of the barn cats raced intently across the field, hopefully after a rat. Keeping rodents out of the food storage sheds was an ongoing battle, requiring several random cats who came and went at their leisure, usually leaving new kitten recruits behind. Cairo raised his head to track the feline, then rested it on his paws again. Since Taliya and Kano's wedding celebration, no one but family and close friends had set foot on the property. But the dogs were still alert and ready.

The tigran community in the Ozarks had not exactly grown since the Gathering, but it had changed. Families from the camp and other parts of the country had relocated there to take over homes and property of tigran who had not survived the purge. Samson had arranged most of it. Each family had a nice plot of land—at least ten acres, usually more—but that meant they were spread out like an old-school farming community.

Taliya's family owned eighty acres her father purchased for his human history projects before she was born. A large chunk of that was the barley and wheat fields—for ale production, bread, or trading. There were bees for honey, chickens for eggs and meat, along with wooded land where Grampa Jai hunted turkey and deer. A small garden provided veggies. Taliya took a moment to appreciate their quiet, mostly self-reliant lives. Kano's comings and goings for government jobs was enough excitement.

A thud of something dropping or being knocked over came from the back of the house, and she swiveled an ear that direction. No crash, so probably nothing broken. Her hackles spiked along the back of her neck. *If they wake the girls . . .*

Kano had helped her get the one-year-old pair to sleep before he'd collapsed, patting one orange-and-black-striped back while she patted the other. Both Luna and Lilly, the L-twins, were excellent sleepers. The five-year-old twins, not so much. Pushing four feet tall now, but still like rambunctious puppies.

Taliya loaded the dishes into the washer and set it to run, then made sure the sturdy oak door was locked and the electronics were all off. She debated picking up the toys scattered around the living room, but that felt pointless. With the youngest four, there were always toys on the floor somewhere.

Marla had brought over her amazing cinnamon rolls, and Taliya gave them a quick sniff, knowing both overflowing baskets waiting on the big kitchen island would be gone when breakfast was done. It was shocking none were missing already. She was tempted to sneak one, but the kits would smell it on her. Maybe once they were asleep.

With order restored to that portion of the house, she shuffled down the hallway toward the bedrooms. The kits thought the giant tiger-foot slippers they'd gotten her for Christmas were hilarious, and Taliya loved how cozy they were. And silly. Also useful on a chilly spring evening.

She heard Kano's even breathing and slight snore as she passed the main bedroom. He'd gone right back to sleep, as males seemed able to do at the drop of a hat. He always slept like the dead for hours after a job. This return would probably be the same, though he'd get up for a cinnamon roll.

She paused across the hall at Aliania's door, but the gentle breathing from inside assured her the white kit was resting peacefully. At eight years old and nearly as tall as her adopted mother, this young one had her own set of issues and battles for independence, but sleep was not one of them.

Three out of five.

Mentally girding her loins, she continued down the hall. The scuffles of the twins scrambling into bed—realizing she was coming to check on them—made her smile, despite how annoying they were at the moment.

"I hope that strawberry butt and that orange butt are in their beds," she whispered as she turned off the bathroom light and gave them a moment to comply. Creaking springs and ruffling of sheets offered hope.

Stopping in the hallway space between their two doors, she dramatically peeked into one room, then across the hall into the other. Amrita and Jai both giggled.

"I know it's hard to calm down after Papa gets home, but you have to at least try. It's too late to be running around the house. Your tiger bits need sleep."

"But my human bits want to play Rampage Roadster," Jai whispered back.

"My human bits want one of Aunty Marla's rolls," Amrita said, her unique tannish-peach tabby-tiger stripe markings contorting into a frown against her white fur.

"No, and no," Taliya said, leaning against the door-frame of her daughter's room. "But . . . you can read, as long as you keep your furry bottoms in bed."

Jai groaned like this was a punishment and flopped over dramatically. But Amrita immediately clicked the little lamp on her nightstand and pulled out a copy of the new teen tigran mystery series. Written by a human, but he got it mostly right. Taliya waited until the kit put on her glasses. Amrita hated them, but using magnification for reading helped her vision. The white tiger DNA routinely involved crossed-eyes, and she struggled with that issue more than Ali or Kano.

Somewhat confident they would stay put and not wake the others, Taliya headed back to the dark living room and stretched out on the sofa. If she was wrong and they started roaming, at least she could avoid waking Kano again. She considered checking her messages, but her communicator was over on the kitchen counter. *Too far.* She sighed and closed her eyes for just a second.

The smell of warm cinnamon, sugar, and buttery dough roused her. Early morning sunlight slanted into the living room through the big bay window. She sat upright, ears perked, and took stock of her household, horrified she'd fallen asleep and left the older twins to their own machinations.

"Morning, Mama," Aliania said from the kitchen.

"Morning, Ali. Is anyone else up yet?"

"The L-twins are starting to stir, but not fussing yet. The pain-in-the-ass twins are out cold."

Taliya chuffed and wondered how late they'd managed to stay awake. The scent of breakfast would have everyone out of bed shortly. Marla's rolls already warming in the oven smelled heavenly.

Aliania moved the basket of eggs next to the electric stovetop and dropped a bit of butter into the cast-iron skillet to melt. Then she pulled a two pound package of bacon from the local butcher out of the cooling unit. Taliya watched in amazement.

"You're being awfully efficient and helpful this morning."

"I'm hungry," the white kit said innocently.

"And . . ."

"And maybe you can drive me to Gracie's later so we can watch a movie at her house?"

Taliya chuffed, glad that was the extent of the bargain. It always made her nervous when Ali went out into the world, but the village and local tigran offered a modicum of safety—friends and school and connections Ali needed.

"We should be able to work that out," Taliya said, stretching and flexing her claws. "I'm sure Grammy can take you. She has to pick up the boys from school for the weekend anyhow."

"Just make sure she drops me off first. The T-twins are big goobers around my friends."

"You have beautiful and delightful friends," Taliya said with a wink. "How could Tuscan and Tyler resist showing off? Especially after all week with *only boys* at school."

"Gross. They're, like, old. It is so not cool."

Taliya smiled at the idea that eleven was old and gross. Though they were the human equivalent of teenagers, which was not a tidy stage of life. And being away at high school now had provided education far beyond their classes on how to annoy their nieces and nephews.

Aliania wrinkled her nose and began breaking eggs into the skillet. She appeared to be preparing for a small army to dine, which was good because the herd would descend on the kitchen any moment.

Happy noises from the L-twins reached Taliya's ears, and she dragged herself from the comfortable sofa to get them before . . . *Too late.* Kano opened the bedroom door and groggily peered out.

"I smell food," he mumbled.

"Your eldest is cooking. Be warned."

He chuckled and yawned. "I miss good food almost as much as I miss all of you when I'm off on a job."

"Are you suggesting the government doesn't feed you well?"

Kano snorted and scratched the white fur of his ruff. "Canned meat is not real food."

The L-twins had begun to chat, and it sounded like they were up and clunking around. Kano glanced at the sound, then back toward the kitchen.

"Go make sure Ali doesn't burn the rolls," Taliya said. "Or burn the house down. I'll get the girls."

Kano frowned for a second before nodding. She knew he felt guilty for being away so much and leaving her alone with five kits, but it was what his job currently demanded. Rebuilding after natural disasters required skilled masons, and she was proud he was considered one of the best. Even if it kept him away from her for long chunks of time. She had her parents, with Marla and her tigran husband Parth just up the road—and a shred of sanity left. The mental list of things to do before lunch danced through her mind. Getting Ali on her transport to school was up soon, though she mostly kept herself on schedule. *What time is it?*

Cairo barked, but it was a happy sound.

"Your parents must have smelled the rolls," Kano said with a grin.

"Ali, unlock the front door for your grandparents," Taliya called to the kitchen.

With a squeal, the L-twins toddled out of their room and slammed into their parents' legs.

"Uppie, uppie," Luna said, reaching her arms for her father.

"Good morning, stinker." Kano picked her up and nuzzled into her neck while she giggled.

"You two, into the bathroom," Taliya said. "Get your business done before anyone else wakes up."

Kano put Luna down, and the L-pair thundered along the hallway.

"We need to build another bathroom," Kano mumbled.

"I'll add that to the list of things to accomplish in all

our spare time," Taliya said, wiping the fur on his sleep-rumpled face so the black lines matched up correctly.

They'd already doubled the size of the original log house, after building a separate house for her parents and brothers across the yard. She and Kano had their own private en suite bathroom, but five kits in one shared bathroom was going to become more and more problematic as they grew older. Especially for Jai, the only boy. She knew he slipped out the back door to pee in the woods more often than not.

Amrita and Jai wandered out of their bedrooms and started complaining about the L-twins already being in the way. The household com in the living room began a rhythmic dinging as Grammy Shreya and Grampa Jai came in the front door.

"Who's calling at this hour?" Kano grumbled.

With a sigh, he motioned Taliya to the kitchen and then staggered toward where it sounded like the L-twins were destroying the bathroom, tail flicking in agitation.

"I'll get it," Taliya sing-songed, heading for the com. Maybe it was about her memoir. Fans were chomping at the bit for all the details of her exploits during the Gathering and in the years after. She was still waiting to hear back from her editor.

With a wave of greeting to her parents and an assessment that Aliania wasn't ruining breakfast, Taliya sat down in front of the video phone and clicked to answer it. She was greeted by Samson, the ligran lawyer—part tigran and part liran, a rare mix. His tan face with distinctive liger spots appeared concerned, and Taliya's chest clenched.

"S-Samson, how are you?" she stuttered out nervously.

"I am fine, but why are you ignoring your messages?"

"I just woke up. What's going on?"

"We found the dragons," Samson said. "We need you in Australia immediately."

2

"I can't go to *Australia*," Taliya said with a snort of a laugh. "And are you sure about the dragons? We've gone off on so many wild goose chases."

"We are positive," Samson said.

"Hold on, then."

Taliya switched the call to the media wall, and the life-size images of both Samson and Reynaldo—the black panthran who had been the head dragon trainer—appeared, sitting at desks in Samson's small beige legal office. Reynaldo helped there from time to time with ongoing cases involving illegally captive creatures. Taliya smiled at her friends. It felt like they were right in the room. Aliania squeaked happily from the kitchen, probably feeling the same way.

"Would you get Kano, please," she asked Shreya, who nodded with wide eyes.

Squeals and arguing carried up the hallway to Taliya

as her mother joined the morning battle for some sense of order among the four younger siblings.

"Okay," Taliya said, settling on the sofa. "How can you be so *positive*?"

Reynaldo clicked on his com, and several images popped up across the middle of the media screen. Photos taken by an overhead drone. They showed vast areas of dried-out grass-land, several large buildings with dark metal roofs, and four white shapes clearly visible outside in a ring of sectioned-off ground in the middle. Taliya looked closely, ready to deny those shapes were Pegasus, Coconut, Polly, and her beloved Bunny—the dragon-like genetic hybrids from the refugee camp who'd been kidnapped, along with Taliya and Reynaldo, right before the end of the war. This wasn't the first time someone had gotten her hopes up about finding them, only to have it all fall apart and prove to be bad intel.

Kano joined her on the sofa and immediately focused on the image showing what looked like the dragons. He was one of the few other creatures in the world who had flown dragon-back, and he was as interested as her in finding the pterodragons.

"I know the photo isn't crystal clear," Reynaldo said. "They didn't want to risk getting too close and possibly setting off security alarms. But the anti-poaching troops on the ground have made visual confirmation and con-tacted us."

Taliya grumbled deep in her chest, excited but still hesitant.

"Where is this?" she asked.

"Deep in Queensland," Samson said. "Middle of nowhere. Troops have witnessed them flying in shipments of food, probably for the keepers as well as the dragons. There is nothing around there for hundreds of miles but dirt and scrub. It is an excellent hiding place."

Taliya grumbled again, and Kano put a comforting hand on his wife's back, rubbing in small circles.

"Australia," Taliya said. "So, there's nothing to be done about it. Who's willing to try to rescue them from another country?"

"We are," Reynaldo said confidently.

Taliya chuffed at him and pursed her whiskers. "Well, of course *we* are. But this is way beyond us. Besides the fact that they are basically under the jurisdiction of another government, can you imagine the cost of returning them to the camp? It's a level of drama and expense that boggles the mind."

"The first part we think you can help with," Samson said. "Call in a favor or two from the president."

Taliya considered this. Surely Padme—President Nakobi, currently running for reelection for her second term—would be willing to help coordinate a rescue with the Australian government. She was a loyal supporter of all genetic creations and their rights. Padme had backed up Samson's work dozens of times and helped get laws passed when needed.

"But what if the Aussie's want to keep the dragons?"

she said. "What if they were part of capturing them in the first place?"

"Then we have a whole different problem," Reynaldo said. "So that makes it the first place to start. President Nakobi can help us determine if we have that government's support or not. Then we can worry about how to get the dragons back to Canada. There will definitely need to be diplomatic involvement."

Taliya wished she could just bring the dragons to her home and their extensive property in the Ozark mountains. In her mind's eye, she could see Kano putting up a building on their land like the one he'd helped construct back at the refugee camp. Maybe they could just keep Bunny and let the Canadians have the other three. It made her wonder where Faria, Nimmy, and Karma—the other dragon wranglers—had ended up.

Kano cleared his throat, bringing her back to the moment. She glanced at him, and he slow-blinked his blue eyes at her, probably guessing what was spinning in her thoughts.

"Will you get in touch with the president?" Samson asked. "If you are uncomfortable with that, I can do it myself with my lawyer hat on, but I think it would be better coming from you. After all the work you two have done together, President Nakobi is more likely to get involved if you ask."

Taliya nodded. "Okay."

The pair on the screen visibly relaxed. They'd clearly been concerned about her refusal. It wasn't that Taliya was uncomfortable asking Padme for help, she just never used that connection to her advantage unless there were no other options. In this case, governments were involved. One of them was going to have to talk to the president, so it logically should be her.

Two tiny screams of frustration came from the bedrooms.

"I've got it!" Shreya yelled.

"Thank you," Taliya called back, and Kano chuckled.

"Maybe you can play on Padme's guilt a bit," he said. "Remind her of the two little gifts we brought back from that visit to the uncivilized Nuche Clan in Colorado."

The others joined him in his laugh.

"She will not take the blame for that," Taliya said. "But I'll gently mention it, if she's hesitant to help."

"She'll have to coordinate with the Canadian government as well," Reynaldo said, "since they're also involved in a sense of ownership of the dragons."

"Who do they actually belong to?" Taliya wondered. "The American government who created them? The Canadians only had them as part of the refugee program. The Australians may think they have just as much of a right to keep them. It's going to get very mucky."

Kano nodded his agreement, but Samson and Reynaldo didn't look concerned.

"Ask Nakobi for help," Samson said, "and let her worry about the politics."

"Gladly." Taliya frowned. "Keep the politics as far away from me as possible."

"Once we have the go-ahead," Samson added, "General Thompson is ready to gather a team and take us in."

Reynaldo grinned at the formal use of his mate Carl's title. Samson threw around the "general" part when he could. Brigadier General was technically correct but too much to say every time.

Kano leaned back on the sofa. "So Carl would actually go to Australia and try to reclaim the animals?"

"He and I would go, yes," Reynaldo said. "I was the head trainer.... But we will need help."

Taliya clenched her jaw, whiskers flared and ears stiff.

"Here we go," Kano mumbled.

"Taliya," Reynaldo said, flaring his own dark whiskers, "we'll need more than one creature the dragons trust. We need you too."

Before Taliya could respond to that ridiculous idea, both sets of twins thundered into the living room and launched themselves onto the sofa. Amrita cuddled into her mother's lap while Little Jai and the L-twins climbed on Kano like he was a jungle gym. Shreya followed behind and mouthed *sorry*. Taliya waved her away.

"Well, the gang's all here," Reynaldo said with a smile. "Good morning, kits."

"Uncle Rey-Rey!" Little Jai said, jumping off the sofa and running up to the media wall. He patted the image of Reynaldo's furry black face. "You're missing breakfast."

"Hello, Jai," Reynaldo said. "I'm too far away to join for breakfast this morning. Maybe another day."

As his Grampa moved him out of the way, Little Jai

whined his disappointment at not having a real visit from his cool panthran "uncle." Aliania quietly sat down next to Taliya and pulled Amrita onto her own lap, but she only had eyes for the magnificent ligran Samson. Ali's childhood crush had not diminished one bit over the years, and Taliya forced herself not to comment about the goo-goo expression on the girl's face. Who could blame her for adoring the smart, kind, glorious Samson? But it was best to pretend no one noticed or Ali would throw a fit.

"As you can see," Taliya said, pulling Lilly off Kano, "I can't go to Australia for a rescue mission. I'll talk to Padme, but that's it."

Samson and Reynaldo exchanged looks. Rey whispered something to the ligran that Taliya couldn't hear over the connection.

"Okay," Samson said, grinning. "Start with getting the governments talking. Then we will see what comes next."

"Nothing involving *me* comes next," Taliya said with assurance.

"Whatever you say." Reynaldo winked at her. "Let us know after you talk with the president."

Samson and Reynaldo waved at the tigran family on the sofa, and the call was terminated on their end.

"Awww," the kits moaned when the images ceased and left a blank white media wall.

"Breakfast," Shreya called from the kitchen, and the kits tumbled over each other, racing to get there first. Aliania followed behind, taking the basket of warm rolls from her grammy.

Kano grabbed his communicator from the side table and started typing.

"What's wrong?" Taliya asked, looking over his shoulder.

"I'm just letting the crew know I won't be able to make the next job in two weeks."

"Why not?"

"Because you're going to Australia. Or Washington. Or something like that."

"No, I'm not," Taliya insisted.

"Whatever you say, Tal." Kano mirrored Rey's words and his knowing wink.

Before she sat down for breakfast at the oversized wood table, Taliya sent a message to President Nakobi about the basics of what Samson had learned and what might be required from the government. The kitchen was clean and restored to order, Ali off to school and kits playing in the yard, before the response came in. The president would request the intel from Samson and be in touch with the Australian prime minister immediately.

Taliya settled on one of the oversized Adirondack chairs on the porch with her chai and watched the kits play tag—a perfect outlet for their unending energy. Elektra sprawled out next to her, but Cairo stayed close to the kits, lying down but ears up and alert. While it might be nice to have dogs that were truly just pets, having backup protection was even better. No one had tried to breach the property line, but Taliya knew fortune hunters and creepy humans were still out there. And two of her young ones were valuable commodities.

When she'd been kidnapped from the refugee camp and tortured by mercenaries, they said the unique kits were worth fifty million to the right buyer. Taliya doubted that value—or interest by certain unscrupulous parties— had diminished. Sending pure-white Aliania to school in town or off with friends was stressful. Every time. But Amrita, with her one-of-a-kind strawberry markings, rarely left the safety of the compound. Taliya had been immensely grateful when the L-twins both turned out to be standard orange tigran. Their futures promised to be more peaceful and normal. As normal as life ever was for a tigran in America, especially ones with an infamous mother.

Within the hour, the president messaged Taliya again. The Australian government claimed to know nothing about the dragons being in their country. They were willing to assist any rescue efforts and return the animals to America. Padme would contact the Canadian prime minister next to begin arrangements for where to deliver the dragons after their successful rescue. Taliya was glad deciding who ended up with the irreplaceable animals was not her responsibility.

A second message came through from the president, and Taliya whuffed. *Shit.*

"What is it?" Shreya asked, setting down a glass of iced tea and settling into a chair next to her daughter.

Taliya aimed the communicator screen at her mother.

> Be prepared to depart for Australia in two
> days. There will be no way to travel
> unnoticed. We will develop an excuse for
> your presence there.

"Well," Shreya said, taking a sip of her drink. "I guess that decides that."

"I can say no to her," Taliya said. "I've resigned from all that government stuff."

"I think we both know that's not how it works, dear. Tigran owe President Nakobi a world of favors for her help getting laws passed to protect us."

"And Samson probably told her I was integral to the operation."

"He probably did," Shreya agreed with a smile. "And it might actually be true. It's going to be no small feat, not only rescuing but getting the dragons out of Australia. They will need creatures the animals trust."

"Are you seriously okay with this? You do realize what it will mean for you."

"Of course, kitten. I can hold down the lair for a week or two."

Taliya's ears flattened at the thought of it. Her mother was wonderful, but her maimed hands and feet —missing the end of each finger and toe from the brutal declawing at the POW camp—made some tasks difficult. Of course, Aunty Marla, with her similar disabilities, would help where she could. As would Grampa Jai. Even with Ali and Kano's help, it was a lot to ask. All four kits ran past—screaming at the top of their lungs for no apparent reason but because they could—confirming all of her concerns.

"Kano should go with you," Shreya said calmly. "It can be a little vacation."

Taliya's communicator dinged before she could respond to that ridiculous idea.

> What if we say you and Kano are going to Australia on vacation? We could add some photo ops and make it a whole thing. It's a perfect cover story.

Taliya sighed, convinced Padme and her mother had clearly lost their minds.

⁂

BEFORE THE DAY WAS OUT, TALIYA FOUND HERSELF RAILROADED into an undercover op involving a pretend vacation with Kano, Carl, and Reynaldo that would conclude in a secret attack by hired mercenaries on the remote Outback location to rescue the pterodragons.

How to get the dragons back to America was still under debate. A trusted human at Australia Zoo, Robbie Powell, was arranging temporary housing for the massive animals in exchange for having them on display to the public for a month. He would also create photo ops at the zoo and around the Sunshine Coast. Samson said Robbie was "keen as mustard" about the plan. Aussies would be "stoked" over the celebrity visit. The continent had its own mixed-species creatures that had come into the public more over the last few years, though they'd quietly been part of the zoo staff for decades. It sounded to Taliya like a whole lot of brouhaha including some of them was in the works. Just the kind of drama she tried to avoid.

While Kano hadn't expected to be pulled into the mission, he seemed happy about it. Certainly more exciting than weeks of home duty without Taliya there for backup.

Before bed, the family sat down in the living room to discuss what was ahead. Aliania looked sad she couldn't go. She remembered flying on Bunny Christmas morning years ago at the refugee camp. While Jai and Amrita had flown as well, they only had vague memories of it. The L-twins were mostly confused.

"Are they real dragons?" Luna asked.

"Well, I suppose there aren't any *real* dragons," Taliya said. "But the scientists called them pterodragons when they were created because they look like dragons from a fantasy story. Most of their DNA comes from pterodactyls, along with a bird called a cockatiel. But no human DNA, like us. That would be terrifying. Do you remember how big they are, Ali?"

Aliania nodded solemnly. "They were huge, with massive wings, like a dragon should be. But all white and covered in feathers."

"The beaks always scared me," Kano admitted. "Very sharp."

"I remember their green eyes sparkling," Ali said, "and the way they yelled words."

"Kaaah! Kaaah! Go!" Kano did a serviceable imitation, and the kits laughed.

"One of them was yours?" Luna asked her mother.

"Yes, in a way," Taliya said. "I was one of the trainers. We hoped to teach the dragons ways they could help at the camp."

"Mama was a dragon wrangler," Shreya loud-whispered to the kits.

Most of them giggled, but Lilly looked more horrified than impressed with her mama's past life.

"So you'll be gone for days and days and days?" Lilly whined.

"Mama used to go away all the time before you were born," Aliania said with a shrug. "No biggie."

"I know it's not what you're used to," Taliya said, trying to smile. She hadn't been away from the L-twins for a single night since they'd been born over a year ago. The idea of it made her heart ache. "But you'll have Grammy and Grampa and Aunty Marla and Uncle Parth. Even your uncles on the weekends."

"Think of all the fun we can have," Shreya said, pulling Lilly into her lap. "And we can watch all of Mama and Papa's adventures along the way on the media wall. I'm sure the Australian news channels will follow the public part of their visit."

"What about the dragon-rescuing part?" Aliania asked with a frown.

"No," Taliya said. "That part is very secret and very undercover. Not a word of it to anyone outside the creatures in this room right now. Not until it's over. Understood?"

"Yes, Mama," all five kits chorused.

Taliya was glad they only had to keep the secret for a short while. Aliania was a worry, but she was old enough to understand the dangers of blabbing. She insisted she'd managed to keep quiet about what she knew when she'd visited her friend after school. The younger kits didn't have anyone to tell. Taliya had been homeschooling Little Jai and Amrita, for the strawberry kit's safety.

"So when do you leave?" Grampa Jai asked.

"Monday morning," Kano said, his tail tip twitching on the sofa next to him. "Two days is barely enough time to pull it all together."

"Samson is worried about the dragons being moved," Taliya added. "So we'll fly to Australia, do the public stuff, and then sneak off to rescue them in the dark of night."

She tried to make it sound very dramatic, but she had no idea how it would all go down. Samson and Carl were making the arrangements. She and Kano were just along for the ride.

Once the kits were tucked into bed—maybe to sleep—the adults met back around the kitchen island. Kano got a bottle of ale for each of them from the refrigeration unit. Taliya pulled out her communicator and swiped on a few messages to share with the family. She sighed and took a long swig of her ale.

"So you fly to D.C. first?" Shreya asked.

"Yeah," Taliya said. "Our flight there leaves early Monday morning. We need to rendezvous with the president and some of her advisors. Carl and Rey will join us there. Then the four of us will make the long flight to Brisbane. Trusted local contacts will meet us at the airport as part of our official tourism visit."

"Someone named Wolfie is in charge," Kano said with a grin. "I mean, it could be a human, but I'm betting on a genetic mixed-species."

Shreya's eyes went wide. "Probably one of the canine hybrids we learned about two years ago."

"I bet those Aussies have come up with some weird stuff." Grampa Jai flared his black whiskers.

Kano nodded and clinked the top of his ale bottle with Jai's. "I'm counting on it."

"President Nakobi says to pack a couple of formal outfits," Taliya said, "along with practical things for sightseeing and trekking around in the Outback."

"I still have my nice suit from our wedding," Kano said, referring to the formal ceremony on the compound in June of 2176, not their impromptu handfasting at the refugee camp so the family could stay together. "That with a couple of tunic and slack sets should have me all set."

"I can't wear my bridal sari," Taliya grumbled. "Too dressy. But I can unpack some of the outfits I used during formal political events. I'll get that box of things from the attic in the morning. You have a blue Diwali outfit up there. Can't hurt to have that too."

Taliya huffed with anxiety over everything that needed accomplishing quickly. "This Wolfie guy is arranging our schedule, but I don't know much more than that."

Shreya placed her hand on top of her daughter's. "Marla will be here for breakfast. Tomorrow, we'll get organized on what the household needs while you're gone and start the packing. The boys can drag themselves away from their gaming and help watch the kits. For tonight, try to get some sleep."

A light came on down the hallway, and tiny feet pattered around. A kit giggled.

"I'll go," Shreya said, polishing off her drink. "It's been a while since I helped get them to bed."

"Godspeed." Taliya raised her ale in salute and chuckled as her mother headed toward the bedrooms.

Giggles flowed down the hall, and then a gasp from Amrita. "*Grammy's* coming."

Sounds of running feet and scrambling back into bed followed. Taliya realized the change in authority might impress the older twins into behaving. For a few days.

3

The flight to D.C. Monday morning was uneventful —besides all the gawking at the pair of tigran in first class, which the flight attendants kept to a minimum. But the motorcade waiting to greet Taliya and Kano was not. Her hackles rose when security met them at the gate, remembering the fuss and bother, as well as the dangers, that came with her role as an ambassador for her species. A role she'd never sought in the first place. Sometimes the news media decided you were important, and that was that.

"Here they are!" President Padme Nakobi herself strode toward them through the airport, surrounded by her Secret Service team, which included two tigran. She wore a bespoke blood-red pantsuit that highlighted her dark skin and hair. Taliya suddenly felt underdressed in the brown tunic and slacks she'd worn.

The click and whirl of old-school cameras came from

somewhere nearby. There were always cameras when Padme was around, though Taliya knew a few passengers on the plane had snuck a photo or two as well. Their trip was likely already splashed around the interwebs. The deception had begun.

The president shook hands with both of them, keeping things formal in the public setting. Even stopping mid-shake to smile at a predesignated camera or two. Then she motioned toward the doors out to the street. Men in black suits had already gathered all of their luggage and were transporting it to the waiting cars. One of the perks of being famous and important, Taliya supposed.

As in the past on political assignments, Taliya and Kano were greeted by a line of imposing black SUVs waiting outside. A man opened the door to one in the middle, and she and Kano climbed in, followed by the president. The middle row of seats was turned backward, so Kano sat facing Taliya and Padme. A Plexiglass divider separated them from the driver.

"Well," the president said with a grin, "that part's over. It's good to see you two again. Been too long."

Taliya grinned back, not admitting she never expected to see the president face-to-face again once she resigned her political role.

Padme checked her com quickly as they settled in. "Reporters were waiting for you two before I arrived. The plan is already going strong."

"That didn't take long," Kano said, glancing out the window.

"Any tigran draws attention," Padme said as the SUV drove off. "But the pair of you are special. And headed to D.C.? Social pages are racing each other to figure out what you're up to. Let them flap around for a while. I'll release a distracting statement in an hour or two."

Taliya took a moment to check her communicator, in case the family had tried to reach her during the flight. Aliania had sent her a video of an otter playing with a ball. *Otters are adorable.* For a moment, she wondered if there were any otterman out there somewhere.

"They've blocked off the streets along our route," Padme said, "as they have to any time I leave the White House. However, locals have anticipated this is about your visit. I'm not sure who they're lining the roads to see: you or me."

As the SUV rolled along, Taliya was captivated by the thousands of people who stood along the roadway, apparently showing up at a moment's notice. But besides the welcoming faces and waves and cheers, some held signs calling them abominations. Freaks. Mutants. A few scattered boos reached her sensitive ears. Nothing new, but it always stung. After one particularly violent sign—with a cartoon image of a tiger being whipped bloody by a gleeful human—Padme placed her hand on Taliya's knee.

"Don't look," she said. "The supportive folks can amp you up, but there's always a couple of crazies in there too. They ruin it all. Ignore them."

Taliya nodded with a huff, but it was hard to ignore. Kano growled and frowned. She had never understood the hatred directed at her species, but then again, she'd never understood the abuse and extortion of tigers and lions and all kinds of other animals. Humans were a tough lot to sort out. A rock pinged off the door, and she flinched involuntarily, her tail puffing.

"Bulletproof," Padme reminded them. "And I'm sure that offender is already on the ground and in cuffs. Forgot who else is in this car. Or maybe it was intended for me." She shrugged and opened her binder that contained a yellow notepad, like something out of an old movie.

Taliya tried to let the plans for the day distract her. They were going straight to a government research facility, where sanctioned programs on mixed-species creation and study were in full swing. She'd spent most of her life thinking there were only a handful of genetically engineered animal/human species mixes, but new ones popped up here and there. Now that the scientific process was out of the bag, regulations couldn't keep up.

"We're meeting Jovita at the lab first," Padme confirmed, "so we can use the secure military lines there."

"*Ho*-vita?" Taliya questioned, pronouncing it like Padme had and looking back at the itinerary on her device.

"It's a Spanish name, so the J is pronounced like our H."

"Ho-vi-ta," Taliya practiced, making sure she said it correctly.

Padme nodded and smiled. "She's a puman—part cougar, what some call a puma, and part human. She has worked with us at the lab for three years now."

Taliya pondered what a puman would look like. *Why aren't they just called panthran?* Sometimes the groups were lumped together. Like she suspected Reynaldo was part jaguar, rather than just melanistic leopard. His build was more muscular, taller, with shoulders that rivaled Samson's, and his face structure was fuller and more "macho," for lack of a better word, than panthran in general.

The president's phone chimed, and she answered immediately. Normally, Taliya would leave the room in case it was classified, but there was nowhere to go. Padme made a *don't worry* swish with her hand.

"It's just my husband," she whispered. "He can't find Gabriel's homework." She winked at Kano. "No, honey, check the media room. He's forever leaving it in there."

Kano chuckled, though Taliya suspected he was more humored by another working mother than he was by his own once again in-demand wife. Taliya glanced back out the window while Padme handled the home-front emergency. She was grateful to only see happy faces along the street, waving and smiling. The crowds had thinned as they traveled farther from the airport.

When they arrived at the government lab, Secret Service agents escorted them from the SUV and ushered them inside through a back door. What felt like an unused hallway, dark and musty, led to a gigantic service elevator.

Padme, Taliya, and Kano stepped inside, but the security team didn't join them.

"Everything beyond here is highly classified," Padme whispered as the doors closed. "We won't need any protection." She tipped her head toward the elevator ceiling and said loudly, "Level two."

"Level two," a smooth female computer voice responded.

The elevator whooshed downward, making Taliya's stomach roil, before it came to a smooth stop. The door opened, and a blast of highly processed, sanitized air smacked her sensitive nose. Her hackles spiked from the tip of her tail to the back of her head. Next to her, Kano shuddered. It smelled exactly like the breeding facility in Colorado, where they'd been paired together by violent, immoral humans.

Kano squeezed her hand briefly and cleared his throat, though she could smell his fearful reaction. Logically, this lab would be antiseptic, like a research facility, but Taliya hadn't been prepared. Clearly, neither had Kano. An image of Colonel Narlin's body on the ground, throat ripped open and spurting blood with each final heartbeat, flashed through her mind. Trying to wash the gore from her claws in the bathroom of that horrible rape room.

Holding her emotions in check, Taliya forced her body to calm down. She focused on the memory of the whole facility exploding and crumbling to the ground. That brought a slight smile.

The trio stepped out into a huge underground warehouse space filled with stations of technical-looking equipment. The floor, walls, and ceiling were bright-white, like most facilities seemed to be. Taliya squinted her sensitive eyes against the harsh lighting.

At one of the workstations, she spotted a genetic crossbreed who must be Jovita. No one else was in the vast room. The creature rose from her chair to greet them. The puman was only about six feet tall—small for a crossbreed, almost dainty—and more grayish-brown than a liran, as much as Taliya could see past the white lab coat and slacks. As she drew closer, Taliya admired the dark markings that resembled elaborate eyeliner. Jovita's wide nose was as pink as Kano's, though probably flushed with excitement at the moment. She did look different enough from a panthran to justify a specific classification.

"Welcome, President Nakobi," the puman said with a fang-filled smile.

"Nice to see you again, Jovita. Let me introduce Kano Rama and Taliya Sharma."

Taliya extended her hand, and Jovita shook it with great excitement, claws popping out a bit, her green-gold eyes sparkling.

"It is a great honor to meet you, Taliya," she said. "I've been following you on all the media channels since the very first story of your kidnapping from the camp in Canada. You are just amazing!"

Taliya's skin flushed and her fur prickled. It was always odd to meet a complete stranger who felt like they already knew her based on events and details of her life shared around the world. And she'd never gotten used to praise and awe she didn't feel she'd earned.

"I'm happy to meet you too," Taliya said, trying to rein in any agitation. "I've never seen a puman before."

"We are mostly south of the border, though there are actual pumas in the U.S."

"I do believe there are some left in the wild," Taliya agreed. "It sounds like a hard life, constantly fighting with humans for territory."

"I've never spent much time beyond our government facilities," Jovita said, "so I'll have to trust you on that."

"Is this the same lab where you were created?" Taliya asked.

"I was born here, not created. I'm a natural Generation Seven. Even though we are free to live wherever we wish, it's safer here in the lab, and I can be of some help instead of fearful about my neighbors. My family and I have an apartment upstairs."

Taliya nodded her understanding. While she might live out in the world, she was grateful for their isolated property and the separation it provided from the human population.

"Jovita has already been talking with her connections in Queensland," Padme said.

Taliya sensed the president wanted to get things moving. "We appreciate your help."

"They claim to be unaware of the pterodragons in their country. It's always hard to know what is true when dealing with governments." Jovita smiled apologetically at the president. "But I sense they are being upfront on this particular issue. The governor says they will support our efforts to bring the dragons back to the Americas."

Taliya hesitated for a moment, not used to the term, but she quickly realized that the whole continent was technically one "America," regardless of how the United States generally considered themselves the only one using that term.

"Can you set up a call right now," Padme asked, "on the secure line so we can work out some details, or would you rather pass it on to us from here?"

"I'd love to help," Jovita said. "If that's okay."

"Absolutely."

Jovita escorted them to a computer station, and they all sat in front of a four-foot-wide monitor. The puman placed the call. In a few moments, the face of a creature appeared. Taliya gasped and hoped it wasn't as loudly as she suspected it was.

"Hullo!" the canine/human mixed-species creature said with glee.

"Hello, Wolfie," Jovita said.

Regardless of the fact they'd expected their contact to be a genetic mix, seeing the evidence in front of her was shocking. All that was visible on the screen was his head and shoulders. The basic physical structure was like a feline/human mix, but his nose and mouth protruded more, with a canine snout, pale-pink nose, and dark whiskers. His fur was a yellowish-ginger color, and he retained the tall ears of a coyote—or a dingo, she corrected herself, remembering the Aussie origin. While his eyes held a glint of gold, they were mostly dark-brown and reminded her of Cairo and Elektra. Taliya blinked slowly, trying to avoid gaping. Kano whuffed, probably assessing this new creature the same way.

"Taliya and Kano are here, as you can see," Jovita said, "so we've accomplished the easiest step in the process."

"No doubt," Wolfie said. "Next leg gets mucky. Long flight from yer capital to Brisbane. Wow, look at ya." He tilted his head and leaned closer to the screen. "Never seen a real tigran in person before. A might bigger than Jovita, there. Especially you, Kano my man."

"Nice to meet you, Wolfie," Kano said with a smile.

"Yes," Taliya choked out. "Nice to meet you." Wolfie was a lot to take in, and his accent reminded her of that loud, wild-eyed guy she'd seen in historical videos who liked to jump on crocodiles and always seemed to be handling some wild animal he probably shouldn't. If Wolfie said "Crikey!" there was no way she was going to avoid laughing hysterically. "Thank you for helping out on your end with this rescue."

"No worries," Wolfie said, seemingly oblivious to Taliya's discomfort, for which she was grateful. "Once ya arrive, I'll grab ya up at the airport, and we'll do all that touristy stuff first. Australia Zoo is right keen for yer visit."

A zoo wasn't top on Taliya's list of places to go, ever, but this particular zoo was in on the rescue operation. It would be rude to say no.

A loud *bing* rang through the room, and Jovita checked

her communicator. "They're here," she said and turned toward the elevator.

General Carl Thompson, in full dress uniform with bars, ribbons, and medals on his chest, and Reynaldo, wearing a simple navy tunic and slacks with open-toe sandals, strode across the room toward them.

"Holy smokes," Wolfie said, his jaw hanging open.

Taliya and Kano rose to greet their friends with hugs and smiles.

"You look ready to impress," Taliya whispered to Carl, adjusting his lapel and brushing off some orange fur she'd left behind as she stepped away from him.

"Shock and awe," he said with a smirk. "Shock and awe, whenever possible."

President Nakobi stood back until the reunion was complete. Jovita looked overwhelmed by the whole scene and hadn't even risen from her chair. Taliya imagined this was quite a lot of creatures and important people to have gathered in her highly classified lab. Reynaldo acknowledged both Padme and Jovita with a nod of his head, but Carl saluted the president formally, his face suddenly the picture of a serious military officer.

"General Thompson," the president said. "I'm so grateful you will be joining this operation."

"It is an honor, Commander."

"Yes, yes, at ease," Padme said with a grin. "I think this little group is long past so many formalities." She motioned for everyone to sit down.

Since there were no introductions—and Padme would

never overlook that—Taliya assumed Jovita had met Carl and Rey before. That brought a sea of questions to mind. Carl removed his beret, and the group sat back across from the monitor.

From the other side of the world, Wolfie watched them all intently through the video feed. Taliya noticed he was panting and stifled a laugh. Canine mannerisms from a part-human creature were going to take some getting used to.

"Wolfie," Padme said, "I'd like you to meet Reynaldo and General Carl Thompson. Rey was the head trainer in the pterodragons program at the Canadian refugee camp, and Carl will be leading this rescue effort."

"Nice to meet ya, mates," Wolfie said with wide dark eyes, his ears tall and alert. "Never met a black panthran either. Jovita, you look like a kit next to those big boys. And girl." He winked an apology at Taliya.

"Feel like one too," Jovita said with a laugh.

Padme gave a head wobble. "You get used to it." The president was only five foot four and petite. Not that it hindered her from commanding every room she entered, tigran at her side or not.

Carl was six foot five and solid muscle. As tall as Taliya, he held his own with Rey and Kano. Today, he was all business, a general in charge of a mission.

"We need to head to the airport soon," Carl said, pulling out his com and tapping on some files to send them out, "so let's review the plan quickly."

The team ran through everything from their arrival, tour of the zoo and the city with multiple photo ops, to the meet-up with a team in Brisbane to head into the Outback to rescue the dragons. It would all take place in a matter of days, and Taliya's head spun a bit as she mulled through it.

"There won't be much more communication that involves the actual rescue once you leave this secure site," Jovita warned. "Only a few coded messages to General Thompson."

"But the rest of it will be public knowledge, right?" Kano asked.

"Yes," Reynaldo said. "We will be super-public about the tourist stuff. Lots of social media postings and stories."

"Then we will load up in the dark of night," Carl added, "and head out into the bush."

"Very cloak-and-dagger," Padme said with a chuckle. "Hopefully, it all works as planned."

"But what happens after that?" Taliya asked. "Once we rescue the dragons, where are they going? How are we going to transport them?"

"Ah," Wolfie said with a smile, "that's where the four of ya are vital. Yer gonna fly them away."

The room was silent for several seconds.

"That's the plan?" Taliya bristled her whiskers. "To just hop on animals who haven't seen us for years and fly away into the desert?"

"We can't exactly drive huge cages out to them,"

Reynaldo said. "There's sure to be some security in place, and definitely nowhere to hide."

"All four of us have flown on the dragons and know what to do," Carl added. "That seems the easiest part of the job."

Taliya sat back in her chair and let the idea process. It certainly made the necessity of Kano's and her presence clearer. They were not just going to rescue the animals, they were going to ride on them in the air. What if the dragons didn't agree?

"Worst case scenario," Carl said, "we take over the facility and then transport the animals at a later date, but I think the main plan will go off without a hitch."

"The kidnapper blokes have been lettin' 'em fly some," Wolfie added from his end. "But we haven't spotted any ridin' 'em."

Kano nodded. "At least that means they should be strong enough to fly with us on their backs."

Taliya shook her head. Any one of them was a hefty load if the animals had been neglected at all. She met Kano's eyes and wondered how he was feeling about the flying part. In her early dragon-wrangler days, he had not been a fan, but he'd thoroughly enjoyed his one flight on Bunny. He'd even shown off and scared Taliya, thinking the dragon was acting up. Now he chuffed to assure her all was well.

"If flying them out is what needs to happen," Kano said, "that's what we'll do."

"For the sake of time," Padme suggested, "let's go with

flying away on those amazing animals. Where are they flying to?"

"Aw, that's the easy part," Wolfie said. "Australia Zoo Trust has thousands of acres of nature reserve about six hours away from where the dragons are bein' held. You'll just fly 'em there. Already have some buildings that'll work well for temporary housin' until we can get 'em to the zoo."

That was part of the deal. Aussie cooperation in exchange for exhibiting the dragons for a while. Getting them to a permanent home was a battle for another day. Just knowing Bunny and the other three dragons would be at a safe, regulated facility made her heart happy.

"What else do you need from us, Wolfie?" Carl asked.

"Just need yer infamous selves to get on the plane and head our way."

4

On the private tarmac in Brisbane, the capital of Queensland, Australia, the flight attendant opened the airplane door and a variety of fascinating foreign aromas flooded the cabin. Flowers and plants and earthy odors. Blinking against the bright light of the autumn May sunshine in the opposite hemisphere of Earth, Taliya took in their immediate surroundings, which were not much to look at. Pavement, as far as the eye could see, some of it marked with yellow paint and red lights. An SUV from the zoo with advertising signs all over it pulled in next to the plane.

Wolfie smiled with gleaming fangs as the group climbed down the airplane stairs. "G'day, mates!"

Taliya froze, catching his scent. Seeing the creature on video was not the same as in person. Wolfie was stocky and stood about as tall as an average human, but his ears added a good four inches to his height, sticking straight up like the dingoes he was related to. He was dressed in the khaki uniform of his job at Australia Zoo, which almost matched his coat, with bare furry feet sporting long, thick, nonretractable canine-like claws. She wondered if he could even wear shoes.

"Taliya," Carl whispered. "Be cool. Keep moving."

She chuffed a nervous laugh and continued her climb down the stairs. Wolfie met them at the bottom and excitedly shook everyone's hand. His hands were the same as his feet—nonretractable claws, like a dog. While trying to be subtle, she could tell he was scenting them each out as well.

"I hope the flight was good," he said. "Private plane and all probably helped. The zoo keeps one for movin' animals and such 'round the country. Came in handy today."

"Very handy. And thank you for meeting us," Taliya said, trying not to gape or examine the dingman too closely. "Your help is going to be invaluable."

"We'll put on a show," Wolfie said, "and then get yer drags back right quick without anyone bein' the wiser."

Taliya nodded and hoped that was true. She knew they would draw attention immediately. There were hardly any tigran in Australia, and Reynaldo stood out like a magnificent sore thumb.

The four of them climbed into the large gray SUV while Wolfie loaded their luggage into the back. Then he sat up with the driver—a dark-skinned man with aboriginal features who spoke in an accent so thick Taliya had no idea what he was saying. It was English. Probably. He and Wolfie chatted animatedly as the car left the airport, and Taliya wondered if there would be a communication barrier in this foreign country, even if they technically spoke the same language.

Once they left the airport, crews with cameras were waiting along the route, as anticipated. Details had been carefully "leaked."

What is Taliya, the famous tigran, up to today? Who really cares, anyhow?

Kano patted her knee. "Wave and smile, Tal. Wave and smile."

She nodded and sighed, obeying. For the next few days, she was going to be front and center and fodder for every camera around—whether professional or random Aussie social media enthusiast.

Camera crews, reporters, and hundreds of others lay in wait at the hotel, as had been arranged. She smoothed the fur on her face and the wrinkles from her clothes, hoping she didn't appear too rumpled. They all still wore what they'd started with, the day before in America. *Showtime.*

The SUV stopped at the front door of the hotel, and the driver jumped out immediately. Wolfie turned around in his seat to give them a thumbs-up, and Taliya took a deep breath, plastering a friendly fang-free smile on her face.

"Here we go," Carl mumbled.

The driver opened Taliya's door for her. The second

she emerged, the crowd started yelling each of their names and chanting what sounded like happy things. There weren't any threatening posters or smells of anger. Maybe the crowd had not only been invited but screened. She waved and smiled and tried to face each camera, one at a time, so they got the shot they wanted. President Nakobi had taught her well.

Kano moved to her side and ushered her toward the hotel entrance. Wolfie made sure only the assigned staff touched their luggage, and Carl brought up the rear, his military posture engaged. Taliya doubted there was any danger, but she was always comforted by that look on his face—alert and attentive to every detail. Still being in full dress uniform and magnetically handsome didn't hurt.

The door closed behind them, blocking the noise from the crowd. Inside the upscale hotel, it was quiet and peaceful, cheery classical music playing over a sound system. Beyond the tan marble floors, everything was decorated in cool shades of brown and blue, with bronze accents. It reminded her of the fancy hotels where she and the presidential team had stayed. Certainly not what she and Kano could afford for a vacation, but she wasn't going to complain. The zoo was covering every expense.

A lovely blonde in a powder-blue uniform hurried toward them, smiling pleasantly but radiating nervous energy. Greeting genetic creations was surely not a normal part of her job.

"Welcome to the Brisbane Grand. You are already checked in as guests of the zoo. Here are your keys for two suites." She handed one set to Carl and one set to Taliya. "We have you up on the eighth floor, for a bit of privacy, but we recommend keeping the curtains pulled when you are not enjoying the view and sunshine. Photodrones are hard to avoid."

Taliya nodded. Not a new problem after traveling with the president or for her own assignments. Things she had definitely not missed. Those photodrones were a menace, and their operators could publish whatever they managed to capture—even through a hotel window.

A bellman had loaded the luggage on a hover cart and led the way to the glass elevator. All of them piled in, and Taliya glanced at the weight limit on the lift. The five of them were much heavier than normal guests. The nervousness she smelled from the bellman was probably more about being in an elevator with the five of them because he pressed the button for the eighth floor without hesitation. Watching the lobby drop away as the elevator ascended made her stomach clench, but it was a pretty view of the atrium and the other floors. The building looked to be open in the center all the way to the top, maybe another ten floors above them.

"Amrita and Jai would insist on riding this up and down a thousand times," Kano whispered to her.

"*Two* thousand," she whispered back. She hoped the strawberry kit somehow managed a few adventures like this in the future of her sheltered life.

The elevator opened, and the bellman led the way to the rooms. Kano used their key to open the door to a huge suite with a dining table and small kitchenette. As with the lobby, it was beautifully decorated in tan, brown, and blue. Through a side door, Taliya could see an enormous bed with a bronze-colored duvet. The bellman cleared his throat behind her, indicating she needed to move so he could bring in the luggage. She laughed and shifted to the side.

"Sorry, just appreciating this huge room."

"Only the best for visiting dignitaries. The toilet is through that way. There's a kitchen, with some snacks in the refrigeration unit and pantry. Room service only runs till midnight since it's a weeknight. Menu's on the table over there."

"That's all perfect. Thank you," Taliya said, selecting their luggage from the hovering cart.

The bellman hung their bag with the dressy clothing options in a closet near the door. Kano moved to get a tip from his wallet, but the man waved him off. "Already covered, sir. Your group has the whole package."

Taliya and Kano exchanged looks, not sure what the whole package involved, but the bellman was already heading the cart next door to Carl and Rey.

Wolfie scanned Taliya and Kano's suite, seeming satisfied. "Right, then. Catch a snooze, shower, grab a snack, relax a bit, and I'll meet ya for dinner here in the hotel at six. Easier than dealin' with an outside situation."

"That sounds wonderful," Taliya said, thinking of both the shower and the meal. She was suddenly starving and exhausted. Traveling, in general, was another thing she hadn't missed at all. Especially internationally. She'd often wondered if you could die from jet lag, and this trip allowed zero time for assimilation.

Wolfie headed off to check on the guys next door and whatever the rest of his day entailed. Kano wandered to the window.

"Amazing view. I think that's Moreton Bay." He pulled the curtains closed. "I'll let the family know we've arrived and all is well."

Taliya waved her hand wearily in acknowledgment. "I forget how much time changes kick my ass. And it's suddenly fall. I guess that's better than an Outback summer."

Kano finished sending his message, slipped off his shoes, flopped down on the long powder-blue sofa, and threw his feet up over the back. Taliya laughed, slipped off her shoes, and collapsed on the other sofa, putting her own feet up as well, flexing her claws a few times to stretch.

"I could use a shower," she said.

"Me too. Before or after some food?"

Taliya pondered this serious question. "Before."

"You go first."

Taliya sighed and swung her feet onto the floor. "I suppose I'll feel better after."

Kano gave her a thumbs-up without lifting his head. She spotted a bag of "crisps" in a basket on the table and tossed them to him. He moaned in gratitude and ripped it open.

Taliya rolled her suitcase into the bedroom. There was a rack next to the big window, so she set her luggage on it. Looking out at the amazing view of the bay before pulling those curtains as well, Taliya wished they could spend a little more time on a true vacation. The water looked welcoming. It had been a long time since she'd enjoyed a good swim. *We should dig a pond on the property one of these days.*

The bathroom was as massive as the rest of the suite. The dark marble walls and floor with gold veins running through them made it feel like something in a mansion. Everything she would need—from soap to shampoo and toothpaste—were laid out on the counter, so she decided to use the freebies instead of what she'd brought. It would be interesting to sample the local brands. She turned on the shower and called to Kano, "There's more than enough room for both of us."

He chuckled but didn't move. Probably just as well. She didn't have the energy for whatever a dual shower with no kits around might lead to.

Taliya stepped under the warm water and let the grime and odors from the roughly 24 hours of travel wash away. It was odd to enjoy a shower without at least one kit interrupting or wanting to join in. She scrubbed and relaxed, relishing the soft eucalyptus smells of the soap until her finger tips pruned up. After drying her fur with a towel, she used the hotel's hairdryer to finish up, hoping she wasn't shedding too much. Then she slipped on the forest-green slacks and tunic she'd picked for dinner, pulling her still damp tail through the hole in the back of the slacks.

Kano had come into the bedroom and was rifling through his own suitcase on a separate rack. "Feel better?"

"Ages better," she said. "All the soap and stuff is provided in there."

"I feel like royalty."

"Wait till you see the bathroom."

Kano glanced that way and then scooped up his change of clothes. "Wow. If only they'd used some marble."

"Yes, it is sad. So boring," she said with a tired grin, setting an alarm for dinner on her device.

Taliya stretched out on the bed, delighting in the silky feel of the duvet. She loved her whole gaggle of kits, but vacations were pretty amazing. Kano turned on the shower and moaned in delight. Closing her eyes, Taliya relaxed into the comfort of the quiet room, where no one was watching or expecting anything from her.

<hr />

DINNER WAS UNEVENTFUL AND MOSTLY SMALL TALK. PRYING EARS could be anywhere, so Wolfie chatted about the zoo, its history, blah, blah, blah. Taliya hated small talk. The dragons were out there. Hopefully staying put. She was away from the kits. Who knows what was happening back at home. There was work to be done here, but not tonight.

Chewing her steak slowly, she tried to pay attention to Wolfie's stories.

She became intrigued to visit the zoo as he listed all the species they had and the efforts toward natural enclosures and animal care. Preservation verses exploitation. Many were extinct or barely hanging on in the wild. Feeding a giraffe with a long purple tongue sounded fun. There was a lot about crocodiles—or crocs, as Wolfie called them—which were a major focus for the zoo. It would be a full day tomorrow, and she tried to get as excited about it as Wolfie. Next to her, Kano all but inhaled his food, even quietly moaning now and then over a particularly delicious bite. She tried to pretend that wasn't an unconscious commentary on her mediocre cooking skills.

"Jaxon will give ya the full tour," Wolfie said. "He's a rooman. Big feller."

"Rooman?" Carl said with a frown.

"Yeah, ya know, part roo, part human. One of our most popular mixed-species."

The four stared at Wolfie for a moment in confusion, but then Kano burst out with a laugh. "A kanga*roo*?"

"Of course," Wolfie said. "What'd ya think I meant?"

Taliya tried to envision what a rooman would look like. Big feet with sturdy legs, maybe. Big ears. *Can they jump? What's their purpose?* Scientists in the U.S. rarely created a species they didn't feel served some need—like tigran were originally designed to be rescuers and builders, stronger and more efficient than humans. As she understood it, kangaroos were as common in Australia as deer in the Americas. And there were no deer/human mixes that she knew of. *Who would bother?*

As the group chuckled over the misunderstanding, the waiter arrived with dessert, his hands shaking slightly as he passed around the plates of lamington. Taliya watched him scurry back to the kitchen, a waft of fear-filled aromas left behind. He was probably trying to play it as cool as he could, but having to serve a table full of huge genetic creations—all from apex predators, no less—was surely unnerving. Even Carl in his casual Army uniform was intimidating.

It hadn't escaped her attention that they were seated alone in a side room of the hotel restaurant—a space for small events or meetings. Was the privacy for their protection from prying eyes or to keep the humans staying at the hotel from being anxious throughout their meals? *Maybe a bit of both.*

After dinner, Wolfie headed home and the four "tourists" decided to return to their rooms for the evening. Kano had suggested some ale at the hotel bar, but just their presence in the lobby discussing the option had brought uncomfortable attention and whispering. And one determined child.

"Mommy, look at the big kitties!"

The group turned as a child of about five barreled in their direction, a focused look on his face, arms extended like he planned to hug them. Behind him, the horrified and panicked look on his mother's face almost made

Taliya laugh. His mom raced to grab him up around the waist before he made it across the lobby, and the boy bellowed an angry scream that echoed around them, thrashing and kicking against her restraint.

"I wanna pet the white kitty! I wanna pet the white kitty! I wanna pet the white kitty!"

Trying to set aside the innocent use of the word *kitty* —which spiked all kinds of bad memories for her and was usually a vulgar insult to tigran—Taliya considered how to handle the situation. Kano moved toward the child, motioning an *it's okay* with his hand.

"If he wants to see what my fur feels like, it's fine with me," Kano said.

The child stopped struggling, but the mother's eyes went so wide Taliya thought they might pop right out. Without a word, she ran from the room, the child in her arms now screaming again at not being allowed to pet the big kitty. The all-too-common odor of human fear was left behind. Taliya sighed. *I should be used to it by now.* The scene—scrutinized by dozens of other humans in the lobby—changed their minds about anything more public that night.

"Do you have to deal with humans being weird when you're away for jobs?" Taliya asked Kano as they both changed into pajamas and got ready for bed. He'd never mentioned anything like that happening.

He shrugged. "No one tries to pet me, if that's what you mean. No. It's usually the same crew I work with all the time. I guess they were weird at first, but it's been years now. And I'm not always the only tigran. We usually stay in private lodgings provided by the company, though I do have to travel back and forth. That's why we tend to drive, instead of using airplanes. Or fly privately. Less attention."

Taliya flopped on the sofa and turned on the media wall. "That kid would have been disappointed anyhow, if he was expecting soft kitten fur." Tigran fur was like a tiger—rough, stiff, more like horse hair than a house cat.

She was grateful they'd decided against having drinks in the bar, but she wasn't ready to sleep yet. Her afternoon nap had taken an edge off the travel fatigue. "I prefer it when we just stay on the property at home and never have to be stared at. Let's get the dragons rescued and go home."

"Try to enjoy this part of the trip." He joined her on the sofa, pulling her into his arms. "Tomorrow, we have a visit to what sounds like a great zoo. No mixed-species in cages at all."

Taliya shuddered. "That would be horrible. I'd refuse to go."

"Of course we would."

She found a rerun of a silly comedy show the kids loved and figured it was good enough. They watched mindlessly for a few minutes before Kano got restless.

"You know," he said, "there are other things we can enjoy about this time away from the house full of kits." He wrapped his tail around her leg and chuffed into her neck.

"Good thing I took a nap."

5

The next day was perfect for a very public display of vacationing: a trip to Australia Zoo. The autumn sun warmed the air just enough but not so much that creatures covered in fur couldn't enjoy a day outside. After a quick breakfast through room service, Wolfie picked them up at nine o'clock. Carl had opted for his casual gray/green camo, and the three creatures all wore tunics and slacks with comfortable shoes. Very civilized and ready for any photo ops.

At the front gate, Wolfie passed them off to Jaxon, their rooman guide, in front of about five hundred screaming fans and members of the press. Taliya did the smile and wave thing, and cameras caught every moment. Meeting Jaxon for the first time so publicly demanded she keep a straight face. She'd done some research on the interwebs the night before, so she wasn't shocked by his appearance.

The rooman could give Samson the ligran a challenge for his size and impressiveness. Taliya had seen photos of full-blooded male red kangaroos that were huge and had abs like a boxer, so adding human DNA to the breed led to a creature who resembled an epic prize fighter. Jaxon the rooman stood over seven feet tall, with a muscular tail spreading out four feet behind him, while his legs were a mix of human and kangaroo, with powerful thighs and long bare feet sporting serious nonretractable claws. On his elongated fingers, they were trimmed but still impressive. He had reddish fur, a protruding snout with a black nose and short whiskers, a square jaw, and ears even taller than Wolfie's. His specially designed khaki outfit designated him as a zoo employee.

Waves of testosterone from Kano at the presence of another alpha male wafted through the air, so Taliya tried to appear unimpressed. But it was a struggle. Jaxon was a burly, magnificent sight to behold.

Once inside the gate and away from the worst of the crowd, Jaxon gave them each a map of the zoo.

"I'll let you explore before we do some behind-the-scenes special tours," he said with a grin, revealing oversized front teeth. "Have a wander. I've assigned two guards to you, but they'll keep their distance and only get involved if humans are givin' you grief."

He pointed out two other equally impressive rooman nearby, who both nodded in response. Taliya supposed being security guys was a good occupation for the brawny creatures.

"Your park has an astounding range of animals," Carl said.

"And many that are extinct in the wild," Reynaldo added, looking at his map. "Polar bears and cheetahs and koalas. It's an amazing mix."

"We work hard to protect all the animals we can," Jaxon said with pride. "But it's a never-endin' fight. Most of the species who used to live freely in the grasslands here can't make it there now. Maybe someday, when the climate starts to cool down again."

Taliya nodded but was less confident that day would ever come. Certainly not within any of their lifetimes. "Thank you for helping us tour your zoo. It's a great start to our vacation."

Jaxon winked. "Right. *Vacation.*"

So he knows. Must be trustworthy.

"What's a Crocoseum?" Kano asked, pointing at a big sign advertising it.

"That's the daily croc show. Been goin' on for centuries, since 2004. Big chance to show off those amazin' reptiles." He hesitated. "You know what'd be great? I'll see if I can get you in as special guests to feed the crocs."

Taliya whuffed. "Like, actually *feed* them?"

"Right on," Jaxon said. "It's part of the daily show. Imagine if fans got to see you out there with one of them big monsters. Crocs would love it as much as the mob. Let me give the boss a bell."

Jaxon stepped aside and pulled out his communicator. Taliya glanced questioningly over at Kano.

"Well," Kano said with a shrug of one shoulder, "it would play into the whole tourist thing."

"I've never seen a real crocodile," Reynaldo said. "Can you imagine if scientists did a human and croc hybrid?"

Everyone considered that for a moment. Taliya shook her head, chasing away the terrifying image. "No, thank you."

Jaxon hopped back over to them with a grin on his face. "Boss was right keen when I suggested it. You're doing the four o'clock. Last of the day. I'll get you there early for some instructions."

"So I guess we're feeding crocs," Kano said.

His nose flushed a deep red, but Taliya wasn't sure if it was from excitement or worry.

"Have fun," Jaxon said, "and don't forget to nab some fairy floss. It's a tourist requirement. I'll join back up with you in a bit."

He turned and hopped off at a leisurely pace, checking exhibits along the way. Taliya had noticed he sometimes walked but seemed to prefer normal roo locomotion.

"What in the world is *fairy floss*?" Kano asked.

"No idea," Taliya said.

Reynaldo and Carl shrugged the same response.

They spent the next hour working their way through the zoo, spending time in front of each exhibit. Some housed animals Taliya never expected to see in real life— elephants, gorillas, hippos, rhinoceros. She was grateful they lived in large, well-maintained enclosures that replicated their natural habitat, with places to hide and open spaces to run. The elephants even had a pool with a glass side so guests could watch the massive pachyderms swim.

"You'd think they'd sink like a stone," Carl said, snapping a photo.

There hadn't been any tigers yet, and that was a relief. Taliya had met a full-blooded tiger. Literally wrestled with it in the Colorado wilds during a capture of the out-of-place feline. It would be depressing to see one trapped in a zoo—however nice the exhibit and no matter how vital it was because there were so few left in the wild.

As they moved toward the Koala Adventure, Kano snorted. She glanced his way, and he pointed to a food stand up ahead. In blue, pink, and orange letters, the sign said Funtastic Fairy Floss. With smiles, they headed toward it. One look inside the booth answered the lingering question.

"Ah, cotton candy," Carl said.

Taliya chuckled. "*That* I've heard of. Never tasted it."

"We'll take four." Carl reached for his wallet. "I mean, how many times are you going to get to eat something called fairy floss?"

"What colors?" the teenager working the stand asked, trying to play it cool. Taliya could smell the truth, even through the pungent sugary miasma. He was terrified.

"Orange," Taliya said.

"Two blue," Reynaldo said, answering for Carl.

"I guess I'll try pink," Kano said. "Does it matter, flavor-wise?"

"Yes, sir," the teenager said. "Pink is strawberry. Blue is blueberry, and orange is, well, orange."

Not being a big fan of fruit or sugary treats, Taliya wasn't sure she really wanted a whole clump of the stuff, but she was game to try. The teenager took the cash and handed them each a large wad of fairy floss on a thin paper cone.

"Thank you, son," Carl said, slipping what looked like a large denomination bill into the tip container.

Taliya wasn't sure about all the colorful foreign money, but it made the teen's eyes light up, so she must have been right.

"Thanks, mate!"

"No worries," Carl said with a slight salute, looking very proud of himself for pulling off the Aussie phrase.

Walking away from the stand, the three creatures stared at the fairy floss, not sure where to start. Carl laughed, ripped off a big piece with his fingers, and popped it into his mouth.

"Best not to bite right into it," he said. "Very sticky."

Taliya hesitantly followed his example, being careful not to get the fluff in her fur. That was going to be a task all on its own. It felt like spider webs, but once it hit her tongue, it melted into a sugary syrup. The orangey flavor didn't really taste like an orange, but it was pleasant.

"I'm not sure whether I like this or not," Kano said.

"We'll certainly get a sugar boost," Reynaldo said with a laugh. "Woo-eee."

Taliya found the more she ate, the more got stuck in

the fur on her hands. The fur around her mouth grew stickier and stickier.

"The kits would love this stuff," she said, licking a finger to get a bit out from under a claw, "mainly because it's so messy."

Looking at Kano, she laughed at the ring of pink sugar bits around his mouth. Reynaldo appeared to be faring better, but maybe she just couldn't see it on his black fur. When they reached the Koala Adventure, Taliya had eaten more than enough of the fairy floss. She tossed the rest of the sticky mess into the garbage and looked around for a sink. There was a bathroom nearby, and that was probably a good idea anyhow.

"I'm stopping here," she said, pointing at the restroom.

"Me too," Kano said. "I really need to wash my hands."

"And your face," she said, motioning to the ring around his mouth.

Kano tried to lick some of it off.

"Your tongue is fuchsia!" She snapped an image to send to the kits later.

They both turned to Reynaldo, and he stuck out his bright-blue tongue.

Carl stuck his out as well, proudly showing off the blue dye covering it. "It's not good cotton candy if your tongue doesn't change color."

After getting photos of all of them, including a selfie of her orange tongue and a group shot, she headed into the bathroom. Washing her hands and face, Taliya could feel the sugar buzzing around in her body. It was the most she'd ever eaten at one time, and it was making her a little dizzy. She used the toilet carefully. No one came in the restroom while she was there, and she suspected the rooman guards had kept others out. They were being discreet, but not one human had approached them for a selfie, which was unusual when in public. A welcome shield.

After checking her reflection in the mirror and washing her hands again, she joined the guys back outside. Their faces and hands were clean as well now, but she suspected all their tongues would be discolored for several hours to come. The rooman guards were hovering nearby, but guests stared and gaped from a distance. Pictures of them eating fairy floss were probably all over the interwebs by now. A public vacation was the intention, so it was hard to complain. Ignoring their spectators, Taliya led the way inside the koala exhibit.

It was a huge section of the zoo, probably because this was one of the few places in the world native koalas still existed. Signs explained that as temperatures in the grasslands grew hotter, koalas couldn't get enough water to survive from the eucalyptus leaves that were the sole source of their diet. Bush fires had become extreme over the decades, killing thousands more. The only way koalas had survived total extinction was human intervention—providing water for them out in their ranges and then providing sanctuaries in captivity when all other hope was lost.

This particular zoo housed fifty koalas in different enclosures and boasted an active breeding program, inter-changing animals with other zoos on the continent to maintain the diversity and health of the species.

The four of them wandered through the exhibit, read all the signs, and observed the few animals who were awake and moving. Koalas didn't really seem to do much but eat and sleep. Photos showed how their young were born the size of a jellybean and grew inside a marsupial pouch. It made Taliya wonder if rooman had actual pouches. At least the females. Had the humans designed that feature out, or had nature kept it in?

At the end of the pathway, there was a booth set up where guests could hold a koala for a photo op, with a queue waiting for a turn. It parted like the Red Sea for Moses at the sight of the two tigran and the panthran.

"We don't need to cut the line," Taliya assured the humans. "We can wait our turn."

There was some shuffling, but no one got back into the queue. Taliya looked to Kano, and he seemed uneasy too. People were sure to post on social media about seeing them, and Taliya didn't want to be rude.

"Excuse me, umm, Miss Taliya, ma'am," a little girl with wide green eyes said. "I'd rather wait and watch *you* hold a koala."

The others smiled and nodded. Apparently, their presence had just made the Koala Adventure even more interesting.

"Okay, then." Taliya looked to the keeper holding a waiting koala. "Is it okay? Do you think I'll scare it?"

"I dunno," she admitted. "You're our first tigran. But let's give it a go. If she's scared, I'll just take 'er back."

Taliya moved to the X on the floor, and the keeper gently transferred the animal from her own arms to Taliya's furry ones. She was surprised by how heavy the koala was. Solid, like a sack of flour. It smelled like cough drops and eucalyptus leaves. The gray bear-like animal tilted her head back and stared at Taliya, nose working overtime, tiny brown button eyes taking her in. The tigran gave her a minute to absorb the unique smell, not sure how else to assure the animal that all was well. After a few seconds, the koala just glanced around at the others and clung to Taliya's tunic like a tree branch.

"She seems content," the keeper said, "so smile for the picture."

Taliya obeyed, keeping her fangs covered. No need to freak out the zoo guests. There were several clicking sounds, and then images of Taliya and the koala appeared on a huge monitor next to them. Pleased sounds of *oohing* and *ahhing* came from the crowd, and Taliya agreed the photos had turned out well. The koala looked toward the keeper, seeming to know she was done with this weird guest, and Taliya handed her back.

"I'll send them all to Jaxon so he can get them to you," the keeper whispered. "Do ya reckon it would be okay to post a few on our public account? Locals will lose their minds over it."

"Yes, that's fine," Taliya said, knowing that was part of the deal. The crowd in line had surely snuck some as well.

Kano took his turn next, looking fascinated by the little animal. Reynaldo made sure Carl went before him so the crowd didn't wonder why this human was cutting the line. When Rey cuddled the koala, Taliya wondered if he and Carl wanted kits—or human children. They were delighted by hers, but maybe they were grateful when visits were over and they could go back to their own quiet, tidy lives. Carl stepped back in, and the pair got a picture with the koala between them.

After taking a few selfie-style photos with guests and signing autographs—while the rooman guards moved closer to assure no one got too overly friendly—the four of them headed out the back of the exhibit. Wolfie was waiting for them on some kind of fancy dirt bike that looked very handy for scooting around the zoo.

"Outstanding shots!" he said. "Mob on the interwebs is going wild. We're pretty used to mixed species 'round here, but not many feline blends."

"Your guests seemed pretty excited by the whole thing," Taliya said. "And it was definitely the highlight of my trip so far."

"You two blokes looked right nice with that koala," Wolfie said to Rey and Carl. "Replace that with somethin' a little closer to either one of yer species, and it's a family portrait."

"Maybe someday," Rey said. "Being able to get married would be a better first step."

His golden eyes looked sad, and Carl stared at the ground, hiding whatever emotions might cross his own face.

"Ya know, it's all legal here, mates. If ya wanna get hitched, get hitched."

"Oh gods, yes!" Taliya's heart leaped and she burst out, "You have to do it. Get married while we're here."

Carl and Reynaldo stared at each other, and Taliya could only begin to guess what was racing through their minds. She'd always assumed they wanted to be married, but what if she'd forced them into an uncomfortable decision?

"I'm sorry," she finally said when the silence lasted too long. "Maybe it was a dumb idea. There's enough going on this trip without throwing anything more in there." Her hackles rose at the stress of her misjudgment.

Carl smiled, and Reynaldo reached for his hand, eyes glowing.

"It sounds like a wonderful idea," Carl said. "We would have done it the moment Rey was rescued, if we could have."

Kano put an arm around Taliya's waist and wrapped his tail around her leg. She copied the tail wrap, rested her head on his shoulder, and chuffed gently.

"Even if it won't be legal in America," Reynaldo said, "it will mean something to us."

"We already think of you as a forever couple," Taliya said. "We'd love to be a part of whatever kind of ceremony you'd like. But we'll have to do it soon."

"We can do it t'day," Wolfie said with a huge canine grin. "Here at the zoo. We do 'em on the daily. One of the first generations of Irwins got married here, and it's kinda become a tradition now. Whadaya say? Nice private spot, and we can do it after closin'."

Reynaldo and Carl exchanged a look, and Carl nodded their acceptance of this plan.

"Oh my," Taliya said. "Today? The kits are going to be so disappointed to miss it."

"We could let them watch over the interweb," Kano suggested.

"Sounds like a right brilliant plan." Wolfie's fluffy tail wagged in excitement. "We could even share it wider."

"I'm not sure about that part," Carl said. "The kits are fine. But sharing with the world? It could be . . ."

"Dangerous." Taliya finished his thought sadly.

"We've stayed under the radar in America," Carl said. "Most folks can handle the two guys part, and some folks can handle the different species part, but both combined is just too much."

"How about this?" Taliya said. "Our family can watch live, and we'll record it. If you want to share that at any time, you can. Otherwise, it will just be for the two of you."

"Sounds perfect." Carl smiled at Rey, and he nodded his agreement.

Wolfie grinned. "I'll get 'er set up."

"I'll send Marla a message," Taliya said. "What time is it there?"

"Fifteen hours behind us," Carl said. "So eight pm."

She pulled out her com and tapped a message to Marla. The kits would be getting ready for bed.

> Carl & Rey getting MARRIED in a few hours at zoo. Around six pm our time. We can live feed you in. Sorry it will be middle of the night for you. Make it a party! More later. Hope all's well there.

She smiled, imagining Marla's reaction.

Wolfie made a happy barking noise. "Now ya just need to let the hotel concierge know what clothes ya want 'er to gather for the event." He hesitated, ears twisting. "Assuming you want to change."

Taliya glanced at the casual outfits each of them had picked for the day of tourist activity. They'd have to do better.

"I suppose we should ask for the dressy stuff," Taliya said with a grin. "That one special outfit Padme suggested we each bring."

"She couldn't have imagined this is why we'd wear it." Kano pulled Taliya in close and kissed the top of her head. Maybe remembering their own wedding not that long ago and the magnificent gift of a bridal sari the president had sent.

All four of them took turns telling Wolfie what they wanted from their hotel rooms as he recorded and sent the messages. Taliya imagined the staff there racing around. It was a tad disconcerting, knowing strangers were going through her things, but she supposed that was an invasion rich people got used to. The high-end hotel staff was surely accustomed to it.

When that was finally settled, she noticed Kano watching a video on his communicator. And looking horrified.

"What?"

He tipped it into her view. "A historical document of those Irwins feeding the crocs during the Crocoseum show. They still do it pretty much the same way."

It took her a moment to process what he was saying. She'd forgotten all about agreeing to feed crocodiles. Kano restarted the video, and Taliya's stomach swirled as she watched humans walk right up to captive crocs, stomp on the ground to get their attention, and throw hunks of meat into their open jaws—from only a few feet away— when the beast finally charged out of the water with a mighty splash.

"We agreed to do that?"

"We sure did."

"Well, that's bound to get us attention."

Kano nodded. "Maybe we should tell Wolfie to keep the whole thing quiet, in case we change our minds."

"Good idea," she said. Her hackles rose at the guttural growling sounds coming from the crocs in the video.

"Could be fun, though."

Holding a koala was more her speed, but maybe a little excitement would prepare them for the rescue operation tomorrow. There wouldn't be any snapping crocodiles, but well-armed humans were expected.

The video popped up text repeatedly saying that no one had ever been injured in a feeding at the zoo, but viewers should not try this at home. Taliya snorted that such a warning was necessary. *Who wanders around tossing meat to crocodiles?*

They enjoyed a quick lunch at the Kookaburra Café. Jaxon treated everyone to fried chicken, french fries, a bit of ale, and some iced vovos for dessert. More sugar, but the frosted cookies, which Jaxon referred to as biscuits, were delicious. Then they resumed their tour of the zoo, trying to stay calm about the two big events still ahead that day, not to mention what unknowns tomorrow would bring.

The crowds had increased, and Taliya suspected all the photos being posted were to blame. Guests gawked at them as much as the animals on display, but the rooman security guards kept the interactions limited. Taliya signed a few autographs, especially for children, and posed for photos. As with many other events since Taliya had become a public persona, people felt like they knew her personally but weren't as attached to Kano, even though he was a much more rare and impressive creature. Visitors seemed curious about Reynaldo, but few approached him. Most snapped photos from a distance, posing so he was in the background of their selfie.

The India portion finally lay ahead. The exhibit Taliya was partly intrigued by and partly dreading—Sumatran tigers, now extinct in the wild, an "ambush" including the parents and several generations of cubs. When they reached it, the group stood along the safety railing in silence for several minutes. Taliya expected the tigers might be curious about their scent, but none even glanced their way.

It wasn't safe for the tiger family to live in their natural habitat, but it made Taliya sad to see them imprisoned—even if it was a vast and lovely enclosure filled with trees and boulders, a large pool for swimming, and a waterfall. She knew how it felt to be locked away, like in the warehouse attic room. Her condo/cell with Kano had supplied all of their needs, but they hadn't been free. Of course, none of these tigers had ever lived anywhere but a zoo, so maybe they didn't miss a freedom they'd never known. Still, it was like finding your cousins in jail for a crime they didn't commit.

"How long can you allow the cubs to stay with their parents?" she asked Jaxon, who'd joined them for the rest of the tour while Wolfie prepared for the wedding in a few hours.

"We have twenty tigers now, who rotate through usin' the exhibits in small groups. When food and territory aren't an issue, family groups of tigers get along right well. At some point the males go on to another zoo, matched with unrelated females. Then they can start their own families and keep the species from becomin' completely extinct. We let the females stay together or house them with a male from another facility when they're old enough to breed."

Taliya winced at that, but she knew the same

emotions from her own experience couldn't be put on wild animals.

"I know, I know," Jaxon said, noticing her reaction. "We preserve the species through selective breedin', but we also want to be sure each and every tiger has a safe home."

Three cubs dashed by, launching themselves onto their mother. She growled playfully and rolled onto her back, swatting at her young while they tried to bite her feet. An older female galloped past the group and leaped into the pool with a massive splash.

"It looks like you're doing a great job," Taliya said. "I'm sure they appreciate it. You let them raise their offspring. That's more than many places would give them."

Jaxon looked sideways at her with a sad smile. Some days she wished she wasn't so well-known, much of her life an open book in the world. She had her kits waiting for her back in Arkansas—all five of them—so she was luckier than many tigran.

"We'd better head over to the show," Jaxon said. "You're on in about thirty minutes."

"It's *croc* time," Carl growled.

6

The Crocoseum sprawled imposingly on the path-way ahead. Making eye contact with Kano, she realized he was excited and tried to let that feeling rise up in her as well.

How many tigran get to hand feed crocodiles? Stop fussing and enjoy yourself.

When they arrived at the backstage area, a stocky human in zoo khakis—only about five foot eight with short, sandy-brown hair, maybe in his late twenties—rolled a large cart holding several metal tubs toward them.

"G'day! I'm Robbie Powell, and I'm gonna get ya through this feedin' with no worries. Yeah?"

They all nodded. Taliya recognized the name as the man from the zoo who was helping with the dragon rescue. Surely, he wouldn't let her get eaten by a reptile before then.

"We've been doin' croc chow-downs like this for over two hundred years," Robbie assured them. "And no one's lost an appendage yet."

Everyone chuckled, and Taliya tried to let his enthusiasm and confidence bolster hers. She just needed to listen carefully and follow his instructions. To the letter.

"I'm gonna be out there with ya. But let's watch a quick video about how it works so ya can see it in action. The crocs know what to do. They've been 'round this block a hundred times. I'm wonderin' if they might even be scared of *you lot*."

Carl smiled and bumped his shoulder into Reynaldo. "Those crocs have never seen the likes of you."

Reynaldo used both hands to smooth the fur along the top of his head like a fashion model, making his sculpted biceps pop in the process, and the group laughed.

"Right, then," Robbie said with a chuckle. "Let's see how it's done. This is the video guests to the zoo can watch durin' the tour, before comin' into the Crocoseum."

He turned on a small com on the wall next to him, and videos of different humans feeding the crocs played. It started with a wild-eyed blond man, the founder of the zoo, who she'd seen recordings of any number of times. Some of it was the same as what she and Kano had watched earlier. Later videos showed his son as a teenager and as a grown man doing the same thing, then it continued through the generations of the family. Taliya lost track of what level of great-great-grandchild the current croc boss, Robbie, must be. The big finish of the show had her really stressed, and her tail puffed in fear just watching others complete the challenge.

When the video was done, Robbie opened the lids of the metal containers, which held whole dead chickens. They reeked of blood, and Taliya could imagine that smell would make the crocs hungry and ready to perform for the fans. He reviewed the basics of what to expect but assured them he'd talk them through every step.

The audience was taking their seats in the large amphitheater, and the rumble of excited conversation carried backstage. Was their participation going to be a surprise? Or had visitors that day figured it out?

"We've kept this kinda quiet," Robbie said, "so we don't have a run on the zoo. It's not unusual to have famous guests join us in the feedin', but this is definitely a first."

"I just hope the crocs behave," Carl said, definitely expressing what was racing through Taliya's mind.

"Nah," Robbie said. "Piece'a cake. They're good as gold, our crocs. Cheeky buggers, but right good."

A voice echoed over the loudspeaker, announcing the show would start in two minutes and guests should find a spot quickly. The hum of voices grew louder as the seats filled up. Two of the keepers started a pre-show routine using macaws and eagles, who flew around the stadium and got the crowd excited. Not like that seemed necessary.

Robbie did a few checks to make sure all the lights and effects were ready, then he peeked out at the crowd. "I'm thinkin' someone got the word out," he said. "Standin' room only. Double what we'd have on a weekday like this. Get ya game faces on, mates!"

Taliya straightened her tunic and took a quick glance in the mirror. Then she noticed Carl and Reynaldo in deep conversation with Kano. "What's wrong?"

"Carl thinks Rey and I should take our shirts off," Kano said with wide blue eyes. His nose was flushed almost red, a sure sign he was either excited or nervous.

"It would be much more impressive," Carl said. "Our mates are pretty fabulous, don't you think?"

Taliya chuckled and nodded. "Absolutely!"

"If we want to make a show of it," Carl said, "we should *really* make it a show."

With fang-baring grins, both Kano and Reynaldo pulled their tunics over their heads and then flexed and posed, challenging each other amid snorts and whipping tails. Rey's dark fur was broken in spots by scarring from whippings when he was still in a lab, and Taliya wondered if the crowd would notice it. *Maybe they should.*

"Holy moly!" Robbie said, joining them again and gawking at the macho display. "That'll get 'em rarin' to go!"

Kano hit a strong-man pose. "Wouldn't want to disappoint the fans."

"Highly unlikely," Robbie said with a grin.

Dramatic music started in the grassy performance area, and they peeked into the arena. Fog and flashing spotlights swept across the pond containing a dozen massive freshwater crocodiles. Holographic images of transport-sized crocodiles that appeared to soar through the air and attack the crowd with open jaws made them whoop and cheer. A voice over the loudspeaker announced the feeding to come and shared some of the history, showing video on an overhead screen along with holographic images of the show through the decades. It struck Taliya that they were participating in an iconic part of Australian culture.

"Here we go," Robbie said. "Just follow my lead. The fans'll be geeked out if ya look nervous and don't quite know what you're doin'. Just roll with it."

The three creatures nodded. Carl was going to come out with them, but he'd be hanging back. Robbie had briefed him on how to help out if a croc became agitated.

"Today," the overhead voice continued, "Australia Zoo is proud to welcome special visitors from the United States of America!"

The crowd cheered and hooted—a few even chanting Taliya's name, clearly in on the agenda.

"Give a big Aussie greeting to Taliya, Kano, and Reynaldo!"

Robbie gave a nod, and the four of them jogged out on the grassy stage at the side of the croc pool, Carl following behind with the "safety team." Everyone in the stands rose to their feet and clapped and whistled. The wave of sound blasted across Taliya, and her fur stood on end as she waved and smiled. Kano and Reynaldo looked perfectly at ease—their furry chests puffed up, both waving and taking in the adoration.

Once the light show stopped and the fog cleared, Robbie adjusted his headpiece mic and started his spiel about the dangers of feeding crocs, repeating some of the things said on the video but with great intensity. Making it all sound very ominous. Taliya understood hyping up the crowd, but it wasn't helping steady her nerves.

"Taliya, are ya ready?" he asked with a grand gesture at the tubs of dead chickens.

She dramatically jumped up and down a few times and shook out her arms, making the crowd laugh and whistle again. Then she walked over and pulled a chicken from the bin by its feet. Robbie moved to the edge of the pond and used a special clicker to call the largest of the crocs closer to the edge of the water.

"Boris is first t'day!"

Boris methodically swam his way toward them, his enormous muscular body undulating just below the surface, spikes from his back poking out of the water menacingly.

"This old man is nearly seventy and measures twenty feet long," Robbie said.

It looked like a cross between a dinosaur and Godzilla coming for her. Taliya swallowed, and a little hiss escaped. Some reactions were just instinctive. That hiss was replayed on the big screen, and the crowd tittered in anticipation. The other reptiles waited their turn. They were well-trained, and Taliya hoped that meant no issues for her.

Robbie coaxed Boris out of the water with lots of stomping and calling, and the croc finally erupted from the pool—thrashing, splashing, and rumbling a growl, mouth agape and threatening. The crowd cheered, and Taliya gawked at the rows of jagged, razor-sharp teeth she now faced.

As the stunning crocodile waddled his way onto the grass, jaws open and ready to bite something, Robbie motioned Taliya over. She could smell the breath of the reptile—like old meat and mud—and her instinct told her to throw the chicken at the animal and run back down the ramp and into the parking lot. Stilling her nerves, she moved slowly toward him instead.

Boris turned his open jaws her direction, made a deep growling noise, and took several lunging steps closer. He seemed completely unconcerned that she was a tigran. She had dinner, or she could *be* dinner. And he wanted it. Now.

Beyond Boris, Taliya could see Robbie tactfully motioning for her to bang the meat on the ground, like she'd seen in the videos. It would make Boris move even closer and come after her in earnest.

"Taliya! Taliya! Taliya!" the crowd started to chant.

She didn't take her eyes off Boris, but she could see Kano and Reynaldo in her peripheral vision, chanting along with the crowd and pumping their fists to the rhythm. Taking a deep breath, Taliya whapped the dead chicken on the ground twice. Boris opened his jaws wider, growled again, and took two strides closer as the theater went silent.

"Come on, Boris!" Taliya yelled. "Come and get it!"

Boris did not disappoint. All twenty feet of him started toward her at a run. The moment he was close enough, she chucked the carcass into his open mouth, and Boris snapped it shut. Then he chomped a couple more times before turning, waddling away, and sliding back into the pond nonchalantly, like he hadn't just scared the crap out of a tigran.

"Taliya and Boris, everyone!" Robbie said, and Taliya took a quick bow while the crowd thundered their approval.

But that was just the beginning. Robbie called different crocs out of the pond, and Kano and Reynaldo each took a turn feeding one in an impressive display. Carl even stepped in for a chance, not wanting to miss out on the fun. Robbie made a fuss about the brave American general facing their Aussie crocs, and the crowd went wild. Taliya panicked for a second when Carl let the open-mouthed reptile get within touching distance, but it made for a good show.

Then Robbie made a big production of giving a croc a leg of meat that he could still hold onto one end of by the bone. Robbie and the croc tugged back and forth on it until he let go and sat down hard as the croc whirled and dragged his prey into the water. Then Taliya, Kano, and Rey together demonstrated a crocodile death roll, holding on to one end of a rope tied to a chunk of meat that the massive croc was determined to have. Of course, the croc won in the end after much rolling and thrashing and splashing, which was amazing if you understood the strength of tigran and panthran. He'd probably never had to fight that hard.

For the big finish—the part that had thoroughly terrified her in the videos—Taliya stood on a tall platform, leaned over the safety railing, and dangled a dead chicken for the last croc.

With a sweep of his tail, the eighteen-foot reptile leapt up out of the water the entire length of his body like a dolphin and grabbed the chicken from her, though she also dropped it when she saw him coming. Robbie had whispered that piece of advice to her. The crowd stood and cheered as a replay of the armored animal leaping and splashing back into the water showed in slow motion on the overhead screen. Taliya laughed at the horrified expression on her face.

Then they waved to the crowd and jogged off stage through the whirling of spotlight beams, bus-sized croc holograms, and the raucous applause of the crowd.

"That was incredible!" Kano said.

Taliya panted for air, the adrenaline wearing off. "It was!"

"Excellent job, mates!" Robbie said. "That video is gonna get lots of attention for the zoo, for sure."

"I hope it brings you extra donations," Carl said.

"No doubt." Robbie nodded. "Now, get washed up

over there, and let's give the fans a few minutes of photos and autographs. You might even mention droppin' a fiver or two in the donation box."

They washed their hands and fur up to the shoulders, used the blowers to dry off, Rey and Kano got their tunics back on, and then they all followed Robbie around to where eager fans were waiting. Jaxon joined them, over the moon at how the demonstration had gone and the reactions coming through on social media. As promised, no one had lost a limb. The whole thing had been recorded, and she looked forward to watching it later on with the kits.

Once they were finished with the meet and greet, Taliya noticed Carl on his communicator.

"What's happening?" she asked Reynaldo.

"He's talking to our contacts here."

"He looks angry," Taliya said.

Reynaldo considered his mate. "No, just focused."

She'd have to trust Rey on that, but she hoped nothing had gone wrong.

Robbie rejoined them. "Now that things are closin' down, let's check out where yer dragons are gonna live."

Taliya grinned, excitement tingling up her spine. "Yes, please."

Reynaldo looked even more enthusiastic. This was his area to shine, and he was determined to have his say if any part of the enclosure didn't meet expectations.

After heading around to what felt like a very "off

exhibit" part of the zoo, Robbie turned to walk backward as he spoke animatedly.

"We've been wantin' to update this section that used to be a hands-on roo encounter. Combinin' that with what was open land, I think we've got enough space for the dragons to be comfortable even long-term, if that's what the powers that be decide."

He stopped and threw his arms wide toward a low fake rock wall and the open space beyond it.

Carl whistled. "Crikey."

Kano chuffed, and Reynaldo laughed and bent over to put his hands on his knees.

Taliya could only stare in shock. "How is this possible?"

"Pretty crackin' for a few days' work, eh?" Robbie said with a grin.

She'd expected something hastily thrown together, barely large enough to hold the massive dragons. Instead, they were faced with an enormous exhibit covered in grass and clover. More than enough room for all four animals to move around comfortably. Heavy netting covered the top, held up by elaborate steel cables. Along the two sides and back was a tall faux-rock wall with food and water troughs. It was dragon paradise.

"Our team's amazin'," Robbie said proudly. "No bludgers allowed. Fortunately, a lot of the basic structure was already in place. Gettin' that netting hung was a stramash, though. We still need to install the Plexiglass along the front here to keep the drags in—and the humans out. On the agenda next."

"Robbie, it's just perfect," Taliya said, giving him a fang-filled smile.

His eyes went wide for a moment, but then he returned her enthusiasm. "Glad to hear it!"

"They won't be able to fly in there," Kano said.

"Yeah, nah," Robbie admitted. "That would take a lot to fashion. But if they stay for a bit, we're gonna put together some kind of show, like the Crocoseum."

Jaxon stopped swiping on his com to add, "Maybe you'll come back and help with that."

Taliya didn't love the idea of the dragons becoming performing monkeys, but she could understand that a demo of some kind would bring in needed funds. Caring for the animals wasn't going to be cheap.

"I'll need to be home with my kits, but you might get in touch with the other former dragon wranglers. Last I heard, they were all still at the refugee camp outside Winnipeg. They might be thrilled to come do a residency here."

Robbie nodded but looked disappointed. Taliya imagined she'd already proven herself to be a big tourist draw. But other tigran and liran could be just as exciting. She could never quite fathom why humans were so enthralled and focused on her specifically.

Reynaldo had the opposite reaction. "Putting together a display of their training and skills sounds great. I'd love that!"

Or maybe a glorious black panthran will be the tourist attraction.

Carl didn't look opposed to the idea. Once they were married, they'd have all of their future to figure out. Maybe time in Queensland would be on the agenda.

After saying he'd see them again soon, Robbie headed to his next challenge of the day—something about training a Komodo dragon. Jaxon led the group to the staff cafeteria for a break while the zoo closed down for the day. Carl followed, talking on his com, but because of the crowd noise, Taliya couldn't hear any of it. The phone wasn't secure, so it would all be in coded messages anyhow—things like "The eagles are flighty today" to talk about the dragon rescue operation.

As they settled at a table in a far corner with some snacks, Carl joined them. Reynaldo slid his tray between the two of them to share.

"So?" Taliya said. "What's happening?"

"The team is almost ready," Carl said. "Satellite images show the cargo still there and no changes in the daily routine, so they don't seem to know what's afoot."

That was excellent news, but Taliya found it hard to focus on her food. It was difficult to wait, now that they were halfway across the world. The day had been full of distractions, but she wanted Bunny and the others to be rescued and safe. Right now! Carl reached over and put his hand on her arm.

"I know it's rough, being patient and all, but rescues

like this take time and planning. It's not my first day on the job, you know."

They locked eyes for a moment, and Taliya's skin prickled at the memory of being held in that small cell and tortured to give up her kits. Carl had managed to find and rescue her then. He'd gotten all of them out of the breeding facility after spending months undercover as a guard. He'd rescued Reynaldo twice and many others too. He wasn't a general now for nothing. She had to trust and be patient. Taliya slow-blinked at him, and Carl smiled, patted her arm, and turned his attention to the snacks.

"Feeding those crocs sure worked up my appetite," Kano said, ripping a chunk of meat from the bone and popping it into his mouth, making large chomps like the reptiles had.

"I'm not throwing a whole chicken at you," Taliya said with a smile, poking at her chips.

Kano eyed her, replicating the crocodile growling noise. She flipped a chip at him, and he caught it in his mouth.

"The show went great," Jaxon said. "No argy-bargy or any dramas. Only one more thing to do before you head to the Outback."

They paused and waited for him to finish. Taliya was pretty sure they had seen all of the zoo. Jaxon was grinning, but everyone else looked confused.

"We're havin' a weddin', aren't we?" Jaxon finally said. "Wolfie said you two blokes are keen to get hitched."

Taliya glanced at Carl and Rey, and they were both

beaming. Reynaldo nodded vehemently, and Carl chuckled.

"Right-o," Jaxon said. "Let me make a couple of calls to be sure we're clear, and we can head on over." He hop/walked to a quiet corner of the big room.

Reynaldo's whiskers flared, and he could barely keep to his seat. Carl grabbed his communicator and typed out a couple of messages. "We can video in my parents."

"I should alert the family that it's almost time," Taliya said. "If they miss this, we'll never hear the end of it."

She pulled out her com and typed in a message to Marla.

> Carl and Reynaldo are tying the knot in
> about an hour.

Even at two am her time, Marla sent back an array of excited emoji images with a trail of exclamation points.

Jaxon was back before they'd gotten their trays cleared into the garbage.

"All set!" he said. "We have some time before we can be sure the area is one-hundred-percent clear. Then you chaps are up. There's a back entrance closer to the chapel area. The shuttle from the hotel with your duds will meet us 'round there so you can start gettin' fancy. Then we can sneak you back in and none the wiser."

Following Jaxon's advice, the group headed for the exit where the shuttle waited. Most of the zoo guests let them pass with only giggles and waves and a bit of applause. They smiled but moved quickly to discourage anyone from interrupting their departure. The rooman guards had to hustle to keep up.

A shuttle the size of a military transport was waiting just outside the back gate, which looked like a service entrance instead of one for patrons. The group climbed aboard and found everything they'd requested from the hotel waiting for them.

Carl unzipped the hanging bags until he found his black dress uniform and Rey's bag. The panthran had selected a dark-purple suit and tie with a lavender shirt. Taliya tucked herself in behind a division wall, and they all set to changing. Her fancy outfit was a bright-blue sari with elaborate black embroidery and a long black dupatta with detailed blue stitching. It had been months since she'd worn a sari, and she hadn't expected to be putting it on in a shuttle. A video on the interwebs helped her remember how to accomplish all the wrapping and pinning. Finally, she emerged to find the men dressed and ready. Kano whistled his approval, and she returned the compliment to her husband. He wore a similar blue Indian-style top and slacks—matching his eyes—with black embroidery.

Kano checked Reynaldo to make sure there was no black fur on the back of his jacket while Taliya adjusted every bar and ribbon on Carl's chest. She paused at the Purple Heart and laid her hand on the special medal.

"I'm glad you didn't die earning this," she whispered.

"Me too. But I would have, gladly, as long as I knew you were safe."

Taliya gently chuffed at him, and he returned his own version of it.

She laughed. "Not bad."

"I've had to communicate with a few tigran in my day," Carl said with a smile.

"And now you get to marry the most amazing panthran on the planet."

Carl gazed over at his soon-to-be husband and grinned. Reynaldo moved to the front of the shuttle with them and gave Carl's uniform the once-over himself. Taliya could smell the excitement wafting from both of them.

Wolfie clambered into the shuttle, wearing a dark suit, tan shirt, and purple tie. "Wow! Lookin' good."

The five of them stepped out to find Jaxon—who'd also changed into a stylish top and slacks instead of his uniform—waiting at the zoo gate.

"Check out you lot," he said, rocking back onto his thick tail. "Looks like you're ready for a weddin' or somethin'."

"A wedding," Reynaldo said with conviction.

Carl adjusted his tie and smiled. "Definitely a wedding."

"Then let's get to it," Jaxon said.

7

Jaxon led the group along the backs of a few different exhibits. Taliya could hear a kookaburra's bizarre laughing, trilling, and cackling cacophony nearby, but based on the smells, she was pretty sure they were passing behind the extensive area with African plains animals. A giraffe lifted its head over the top of the bamboo fencing, chewing slowly and gazing at them with massive brown eyes, confirming her suspicions. His long purple tongue stripped the leaves off a nearby branch before he lowered his head below the fence line, unimpressed with the group of creatures walking by.

Before long, they arrived at a small park area with a pagoda-style archway covered in beautiful flowers. Taliya recognized wisteria and jasmine from Shreya's garden back home. In a lake behind the arch, dozens of swans—black and white—floated gracefully. The males and females were in pairs, side by side, facing opposite directions. Jaxon noticed Taliya watching them and added, "They keep an eye out for each other."

"Very supportive."

"They mate for life. If one of 'em dies or even gets sick and needs to go to the clinic, we have to use a fake swan stand-in to keep the one left behind calm. They seem to know it's not real, but it works anyhow."

Taliya watched the swans a little longer, one black pair preening each other's feathers and laying their necks across the other's back. It was quite a poetic thing to have behind the zoo's wedding venue and definitely made her think of the pair preparing to tie the knot.

Mates for life.

She hadn't been sure of a lifelong commitment to Kano when they were handfast, but she was absolutely sure by the time they'd had a formal, legal wedding and celebrated with their community at home.

Definitely, mates for life.

The white tigran in question slipped up beside her and wrapped one arm around her waist. He looked magnificent in his Indian ensemble, and she hoped they could get some pictures of just the two of them together while they were looking so outstanding. Life at home rarely led to events that justified fancy clothes.

Taliya was in charge of making sure those who were far away could watch the wedding ceremony. She confirmed she had her communicator and Carl's. Someone from the zoo would record a video, but her family would want to be there live. There was a special shelf in the ceremony area for personal recordings, where Taliya set up the coms and called Carl's parents and her own family.

"Mama!" all five kits yelled at the sight of her.

"My kittens!" she yelled back at the screen.

They were all settling onto the sofa in front of the media wall. Marla had managed to get the four youngest kits into their nicest outfits. Ali had pulled her red Diwali sari out of the attic and looked ready for a party. Shreya and Grampa Jai were there as well, along with Taliya's twin brothers, Tuscan and Tyler, who at least weren't wearing their standard sweatpants and hoodies.

"Y'all look amazing!" Marla said, sitting with Amrita on her lap.

"Thank you," Taliya said, turning and twisting to show off her outfit. "You all look ready for a wedding as well. I'm going to mute you for now, but once the ceremony is done, I'm sure the happy couple will want to chat."

As she clicked on the mute setting over the protesting calls of the kits, Carl's parents appeared on his screen, and she greeted them before muting their call as well.

"Is anybody walking down the aisle?" Jaxon asked.

"No," Reynaldo said. "We'll just stand up together."

Jaxon motioned the group over to the lovely pagoda area and arranged Carl and Reynaldo facing him. The white and purple flowers hanging around them would make for excellent photos. The zoo's media guy, with Wolfie's help, was already all over it. Video cameras were set up in three locations to catch the wedding from several angles, and he was snapping away for still images.

"Those are not to be shared publicly," Kano whispered to him in a firm voice.

The media guy nodded and smiled, but nerves tingled along Taliya's spine. She trusted Wolfie, but organizations often did as they pleased, regardless of what they promised. She, Reynaldo, and the dragons were kidnapped because of the documentary at the refugee camp. Her tail puffed, and she tried to tactfully wipe the fur back down by dragging it between her fingers.

"Kano and Taliya," Jaxon said, "come stand next to your friends to act as witnesses."

Without discussing it, Kano stood next to Reynaldo and Taliya moved next to Carl—even though Carl had served as Kano's best man at his marriage to Taliya. It still felt right. Carl turned to her with a huge grin on his face. Taliya grinned back and pointed at the coms on the shelf so he could see his parents there. Carl waved to them, and they waved back, as did Taliya's family on her screen.

"Are we ready, then?" Jaxon asked.

"Yes," Rey said, rubbing his hands together and grinning. "*More* than ready."

Everyone laughed at his enthusiasm, and then Jaxon shifted himself to stand more formally, though he rocked back on his tail now and then out of habit.

"Friends," he began, "we are gathered here today at the beautiful Australia Zoo to unite Carl Thompson and Reynaldo Thompson in holy matrimony."

Taliya's heart blazed with happiness. She hadn't realized the panthran had already adopted Carl's last name.

Jaxon continued. "Do you both enter into this agreement of your own free will, without any promise of financial benefit or fear of punishment?"

All four of them startled at the specifics of that. Carl and Reynaldo nodded slightly and then glanced at each other.

"For interspecies weddin's," Jaxon whispered, "we're required to include that."

"I enter into this agreement of my own free will," Carl said quickly.

Reynaldo adjusted his jacket and nodded. "I do as well."

It was a sad thought—that some creature could be forced or paid to marry a human. Of course, anyone marrying under that kind of duress would just lie. Taliya shook off the thought and focused on her friends.

Jaxon turned the page in the folder he was holding. "Reynaldo, do you take Carl to be your partner? To love and to cherish, in sickness and in health, forsakin' all others, until death parts you?"

"I do," Reynaldo said, reaching out and holding Carl's hand.

"Carl, do you take Reynaldo to be your partner? To love and to cherish, in sickness and in health, forsakin' all others, until death parts you?"

"I absolutely do," Carl said.

"Witnesses to these agreements, do you swear to honor and protect this union?"

"Yes," Kano and Taliya both answered. "We do."

Taliya spotted the kits on her com screen, waving and cheering silently and agreeing as well.

"Carl and Reynaldo," Jaxon said, "do you have any vows you'd like to share before we finish?"

Carl nodded and turned to Reynaldo.

"Rey, since the first moment I locked eyes with you in that horrific lab dungeon, I knew you were special. It's logical we would feel a bond after surviving that escape together, but I never anticipated the true love that developed after I was assigned to the camp. That I could be deserving of your love seems unfathomable. You are brave and strong and honest and every wonderful quality any human could look for in a mate. Never in a million years did I expect we would have this moment. You are my heart and my soul, and I am honored you would choose to spend the rest of your life with me."

A lump formed in Taliya's throat, remembering those first few media nights at the school when she'd spotted them sitting together and wondered about their relationship. Them celebrating the first dragon flights, jumping around the arena and hugging. The pair in their home together in D.C., lounging on the sofa or bickering over a game. *How can any government forbid love like this from being made official and legal?*

Next, Reynaldo spoke from the heart, but Taliya had no idea what he was saying. Some of it was more growls than words. She glanced at Kano, who seemed just as confused. Carl, however, smiled like he'd just won the lottery. Whatever language it was, Carl understood. By the end, he was teary, and Reynaldo was sniffling. They turned back to Jaxon.

"No idea what that was, but it doesn't matter," he said with a laugh. "The vows are for the two of you alone. Now . . . by the power vested in me by the city of Brisbane, I pronounce you legally married."

Reynaldo grabbed Carl by the sides of his face and pulled him in for a serious kiss, and Wolfie howled loud enough to rival the kookaburras. Taliya laughed at the silent celebrations and clapping from the coms. She headed over to the shelf and unmuted the wedding guests. Cheers immediately echoed out around them, making the swans lift their heads and gaze at the wedding party.

"Congratulations!" Marla yelled. "We are so happy for you!"

"Yay for Uncle Carl and Uncle Rey-Rey!" Aliania called out.

Taliya wondered if she could remember "Uncle Carl" lifting her out of her crib at the breeding facility, carrying her to safety through a war zone, and returning her to her father. That was the moment Taliya, Kano, and Ali became a family. Carl had been there for so much of it. Ali continued to be his little "marshmallow," even as she grew too big for such endearments. Amrita was his strawberry sundae. The L-twins knew him better than most anyone in the world. Taliya was thrilled they could be a part of this milestone in his life.

The happy couple chatted with Carl's parents while the kits talked over each other in a happy chatter, impatiently waiting their turn. Jaxon pulled a paper from the back of his binder.

"We'll get 'em to sign in a jiff," he said, showing Taliya and Kano the official document, "but you two can give us your siggy now as witnesses. When they file this at the courthouse, it'll complete the legal process."

Kano growled. "Not like it will matter back home."

"They should move here," Jaxon suggested.

Kano handed Taliya the pen so she could sign, and the look in his eyes suggested he thought that was an excellent idea. Carl and Rey joined them, and Taliya said goodbye to everyone on the coms while the pair signed their marriage license.

"Maybe someone from the hotel can drop it at the government offices," Kano said. "We'll be long gone before they open tomorrow."

Carl and Rey didn't look like they really cared if that happened or not, but Taliya hoped it did. At least somewhere in the world they could claim to be legally married.

The photographer took what felt like two hundred pictures, even some fun ones with giraffes, zebras, and rhinos in the background. Kano and Taliya posed for a few on their own, and she hoped one was good enough for displaying on the wall at home.

Finally, as the sun began to set, Jaxon said goodbye—

along with whispered wishes to see them again with dragons in tow. Wolfie assured them he'd meet them at the designated post-rescue location. Then the two couples climbed into the shuttle to head to the hotel for the night.

"Well," Kano said, "this day was a lot more interesting than the agenda suggested."

"To say the least." Carl leaned back into Reynaldo, resting his head on the panthran's shoulder. "I mean, feeding those crocs was right exciting."

Reynaldo playfully shoved him away. "Oh, *that* was the most exciting event of the day?"

Taliya joined the game. "I thought the most exciting thing was holding a koala. Didn't you, Kano?"

"One-hundred-percent," he said.

"Cheeky buggers," Reynaldo grumbled. "None of you are getting any of that cake Jaxon said he sent to the hotel."

As they drove along, the mood shifted to more somber thoughts. The trip so far had been all fun, amusement, and happiness. The next few days held their real purpose for visiting Australia, and *fun* was not the first word that popped into Taliya's mind to describe what lay ahead.

When they arrived at the hotel, two men in uniforms whisked their bags upstairs. The four followed at a slower pace. Adrenaline was wearing off, and it had been a re-markably busy day, not considering jet lag and big cat DNA in the mix. Taliya suggested calling the kits to tell them about feeding the crocs.

Kano flopped down on the bed and sighed. "They're probably back in bed by now."

Taliya wasn't sure Marla and her mother had gotten that lucky.

Before she could respond, Carl knocked on the door. "Jaxon sent way more than cake." He motioned them across the hall to the newlyweds' room.

A young man in a waiter uniform was uncovering trays of all kinds of food that were arranged on several carts.

"G'day," he said to Taliya and Kano. "Right, so here we have some meat pies, venison off the barbie, and a few delicious side dishes. I'm not sure who to say congrats to, but there's a fancy cake here for a newly married couple."

"That would be them," Taliya said, pointing to Carl and Reynaldo.

The young man swallowed hard and then nodded politely. "Congrats," he said, eyebrows raised but clearly trying to be enthusiastic.

"Not something you see every day?" Carl grinned proudly.

The young man shook his head, then looked to Reynaldo. "Never seen a creature like you at all."

Rey smiled sadly. "There aren't many of us."

"You must get a lot of attention when you walk down the street," the waiter said. "And well done, you," he added, looking at Carl. "Nabbed a good one, yeah?"

"Most certainly did," Carl agreed.

The two couples settled in for a delicious dinner and

white wedding cake with purple icing flowers for dessert, fortunately not too sicky-sweet. Taliya had already made a note on her com to host a party for the newlyweds once this rescue was over. Weddings deserved a celebration. Then Taliya and Kano staggered back to their room to sleep for a few hours. Celebrations aside, they needed to be up and gone long before the sun rose in the morning. The dragons were waiting.

8

The alarm started beeping far too early, and Taliya tapped it off with a groan. Kano chuffed sleepily and rolled away from her. She forced one eye open. No light peeked around the curtains they'd pulled closed to avoid any photodrones. She tried to stir her nocturnal instinct to get excited about being up before the sun, but her internal clock was completely wonked-out about what time or day it was. Dragging her legs around to sit up on the side of the bed, she yawned and stretched, then collapsed back into herself.

"Five minutes," Kano mumbled.

Taliya agreed, but then she thought about Bunny and the other dragons, maybe suffering under cruel captors, and a spark of energy pushed her into action. After washing up and getting dressed in her most practical tunic, slacks, and heavy-duty boots, she patted Kano on the hip.

"Rise and shine, mate," she said with a chuckle. "We've got dragons to save."

Kano grumbled. "That sounds like a bad line from some old science fiction movie. Set in Australia."

"Yesterday we witnessed a kangaroo hybrid perform the wedding of a jaguar hybrid to a celebrated human military general while a dingo hybrid watched from the sidelines. Our lives are science fiction, with or without dragons." Taliya organized their travel packs, preparing to leave. "The transport will be here in thirty minutes."

Kano sat up on the edge of the bed and stretched, scratching his ruff and the rumpled fur on his chest. "It's a long drive. We can nap on the way."

There was a knock on the door, and Taliya opened it to a young woman from room service with a light breakfast they'd ordered the night before. They ate quickly and finished packing before an alarm went off on Taliya's com.

"We need to be at the front door in ten minutes," she said.

It seemed a waste for the zoo to pay for a few days of hotel stay when they wouldn't actually be there, but it helped with the cover story. After giving the room and bathroom one final check for anything they might need during the mission, Taliya opened the door to the hall to head downstairs.

Across the way, a groggy-looking Reynaldo was hurried out by his alert, ready-to-roll husband, who carried both of their travel bags. "G'day, mates."

Reynaldo gave them a sideways grin and rubbed the scar that ran from one ear to under his tunic. "Up with the sun."

"Up *before* the sun," Kano mumbled, closing the door behind them.

"Come on, you bunch of whiners," Carl said. "It's go time."

"Go time?" Taliya laughed.

"'Everyone fights! No one quits!'" Carl said with way more enthusiasm than Taliya could handle that early. She sensed he was quoting something but didn't know what. Or have the energy to get into it.

The group took the elevator down and found the transport waiting for them at the front door. The vehicle looked military, ready to withstand a bomb blast, and rust-colored to blend in with the Aussie landscape. The human driver was as large as any of them, and even in a generic black top and slacks, he looked like he knew his way around a battle. Everything about him—from his haircut to his posture—screamed soldier.

Taliya had been worried that media folks or fans might be waiting outside the hotel after all of the publicity the day before, but there was not a soul in sight except for the hotel staff. Maybe no one expected them to be up and about so early. Maybe no one cared. Either way, she was grateful. This was the part of their time in Australia they needed to keep secret. But if anyone asked, they were taking a tour of the area today.

The media wouldn't know more until they returned with the dragons.

Carl sat up with the driver, while the other three climbed in the back seat and put their packs at their feet.

"Ready?" the driver asked Carl.

"Yes. Everyone else is meeting us outside of town?"

"Affirmative," the driver said. "Another vehicle and the ammunition truck will rendezvous with us at zero nine hundred." He glanced at the other three passengers.

Carl made the introductions. "Rico, this is Taliya, her husband, Kano . . . and Reynaldo, my husband."

Rico glanced back at Carl with a frown after the use of the word *husband*, but he nodded a greeting and turned around to get the vehicle moving. Taliya felt it elevate and the tires tuck underneath.

"Buckle up and settle in," Rico said. "If you need to stop for a break, it'll be at the side of the road. There's not much along the way where we're going."

"Think of it like camping," Carl said.

"We lived under the stars with the wild tigran for weeks," Kano said. "We can manage."

Taliya didn't relish the idea of having to pee in some Outback weeds with venomous snakes, giant spiders, dingoes, and roaming bands of feral camels. Not to mention emus, who stood as tall as a tigran and could gut you with a kick. The joke that everything in the Outback—or all of Australia—will try to kill you was not lost on her.

In under an hour, the transport was clear of civilization and heading north. Fortunately, the ride was uneventful. All of them dozed, though Carl spent a great deal of time answering emails and dashing off messages here and there, probably too amped up to relax.

Before long, the landscape zooming by was bare, red dust, and unending, with only a peek of mountains and trees here and there in the distance. Nothing to hold the attention. It didn't seem like much lived out there but snakes and insects. Too many wildfires had decimated the area time and time again, destroying small towns and wildlife habitats. What had once been a way to refresh and cleanse the land had become devastating.

After over four hours on roads that never seemed to end and a few turns onto dirt roads that led nowhere, they finally came to a stop near a large dark-red transport parked by a stand of eucalyptus trees. Getting out with quiet moans and groans, the five of them were greeted by an assembly of seven male humans, who looked ready to storm a fortress, and a rooman dressed in zoo-style khakis.

Rico immediately checked in with what seemed like the leader of the group and the rooman. Carl moved to join him, so Taliya and the others followed.

"This is Quinn," Rico said, nodding at the rooman as he handed out weapons from the truck. "She's head of the Wildlife Conservation Team in Queensland and has been monitoring the situation."

Taliya smiled and nodded at Quinn. The creature

smiled shyly in return. She stood around six feet tall, with the reddish fur of her kangaroo DNA. Taliya's question about the species was answered in the next moment as a small face with tan fur peeked out from under Quinn's shirt. Big black eyes stared up at the tigran, blinking slowly.

"And this is my roo, Mila," Quinn said.

Taliya leaned forward, and the little black nose went wild, trying to gather up the unknown smell. "Nice to meet you, Mila."

The little roo blinked twice, then ducked back under her mother's tunic and, Taliya assumed, into a pouch. Was there really a physical pouch, like a kangaroo, or had they simply devised some clothing item to mimic it for the rooman? This didn't seem like the moment for that conversation, so Taliya simply stood up and smiled.

"She's adorable."

Quinn placed a hand over where Mila was hiding. "I've seen photos of your kits. They are just remarkable. Little Amrita is so stunning."

"Yes, she is." Taliya desperately wished the world didn't know anything about the rare strawberry tigran.

Rico approached with an open case of handheld laser guns in front of him.

"Carl says you're handy with a weapon. Take your pick."

Taliya had seen, and skillfully wielded, most of the options presented—and had many of them in their arsenal at home. As she understood it, they would be hiking for several miles before the actual rescue, so she selected two handguns that were light but had good range. Nodding at her choices, Rico handed her a belt with holsters to carry them and several extra power clips for recharging. No one knew exactly what they were walking into, so better to be prepared for a long fight, even if the mercenaries would handle most of the shooting part.

"Quinn'll be leading the way through the bush," Rico said. "She knows this territory better than any of us."

"Have you actually seen the pterodragons?" Taliya asked.

"Yes," Quinn said. "They've let them fly around, but kept them tethered to the ground. That's how I spotted all four the first time. I hid in some trees, and that's good because if they saw me, well. I'd probably be dead."

"Let's not have anybody gettin' dead today," Rico said. "Except maybe those scumbags who've got your drags."

Carl and Reynaldo both selected larger continuous-blast laser weapons. Kano inspected what looked like small explosive devices. They had that at home too, but it was only for shooting into the woods to scare off any unwelcome visitors. Thinking of that made her hackles rise along her spine. She tried not to worry about her kits a world away. Padme had assigned four security guards around the family compound. Competent adults were there with the kits. But the mission was dredging up trauma and fears Taliya normally tamped down. Mila poked her head out again to say something to Quinn, and her heart clenched a little more.

"That's a cute little roo," Kano said, coming up beside her. Then he noticed her expression. "Taliya, the kits are fine. We have our coms. If anything was wrong, Marla wouldn't hesitate to tell us."

"I know, I know," she whispered. "I can't help it. When we're in the middle of the rescue, we'll be out of reach."

"Then Marla, your parents, or the guards will take care of things."

Taliya shrugged one shoulder, only mildly comforted, and added another smaller gun and more clips to her belt. Hopefully, this would be the last time she'd have to step into this role and leave her kits. Once the dragons were secure, she planned to stay home for a year or more and never leave their property.

"Find a bush, then find a transport," Rico shouted to the group. "Remember to stomp around and scare off the taipans. No help for you here if one nabs ya."

"Taipans?" Taliya glanced nervously at Quinn.

"Snakes," she said without flinching. "Very deadly. Also very rare and reclusive. Just stomp anyhow. Lots of snakes out here."

"*Lots of* snakes. Great," Taliya said, smiling at Kano.

He laughed and headed off.

"Stomp, Kano! Stomp!" she called after him.

He waved her away with a laugh.

"A tiger snake getting you would be more ironic, I suppose," Quinn said. "Let's head over here."

She led Taliya away from where the men were walking. Not like there was much privacy to be had. There were trees and a bush here and there, but it wasn't like the forest at home.

Quinn called over to her, "Kick some dirt on it when you're done. Local critters are gonna carry on like a pork chop over all these weird smells."

Taliya wondered how a pork chop carries on but obeyed and then headed to the transports, storing her ammo belt with her pack. The intense-looking soldiers loaded into the back of the larger vehicle, while Taliya and her group loaded into the one they'd arrived in with Taliya and Quinn in the first row and Rey and Kano in the seats behind them. The rooman's thick tail took some maneuvering to get comfortable. Carl and Rico manned the front.

"We'll stick with the transports as long as we can," Quinn said to all of them, "but the last five miles we should go on foot. They won't be expecting it."

"From what we can tell," Rico said, "they only have minimal security. Probably assumin' they're too far out for anyone to find 'em. We'll mosey in once it's dark."

Taliya huffed. "But they have to know, however much they paid, those dragons aren't really their property."

"Sure enough," Rico agreed. "Or those gronks wouldn't have 'em tucked in woop woop."

Taliya and Kano looked at each other, confused, as Rico turned on the transport. It elevated, and the other transport rose up next to them.

"Onward," Rico said, accelerating the vehicle with a whoosh.

Quinn glanced out the window nervously. "Watch out for wildlife."

"At home, we have to avoid deer," Taliya said. "They sometimes run right into the side of a vehicle."

"It's roos for us," Quinn said. "Though the mobs are rare out here."

"I've got the radar on," Rico assured her. "It should warn 'em off and give me a beep if something's in our path."

After a hesitant nod, Quinn leaned back, and Mila stuck her head out from under her mom's tunic. This time, sitting right next to her, Taliya could see there was indeed a natural pouch opening in the fur of Quinn's belly. Mila leaned back, stretched one leg out, and rested her long foot on Quinn's shoulder. Taliya loved that rooman still had the big feet and strong hopping legs of their wild cousins.

"Settle in," Quinn said to her roo. "It will be a few hours before we reach our stopping point. Are you hungry?"

Mila nodded, and Quinn opened a cooler pack on the floor. She handed Mila some kind of compressed food bar and then rested her head against the back of the seat while Mila munched contentedly.

"Rest up, Taliya," Quinn said. "We have a long day and night ahead of us, even if the plan goes perfectly."

Taliya leaned back. In the seats behind them, Kano

was already asleep. He could conk-out anywhere. Rey's breathing sounded like he was close as well. She doubted she'd be that lucky. Too many details raced around in her brain.

The plan was simple and direct. They would drive as close as they dared to the building where the dragons were being held, then hike the rest of the way in. Under the cover of darkness, the mercenary team would enter and secure the premises. Taliya hoped that didn't involve killing anyone, but she knew it might. Or anyone on their side dying, which she refused to consider.

That would all be complete before she was called on. Her job was to keep the dragons calm—expecting they would remember her, or at least Bunny would—and help fly them to safety on land owned by the family from Australia Zoo. The dragons knew Reynaldo too, and Carl and Kano to some extent. Depending on how scared or traumatized the animals were, they might let the four-some ride them during the escape. If not, the team would have to hold the compound until trucks arrived. She prayed to the gods it didn't come to that.

If all went to plan, the dragons would be transported from the Irwin reserve to the zoo and put on display temporarily. The exhibit they'd seen was ready, though it was listed to be for a group of quokkas—adorable beaver-sized animals that always looked like they were smiling. The zoo staff had no idea what was coming.

From there, details weren't clear, but at least the dragons would be back in safe hands. Would the government move them from Australia back to North America? The thieves had gotten the animals across the ocean in the first place, so it was obviously possible. A really big boat or plane would be required. Leaving the dragons in Australia sounded like the easiest choice to her, but she wasn't sure exactly who got to make that decision. Did the animals belong to the U.S. government? To the Canadians?

Even with her thoughts racing, Taliya managed to get some sleep. During the two breaks they took along the route, Taliya never saw anything alive but them. She was grateful for the jugs of water Rico had packed because there were no wells, lakes, or rivers. Just dried-out dusty acres. Which also made her grateful it was fall and a bit more temperate. She and Quinn chatted a bit about the day before at the zoo and what her job involved, but mostly they tried to rest.

The sun was low on the horizon when they finally came to a stop near a small cluster of trees in the middle of nowhere—or woop woop, as Rico called it. Everyone grabbed a quick meal of dried meat, bread, and water, with little conversation beyond grunts. Camouflage nets were thrown over the vehicles. Taliya checked her own gun and equipment, stomped her way to a nearby thorny bush area, and then returned to wait for directions. Carl and Reynaldo leaned against one of the transports, talking quietly between themselves, and Kano joined her on a boulder, rocking back and forth in anticipation.

An alpha-looking hired soldier—a massive man who

stood as tall as Kano and maybe weighed as much—made a whirling motion with his hand, and that seemed to be the signal it was time. The whole group moved toward him. Taliya sensed the mercenaries had worked as a team before. She'd noticed a lot of communication with only hand motions, nods, and eye contact. Giving them each a quick inspection, the leader seemed satisfied they were ready.

"I'm here as your bush guide," Quinn said, "but Mack is the man with the plan . . . and the big guns."

That brought some snickers from the group. He did, indeed, have two enormous repeating laser guns hanging on straps across his body like a destroyer out of some military virtual game, ready to take on alien scum.

"Right, then," he said in a deep, booming voice with only a mild accent, "me and Quinn will take the lead. Everyone else, pair up. Never leave your partner. Two sets of eyes are always better than one. It's about a five-mile hike to the facility. Rico will stay with the vehicles, get them to us if necessary, and let us know if we've been spotted. We know what frequency they use."

Rico nodded and held up his com. "I'll be eavesdroppin'."

"Tigran," Mack continued, "once it's dark, we'll need you up front with those good eyes of yours."

Taliya and Kano both nodded. They could see in moonlight many times better than the humans. As could Reynaldo. She assumed he was in on that request as well, but Mack didn't even glance his way. The group shifted into various last-minute duties. Taliya wasn't sure what else to do. She was as prepared as she was going to get.

Mack, with Quinn hop-stepping next to him, headed out, and the rest of the group fell in line. Leaving the transports behind was unnerving. There was nowhere to hide except a few trees here and there. Vast expanses of nothing but red dust. Seeing Quinn against the ruddy earth explained the natural selection of that fur color for some kangaroos, even in the dim light.

Little by little, the group spread out in pairs. Carl and Reynaldo gradually drifted to the front. Taliya suspected it was disconcerting for Carl to be in a military-style operation and not be in command. Mack frowned when he noticed the newlyweds second in line behind him.

"You blokes bring up the rear," he said sharply. "Keep watch."

Carl and Rey hesitated for a second, and Rey's tail puffed. It didn't seem like an offensive request, but the reactions from her friends suggested otherwise. The scent of testosterone and anger permeated the dusty air. Carl nodded, and he and Rey let the rest of the group pass, taking up the last spots. Taliya and Kano held back as well since it wasn't fully dark yet.

"Good to know," Kano grumbled.

"I feel like I'm missing something," Taliya whispered to him.

"Mack the man there's a bigot. You can see it in his eyes, smell it on him. Carl and Rey agitate him. Or worse."

Taliya flattened her ears, and her tail swished in agitation.

"Sensed it from Rico too," Kano said. "Guess you can change laws but not the hearts and minds."

Taliya glanced back at her friends. They hiked along like the rest of the group, though she sensed a sadness in the way Reynaldo's shoulders slumped. Carl met her eyes and grimaced, then resumed scanning the landscape for trouble.

How big a problem is Mack? Not a fan, or downright hateful? Dangerous, even?

Reynaldo had suffered through enough of that bullshit during the years he was living in a horrible lab, where disciplinary whippings left scars and almost killed him, and when he was held captive by the fanatical rednecks in Mississippi. Taliya extended and retracted her claws, trying to contain the anger over her friends having to deal with prejudice in the middle of a rescue operation. Mack was being paid. He had no right to exclude or demean.

Could Mack put Rey or Carl in unnecessary danger? Intentionally risk them? It was important to trust the leader, and she no longer did. *What about Quinn?* It had Taliya second-guessing everyone.

A rumble from Kano, too low for even tigran ears, vibrated across her skin. She met his gaze and felt assurance there. Taliya chuffed, and Kano slow-blinked in response. Regardless of who was in charge around them, they would always have each other's backs.

As the sun finally dipped below the horizon, Mack

motioned for Taliya and Kano to come to the front. They followed his direction, though she was less enthusiastic now.

"Use those sharp eyes and noses to watch for critters or hidden wires," Mack said. "We've gone more than two miles, and it's unclear what we'll face when we get closer."

Kano frowned. "Like explosives?"

"Doubt that," Mack said. "There's no direct path. They wouldn't waste the ammo. More like trip wires that signal an alarm or laser scopes. Anything that doesn't belong, point it out."

"And critters?" Taliya clarified. "You mean snakes?"

"Yup. They'll be sleeping. Give a little stomp now and then."

Mack motioned them on. The two tigran were now the leaders, with Quinn behind them, Mila staying hidden in her pouch. Taking a moment to tune in to the environment around her—focusing more on the smells of the desert and the taste of the night air—Taliya started off in the same direction they'd been going. The group lined up more directly behind her and Kano as they headed forward, nearly single file. Taliya whuffed and adjusted her ammo belt, tense about being the pair to clear the way. Kano grumbled next to her and stayed close, as intent on the surroundings as she was.

Trip wires. Land mines. Snakes. She tried to keep up the pace while watching for threats in the dark. Maybe this was also part of why she and Kano were there—one of the skills they'd been bred for. The humans pulled out night-vision, heat sensitive goggles.

After around thirty minutes of stressfully hiking through dark terrain, Mack placed a hand on Kano's shoulder, pulling him to a stop. The whole group froze. Mack pointed up ahead at the dim glow of buildings in the distance.

"First-wave team, let's roll," he barked.

9

Taliya scowled at the light from the buildings on the horizon, where the dragons were being held, as the mercenaries opened packs and pulled out extra guns, explosives, and a videodrone that would monitor the rescue and transmit to them, along with Rico back at the transports. Mack checked the charges on his two repeat laser rifles and added extra charges to his ammo belt. The fur spiked along Taliya's spine, all the way up the back of her head, and her ears flattened, absorbing the adrenaline from everyone around.

"You two," Mack said, motioning to Carl and Reynaldo, "lead the way."

She hadn't realized the pair were part of the first wave of attack. Taliya's chest clenched as Reynaldo scoped out the land ahead of them, then started off at a jog. Kano tensed next to her, maybe worrying about the same thing. Would Mack's prejudice put them in harm's way?

Carl was understandable. He was a highly trained soldier. But Rey? A shudder ran across her skin.

"No worries," Quinn said, misinterpreting their concern. "Mack's a pro." She turned away and gave Mila a snack bar while they found a place to settle in.

The last members of the invasion team disappeared into the dark, and the two soldiers remaining with them watched the coms to monitor the drone feed from the assault. The team had done reconnaissance work, but the threat level was still high. There was no way to predict exactly what they were marching into. It was all ridiculously stressful.

Taliya spotted a boulder nearby, made sure it was clear of snakes, and half leaned, half sat on it. Kano perched on the far side, leaning back on her. She could feel his impatience matching hers.

It felt like forever before flashes of light came from the buildings.

"Looks like we've got a firefight on our hands," one of the soldiers mumbled.

Taliya lurched up and joined them watching the video feed, with Kano and Quinn right behind her. The team was launching an attack, and the kidnappers were defending the facility. Laser gunfire continued for several minutes. With the night-vision of the drone and the wide shot, it was hard to tell exactly what was happening. Red blasts came from both directions. Bright figures were lit up by their body heat.

Floodlights snapped on around the building, temporarily blinding the drone and the group watching. Taliya's heart raced. The rescue team had nowhere to hide. As the video feed adjusted, she watched the team rush the facility with guns blazing. The enormous form of Mack stood out from the rest, firing a constant stream of crimson from both huge guns—one in each hand—as he stormed the building.

Once they were inside, the silence was unbearable. The drone showed a clear field, so no one had been killed. So far. Pops of light from laser fire shone through a window here and there.

"I wish we could see inside," Taliya whispered.

A large explosion lit up the sky, blinding the drone again, and vibrated the ground around them. Taliya's tail puffed. Kano whuffed next to her, adrenaline flowing from every pore. Their attention shifted from the drone feed to the building in the distance. More than once, Taliya had been the one waiting for rescue. The pterodragons probably didn't feel the same worries she had—maybe didn't even understand they were captives—but it was all frustrating and unnerving.

After a solid minute of no sound or lights, Taliya turned to Quinn. "What now?"

"We wait," she said with a shrug. "Unless it's safe, you two aren't going anywhere near it. Can't have them capturing you as well."

Taliya nodded her understanding, but she wanted to run and help somehow. Reynaldo had gone in. Was he expendable in their eyes? The panthran was more "valu-able" than her by a mile.

Quinn's com beeped. "It's Rico." She held it out so they could all hear.

"There was a lotta chatter for a bit there, warning each other, but it's gone quiet now. Hang tight till Mack gives us the all clear."

"Roger that," Quinn said.

Taliya spotted something in the air, heading their way. *A drone? A small plane?* Instinctively, she hunched down. The soldiers readied their guns, taking aim, and Kano instinctively moved to block her from an attack.

"What the hell is that?" Quinn said, clutching at Mila in her pouch. A strange chirping noise came from the roo, and Quinn growled a terrifying rumble deep in her chest.

Taliya caught a familiar musty scent on the wind.

"Wait!" she yelled. "Don't shoot! Don't shoot!"

"Kaah! Kaah! Kaah!"

The enormous shape seemed to glow against the dark sky as it swooped low over their heads. With a high-pitched scream, Quinn ducked behind a boulder.

The white pterodragon banked and headed back their direction with lazy beats of its wings. A moment later, the golden eyes of Reynaldo came into view, and Taliya could just make out his shape on its back.

"Down, Pegasus!" Rey shouted, and the dragon obeyed, landing a few yards away from the small group with a whoosh of tumbleweeds and rust-colored dirt.

Taliya's whiskers tingled with joy at the sight of them

both. It was like being right back in the training arena when the animals did something impressive. There was no other thrill quite like her days as a pterodragon wrangler.

Pegasus stomped his clawed feet back and forth a few times, spread his massive wings, and called out like a parrot in the rain forest. "KAAAH!"

The alpha dragon looked healthy, from his strange pterodactyl-shaped head to his sparkling green eyes and white feathered wings with a clawed joint midway, like a bat. Her head only reached the middle of the animal's chest, and his wingspan could swallow up a whole transport vehicle.

Moving slowly toward Pegasus, Taliya smiled and reached out her hand. He leaned down, gave her a sniff with his sharp hooked beak, snorted at the dust in the air, and set to nonchalantly preening the feathers of one wing.

"That was quite an entrance," Taliya called up to Reynaldo. "They almost shot you. Probably should have warned us."

The panthran swung one leg over so he sat sideways on the dragon's back, his white teeth and gold eyes glowing in the darkness. Taliya realized he'd been riding without any kind of harness or saddle and was shocked until she remembered he preferred it that way. He insisted it blocked the animal's flesh and made it hard to communicate with the dragon. The riggings had been for the tigran and liran who were trainers, but Reynaldo had usually flown without.

"All four dragons remembered me like it was yester-day," Rey said. "I couldn't resist personally bringing you the message of our success. We have the place locked down. There were only a few guards. Pretty cocky, frankly."

"But the explosion?"

"Taking down the communications tower. But we're not one-hundred-percent sure they didn't get a message out first, so let's get moving. Meet you there!"

Reynaldo swung his leg back over Pegasus and grabbed hold of a rope around the dragon's neck. "Go!"

Pegasus obeyed and flapped into the air, jogging forward and stirring up dust like a helicopter before soaring back to the facility. Taliya covered her eyes until it cleared, then turned to the group, who were already gathering up packs and supplies like nothing unusual had just occurred. She and Kano led the way at a trot, careful not to stumble in the dark on a rock or a snake. In fifteen minutes, they reached what was not much more than a circle of enormous metal sheds.

Mack was waiting for them outside. "No worries. Five men were on duty, but we got 'em."

Taliya suspected that meant all five were dead, but she didn't ask.

He motioned to follow him inside. "We'll gather up whatever boxes, tech, and research we can carry in the transport and deliver it to the zoo. Scans don't show any trackers in the drags, so you should be clear there."

A few lights were on inside the cavernous building,

and Taliya spotted four cages, barely big enough for the animals to move around in. One was empty—Rey and Pegasus were outside somewhere—and the others held Coconut, Polly, and Taliya's lovely Bunny. Relief flooded her, knowing they were all accounted for, finally.

"Kaah! Kaah! Kaah!" all three of them bellowed, echoing off the walls.

Taliya laughed with joy and ran toward the cages. One of the mercenaries was already swiping a key card over the locks to free the dragons. They each waddled out and sniffed at the team.

After catching Taliya's scent, Bunny raced directly to her former trainer in her funny bird-like hop/walk, wings spread in excitement. "Go! Go! Kaah! Go!" Bunny called out. "Taah-yaa! Taah-yaa!"

Taliya stopped for a second, but the instinctive shock of an animal that big racing toward her was quelled by the memory of their time together at the refugee camp—and the realization that the last two calls sounded rather like Bunny trying to say her name. The tigran met her dragon halfway and hugged her around the chest, scratching all the dragon's favorite spots and cooing. Bunny leaned down and preened the fur on top of Taliya's head.

Mack pushed the huge exit door open. "Move 'em out." Members of the team had found ladders and were heading her way.

The reality of accomplishing the next stage was daunting. Carl double-checked the directions and GPS on his com, making sure everyone had a copy in case they became separated, while Kano shifted around nervously. Pulling the harnesses out of a bag, Taliya let the dragon smell one and then climbed the ladder to start hooking her up. Kano came to help, and the dragon gave him a quick sniff. He was the one set to fly on Bunny since he'd ridden her once before.

"This is different than in the building back at camp with a soft floor . . . and a roof," he whispered.

"I know. But they clearly remember us. Would you rather ride one of the others?"

"Not exactly," he said.

Taliya knew the full answer was that he was nervous to ride *any* of them, but Bunny was his best bet. She was pretty sure the dragon would behave. Pegasus hadn't missed a beat. After seeing how they'd been held, she was more worried they were going to be malnourished and unable to make the whole trip to the Irwin property. Or simply fly off and refuse to be directed, but she didn't admit that out loud.

The dragons could see the open door, smell the fresh air, and were starting to get antsy. Taliya quickly got riggings around the other two animals, and Carl and Kano helped secure it all in place. Polly squawked and flapped a few times, slowing the process down. Coconut grumbled but mostly held still.

"Remember," Taliya said to Carl, "Pegasus is the alpha, so he needs to be in the lead. Since Rey is on him already, you're going to have to let them take the helm."

Carl chuckled. "Rey can boss me around anytime."

Two soldiers held the ladder for Carl and then Kano. Taliya could smell stress from both of the riders as they settled in and adjusted their backpacks. Her heart thudded, and she undoubtedly smelled the same. They'd never flown outside of the training building and were heading into the dark night of the Australian Outback. Besides whether or not the dragons would behave and take directions, there was still the fear of being attacked before they got to safety.

The soldiers helped her up on Coconut as the other two dragons headed for the doorway, where Quinn stared in awe. Mack waved from across the building.

"Fly safe," he called out.

His part of the rescue was nearly done. Rico was heading their way with a transport. He and the mercenary team would now gather what they could and disappear into the night. As Taliya passed Quinn on her way out the door, she called down, "Thank you!"

Quinn looked overwhelmed by the massive dragons, but there was a smile on her long-nosed face. Mila peeked out from under her mother's tunic with wide brown eyes.

"Be careful," Quinn said. "And get them the hell out of here!"

"You too. Don't wait around."

"Nah, yeah, we're outta here." Quinn hopped toward Mack and the rest of the team, who looked to be gathering boxes of research papers.

Taliya made eye contact with Kano. He looked scared

but focused. Pegasus appeared inside the doorway open-ing.

"Ready?" Rey asked the group.

Taliya nodded and wrapped the strap tighter around her hands, trying not to let her nervousness transmit to Coconut. The dragons had already started stomping and *kaahing*, excited by all the energy around them. Rey leaned down and said something to Pegasus, then grabbed his own rope tightly, leading him away from the building so they had room to launch. Taliya could feel Coconut huffing and scenting the air as the other three followed their leader out the door.

"Go!" Reynaldo yelled.

"Go!" the other three riders ordered.

"Go! Kaaah!" all four dragons called into the night.

With a massive hurricane of flapping and dust and cheers from the team left behind, all four dragons rose into the air and flew off into the dark. Taliya leaned close to Coconut's neck, taking a moment to enjoy the whoosh of the wind blowing past her, the thrill of soaring to freedom tingling her skin. No roof. No limitations.

Behind them, the building was already nothing but a faint glow in a blanket of blackness. She couldn't see any vehicles approaching except for Rico in the transport, so it seemed they'd escaped in the clear. Coconut's flight didn't feel stressed, and his breathing was normal. The other dragons looked fine as well. With a sigh, Taliya gave Coconut's shoulder a pat and took a deep breath, pre-paring for the night ahead and the unknowns it still held.

10

Nothing on Earth adequately compared with the feeling of flying on a dragon through the dark night air over the silent desert. Wildness. Freedom. Something sparked deep in Taliya's tiger DNA. She couldn't help but be enchanted by the bizarreness of it: two tigran, a panthran, and a highly decorated American Army general on genetically created dragons, soaring over the Outback.

In the moonlight, it was difficult to see the desert and how far below it was. They weren't as high as a helicopter would travel, but it was far enough to be a quick death. Taliya had worried the dragons wouldn't want to fly in the dark, but maybe they could see better than she expected. Or they were willing to risk it to escape those small cages.

The other riders and dragons were keeping an easy

pace. Kano appeared to be doing fine. Carl and Rey were too far away to tell. The others were following Pegasus's lead, as she'd anticipated, and Rey was keeping them fairly low. They seemed content with riders on their backs and were staying on course together.

The reality was that one dragon—or all of them—could decide to dump off their rider and fly freely at any moment. It was probably for the best Reynaldo had ended up on Pegasus because his way with animals bordered on psychic, downright magical. The dragons had always adored him and been willing to follow and cooperate. Taliya fleetingly wondered if he might want to stay with the dragons in Australia when the rescue was complete. It could solve several dilemmas for the newlyweds.

After roughly thirty minutes, when she was beginning to feel confident about their escape, chatter drifted back to her from Carl's com. It was hard to tell exactly what he was up to, but unless it was an emergency, he wouldn't be on his com while dragon-back hundreds of feet in the air. She spotted the light of an incoming message on Rey's communicator in the panthran's hand. Her claws flexed in and out involuntarily. Kano adjusted his hold on the harness, clearly anticipating something as well.

Reynaldo banked to the left and downward, and the other dragons followed. Pegasus sped up considerably, and Taliya's heart stuttered.

Are we being followed? Have we been spotted?

She held on tight and lowered herself on Coconut's back, hoping to avoid as much air resistance for the animal as possible. Wind whistled sharply in her ears, and she tucked them back.

After several minutes of sprinting, Pegasus angled downward for a landing. Taliya considered yelling "down," but it wasn't necessary. She just hung on while the dragon sailed toward the ground, made a running landing, and then came to a stop. Bunny hopped closer to her and Coconut while Carl and Rey talked from the backs of their dragons twenty yards away.

"Some kind of alert must have gotten out," Carl called over to them, "because several vehicles have pulled up to the building. The team's clear, but Rico's worried we'll be easy to spot in the air, the white feathers and all."

"Would they expect us to fly them out?" Taliya asked.

"Unclear," Carl said, "but the team's watching and monitoring the frequency. Rico thought it would be best if we stopped and waited to see what comes of it."

Taliya considered the area around them. There were a few trees, but nowhere to hide. The dragons were big mounds of glowing white on a dark sea of dirt and shrubs. She smelled a pond or lake about fifty yards away—an oasis in the desert, bits of greenery around the edges— and things like soap and machinery that indicated a homestead nearby. Sheep too, but not close at hand. Maybe a small farm. Carl pulled out his night-vision glasses, scanning the surroundings.

"There's a house over there, maybe half a mile." He pointed to his right. "No lights on."

Bunny started sneaking toward the pond with sly

bird-like side steps, and Kano chuckled. "I think she's thirsty."

Taliya sensed the same eagerness from Coconut, but she hesitated to dismount. How would they get back on without a ladder or someone to help? What if the dragons decided to fly away without them? Carl either hadn't thought it through or had a plan. He stowed his glasses and swung off Polly's back, encouraging the dragon toward the pond. The others followed with their riders still aboard.

"Watch out for crocs," Reynaldo warned, and Carl froze for a second.

An image of her time in the Crocoseum—a massive armored reptile jumping fully out of the water to grab a dead chicken from her hand—flashed through Taliya's mind. "Would they be out here?"

Carl shrugged. "Better safe than sorry. But I bet the dragons scare them off. Either way, let's not feed any crocs tonight."

All four animals drank from the pond using the odd scoop and head-tip-back method their beaks required. Then they squatted down on the bank to rest. The four riders sipped from their canteens, which seemed safer than the unknown water source—though the dragons clearly thought it smelled okay. Taliya tested the air but didn't sense anything for the dragons to eat. Carl's com buzzed, and he answered on speaker.

"The kidnappers are lookin' for tracks," Rico said.

"Won't be long 'fore they figure out the drags flew off. We shoulda driven around at the exit doors for show."

"Seems better if we keep going, then," Carl said. "Otherwise, we're sitting ducks."

"Up to you, mate. That end of the operation's your call."

Carl looked to Taliya. "Stay or go?"

"Careful with that word," she warned. "Polly might take off without you."

"Stay or *leave*, then," Carl corrected himself.

"Leave, definitely," Taliya said. "The farther away we can get, the better."

Rey and Kano nodded their agreement.

"Okay," Carl said into the com. "Rico, we're moving on."

"Roger that."

"You should get far away too."

"Already on it. Rico out."

Carl took a swig from his canteen and wiped his mouth. "Give the dragons a couple more minutes to rest, and we'll get back to it. At the rate we were going, it'll take us over four hours. Whole lotta nothing out here." He looked around in the dark. "Not like I can see much."

"I can," Rey said, "and you're right. Glad I spotted this pond. Who knows where we'll find more water."

Dogs started barking, and a light came on at the farmhouse in the distance.

Taliya tightened her grip on the riggings in case

Coconut startled. Her stomach roiled at the idea of some midnight interweb post that led the kidnappers right to the escape route. Otherwise, they'd have no idea which direction to start the search. Taliya spotted the lights of a vehicle pulling away from the house. "Shit."

"Well, that settles that," Carl said.

Without hesitation, he ran to Polly and took a leap at the rigging. Grabbing on with one hand, he pulled himself up. Taliya wasn't sure how he'd have managed it if the animal wasn't hunkered at the edge of the pond. The dragons all stood, and Coconut stretched his wings, ready to go.

Rey adjusted his position. "First star to the right, and straight on till morning."

Carl laughed and wrapped the riggings around his hand.

"What?" Kano frowned, clearly not up on his ancient-Disney-movie lore.

"Poor Tinkerbell's gonna need some extra clapping to recover from that slight," Taliya said with a smile at her husband.

"Go!" Rey shouted.

All the dragons *kaahed* and flapped their wings, took a running start, and hit the air together. Taliya looked back as the truck pulled up to the pond. Several dogs raced around the edges, smelling the air and wagging their tails in excitement, baying and howling. A man got out of the truck holding a rifle. Fortunately, it didn't occur to him to look up. The last she could see, he was shining a spotlight around the edges of the pond, probably very bewildered.

Four hours was a long time for the dragons to fly. She trusted Reynaldo to make the call when to land again. They were remaining at a lower altitude, so maybe he was keeping an eye out for opportunities. How far would the kidnappers go to get the dragons back? She couldn't imagine them taking up a helicopter in the dark, especially having no clue where to search.

After a while, the rhythmic sway of Coconut's flying started to make Taliya drowsy. Staying awake would be challenging for all of them. Giving Coconut a signal with her legs to slow down some, Taliya put herself at the rear of the group.

"You okay?" Kano called back.

"Yes, just keeping track of you males. No napping."

"Okay, Mom."

She chuckled to herself. No denying she was a mother. Many times over. No one was falling asleep and falling off on her watch. Worrying over them gave her something to focus on.

The faint sound of Carl singing floated back to her, a favorite fireside melody from the refugee camp. They called it the "Walk On" song because that was the main refrain. Taliya had seen the ancient musical movie it came from many times because it fascinated her father and his love of human behavior back when men actually risked their lives in boats, fished the ocean, and murdered whales—though carousels still existed as part of zoos and parks. As a teen, she'd found the plot a cautionary tale about choosing your life partner with great care. Then there was Kano, and that was that.

Rey soon joined in the song with his deep bass voice to harmonize the chorus but changing the words to "Fly on! Fly on!" and belting it out like he was back around that campfire and a bit drunk on ale. If it kept them awake, she didn't care if they put on a whole concert. There was no one around to hear.

She watched the world flow by beneath them. Mile after mile of shrub and bush with a few random trees in the moonlight. So many animals used to live there. Taliya imagined mobs of kangaroos and dingoes—without any human DNA—koalas in the eucalyptus trees and dozens of other species populating the Outback. As the team got closer to their journey's end, there would be dense trees and even the remnants of a rain forest, but not here.

They stopped once more, giving the dragons a chance to rest and sharing water from their canteens, but reaching safety before sunrise was vital. It was unlikely anyone had spotted them so far, but they'd have to pass over ranches and farms near the end. Those humans tended to rise early. The less notice of their adventure, the better. The landscape below was slowly shifting to sparse forests and even a small lake here and there, so she knew they were getting close to the 350,000 acres of the Irwin Nature Reserve and Research Center.

As the first bit of sun started to show over the horizon, Reynaldo steered Pegasus downward. A sprawling homestead lay in a clearing among the trees ahead. Several humans milled about in a field not far from a grouping of large buildings. There was a massive barn, at least 20 yards square. It wouldn't do for the long-term, but they only needed to hide the dragons for a day or two, until the trucks from the zoo arrived to pick them up. As they neared landing, Taliya spotted Robbie Powell and Wolfie among the dozen or so humans waiting for them in the early dawn light.

Pegasus aimed for strip of open roadway near the buildings, and all four dragons took turns for a running landing. The team on the ground greeted them with cheers and applause.

"Kaah! Kaah! Kaah!" Coming to a stop, the foursome announced their arrival with ear-splitting cries.

Coconut spread his wings and strutted around, either showing off or telling the crowd to keep back. Taliya laughed and patted his side to calm him down. The other three animals settled their wings as well, but there was still snorting and clawing at the ground.

"Stay aboard," Reynaldo called out. "Until we have them secured."

Robbie was the first one brave enough to come close. "These dragons deserve a full-on *Crikey*!" He put his hands on his head and grinned. "Bonzer!"

Taliya chuckled. "They are amazing."

"That's the understatement of the century, mate."

When Robbie urged the dragons to some livestock troughs with food and water, they didn't hesitate—trotting over and digging in. While they fed messily and tossed around as much seed and berries as they consumed, humans in khakis moved in and looped ropes around the dragons' necks, in case they got it into their heads to fly away. Taliya doubted they would. The last few hours had probably been more flying than they'd done their whole lives put together.

All four riders slid to the ground and stretched wearily, handing their packs over to young humans buzzing around them. Now that it was over, Taliya was sure she would fall asleep right there, leaning on Coconut. But she wouldn't rest until the animals were well hidden.

Once the dragons had their fill, the riders led them into the massive barn. They barely fit through a side sliding door. An open area in the middle could hold all four and keep them out of sight of any roving drones or helicopters. The ground was covered with hay and some soft mulchy bedding. Checking each of them over, Taliya gave Bunny a few extra pats and scratches to thank her for not dumping Kano off. Bunny groomed the hair on the tigran's arms before settling down into the straw. Taliya staggered over to the door, watching the animals until it was shut behind her. Several of the humans stationed themselves around the building to be on watch and keep an ear out for the dragons.

"They'll be fine now," Wolfie assured her. "From what we've heard, the kidnappers have no idea where ya went. No reason they'd suspect here."

"Maybe we shouldn't have gone to the zoo yesterday," Taliya fretted. "Someone might make a connection."

"Yeah, nah. Not all the way out here. Not a chance."

She nodded reluctantly and followed Robbie to the main building. The smell of breakfast—bacon and eggs and that weird Aussie veggie spread—wafted out of an open window. Her stomach rumbled in response.

Inside, they met more members of the human team and Connie, Robbie's mom—a sturdy blonde with smile lines around her brown eyes. The lodgings were nothing fancy. Beige metal buildings filled with several large open rooms, the kitchen and dining area, and the barracks and bathrooms. It appeared practical and efficient, more for conservation work than a cozy home. Connie led them straight to the utilitarian kitchen and set them up with food at one of the many big wooden tables. A few humans from the zoo team joined them, but most were done eating and off elsewhere, busy with the tasks of the day. Even Wolfie had jumped on his motorbike and headed out on the property once he knew they were comfortable. He and four other dingman would be standing guard.

While they ate, Connie gave them an update.

"All info we have suggests you are totally in the clear. They're probably searching and ready to check satellites this morning, but since we've got the dragons tucked away, it's unlikely they'll find a trace. No one saw you?"

"Not as far as I could tell," Carl said. "We had one close call with a farmer and his dogs, but he didn't think to look up."

"Good," Robbie said. "The plan's to move 'em tomorrow night. That will give ya a rest before the next leg. Shouldn't set off alarms for anyone in the area. We do overnight transports like that all the time to avoid traffic."

Taliya wanted to ask for details and have it all spelled out, but with a full stomach now her eyes felt heavy and her brain too fuzzy to process.

They'd made it. The dragons were safe. The full plan could wait a few hours.

"You must be plumb tuckered out," Connie said with a smile. "Bet your feline genes are ready for some sleep."

"About four hours ago." Reynaldo grinned and then yawned, covering his mouth politely—and probably so his teeth didn't scare the humans.

"Finish yer grub," Robbie said, "and we'll get ya to a cot. We have a whole bunkhouse available for workers."

The foursome finished eating and headed for bed. Reynaldo decided he would sleep in the barn with the dragons. If they grew restless, it would be good to have someone they knew on hand.

The bunkhouse looked rather like Army barracks. Over two dozen simple metal bunkbeds were lined up in two rows with an aisle down the middle. At the far end of the room was a large bathroom. It was nice to have a real toilet again, but a shower was going to have to wait. She didn't have a change of clothes handy anyhow, not sure where her pack ended up.

"I don't think I've ever been this tired," Kano said,

pulling off his boots with a groan and tucking them under the bed.

"Not even when the twins were born?" Taliya asked.

"Which set?"

Carl chuckled from across the room. "I'd warn you I snore, but I don't think it'll matter."

Taliya felt like she'd sleep through that and pretty much anything else. Exhaustion pulled her down, and she sighed. *The dragons are safe. Everyone's safe.*

11

Taliya rolled and stretched. Whuffing, she pulled the covers up around her, hoping to fall back asleep. Muscles she didn't even know she had ached throughout her back and legs, reminding her of the successful rescue. After flopping around uncomfortably for bit, Taliya cracked one eye open. Her pack was resting next to the bed. Checking her com, she realized it had been six hours since their arrival.

"Morning, sunshine," Carl called from the doorway.

She groaned deep in her throat and considered finding something to throw at him, but that felt like too much effort. He was up and at 'em, fully dressed in casual camo and sipping a mug of what smelled like strange coffee, bitter and earthy. He made a motion to offer her some.

"No thanks," she mumbled.

"This brew'll get your heart going," he said with a laugh. "Whew."

A shower turned off in the bathroom. One whiff told her Kano was in there.

"Robbie said to relax today. I'm definitely looking forward to just sitting in a transport and getting back to the Sunshine Coast without worrying about falling to my death or being shot."

Taliya agreed. Another long flight did not sound appealing.

"Rey's still out with the dragons," Carl said. "Haven't heard any fuss from them. Probably exhausted. They did all the work."

Taliya sat up and remembered she'd slept in her clothes. It wasn't a pleasant smell—dust and stress pheromones embedded in her fur.

"I'll let 'em know you're moving. Connie is determined to feed us all until we bust. You missed an excellent pork roast for lunch, but they saved you some." He tossed a bottle of pills on the end of her bed. "Take two. It'll help with the aches."

"Thanks."

Carl headed out the front door of the barrack as Kano emerged from the shower in a pair of black slacks. "Does every bone and muscle in *your* body hurt?"

She chuckled. "Yup. Carl said to take these."

"Already did. Takes a bit to kick in."

She glanced at the pill bottle and frowned. Tigran rarely needed any kind of pain relief. Today was definitely an exception.

"A shower'll help. The basic stuff is in there, soap and

such." He dropped his pack by his bed and put his boots on. "But don't drink the weird coffee. I swear, it's got that veg spread stuff in it."

"I'm going to need something," she admitted. "And I'm beyond grateful we have a quiet day ahead. 'Vacationing' is exhausting."

"If we ever get a *real* vacation that doesn't involve you working, I bet it'll be relaxing."

She nodded in agreement. Once they left the dragons in the care of Australia Zoo, they deserved a few days of actual rest. Thoughts of a quiet beach or snorkeling around the reefs off the coast helped unclench the knot between her shoulder blades. She popped two of the pills and swallowed them with warm water from her canteen.

Kano slipped on a black tunic and headed to the main building for food while Taliya showered. He was right, she did feel better afterward. It helped to ease out her sore body, but it was too warm to get the water more than tepid. The barrack had air conditioning, but not set low enough for creatures with fur. Still, it was better than outside, which her com said was near 85 degrees Fahrenheit, despite being autumn. *Much hotter, and I'll end up panting and looking silly.*

There wasn't a hair dryer, so she did the best she could with the towel before she dressed in the navy tunic and slacks from her pack, pulled her dusty boots on, and followed the smells of food.

Kano was still finishing his meal in the commissary and chatting with two young women in zoo uniforms at a long wood table. Their eyes were wide, and Kano was clearly making an impression. Taliya chuffed at him, and he chuffed back. The girls giggled.

"We'll see you later, Kano," one said, setting her mug in the sink along with piles of dishes from lunch. She smiled hesitantly at Taliya, and the pair hurried out of the building.

"Entertaining the locals?" she said with a fang-filled grin, loading a plate with leftover roast, potatoes, and a hunk of brown bread.

"They've never met a tigran before."

She joined him at the table, though his plate was nearly clean. "Certainly not one as magnificent as you."

"Why, thank you, wife. Do you want some tea or funky coffee?"

She squinched her nose at the aroma from the coffee pot. "No, just water, I think. The shower woke me up." She poured herself a glass from the pitcher on the table. "I can't get over how arid everything is here."

"They're apparently starting the dry season, though it's hard to imagine being drier than what we've already seen."

He hung out and sipped tea while Taliya enjoyed a quiet meal. After the last twenty-four hours, her stomach appreciated the leisure. As the protein rushed through her bloodstream, she felt more like herself. Taking their empty plates over to the sink, she hesitated. The workspace was a mess. She would've chewed the kits out if her kitchen ever looked like that.

"Robbie says to just leave them," Kano said. "An intern will see to it."

She put her plate in the sink and started running water over things. Just leaving it seemed rude. A teenager in khakis came in through the back door, and he immediately looked horrified.

"Nah, mate, I'll get that. My duty today."

She turned off the water. "Sorry."

"No worries, but guests don't do the scrubbin'. And it's a complicated process out here. Gotta ration the suds."

She nodded and moved out of the way, but she wasn't sure why the kid thought dishes were complicated. And why did they need to ration detergent?

"Thanks to whoever made the food," she said. "It was fantastic."

"That's all Connie. Showin' off a bit, I reckon." He beamed a huge smile at her. "Those dragons. Man, oh man. I've wrangled some cool critters, but nothin' like them babies. Once we're clear to tell the tale, my friends'll never believe it."

Taliya nodded. "I remember the first time I saw them, when they arrived at the refugee camp. Most amazing sight ever. If I'd known in that moment what Bunny would mean to me and how that day would change my life, I never would have believed it either."

"It brought ya to Australia, so that's a bonus."

"It is, indeed."

He turned to his work, filling a section of the sink with water, and she met Kano at the door. They headed out to the barn to check on the dragons, but the sight outside made them both pause. What looked like a whole flock of weird ostriches stood at attention, necks stretched and heads high, orange-brown eyes inspecting them. Her tail puffed instinctively.

Robbie called from across the field. "Don't let the mob worry ya. Just curious. Never seen a tigran before."

"Female ostriches?" Taliya asked, still not moving from the porch.

"Emus," Robbie corrected. "No ostriches 'round here."

"Right." Taliya shook out her tail. "Emus. Birds that can kill you with a good kick. But just curious birds."

Kano whispered behind her. "*Big-ass* birds."

Hoping they couldn't fly, Taliya stepped hesitantly down into the yard. The emus backed out of the way, but they also lowered their heads and continued to check out the pair of strangers. Robbie met the pair halfway, shushing the mob to the side as he went.

"These blokes shouldn't worry ya much," he said, "after flyin' all night on those dragons."

Taliya laughed and realized it was true. If she didn't know the dragons, they'd certainly be terrifying. But something about birds always made her stomach swirl. They were so unpredictable.

"If ya want, I can take ya on a tour of the refuge later. We release all kinds of animals here, since we know they'll have access to water and food. Water's always an issue in these parts."

Taliya nodded and smiled. "We'd love that."

"Go check on ya drags, then let me know if ya need anythin'." Robbie gave a quick salute and headed into the main building.

Taliya looked around past the emus, who were wandering off and pecking at the ground, and noticed a mob of kangaroos and smaller wallabies drinking from a trough nearby. Thinking about Robbie's comment on the water supply, she felt guilty for taking a long shower. That was probably why the dishwashing kid had gotten so excited. Water was in short supply. It needed to be used wisely.

Working their way through the animals milling around the yard—who seemed as nervous about the pair as they were about them—Taliya and Kano headed to the barn. It was dusty and stuffy in there, but there was a breeze from some kind of cooling unit. The dragons were awake but still hunkered where she'd left them, and Reynaldo was checking each over with his trained eye.

"No worse for wear," he said.

A few more knots in Taliya's muscles relaxed—partly from seeing the dragons again and probably also from the meds Carl provided. "When do the transports and cages arrive?"

"Should be around dusk tomorrow, so the move can be done overnight, like they routinely do them. Robbie didn't want to have activity right away because that might grab attention. The drive will take fifteen hours, if all goes to plan. Hopefully, we can sneak them in and have them settled before the media finds out."

"Fifteen hours?" Kano whuffed. "Glad we don't have to fly again."

"Amen to that. And the kidnappers or someone else would spot them when we got closer to the city," Rey said.

Taliya flared her whiskers. "That could cause a panic. Though, this is Australia. Maybe not."

Rey chuckled. "They're not secure until they're at the zoo. In the transport enclosures, they'll be all but invisible. Just truck 'em down the highway."

Taliya ambled over to Bunny, and the dragon greeted her with a quiet "Taah-yah."

"Hello, my friend," Taliya said, leaning into Bunny's musty-smelling chest. "Are you as sore as me?"

Bunny lowered her head and fussed with the back of Taliya's shirt, then stretched her wings and settled again. The other three dragons looked content. Maybe they'd gotten used to being so contained. It was unclear how long they'd been at the kidnappers' facility. Since their original capture four years ago?

"Bunny and Polly were anxious and fussy when we first arrived," Rey said. "Lots of squawking and shifting around. Seem fine now. Slept for hours. I'll get them some fresh hay."

Taliya started to offer help, but her back disagreed. Maybe she could recruit a couple of those young humans who seemed so useful. Rey came back with a pitchfork and started to move the hay around Bunny, but Taliya sensed agitation from the dragon.

Bunny stood up, spread her wings, and squawked, "Stop! Stop! Stop!"

All three of them stared in shock at the spot where she'd been sitting.

"Is that an *egg*?" Kano said.

Taliya nodded slightly, her brain still processing. It was clearly an egg—light-brown, about a foot wide.

"Well, that explains the fussiness," Rey said as Bunny settled back down on her prize.

Kano snorted. "I guess the bad guys had an agenda."

"Puts a big ol' wrinkle in our plans." Rey frowned.

"To say the least." Taliya leaned on the barn wall with a sigh. *Shit, shit, shit!*

Rey's face looked like he was thinking the same thing. "We'll need to find a safe way to move it with her. I'll get Robbie. He seems to be the man with the plan around here."

As Rey rushed off, Taliya patted Bunny on the chest. "How'd you make that whole flight with that giant egg inside of you?"

"Can you imagine if she'd laid it while we were traveling?" Kano said. "Or when we were flying? Can you lay an egg while flying?"

Taliya snorted. "I can't lay an egg at all, so don't ask me."

Robbie jogged into the barn with Reynaldo and a shocked-looking Carl following close behind.

"An egg?" Robbie said with a gasp. "No doubt?"

"*No* doubt." Taliya wasn't sure if she could get Bunny

off it again, but she lifted up the feathers on her side enough for him to get a peek at the egg. The dragon glanced back at her with one green eye.

"Ya little ripper!" Robbie said, bending over to see better.

All five of them stood there for a solid minute. Taliya considered how or even if they should move Bunny and the egg to the zoo. It seemed perilous for the egg to be in the transport container with the dragon. She could accidentally step on it, or it could break from the roughness of travel. But Bunny couldn't stay in the barn until it hatched —whenever that might be.

Carl broke the silence. "So, we need a plan. Ideas?"

"Right," Robbie chimed in. "We move eggs now and then, just not usually ones this big. Or with broodin' mamas this big. I bet there's an incubator meant to hold a batch of eggs that'd be large enough. But will she let us take it?"

"What if she doesn't know?" Kano said.

Taliya frowned and put her hands on her hips with a huff. "She's going to notice if we steal her egg."

"Not if we replace it with a dummy egg," Kano said. "I've seen it on dozens of zoo shows. They take the eggs away from penguins and other endangered birds and put a fake one in its place, so they can be sure it hatches. They give the chick back to the parents to raise."

"He's right," Robbie said. "Standard practice fer rare animals."

"So what could serve as a dummy egg, at least for the trip?" Reynaldo asked.

"Ah," Robbie said with a grin, "this is where zoo interns come in handy. Time to rally." He jogged from the barn.

After patting Bunny and praising her accomplishment, they followed after him. In the yard, Robbie already had four young humans in a huddle. One of them peeked toward the barn with wide eyes and then tucked back into the group again. After another few seconds, they all turned toward Taliya.

"We're gonna need to really see that egg," Robbie said.

Taliya nodded and led the way back into the barn. Bunny had always been food motivated, and she hoped that hadn't changed. The interns all hovered near the door while Taliya scooped some grains and nuts into a nearby feeding trough.

"Hey, Bunny," she said, hoping not to disturb the other dragons, who were napping again. "Hungry?"

Bunny tipped her head questioningly, then stood up, spread her wings for a stretch, and hop/walked over to the food, leaving the glorious egg behind.

"Don't get too close," Taliya warned as the eager interns started to creep forward.

Pulling out communicators, the team snapped photos and made estimates on size and shape.

"Is it warm?" one of them asked. "She might notice if we give her somethin' that doesn't feel right."

Everyone looked to Taliya. She supposed if anyone

was going to be allowed to touch the egg, it would be her. Keeping an eye on Bunny, she moved slowly away from the dragon and closer to the egg. When the munching mama didn't react, Taliya gently put one hand on top of it. An intern gasped in shared excitement. It felt slightly warm to the touch, but not particularly hot. The shell had tiny pock marks, like a hen's egg, but she doubted Bunny could feel that. Stepping back before the dragon noticed the invasion, Taliya joined the team.

"It feels like it's just warm from her body, not necessarily radiating heat. So it would need to be a substance that can pick up her body heat. Otherwise, it's like a chicken egg."

"Just a whole lot bigger," one of the interns said with a chuckle.

"With a dragon inside," another whispered with awe.

"Research carefully," Robbie warned the group, "and only with a hidden identity. Just in case. We don't know if the captors knew she was brewin' a baby. We've got twenty-four hours."

The interns nodded and rushed off to design a fake egg. Bunny hopped back over and settled down on the real thing. Part of Taliya was proud Bunny was being a good mother, keeping her egg warm. The other part had no idea how they'd get it away from her, fake her out with a dummy egg, and complete the transfer to the zoo.

"Leave it to the team," Robbie said. "I'm gonna see what incubators we have at hand. Emus lay pretty big eggs, but we usually leave that part to nature. It's not too late to have the zoo team bring us somethin' with the transports." He clapped his hands and rubbed them together. "Never a dull day."

"What about Polly?" Reynaldo walked over to the dragon in question. "Do you suppose she laid an egg too? She was fussy."

Everyone stared at Polly, but she was oblivious to their attention.

Carl slapped a hand across his forehead. "*Two* eggs?"

"There could be one under her now." Taliya felt stupid for not checking right away.

Reynaldo circled Polly once and then shrugged. "I guess we get her to stand up."

Taliya grabbed a tub of food and took it to Polly, shaking it under her nose. The dragon opened her eyes but didn't move.

"Come and get it, Polly. Aren't you hungry? Polly want some breakfast?"

The dragon watched her but still didn't budge. Maybe because she was sitting on an egg.

"You keep her distracted, and I'll check," Rey said.

Taliya continued shaking the food and talking to Polly while Reynaldo slowly reached under the dragon with both hands. Polly squawked but didn't turn around to bite him. Reynaldo paused a second and smiled before pulling back out.

"Egg?" Taliya asked.

Rey grinned with delight. "Egg."

"Well, we always assumed that's why there were two pairs, for breeding, but I never expected this."

"So we need *two* huge incubators," Robbie concluded. "And a second dummy egg." He headed off at a trot to handle it.

Taliya put the food in front of Polly, who leaned down to take a few bites. She rubbed the sides of Polly's face and scratched between her eyes.

Taliya let her mind wander to what was growing inside those massive eggs. How cute would little pterodragons be? What could be accomplished with their training when you could start out young? Sadness settled in her heart, knowing she wouldn't be part of any of it. She already had her hands full. Being a pterodragon wrangler had been complicated with three kits, but it would be impossible with five. And the whole not-living-in-Australia thing, of course.

"Thinking about the chicks?" Kano said quietly, stepping up to wrap an arm around her waist.

"Is that what they'd be called?"

"Hatchlings? I guess the zoo will be the one to decide. Naming an animal that hasn't been named before."

"Well, maybe the scientists named them," Taliya said, "because these dragons must have come from eggs at some point."

"True, but who cares what they called them. I bet it was something boring and clinical."

She smiled with a huff. Robbie and his family would come up with a good classifier.

Leaving the dragons to rest—and incubate their eggs —they headed out to the open field and all the animals there. Two interns stayed on duty just outside the barn door, in case the dragons became agitated.

There were a couple of hours before dinner, so Robbie showed the four visitors around the complex. The mob of kangaroos and wallabies were hesitant about the tigran and panthran, but they eventually gained enough confidence to eat out of the creatures' hands. Their tongues tickled Taliya's palm, and it felt odd to feed something so similar to Quinn and Mila. The emus were more wary and simply headed off into the bush. Taliya was okay with that.

See ya, huge freaky birds.

Robbie led the way into a nearby building and introduced them to some spiky echidnas and three baby wombats that had been found orphaned. The wombats, which reminded Taliya of stocky American ground hogs, provided a lesson in square-shaped poop. Robbie explained the how and why of their digestive process, but it was like an old joke. Apparently, in wombat world, you could pass a square object through a round hole.

There was an enclosure of fruit bats recovering from injuries, who were munching greedily on wedges of watermelon, and an injured kookaburra. Robbie sounded a startling imitation of the kookaburra's multi-faceted call —like he spoke the language—and the bird joined in with great gusto. Near the back of the building, there were kangaroo joeys being hand raised by a team of volunteers.

"Back in the day," Robbie said, "we only had the wildlife hospital at the main zoo, but our facility services orphans and injured animals from this part of the country."

One of the interns bottle-fed a joey while it lounged in a cotton sack meant to feel like a mom's pouch. When she was done, the visitors were given a chance to hold him. He was heavier than Taliya had expected and all legs. One foot or another stuck out of the bag constantly. The joey sniffed her face and nibbled on her fur. Her chest tightened, and she wondered what her kits were up to right then. Just waking, maybe, a world away at home with Marla and their grandparents.

Behind the building were five-foot-tall, bizarre-looking birds. Unlike the roaming emus, these four were in a large fenced-in area, each with their own specific territory full of grass and trees. Their heads sported a gigantic crested bone, reminding her more of the pterodragons than emus, but these birds were colorful: blue-black feathers, turquoise necks and faces, and red wattles hanging from their chins. The three-toed feet with sharp claws—one toe sporting a nail five inches long—were very much like the dragons.

"These're our cassowaries," Robbie said. "They can't thrive in the wild anymore. The old rain forest areas are too dry. They're highly territorial, and their kick can pack a wallop. Most dangerous bird in the world, so they say."

"That's quite a colorful mob," Carl said, using the

word that seemed to apply for every group of Australian animals.

"A shock," Robbie corrected. "Not like they hang out together."

"A *shock* of cassowaries?" Taliya asked.

"Right. Maybe 'cause a their nasty kicks. Maybe 'cause a the sounds they make. Most of it we can't even hear. Well, maybe you lot can."

One of the birds strutted toward them making a low noise like a bullfrog croaking. Another in the distance emitted barking snorts, like an agitated pig. Vibrations tingled in her body that must come from sounds lower than she could perceive. The same way she'd felt at the elephant and giraffe exhibits at the zoo—feeling the animals communicating but not hearing it. Kano could make that low, inaudible rumble too, but she'd never gotten good at it.

Giving the cassowary enclosures a wide berth, the foursome followed Robbie into the main building. Dinner prep was in full swing, delicious smells wafting through the air, and sounds of a media wall came from a room in the back. It seemed odd that life was flowing along normally for a huge portion of the staff members. Maybe they were used to weird animals showing up and visitors coming and going. This group was just weirder than most.

"They're watching the second Dragonriders of Pern movie," Kano said with a smile.

Taliya listened for a moment and had to agree on the subject if not the exact movie in the series. She'd watched all six of the Dragonrider movies more times than she could count. "I guess they thought it was appropriate."

"I'm glad our dragons don't breathe fire," Carl said with a grin. "But I wouldn't mind watching a movie about ones that do."

After a delicious dinner of lamb and veggies, the evening was spent watching fictional genetically created dragons burn thread from the skies of Pern on the media wall in the lounge area, though each of them slipped out to take turns checking on their pterodragons. When the movie ended, Connie announced it was time to shut things down because tomorrow would be a demanding day.

Heading to bed this time, the barrack was nearly full with two dozen interns, male and female, all young and brimming with energy and activity. For creatures sensitive to smells and atmosphere, it was unnerving. Taliya hadn't really thought about the fact they were only alone before because it was daytime. *I've never had to sleep surrounded by so many humans.* Looking around the room more carefully, there were dressers and personal belongings next to the bunks. She'd been too tired earlier to notice. Fortunately, she and Kano had both selected beds at the end of the row that appeared unclaimed.

Carl decided to join Reynaldo in the barn for the night. Maybe he felt the same way about being surrounded, despite his years in the Army. Maybe the newlyweds just wanted time alone.

Taliya and Kano waited until the humans settled

before they ventured into the bathroom. The showers were separated into male and female sections, but some parts—like sinks and toilet stalls—were shared areas. She changed into light pajamas that had fit in her pack, as did Kano. She made eye contact with him in the mirrors as they cleaned their teeth, and he slow-blinked. At least they didn't have to sleep in separate barracks.

When they emerged, there was nothing but dim lighting in the sleeping area. Each returned to the bunk from earlier in the day and settled in. Taliya immediately noticed that her sheets had been changed. Connie, she suspected, had wanted to remove the dust that certainly came off the clothes Taliya had slept in that morning. The clothes from their nighttime flight were also cleaned and folded, ready for the adventures to come.

Most of the men were already asleep, but she could sense most of the females were not. The one closest to Taliya rolled on her side and whispered, "What does it feel like to ride on your dragon in the sky?"

"Well, nothing like the dramatic swooping around and diving while fighting thread in those movies. Their wings are quiet. It's thrilling and peaceful at the same time. Maybe you'll get to find out someday."

The girl sighed and tucked the covers up to her chin. "Maybe."

"I hope so," Taliya said honestly. "It's amazing."

12

Taliya woke to the interns bustling around her, even though it was barely dawn. Focusing on Kano's breathing, she could tell he was still asleep. She rolled over and decided to wake him when the staff had cleared out. But it was Kano who woke her with a kiss on the forehead. She snorted and sat up. The barrack was empty except for them.

"These kids are going to think we are very lazy," he said. "It smells like they've all been gone for hours."

Taliya glanced out the window at the sun. "Not that long. Maybe an hour. Remind them we're part feline."

"Let's go see how we can be useful today."

After dressing and preparing their packs to leave, they headed for breakfast. Scrambled eggs, bacon, rolls, and smoked salmon rested on warming plates for them, along with coffee and tea.

"G'mornin'" Robbie said, entering the building with a

grin, looking like he'd been awake and busy for hours. "No criminals stormed the gates. No dragons got rowdy and wrecked the barn. All's well."

Taliya wiped her mouth with a bamboo napkin. "I don't think I moved all night."

"Outstandin'! Once you've checked on the drags, how 'bout I take ya on a tour of the reserve?"

"That would be great," Kano said.

Carl and Rey joined them, though they'd had breakfast already, and said the dragons were doing fine. Brooding the eggs might actually be serving to keep them settled and calm. Taliya still took a quick peek to assure herself all was well before the foursome set off with Robbie to explore.

For the next few hours, he drove them around the extensive property in an old-school jeep with no doors. In the open grasslands, they spotted kangaroos sprawled out in the sun, fruit bats sleeping in a tree, and a mob of emus pecking around for breakfast, though spread out because they don't normally live in groups. There were wetlands and streams. Crocodiles lounged on a riverbank. Robbie said they studied those but never hand fed the wild ones. Taliya was fascinated by all the different ecosystems in the same territory.

"Here on the peninsula," Robbie explained, "the seas around us keep things healthier than what ya saw in the Outback."

Returning to the main house for lunch, they enjoyed a casual meal of make-it-yourself sandwiches and baked beans, with different interns coming and going as they handled their daily chores.

"The trucks'll be here around six," Robbie said, checking his communicator after slipping his plate into the sink. "The cages are collapsible, so they won't look like anythin' suspicious on the road. Once they arrive, we'll get it all assembled, load 'em up, and head 'em to the zoo."

"And you trust everyone involved in this?" Carl asked, shifting into protective mode. "On the road, we'll be out in the middle of nothing most of the time. Nowhere to hide."

"One-hundred-percent," Robbie assured him. "Mostly because only a handful of people actually know what's happenin'. Interns here are on media silence, and we're not askin' for supplies or things that are unusual. All routine for animal transports."

"And the fake eggs?" Taliya asked.

Robbie nodded. "In process. We got it."

"All right, then," Carl said, getting up from the table. "I'm gonna try to get some shut-eye. It's gonna be a long night."

Reynaldo nodded in agreement and took their dishes to the sink before heading to the barn. They'd slept on cots there, and it would probably be the quietest place around if the dragons behaved. Soon Taliya and Kano were the only ones left at the table.

"I could use a nap too," Kano said, stretching his arms up high. "I doubt we'll sleep much tonight."

"I saw some hammocks on the porch," Taliya said.

"Excellent idea."

After making sure all the dishes were in the sink—and forcing herself to walk away and let an intern handle it with all the proper water protocols—the pair stretched out in the hammocks and watched the freaky emus peck at the ground nearby. A small mob of kangaroos sprawled in the brown grass under a tree across the field. It was hot that afternoon, and in the shade of the porch with the swing of the hammock, Taliya found herself quickly lulled to sleep.

She woke to the voices of interns coming back to the main house for dinner. Kano's spot was already empty, and she could smell beef stew wafting from the kitchen. It was amazing that alone hadn't woken her. Her stomach grumbled, and she rolled carefully out of the hammock. The interns smiled at her as she stretched and groaned.

"Those hammocks'll suck ya in," one of the guys said.

Taliya smiled back, careful to keep her fangs mostly hidden, and followed the interns to the dining hall. The room was full to overflowing, with the cooks still fussing as Connie ran the kitchen and everyone waited around the big tables impatiently. Taliya suspected this was an earlier dinner than usual and people were excited about what lay ahead. If this truly was every member of the team at the reserve, there were forty humans of varying ages. She hadn't seen Wolfie or his dingman guards since they'd arrived. Kano, Carl, and Rey were chatting with a table of rapt interns, so she joined them. Robbie spotted her arrival and waved.

"Right-o," he called out, like they'd been waiting for her. "Let's have a chat before the grub's on."

Everyone except the three cooks settled down onto window ledges and chairs and gave him their full attention.

"The trucks're on schedule and will arrive at six. Two incubators should be here soon, so we'll have everythin' we need to make this move successful. Taliya and Rey are in charge of convincin' the dragons to load into the crates. A challenge we weren't expectin' is the two eggs. We're gonna do the swap out with the dummies right after some tucker."

He opened a large box at the end of the table and pulled out what looked remarkably similar to the dragon eggs. After enthusiastic chatter and even some applause for the hastily but accurately made substitute, he continued.

"Taliya, we want ya to make the switch while Rey distracts 'em."

"Okaaay," she said hesitantly. "Bunny walked right off her egg, but Polly seems very attached."

"I'd hate to scare her off and have her reject it later." Robbie considered it a moment. "Let's start with Bunny. Ya can trick birds with a rock sometimes. Let's hope that holds true for these avian-style drags. And remember . . ." He looked all around the room. "Not a peep on the webs or to your friends. Not a hint or suggestion that anythin' is goin' on, even after we've headed out. Not till ya get the all clear. Got me?" The crowd nodded with solemn faces and wide eyes. "Any whiff of anythin' from a one of ya, and you'll be sacked on the spot. You'd be puttin' the lives of our team in grave danger. Total. Silence."

Robbie let that hang in the air for a very long minute while he made eye contact with each person. Taliya tried not to chuckle because he was right about the danger, but it was humorous to feel the angst of young people denied web postings when they were surrounded by such epic goings-on.

Finally, Robbie announced dinner and indicated that Taliya, Kano, Reynaldo, and Carl should go first. That seemed wrong to her. The workers around camp had been hustling all day. But she was a guest, and guests ate first in most cultures. Moving quickly through the buffet set-up, she got a bowl of stew and some bread, along with a glass of very dark ale she wasn't quite sure about. The meal was filling and made her feel more prepared for the demands of the evening. Then the four of them headed out to prepare while the others finished.

In the barn, Coconut and Pegasus had moved to new positions, but Polly and Bunny were still firmly ensconced on their eggs.

"I'm not looking forward to making the swap," Taliya admitted.

"They may not even notice," Carl said. "They trust you."

"Maybe not for this."

Taliya knew what it meant to worry about danger to your young. Most of her first pregnancy, she'd lived in constant fear the kits would be taken away from her. Even now, if she let her thoughts open to the ongoing dangers to her young ones, anxiety bubbled up inside her. Being thousands of miles away didn't help.

"You're not stealing their babies," Kano said, pulling her in close to his chest. "Just helping them make the transfer to a safe place. Keep that in mind, and don't let the stress take over. The dragons will sense it."

She knew he was right. They might not smell things the way the tigran did, but they were highly perceptive. She'd need to find a way to stay calm, as would Reynaldo.

"Let me do a test first," Taliya said. "See if she'll let me touch it at all."

Moving over to Bunny, she greeted the dragon and then ran her hand along the animal's feathered side. Stopping where she suspected the egg was, she sat down. Bunny glanced back at her, shifted her bottom, and closed her eyes. Taliya leaned her head against Bunny's side and then slid both arms under the dragon, like Rey had done to Polly earlier. Bunny squawked sleepily but didn't move. Taliya could feel the egg, could get her hands around it. It was tucked under the dragon's wing instead of directly under her body. Bunny stayed calm. That was a great sign.

Taliya pulled her arms out and stood. "That went well."

They all looked at Polly. Dealing with her was daunting.

Taliya wished Karma, the tigran from the camp team, was here. Having the original four trainers all in on the

rescue hadn't seemed necessary. But no one had anticipated eggs.

"Rey," Taliya said, "she let you mess with it earlier.
Maybe you should be the one to get it from her. She knows
you better than she knows me, really."

Reynaldo approached Polly, following the same steps
Taliya had tried. Polly was cooperative as well and let him
touch the egg. After backing away, Rey joined the others
near the door. "So, we have a plan?"

"As solid a plan as we can hope for," Taliya agreed.

Noises in the yard outside indicated a transport had
arrived. The foursome peeked out of the barn windows.
Robbie was unloading two huge incubators.

"Got a stray batch of emu eggs, eh?" the driver asked
Robbie while handing him a com to sign for the deli-
very.

"Nah, yeah," Robbie said without pause. "Thanks for
rushin' these over."

Taliya worried the driver might be curious or want to
help, but he hopped straight back up into the cab. Before
the interns had rolled the machines to the barn, the transport was nothing more than a trail of dust on the road.
The incubators were plugged in outside of the barn door,
and the dummy eggs warmed up.

Robbie jogged to where the crew stood around the
incubators. "All on you, now," he said to Rey and Taliya.
"Go get 'em."

Carl, Reynaldo, Taliya, and Kano huddled up just
inside the barn entrance.

"Deep, calm breaths," Carl said. "Never go into battle wound up."

Taliya laughed at the idea of combat with the massive pterodragons, but she understood the sentiment. They needed to move stealthily and avoid alerting the animals to anything amiss. "Bunny first," she said. "I doubt she's going to make a fuss. If things go badly with Polly, though, she might."

The others nodded agreement. Reynaldo sauntered into the barn and grabbed the waiting bucket of food.

"Hey, Bunny," he said calmly, rustling the seeds and fruit. "How about a snack?"

In Taliya's experience, Bunny never refused a snack, and today was no different. She leaned right into the bucket, but she didn't stand up. Taliya took the first warmed-up dummy egg from one of the incubators and hid it behind her back before walking over to the dragon. The egg was a foot wide, but concealed enough. Carefully, she repeated the exact same motions as earlier, ending with both of her arms under the dragon and her head pressed against Bunny's side, the fake egg beside her. The dragon paused for a moment to glance back at her, then continued eating.

Taking a deep breath and counting down from three, Taliya slid the dummy egg under Bunny with one hand while pulling the real egg out with the other and tucking it under her tunic. Bunny spread her wings slightly, whapping Taliya in the head, then glared back at her trainer with one green eye.

"It's okay," Taliya said in the most relaxed voice she could muster.

Bunny believed her—or at least wasn't concerned—and relaxed her wings before going back to eating. Taliya tenderly and surreptitiously carried the egg outside. Kano glanced down at her middle, which looked like a pregnant belly, and chuffed a laugh.

Taliya whuffed in horror. "Don't even *think* it."

Robbie had placed notes in each machine, to make sure the eggs were replaced under the right dragon at the zoo. Taliya tucked Bunny's inside the correct warm chamber and sealed the door.

"One down," she whispered to Kano and Carl as she headed back into the barn.

Reynaldo handed Taliya the bucket and collected the other dummy egg from the second incubator, hiding it behind his back. With a nod, they both moved over to Polly.

"Polly want some munchies?" Taliya said, shaking the food like Rey had done for Bunny.

Polly eyed her with a tipped head. Reynaldo patted the dragon on the chest and started running his hands along her sides, like he used to for health inspections. That seemed to relax her, and she bent down to take some bites from the tub Taliya held out. It was intimidating, being that close to the crested head and sharp beak—knowing Reynaldo was possibly about to piss the animal off.

He fussed with Polly's wing and then kneeled next to

her. Taliya could feel nervousness radiating from Carl and Kano and wished they'd settle down. Finally, Reynaldo slipped one arm under Polly but seemed to be having trouble finding the egg. Taliya rattled the seed bucket to distract the dragon.

The next moments unfurled in a horrifying blast.

Reynaldo found it and started to make the swap. Touching the egg had been allowed, but taking it was not. Polly spread her wings with a deafening "KAAH!" and knocked Rey over. Then lunged at Taliya, the closest creature she could reach.

The tigran screamed and ducked away from the stabbing beak. It slammed into the hay inches from her feet. The bucket of seeds scattered in the air, and Taliya growl/hissed as the dragon spread her wings and screeched repeatedly like a macaw in the jungle.

"KAAH! KAAH! KAAH! KAAH!"

Then chaos erupted as all four dragons flapped and stomped and squawked and generally flipped out, strong wings flapping and bashing into the walls and each other.

Taliya desperately crawled to the side. A whoosh of air ruffled her fur as one of the dragons careened past her, missing her by only inches. Jets of beige poo squirted the walls. Hay scattered and filled the air.

When she reached a wall, Taliya curled up in a ball and covered her head. Rey yelled something, and Carl responded, but she couldn't understand what they were saying.

"Taliya, stay there!" Kano shouted.

She held her breath and waited for the dragons to calm down—or stomp/claw/peck her to death, whichever came first.

Kano threw his body over her. She growled deep in her throat and tiger moaned as he wrapped her in strong arms.

"It's okay, it's okay, it's okay," he whispered in her ear, though she could feel his heart thundering.

There was a loud thud, followed by what smelled like bits of the barn raining down around them. All four dragons screeched and *kaahed* and threw bedding up with their feet.

Then the barn was suddenly silent except for the rapid breathing of all eight of them.

Kano rolled off and sat down next to her but kept one hand on Taliya's back. She lifted her head and dared a glance around.

The dragons were all back in their original spots. The only evidence of the mayhem was bits of bedding and white feathers floating around, poo on the walls, and dust in the air. And a hole in the roof where one of the dragons must have tried to break free.

Polly glared at Taliya from across the room, green eyes sparkling.

Carl hovered near the door, coughing and wiping dust from his face. Reynaldo was flattened against the far wall. He smiled at Taliya and gave a thumbs-up, then lifted his tunic slightly to show an egg there. He must have managed the switch.

Moving slowly, sneezing a few times, Rey took his prize outside to the second incubator—Polly none the wiser she was sitting on a fake. Kano helped Taliya up, they both dusted off, and then met the others outside. Polly shouted a "Kaah! Go!" at them before the door closed.

"Well," Carl said, "that was interesting." His words were routine-sounding, but his eyes took in every inch of the three creatures, ensuring they were unharmed.

Taliya chuckled at the understatement, running her fingers along her tail to confirm it was in one piece. Her claws extended and retracted several times involuntarily. She'd need to get her heartrate and adrenalin under control before going back in the barn.

Robbie, who'd been watching through a window, jogged toward them. "What a stramash!"

"No harm done in the end," Taliya said, "except for the roof. We got the eggs. That was the mission."

Rey nodded. "I was able to make the swap when she jumped up."

"Brilliant." Robbie admired the two dragon eggs safely tucked in incubators for the trip to the zoo.

"I would *not* have been able to stay that calm and get it done," Taliya admitted. "I thought she was going to snap the whiskers right off my face."

Kano moaned, and she chuffed reassuringly.

"That raises a serious issue," Carl said. "How the hell are we going to load Polly? I hate to tranq any of them, not knowing much about the species, but I don't see how we're going to get Polly safely off her egg and into a crate."

Robbie frowned. Taliya knew he did this kind of animal work all the time. However, the dragons were not only unknown but also three times the size of anything the zoo had dealt with before.

"Sometimes we just grab and stuff," Robbie admitted, "but there's no way to do that with those four. Even once we got her sedated, how'd we move her out of the barn and into the crate? We really need 'em to walk."

"It's gonna have to be a team effort, then," Carl said. "And we'll leave Polly to last. Maybe once the others have gone, she'll want to follow."

"We've got about an hour to make a plan," Robbie said. "Or a titch longer 'cause the crates gotta be assembled." With a firm nod, he headed out to gather interns and prepare for the transports' arrival.

"I'm glad we got those eggs tucked in," Carl said, "or they'd have been smashed in that bruhaha. I saw Bunny step on her dummy egg twice, and Pegasus stomped on Polly's."

"They're just animals, after all," Reynaldo said. "Logic and reasoning aren't going to flow like we wish they would. No human DNA in the mix."

"*No thank you* to a part-human pterodragon." Taliya's hackles raised along her neck. "That sounds terrifying."

"No kidding." Kano shook his head and scratched his ruff, coughing at the dust that released.

"Well," Carl said, "time to adjust the plans. One way or another, they leave for the zoo soon."

Taliya huffed. "Whatever we decide, I need to stay clear for Polly's transfer. I'm on her shitlist now."

13

After getting a drink, calming down, and making sure the dragons were staying settled, the foursome joined Robbie and the interns in the yard. They were deep in conversation but parted when the group joined them.

"So, we do have quite a bit of ketamine on hand," Robbie said, "to conk 'em out. But let's leave that as a last resort. Our immediate issue is that we may not be able to just walk 'em through the slidin' door, like we did when ya arrived. They were tired then, and very cooperative. No eggs. And the angle is wrong for a truck to line up with the door."

Wolfie arrived with two other dingman, and Taliya smiled at the way they moved around each other, bumping and jostling like she'd seen her own dogs do in friendly pack play. Wolfie snapped at another of the dingman, then jogged across the yard to join them.

"Hey, mate," Robbie said. "How's it doin'?"

"All clear so far. Trucks'll be here in about fifteen. Where should they park?"

"Line 'em up on the road, startin' here," Robbie said. "Unless someone has a better idea, I'm thinkin' we need to slice open part of the barn so we can back the crates right up to it and wrangle the drags in that way."

No one had a different suggestion, so two interns were assigned to decide the best way to cut the barn open on the side facing the field. That could be done quickly once the crates were assembled. Taliya felt bad about the destruction they were leaving behind—between the hole in the barn roof and the soon-to-be missing side—but she couldn't see another way around. She had formulated a plan for getting the mamas and eggs into the trucks, and it worked with the open-side strategy.

Before long, four high-tech solar semitrucks drove up the main road to the property, scattering the few emus and kangaroos who were hanging around. Each truck pulled a flatbed with a stack of metal sections strapped down on it. Pieces the zoo used for transporting giraffes and elephants were being quadrupled in size for the drag-ons. Even then, it would be a snug fit. Robbie assured them this was best to keep the dragons from moving too much and hurting themselves on the journey.

The interns split into two groups and attacked the sections like their lives depended on building those crates as fast as possible. Taliya was impressed with the efficiency. The clanking and smell of steel, whirring of drills, and shouted words of direction filled the yard. Ropes and pulleys hauled massive pieces into place to form metal boxes just big enough for a dragon but short enough to fit under bridges as they traveled. There were small slit openings here and there on the sides for ventilation, but the tops were one solid piece. Any drones flying overhead during the fifteen-hour race to the zoo would be hard-pressed to catch a glimpse of the white dragons inside.

The frenetic energy of the intern construction project made Taliya's skin tingle and heart race. They were like army ants swarming. She forced herself to take deep, relaxing breaths, but the scent of anxiousness was every-where on the slight breeze. Reynaldo stretched flat-out on the porch with his hands across his belly, probably calming himself down as well, while Carl paced and observed from a distance. His role in the rescue was shifting from being part of their team to part of Wolfie's security team. Taliya wondered if he'd snuck off to chat with the dingman where he'd been keeping watch to compare notes or formulate a plan. It seemed like a very Carl thing to do.

Within the hour, all four enormous crates were assembled on the flatbeds and the trucks positioned to move into place one after another. Robbie had it all coor-dinated, though it was clear the drivers didn't know exactly what was going into the crates. Every now and then, one would glance at the barn with a concerned look.

Taliya hoped they'd keep quiet about what they saw for a day or two.

The sun had nearly set now, but only a few solar lanterns were put up in the yard. If a drone or helicopter flew over, it would be difficult to see what they were up to.

Robbie waved Taliya and Reynaldo over, with Kano following along for support. Remembering how terrified he'd been of the dragons for the first few months she'd worked with them, and after the egg-snatching drama, Taliya was grateful he was still willing to help and jump right into the fray. Most likely to ensure she stayed safe.

"Okay, mates," Robbie shouted across the field. "No time to muck about. The back of the truck bed lowers down to the ground, so we just need to run 'em up into the crate. Normally, we'd go calmest to spiciest. Then the animals don't get more worked up than necessary."

"I agree," Reynaldo said. "Polly would spook them all if we tried to get her first. I'd start with Bunny. Then Coconut. Then Pegasus. Maybe Polly will feel left out and want to follow him."

Taliya thought that was highly optimistic based on the chaos Polly had created earlier. "To be honest, I have no idea how this will go. They are used to being in stalls and might see it as the same thing. And we know they were crated when they arrived at the refugee camp, so it's not a totally new experience for them. But maybe start with Coconut. If Bunny gets upset, we'll have at least one out of the way."

"If she even starts to fuss," Rey added, "we'll leave her and go to Pegasus instead. Then we can deal with the mamas."

With the plan set, two interns took laser cutters to the side of the barn, slicing along one corner to the floor, down a section in the middle, and across most of the top. Wedging it carefully so it wouldn't fall in on the dragons, the last cut was made and the section of barn wall dragged out of the way.

Taliya peeked in, and all four dragons glowered at her through the dim overhead lighting. Pegasus was on his feet, wings slightly spread, stomping in agitation. Despite the quietness of the lasers, he knew something was afoot.

"What is that?!" one of the drivers shouted after getting a look inside the barn.

Robbie patted her on the back, explained a bit, and assured the drivers there were no worries. "All in a day's work."

After moving out of the way so the first truck could pull up, Taliya decided to go in through the side door and help calm the animals. Reynaldo was already a step ahead of her.

Pegasus was not remotely interested in being calm.

Rey approached him, hands up, reaching toward the dragon and speaking in a soothing voice, but the alpha male was having none of it. He stabbed his beak at Rey and spread his wings, banging into Bunny still hunkered on her fake egg, and *kaahed* at the ceiling in anger.

"I know, I know," Reynaldo said, venturing closer still. "The last few days have been a lot. But it's almost over."

The truck had backed into the open space, lowered the tailgate, and the crate was now open, waiting for the first dragon.

"Taliya," Reynaldo said, not looking away from Pegasus, "I think we'd better get him out of here first."

"Good idea," she said quietly, not sure how much effort it would take for Pegasus to break out of the barn entirely if he got mad enough.

"Let's see if we can guide him that way. He might see it as a chance to escape."

Taliya trusted Rey's experience with herding and waited for directions. The panthran had stopped advancing on the dragon and seemed to be evaluating the best strategy. He motioned Taliya to move around to the left of the animal, and as she did, Pegasus shifted away and *kaahed* at her, but he also started backing toward the opening. Reynaldo moved forward, which encouraged the dragon to continue his path away from the two creatures. Taliya kept her eye on the other dragons, but they just observed the proceedings intensely.

As Pegasus got closer to the opening, he turned. In the dark, it was hard to tell what was beyond the gap in the wall. With an ear-splitting squawk, he raced right into the crate, which was immediately slid shut behind him. Screams filled the air, and he thrashed against the metal sides. Taliya watched in amazement as the heavy crate tipped and swayed. It was latched down tightly on the flatbed, ready for the long trip ahead. *But how sturdy are those straps? Is he strong enough to tip the entire flatbed over?*

As the crashing around inside the crate continued, Robbie approached with a long tube-like contraption. He slid it through a slit opening at one end, paused to take aim, and shot a dart into Pegasus.

Taliya's heart sank, but she didn't blame Robbie for making that call. They couldn't risk Pegasus hurting himself, breaking the crate, or escaping. The sooner he was calmed down, the better for the other three who still needed to be loaded. Fortunately, they seemed to be more scared than agitated, though she sensed Coconut was ready to shift any second.

The banging and bird-like screeching from Pegasus didn't stop immediately, but after a few minutes, it slowed. When all was quiet, Taliya and Reynaldo approached the crate. Pegasus hunkered inside, his head under one wing. Robbie had been watching from his position at the far end and smiled at the pair.

"One down, three to go," he said, like it had been no big deal.

"What if they're all like that?" Taliya said.

"Yeah, nah," Robbie smiled, "he's just the papa. Tryin' to protect his flock. That'll keep him tidy for the next few hours."

Rey nodded and turned back to the other three dragons. They eyed him warily. At Robbie's order, gears whirled and lifted the back of the truck so it was ready to travel. The semi with its sleeping cargo pulled out and drove partway down the long driveway, ready to start the trip. That left the opening in the barn bare for a few minutes, but Taliya and Reynaldo blocked the way. After watching what had happened to Pegasus, none of the dragons seemed interested in making a break for it.

As the next truck backed in and then lowered the crate to floor level, Taliya considered the remaining three. "Bunny next?"

Rey flared his whiskers. "I'll follow *you* on that one. You have a plan for the egg?"

Taliya nodded, straightened her tunic, and took a deep breath. *Calm. Stay calm.*

Two interns slid the crate door open. Robbie nodded that they were ready.

Walking slowly over to Bunny, Taliya greeted her dragon with pats to the side and chest. "Hey, Bun-Bun, it's okay." The dragon looked down at her, and Taliya felt the animal's agitation melting.

She suspected that wouldn't last long.

Sliding her hand along Bunny's side, Taliya bent down, reached her arms under the dragon, and pulled out the dummy egg. She jumped clear as Bunny squawked and leapt up on her taloned feet. Taliya held up the egg so the dragon could see it.

"It's safe, Bunny. I'm not going to hurt it."

Bunny did not look convinced and spread her wings,

lowering her head aggressively. "Kaah! Kaah! Kaah! Taah-yaa!"

With a yelp, Taliya ran the egg right into the crate. She heard Bunny following and set it down in the middle of the bedding as the animal stormed into the box. The tigran suddenly realized a glitch in her plan. She was now on the beaky end of an angry, broody dragon. Even though it was her Bunny, there were no guarantees of what would come next.

Taliya flattened herself against the back of the crate, every hair on her body standing on end. The massive dragon hovered overhead. Rearing back, Bunny pecked at her former trainer. Taliya jumped to the side and darted past her toward the open end of the crate. Fortunately, the cage was too small for Bunny to turn around. Taliya leaped out of the back—where half of it had been left open for her—and heard the steel door clang shut on dragon number two.

Kano rushed to her, his blue eyes wide with panic and nose so flushed it looked purple in the dim light, hackles raised all the way up the back of his neck.

She waved him away. "I'm fine. It's all good." She leaned over with her hands on her knees, trying to catch her breath and pretend she hadn't just had her fur scared off. The full puff on her tail was evidence enough.

Bunny stomped around, then settled on her fake egg, leaning forward into the incline of the flatbed.

Taliya let her husband wrap her up in a big hug, tail around her legs. "She got much angrier than I expected.

She hadn't seemed that protective of the egg. Maybe Pegasus got her riled up."

"No more putting yourself on the stabby end of a furious mama dragon, please."

"If you insist." Taliya nuzzled her face into the fur of his neck and chuffed.

"I do," he said, squeezing her a bit too hard and growling.

The truck driver was already lifting the back end and preparing for transport. Taliya and Kano joined the others off to the side for a quick drink of water—though she'd have preferred some ale at that point—and a strategy session for the next two.

Reynaldo smiled at Taliya, but she could smell he was highly alarmed. "I should have insisted you elaborate on your getting-the-egg-into-the-transport plan. That was a *terrible* idea."

"Ya think?" Taliya drained her glass and set it down on a nearby table. "Definitely not the strategy for Polly."

Rey huffed and shook his head. "Definitely not."

"I say you still go for Coconut next," Carl suggested. "Maybe when she's left alone, Polly will go more willingly, like we'd planned."

"I have no idea what to expect from her," Taliya admitted. "Bunny's reaction totally shocked me. She was *furious.*"

Rey sighed. "We don't know what the last months of their lives have been like. I'm not sure their level of trust is very high. Even in us."

"Should we just drug and drag?" Robbie asked. "They're mighty big beasts, but it can be done."

"Drug and drag?" Taliya's ears lay flat in horror at the casual attitude over something traumatic that had been done to her twice. Her claws flexed in and out.

Robbie glanced down at her hands and frowned. There was no way he didn't know about her experience with a tranq gun. The media loved to retell the story of her capture from the warehouse attic. Of course, those Enforcers would still be alive if they'd drugged and dragged her quickly instead of trying to reason with her. Knowing that logically didn't help.

"Sorry, mate," Robbie said. "It's a last-resort strategy, to be sure, but it's one we've got to use now and then. Especially when time and safety of the crew and animals are concerns. . . . Like now."

She caught his meaning. If they were going to get all four dragons safely loaded and ready to roll in the next few minutes, which they absolutely needed to, they couldn't "muck about" for long.

"Let's try Coconut, then." Taliya took a deep breath and shook the tension from her hands. "See if we can just herd him in."

"Watch ya tails in there," Robbie said with a nod. "No time for sewin' 'em back on."

Taliya chuckled, but his worries over physical danger weren't unfounded. Coconut wasn't as big as Pegasus, but he was still a huge, powerful animal—agitated and scared.

The driver of the third truck indicated the crate was in place, so Taliya and Reynaldo headed back through the barn door. Polly still squatted on her egg and snorted at them. Coconut was standing and glaring, clawed feet slowly and rhythmically stomping.

"I'm guessing Polly is his mate," Reynaldo said, "based on his posturing."

Taliya nodded her agreement. *Will he leave her behind? Attack us if we touch her?* "Then I definitely think we should get him first. He may not be happy about us messing with Polly and come after us while we're dealing with her."

With a glance at the side of the barn to confirm the crate was open and ready, Reynaldo started to move around behind Coconut, to urge him in the direction of the crate. They'd gotten the drop on Pegasus before the dragons realized what was going on. Bunny had chased Taliya to save her egg. But now they faced a dragon who knew exactly what was on the agenda. And he was not on board with it.

Coconut took a couple of steps away from Reynaldo and spread his wings, lowering his head at him, then Taliya. A rumbling noise vibrated deep in his throat. Both creatures froze.

"Never heard that sound before," Taliya whispered.

"Me neither," Reynaldo admitted. "Not good."

As they considered changing approaches, Coconut lost his dragony mind.

Kaahing in rage and wings flapping, he leaped at Taliya. She instinctively dropped and covered her head.

Coconut soared over her and landed with a resounding thud against the far wall of the barn. The whole building rattled.

The moment he was up, the dragon threw himself against the wooden wall—screeching and stabbing it with his beak. Glass from a window crashed. The roof swayed, unsteady from having a large chunk of one wall removed.

Taliya crawled to the back near Reynaldo. He pulled her in behind him, shielding her with his body.

"He's going to smash through right on top of the incubators!" she yelled. *Shit. Shit. Shit!!*

Reynaldo screamed like a panther—a sound she didn't know he was capable of—and spread his arms wide, trying to distract the animal. But Coconut was no longer paying any attention to the two creatures. He was bent on escape.

As Coconut battered the wall and bits of wood from the swaying ceiling rained down on them, Taliya spotted Robbie peeking around the side of the crate into the barn. A sharp whistling noise, and Coconut *kaahed* in anger. He spun around, wings spread and head low. Another whistle, and Polly squawked, spreading her wings.

"Get outta there!" Robbie yelled, lowering his dart-shooting stick.

Reynaldo screamed again and dragged Taliya out the side door. The panthran didn't stop running and pulling her along—half on her feet and half not—until they were well clear, the dragon crashing and screeching inside the barn.

Kano raced to them and helped Taliya stand. "You okay?"

She nodded and tried to catch her breath. Robbie stood next to the truck, shouting directions to two interns. They rushed off, and he peeked back into the barn. Seeming happy with what was going on inside, Robbie jogged over to join them.

"He's a cheeky bugger, eh?"

"That's an understatement," Taliya said, adjusting her clothes and sighing deeply. "He was ready to kill me." Her heart still pounded, and her tail thrashed. The reek of human and creature stress filled the yard.

"Won't be long now," Robbie said, glancing back at the barn. "Got darts into both of 'em."

"Polly too?" she asked sadly.

"Nah, yeah, seemed safest. Makes it rougher on us, but that bloke was gonna hurt himself, one of us, or even his mate. There's always a risk, conkin' 'em out, but it's a light dose. Best way ta go."

"Okay," Taliya mumbled. Ultimately, the decision wasn't hers to make. She was there to help the zoo take possession of the pterodragons, not the other way around. It was Robbie's call, and he'd made it swiftly and professionally. If Coconut had broken out of the barn, who knows what kind of damage he might have done, assuming he didn't just fly off into the night with Polly behind him.

Robbie seemed to sense her hesitancy with the turn of events. "Look, I've thrown myself on top of wild crocs more times than I can count, but these dragons are just so massive. All of us together couldn't take 'em down. This is the safest way."

Taliya nodded and sat down on the porch step. Kano joined her, wrapping a strong arm around her and chuffing quietly. Reynaldo paced nearby, probably fussing about the whole situation and how he could've handled it differently. Carl hovered but let his mate work it out himself.

For his part, Carl was now armed with a belt holding two laser handguns. *Is that prep for the trip ahead, or was he ready to shoot one of the dragons?* They'd never discussed that option, but she realized it certainly had to be in Carl's thoughts. If it was a choice between Reynaldo and one of the dragons, she knew he wouldn't hesitate. He would have protected her the same way. The skin along her spine tingled.

The dragons had gone quiet, and interns were starting to peek into the barn. Reynaldo headed to join them, and Taliya followed wearily, Kano and Carl right behind.

In the barn, both dragons were asleep, heads tucked under their feathery white wings. There was a concerning lean to the huge structure now. Between the hole in the roof, the opening cut in the wall, and the furious attack from Coconut, Taliya was grateful it hadn't collapsed. It was built to hold groups of kangaroos, emus, and normal-sized animals, not enormous genetic creations that attacked it. Robbie and three interns headed into the barn through the wall opening lugging a giant brown tarp, and the foursome followed.

Kano eyed the building warily from top to bottom, probably trying to figure out a way to shore it up quickly before they went back inside—territory where he was the expert. The white tigran huffed and frowned, drawing the black lines on his forehead into a V. Since he didn't offer a suggestion, she assumed it was sound enough. Or it would take too long to fix.

He met her gaze. "It'll do. Try not to bang into the walls."

Robbie gave a nod. "Let's start with Polly, since she's closest to the door."

The tarp was stretched out next to the dragon, and the interns rolled the huge animal over onto it. Polly flopped and lay motionless, taloned feet sticking straight up in the air.

"Is she breathing?" Taliya whispered to Reynaldo.

"Yes," he said confidently, like he'd already worried about that himself.

"Okay," Robbie said, "everyone grab a spot, and we drag her into the crate."

Carl hesitated. "Can't we rig up some of those ropes and pulleys you used to put things together?"

"If ya wanna delay an hour."

"Not really an option, is it," Carl said, hands on his hips. "Heave ho we go."

Following Robbie's directions, the whole group

surrounded the tarp, grabbed a chunk of fabric, and worked to drag the deadweight of Polly across the barn and up into the waiting crate. Being genetically mostly bird, the animal was lighter than an elephant or large mammal, but still heavy.

The team didn't all fit inside the crate, so by the end only Taliya, Kano, Reynaldo, Carl, and Robbie were left hauling her—those genetically designed to be strong calling on every ounce of it. Once Polly's tail was inside, all five of them collapsed against the walls. Taliya panted in exhaustion, and they all worked to catch their breath. Robbie wiped sweat from his forehead.

"Just leave the tarp under her," Robbie said between gasps for air. "We've got a second one, and there isn't room to budge her off it in here."

They climbed out around Polly's sleeping body, now on her side. Taliya picked up the dummy egg from the barn floor and tucked it in under Polly so it would be there when she woke up. Based on Taliya's experience, Polly had a mighty headache waiting for her. Best to have the egg right where she'd want it.

The crate was closed, the back end lifted up, and truck number three pulled into line on the driveway behind the other two. A dingman loped into sight, then into the shadows again, keeping watch. Taliya noticed the drivers were having an animated chat while waiting by the animal clinic. She could only imagine the "What the hell are those things?" of the conversation. Robbie had assured her the drivers would keep quiet, and she hoped he was right. They could spill their whole story in a few days.

The dragging process was repeated with Coconut, though he did kick valiantly a couple of times without actually waking up. Kano mumbled he was going to feel this in his back tomorrow, and Taliya agreed. Being strong didn't mean you were in shape to drag dragons around.

With all four trucks loaded, the incubators were rolled into the back of a smaller transport. Taliya looked around the yard one last time. It had been a fascinating visit, but she was ready to go. Carl gathered their backpacks. There was nothing left to do but find a spot for the long ride to the Sunshine Coast and Australia Zoo.

Connie had provided tubs of food for the trip and gave each of them a hug. "The zoo will take good care of your dragons," she assured Taliya. "I promise. *Our family* will take good care of them."

"Thank you. For everything."

Carl checked his com and then tucked it away. "Rey and I are riding in the lead transport. Robbie's will be at the end with the incubators. Dingman are positioned in each truck with the drivers. You and Kano can pick a spot."

"Why don't we go with the eggs?" she suggested.

Kano shrugged, like either way was fine.

A loud crack resonated across the yard. Everyone froze. Taliya glanced around, but she didn't see any danger. Then a long, excruciating moan erupted from the barn as the whole frame shifted to the right.

"Get back!" Kano yelled.

Those still close to the structure scattered as the building groaned and leaned even more precariously. Taliya held her breath, but there was no way to stop the inevitable. With a massive screech and crash that threw straw and bits of wood into the air, the abused structure collapsed. Windows shattered, and what remained of the roof landed on top of the pile of boards with a bang that whooshed a cloud of debris into the air.

Everyone stared as the dust settled.

"Well," Robbie finally said. "Guess we know what the team'll be up to t'morrow."

A shout of laughter burst from Taliya, and she clapped her hands over her mouth.

Robbie chuckled. "Sometimes all ya can do is find the humor."

"I'm grateful no one was still inside." Kano huffed, maybe upset he'd allowed anyone back in.

"She'll be right," Robbie said. "But we're gonna need to rebuild quickly. A family of dingoes is headin' our way in two days 'cause they've been pickin' off a local's sheep. They'll need to quarantine in there before they're relocated to the property."

"What about all the prey animals here?" Taliya asked.

"We don't stop nature from takin' its course. We just try to keep water and food available. We don't have many dingoes on the reserve, and that makes it out of balance. Nature likes balance."

Taliya thought of all the emus and kangaroos and

other creatures she'd seen. Wild dogs having access to them made her sad, but she also knew he was right. Balance is important between hunters and the hunted. She'd watched enough nature specials to understand that. Take away one part, and the other struggles.

"I suppose our dragons were just one more animal rescue to your team," Kano said.

"Well, a bit spicier than most." Robbie grinned and clapped the white tigran on the back.

"I feel like we should stay to help rebuild," Kano said, whiskers flared and tail thrashing as he stared at the devastated building. "Or at least I should. I'm a skilled mason. This is what I do."

"So I've heard, but the interns can handle it. No worries. Let's get these drags safely to the zoo."

After quick bathroom breaks and hugs and hand-shakes with the team, Carl and Reynaldo loaded into the back seats of the lead transport with two interns in front to handle the driving. Taliya suspected there was more armory on board than the two laser handguns on Carl's belt. An attack on the trucks seemed highly unlikely, but Carl would be prepared. The four semitruck drivers were already in place, and the solar trucks vibrated slightly, ready to roll. All four dragons were still quiet, even wide-awake Bunny. The tranquilizers wouldn't last the whole trip—though they'd packed backup doses—but hopefully the animals would be groggy enough to stay calm when they woke.

Robbie and a female intern settled into the front seats

of the final transport that held the incubators with the real dragon eggs, so Kano and Taliya climbed into the back seats and closed the doors behind them.

"Have a kip," Robbie said, looking at them through the rearview mirror from the driver's seat. "We've got it from here. Smooth sailing ahead."

Taliya hoped a kip was something like long, uninterrupted sleep. She closed her eyes, laid her head back on the seat, and prayed to the gods he was right.

14

The trip to the zoo had been uneventful for the first few hours. Taliya and Kano even managed to get some much-needed sleep while Robbie and the intern listened to a memoir by David Attenborough, the legendary biologist. But around midnight, three drones zipped up alongside the transport.

"Prepare for trouble," Carl's voice warned over the vehicle's radio.

Taliya's chest tightened like it was in a vise. The general was in the lead transport, so maybe he was already seeing something they couldn't. Looking out the tinted windows, she spotted dozens and dozens of drones buzzing around the convoy of semis trying to carry the dragons to safety, keeping pace with their highway speed.

"Hell's bells," Robbie mumbled from the driver's seat.

Carl's voice came again. "Road's blocked up ahead."

Robbie cussed with a string of Aussie words, and the intern riding next to him whimpered.

Taliya leaned toward the front seat. "How in the world did they find us?"

"No clue," Robbie said, "but it's on now."

Taliya turned to Kano, still sound asleep. "Wake up!" She shook him, but he didn't stir.

An explosion quaked the ground, slamming Taliya's head into the side window as the transport almost flipped. Screams and shouts came from outside. Bunny *kaahed* in rage. It took a few seconds for Taliya to see clearly again, and her skull felt like it was splitting in two.

Shweps of laser gunfire flashed, and more explosions came from the front of the convoy. She reached for Kano… only to discover he wasn't there. The front seat was empty as well, with no sign of Robbie or the intern. Attenborough's voice droned soothingly on. Something about natural selection. She searched for her pack, which still held the laser guns Mack had given her during the raid. That was gone too.

Panic raced up her throat, but she tamped down the scream. Checking the back of the transport, she found both incubators overturned—the eggs smashed on the floor, bright-yellow yolks splattered across the windows. Tears sprang to her eyes, but that was the least of her worries.

Another explosion rocked the transport and slammed her against the door. Something in her shoulder cracked with a sickening sound, and pain radiated through her body. Clangings of metal being moved around reached her sensitive ears through a dull ringing.

The dragons! It sounded like the cages were being attacked. All of the animals but Bunny had been sedated. *They can't defend themselves!*

She struggled to open the transport door, but it wouldn't give. Crawling across the seats, she tried the other door, but it was just as firmly stuck. Banging on the windows didn't work either. What seemed like a hundred drones buzzed around the vehicle and the flatbed ahead of her.

Taliya screamed in rage and frustration, throwing her good shoulder into the door over and over again.

She couldn't get out. Couldn't help.

A male voice urgently shouted directions over the radio, but she couldn't make out the words. Nothing made sense.

The transport door flew open, and Taliya faced an enormous human dressed in black, his face shrouded. With a sinister laugh, he aimed a tranq gun at her face and fired. . . .

Taliya stirred awake with a snort at Kano's hand on her knee.

"Just a nightmare," he whispered.

She blinked frantically, his face coming into focus, frowning. It wasn't dark outside, with the sun solidly over the horizon. She flexed her claws a few times and tried to settle her hackles, the tip of her tail flicking in agitation.

Rotating her shoulder, she tested for the injury that

felt so real moments ago. They hadn't been attacked. Everything was fine. Robbie was driving, and the intern was asleep against the door. Glancing behind her, Taliya found both incubators in place and the eggs safe. It took a minute to settle her heart rate and bring her mind back to reality. They'd been on the road over twelve hours last time she fell asleep. She vaguely remembered stopping twice for bathroom breaks and snacks at primitive spots along the side of the road. It was only a dream.

Kano chuffed. "Want to talk about it?"

Nightmares for both of them were fairly common events, and sometimes it did help to talk through the horrible dreams based on legitimate horrible events they'd both survived.

"The kidnappers found us." She shuddered. "They were blowing everything up."

He flared his whiskers. "Part of that may be true."

Nothing was wrong inside the transport, but nervous tension radiated from her husband.

"Drones," he said more calmly than he must actually be feeling, nodding past her to the road.

Knowing the windows were tinted and they couldn't possibly see inside didn't stop her from wanting to scrunch down in the seat. After her dream, she expected to find drones covering the road around them, but only one zoomed along, keeping pace with their transport.

"Robbie says it's probably just media, looking for a story on what the zoo is up to."

"No worries," Robbie said from the front seat. "Almost

there anyhow. If it's the baddies, too late for tryin' to get their drags back."

"We're expecting a police escort any second," Kano explained, "to help navigate through the city. I doubt even the boldest kidnappers will try anything at this point. It's over."

Staring out the window, she realized there were buildings now and then among the trees, and the highway had expanded to multiple lanes. They were heading into Brisbane.

Taliya sat up and tried to compose herself, but adrenalin still tingled her skin.

"Get ya game faces on," Robbie joked. "Won't be arrivin' quietly, like I'd hoped. Whoever those drones belong to, they know somethin's up."

Taliya grumbled deep in her throat. "Did someone break the media silence?"

"Maybe, but I doubt it. The size of these cages probably caught some news hound's attention. Always lookin' for a story."

The drone that had been hovering outside their transport window zoomed off, maybe to get a wider shot of the convoy. Taliya was grateful it couldn't get photos of them inside the vehicle, but their presence would be obvious once the team arrived. All the fanfare planned in a few days would have to take place now.

"Looks like backup's here." Carl's voice crackled over the transport's radio.

Unexpected relief flushed through her at the sound of

his confident voice. Bits and pieces of the nightmare flashed through her mind, and she shuddered again. Kano glanced at her, but she motioned that it was fine.

Police cars with flashing lights but no sirens pulled up on either side of their transport, and Kano sighed in relief. Taliya turned to spot another behind them. The traditional white cars with blue-and-white checkerboard designs were remarkably different from black police vehicles in the U.S. Easy to spot if you needed one, instead of trying to hide and catch.

"Looks like Officer Hutch in the car behind us," Robbie said. "He's not lettin' *anyone* through."

Taliya looked back again and could just see the stern face of what must be Officer Hutch—a massive, thick-necked Black man in full uniform and aviator glasses. He certainly looked like a serious dude, ready to handle whatever needed handling. The Aussie version of Carl.

As they continued along, Taliya noticed crowds were starting to gather along the route, waving and taking photos. The speed of media and how humans reacted to anything unusual always surprised her, though it really shouldn't anymore. They were on the outskirts of the city, and traffic was being redirected or stopped so the semis didn't have to.

"We're goin' in the back way," Robbie said, "like ya did for the weddin'. But I'm bettin' there're drones hoverin' all over the zoo right now. It won't be private."

"Understood." Taliya swiped both hands across her face, making sure her fur was as tidy as it could be, though her clothes were still dusty from getting the dragons into the crates. She looked forward to a long, hot shower in the hotel's enormous marble bathroom later in the day.

Turning to Kano, she assured he was presentable, wiping all the black lines on his face until they lined up properly. His nose was flushed red, and he smelled nervous.

"I know you hate this stuff," she whispered. "It'll be over soon. Then we can go home and just sit on the porch with the kits."

"That sounds perfect." He glanced down at the state of his clothes and sighed.

She chuckled. "At least we look like we helped."

"Do you suppose we'll still have to be there for the formal unveiling if we've already gone through this?"

"Maybe not," Taliya admitted. Big public events always made her nervous too. So many humans. All staring.

The convoy drove through the back gate into the zoo, and their transport continued past the three flatbed trucks before coming to a stop next to the lead vehicle. Wolfie climbed out of the first truck's cab, and the back doors of the other transport opened as Carl and Reynaldo stepped out. Carl's head was on a swivel, despite a dozen police cars surrounding them and being inside the zoo grounds. She doubted he'd stand down until the dragons were secured and the new team of dingman in place. Rey hurried to check on each dragon. Robbie and the intern got out and headed around the back, to get the eggs.

"Showtime," Kano mumbled, opening his door.

Taliya chuffed and swung hers open too. Her legs were stiff from being in one place for so many hours, and she groaned, stretching her back. The fresh air was welcoming and carried the scents of hundreds of different species housed at the zoo. Now the pterodragons would join the menagerie for who knows how long.

Before she'd taken a step, a photodrone dropped in front of her face, hovering intently. She startled back, but Carl grabbed the drone, slammed it to the ground, and gave it two solid stomps with his military boots.

"That one was ballsy," he said, watching it sputter and die.

Taliya frowned. "Wonder what kind of pictures it got."

"Hopefully, nothing usable. This is private property, after all. I'll kill any I can reach."

Taliya chuckled at the image of Carl doing battle with a mass of photodrones. It would be the easiest fight he'd ever taken on to protect her.

"Let's not assume they're all enterprising journalists and media scum," Carl said, scanning the skies above them. "Drones can hold laser weapons just as easily."

Her stomach roiled, realizing he was right. Bits of her nightmare flashed through her thoughts again.

"No worries," he said with a wink and an Aussie accent, patting his guns. "Nothin's gettin' past me. Or gettin' me."

"Good. Let's not have your ultimate demise be at the

hands of a *drone*. That's a terrible way for a war hero to go."

"No chance." Carl took a deep breath and puffed out his chest. "Blaze of glory for me."

Taliya glanced up at the currently drone-free sky. "But not today."

At the sounds of clanking metal, they both turned to see flashes of white shifting inside the closest crate. Robbie was jogging around and giving directions to the handful of zoo employees nearby. They all looked gobs-macked but were nodding and following him.

Jaxon, the rooman who'd helped them tour the zoo, hop/walked over to greet them with a massive grin on his brick-red furry face. "Aw, well done, you! Can't wait to meet the dragons!" He shook hands with Carl and Kano, then gave Taliya a fancy bow, like she was royalty. "The word's definitely out that several somethin's have arrived, and folks are linin' up outside the doors to get in."

Taliya glanced toward the front of the zoo and sighed. "It's not like they'll be on display yet. Once we get them unloaded, that exhibit will be blocked off and under quarantine."

"Sure," Jaxon said, "but that doesn't mean the mob won't claim to have been here when it all went down. Get a photo of somethin' interesting to share and boost their social. Wait till they figure out you're here again. Maybe gonna feed another croc."

"Showboating is not on my agenda for the day."

Kano chuffed his agreement, and Jaxon chuckled as Reynaldo joined them.

"They've got the area all roped off in front of the exhibit," Rey said. "As long as the drones keep a respectable distance, we're supposed to let them do their thing." He noticed the smashed one on the ground, made eye contact with Carl, and smirked, whiskers flaring. "Tech is scanning them for any danger. So far, only photodrones. Robbie says it's best to just let it roll because 'The joey is outta the pouch.'"

Taliya snorted a laugh. "It definitely is."

Rey glanced at the bustle of activity around them, probably making sure no one was messing with his dragons. Six dingman in zoo security uniforms arrived and began directing traffic, yipping directions at each other, and the first of the semis inched forward along the wide path.

"Here we go," Rey said with a gleam in his golden eyes.

Taliya followed down the road. "There are no words for how grateful I'm going to be when they are all safely tucked in with the correct eggs under the correct mama."

Reynaldo cracked his knuckles, looking more excited than tired. "I hear that."

Kano fell into step next to her as Reynaldo and Carl hurried ahead. He slipped a hand in under her tunic and gently rubbed her back. "Almost done."

She sighed and nodded. It had been too long since she'd tried to differentiate the animals by scent, but she suspected it was still Pegasus on the first truck. Whichever dragon, the captive was stomping but not causing too much ruckus. They followed along until the semis came to rest behind the exhibit. Zoo staff opened a back door that led to behind-the-scenes hallways. Then one of the trucks backed up to a huge gate, leading directly to the exhibit. Keepers began hooking the cage up securely to the sides of the gate.

"Why don't ya go 'round the front," Robbie suggested. "Then you can watch 'em go free."

Free wasn't the first word Taliya would use for the situation. But it was as close to free as they'd probably ever get.

She and Kano hurried around to the front of the exhibit. A small media tech team from the zoo was positioned in the center of the viewing area, ready to officially document the dragons' release. Unofficially, five photo-drones hovered nearby, but they kept their distance. Telephoto lenses would have to do, she supposed. If one got too close, she'd be happy to smack it down.

Clanging of the crate being opened came from the back area, and Taliya held her breath.

"Look there, Tal," Kano said, pointing to a small mound of hay on the right-hand side of the exhibit with an egg settled into the makeshift nest.

Before they could discuss it further, Polly flapped and screamed her way into the exhibit. She raced in circles, her wings spread wide, and then stopped in the middle to let everyone know her feelings about the last few days.

"KAAH! KAAH! KAAAAH!"

Her wings beat the air, stirring up dust and making an impressive display. The photodrones swept low over Taliya and Kano's heads, capturing images through the Plexiglas front. One swung high and went for an overhead view through the netting. Taliya couldn't really blame them. *Media folks must be losing their minds.*

Her rage abated some, Polly stalked around until she spotted the egg. With a snort, she hunkered down on top of it, ruffled out her feathers with a shake, and settled in on the nest.

Hoots and cheers came from the back of the enclosure, where the rest of the team was watching. The sound of the semis moving around indicated preparations were underway for the next dragon's release.

One down, three to go. Taliya hoped they were getting the brooding mamas out first. No chance for one of the males accidentally stomping an egg before it was safely tucked under the correct female.

As if to prove her point, Reynaldo crept into the enclosure, the second egg clutched in front of him. Polly seemed oblivious to his presence. Moving stealthily, he placed the egg on another makeshift nest on the left-hand side of the exhibit. When the panthran came more into her line of vision, Polly snorted again and glared at him, but she didn't get up. Maybe she didn't associate Rey with all that had gone on because she'd been drugged. Either way, he was able to leave without disturbing her.

"There's another one?" The media guys gawked at Polly.

Taliya chuckled deep in her chest. "Oh yes."

The two men turned toward her with wide eyes.

"And are those eggs *real?*" the other one asked.

"Yep. Laid them at the Outback reserve yesterday. I hope they survived the trip."

The men looked totally dumfounded. Taliya had to hand it to Robbie and his team. If even the media guys for the zoo hadn't known what to expect, a tight lid had been kept on the whole operation. She'd have to send a thank you present of some kind to the interns out at the reserve. *Maybe a replacement barn?* That made her smile. *Probably already have the new one halfway built.*

"So huge!" One of the media guys snapped photo after photo. "Bizarre!"

Taliya's hackles spiked at the dragons being called bizarre, even though she understood that was a logical reaction.

"Here comes the next one," Kano said before she could respond. "Probably Bunny."

"Bunny?" one of the media guys mumbled.

Based on the unclaimed egg, Kano's guess was a good one. After more clanging of metal doors, a squawk came from the backstage area. Then Bunny—who'd been awake and alert throughout the move—hop/walked into the enclosure, head low and threatening, wings spread. "KAAH!"

Taliya climbed over the safety railing and moved up to

the Plexiglass, hoping Bunny would notice her. And wasn't too angry about the whole pretending to steal the egg and tricking her into a cage thing. After stomping around the exhibit for a minute, stopping to touch beaks with Polly, Bunny eyed her former trainer.

"Kaah! Taah-yaa! Taah-yaa!"

The tigran put both hands flat on the glass and looked up at her dragon. "It's okay, Bunny. This place is safe. Go find your egg," she shouted loudly enough for her voice to carry over the barrier and through the netting.

Bunny tipped her head and sniffed the air, probably catching Taliya's scent. Polly made a soft chirp, and Bunny turned toward her. The two chatted back and forth with little chirps, trills, and clicks. After a long string of sounds from Polly, Bunny turned and looked directly at her egg in the makeshift hay nest. Without hesitation, she hurried over to it, wings flapping. After poking at the hay with her beak, she settled down on top of the egg and made a happy-sounding chirp.

Kano stepped next to Taliya and put a hand on the glass as well. "Have you heard them do that before?"

Taliya shook her head, stunned. It had been years since she'd been around the animals, and they'd clearly learned some new skills. "It looked like Polly told her about the egg. Like they had a *conversation*."

Her com dinged, and she pulled it out of her pocket. "Rey is excited too," she said, showing Kano the text full of exclamation marks. "Says he's never heard it either."

"Are you saying those things can talk?" one media guy asked.

"It's the first time I've seen that behavior," Taliya admitted. "Your keepers get the fun of deciding what it means."

They'd captured that dragon chat on video, so the folks in charge could replay it and draw their own conclusions. A surge of jealousy rose up, and Taliya took a deep breath to quell it. Kano wrapped his tail around her leg and chuffed quietly, knowing her well enough to sense her frustration.

"We can all come back to visit," he said.

She nodded but doubted that would happen. At least not with the kits. The thought of what security would be required to take the girls out of the country was overwhelming. The president would definitely try to talk her out of it.

"Maybe the dragons will come back to North America someday," she said. "Or their offspring will."

Clanking came from behind the scenes, and the media pair jumped back behind their cameras. Coconut burst into the enclosure, and all attention went to him.

All three dragons *kaahed* and chirped. They seemed to be discussing the new situation. After taking his own tour of the exhibit and a check-in with both females, Coconut settled on the ground next to Polly. They tipped their heads together, making tiny cooing sounds. More conversation for the experts to decode. Taliya suspected they were comforting each other.

Bunny didn't have to wait long for her mate. By the time Coconut had calmed down, the next truck was ready. As furious as Pegasus had been in the cage, Taliya was sure his arrival would be exciting.

The alpha dragon did not disappoint. Crashing and shouts from backstage announced he was being unloaded. Bird-like screaming and *kaahing* followed. Pegasus burst into the exhibit—wings spread and hollering to wake the dead. He stomped around and sprayed cream-colored jets of poo on several back walls, marking the new territory. The familiar scent wafted past Taliya and made her chuckle. When he reached the center of the enclosure, Pegasus froze and glared at her. He snorted several times, staring her down.

"Guess he's holding a grudge," Taliya whispered in awe at the magnificent animal.

Throwing his head toward the sky, Pegasus *kaahed* so loudly the tigran covered their ears. Seeing him in the middle of the field, wings spread and head high, reminded Taliya of the end of that dinosaur movie, where the T-Rex trashed the welcome center and claimed his domain. Pegasus wanted everyone to know he was still the boss.

When he finally stopped, the media guys laughed nervously. Bunny made gentle chirping noises at her mate, and Pegasus settled in next to her. They did the same tilted-head chirping conversation until all four dragons finally went quiet.

The photodrones overhead moved around, trying to get different shots now that the big show was over. The whole world would soon know about the dragons and where they were. From now on, the dragons' safety was up to Australia Zoo, the responsibility of Wolfie and his dingman team.

Taliya stepped up to the glass one more time, and Bunny focused green eyes on her.

"Time to say goodbye," Taliya called out. "Take care of that egg."

"Taah-yaa, kaah," Bunny responded calmly.

Both media guys stared at Taliya, probably wondering if the dragon had actually said her name. She didn't know the answer for sure but held a yes to that in her heart.

Robbie, Carl, and Reynaldo jogged around to the front of the exhibit to join them. They all stood for a moment, taking in the sight of the white pterodragons in their new extensive enclosure. Taliya appreciated how the zoo had made the background look like rock walls and trees in the distance, despite some of them now being splattered with poo. She snapped several pictures with her com. Kano took one of her standing at the glass with all four dragons in the background, even though the media team must have taken thousands of images. She'd ask for copies of the best ones later.

"It's a bonza start," Robbie said. "We may have to adapt after we get to know 'em better, but now they're safe."

"Promise you'll send me videos of the eggs hatching," Taliya said, getting a bit misty-eyed at all she was going to miss. "And exciting things along the way."

"You know it. We'll take good care of 'em." Robbie tipped his head thoughtfully. "Hadn't considered breedin' the dragons, but I suppose the more of 'em there are, the less valuable these four'll be."

"I hadn't thought of that," Taliya admitted, though she doubted it would hold true. Unless there were thousands, unscrupulous collectors would always be after them. Probably even then too. Humans adored owning animals.

"Wish ya could stay longer," Robbie said. "Help us with what's to come."

Kano chuckled. "We have our own zoo of kits at home who would not be happy about that."

A man in a business suit—very official-looking—came around the corner and gave them a nod.

"Ya wanna be part of the announcement, like we planned?" Robbie asked. "Now's the time."

The foursome glanced at each other—taking in their dusty, rumbled state—and Taliya shook her head. "I think we'll stay off camera. You can have all the glory."

Robbie frowned but nodded. "When I use words like *team* and *amazin' cooperation between countries*, know that I'm talkin' about you lot. This absolutely could not have been accomplished without your help." He hesitated a moment, then nodded conclusively. "Tah muchly, then."

He jogged off to join the bigwig from the zoo in letting the world know about the successful rescue operation and the dragons.

"So . . . what now?" Carl asked, looking at each of them.

Taliya shrugged. After the stress of the last few days, it was odd for the mission to be over. "No more grand unveiling. We could reschedule the flight."

"Honestly, I could use a nap and a nice swim," Reynaldo said, stretching and twisting his body side to side. "It's been a while since I saw a real bed."

"We suddenly have the next three days free." Taliya thought a swim sounded fantastic. Nap or swim, she was up for anything relaxing.

Kano wrapped an arm around her waist. "Maybe we can actually enjoy a *real* vacation."

Carl stretched his neck and shook the tension out of his shoulders. "That would be outstanding."

"What about visiting the coral reefs and doing some snorkeling?" Reynaldo's golden eyes glimmered with excitement. "The most amazing man-made ones in the world are not far from here."

"Tomorrow?" Taliya suggested.

Kano chuffed. "Yeah, tomorrow. I'm sure the hotel has a pool for today."

Rey agreed, though he looked disappointed. "Maybe I'll stay here for a bit, then. Make sure the dragons are calm and settled in. Get the crew through the first feeding." He looked to Carl, who nodded agreement.

"Okay," Taliya said. "We'll meet you at the hotel later."

With a last glance at the dragons—who were alert but

all still in the same spots they'd picked—Taliya and Kano climbed back over the safety barrier and headed to where the transports waited.

Taliya felt like a huge weight had been lifted. She was now free to enjoy Australia and then head home. But it was somehow anticlimactic.

"I don't remember how to relax and have a vacation," she whispered to Kano as she tucked in under his arm.

He chuckled. "It's okay to let down your hair and enjoy yourself now and then. Not Mom. Not ambassador for our species. Just Taliya."

The human idea of letting her hair down made her snort a laugh, but he was right. "I vaguely remember her. That innocent tigran girl whose mother was afraid to warn her about the breeding facility. She's been MIA since . . . well, since that Thanksgiving during the Gathering, when everything changed forever."

Kano grumbled deep in his throat. "We have three days." He kissed her on the top of the head. "Let's enjoy it."

"In the swimming pool?"

"Sounds like a good place to start."

15

Taliya rolled over and stretched, totally at peace and relaxed. The afternoon at the hotel pool yesterday had been delightful, even if their presence alarmed some guests. Mostly, the humans were curious. She'd noticed more than one looking at their devices, probably media reports from the zoo, and then glancing her way. However, no one approached or asked for a photo, which was fine with her, though she caught a few taking stealthy ones. Benefits of a swanky hotel. At least they pretended to be respectful.

She'd never owned a bathing suit, so the lightweight top and shorts she'd brought to sleep in had to do. Maybe the gawking was more about Kano—all seven feet and four hundred pounds of muscle—in his black swim trunks, effortlessly backstroking and relaxing in the sun. They'd taken turns catnapping on lounge chairs, relaxed but not quite letting down their guard in public.

After that, they showered and collapsed in the room to video chat with the kits and update Marla about the rescue and their schedule. It had taken several tries to get through, which panicked Taliya for a good thirty minutes, immediately jumping to dire conclusions. But all was well. The family had loved seeing media posts about their parents and zoo photos of the dragons because, of course, whatever was shared in Australia found its way around the planet in moments. Taliya spent some time sorting through it all as well, saving her favorites. Fortunately, nothing about Rey and Carl's wedding had surfaced. It was a sad fact, but sharing that joyous event would only lead to problems.

Carl texted that evening to say he and Rey were back at the hotel but ready to crash out. They'd connect in the morning for a vacation adventure at sea. Sounds Taliya's sensitive ears picked up from across the hall made her suspect the newlyweds were up to more than sleeping.

Taliya and Kano had finished the day with massive steaks for dinner from room service and a quiet evening in front of the media wall, the perfect ending to an intense mission.

A wake-up alarm beeped, and she tapped it off. Kano shifted, pulling her in to spoon, breath tickling her neck. Reminding her that their after-dark vacation activities had been quite delightful as well. A rumble vibrated through his chest, and she smiled.

"We have to get up soon if we're going to join in the snorkeling," she said.

"But not yet. Not quite yet."

Rolling to face him, she pulled the covers over their heads, like they used to in their first days together, kissed him on the pink nose, and smoothed the black lines of his fur into some kind of order. "You're very rumpled."

"May as well roll with it before we get cleaned up." He ran the length of her tail through his fingers.

Taliya chuffed. "May as well."

⊰⊱◆⊰⊱

THE ZOO HAD ARRANGED FOR A HELICOPTER TO PICK THEM UP ON the hotel roof and take them to the reef in the Coral Sea northeast of Brisbane. It would get them out of the hotel without a media crush at the front door. Taliya gawked a moment at the fancy machine with eight smaller rotors and barely any noise, unlike what the military still used.

Regardless of the upgrade, Taliya wasn't thrilled with the prospect of a helicopter ride. It stirred up serious traumatic memories. After her rescue from the kidnappers, Carl, skin gray, slowly bleeding out on the floor of the loudly whopping machine. Her body wracked with pain from the cattle prod and dental torture. She remembered the sounds and smells like it was yesterday. As they ducked under the rotating blades to board, she caught Carl's eye. He grinned—undaunted, as always—and she pursed her whiskers in return. Kano didn't seem to be flustered either, maybe not making the connection like her brain was.

She focused on the promise of several dolphman leading their diving tour. Yet another hybrid species she'd never known existed—and didn't outside of this part of Australia. They'd been designed for working in the seas but were complicated to create. Not worth the effort and expense for the government. Any currently alive were the result of natural births as this species found their own place in the world.

"All buckled in?" the pilot asked.

They each gave a thumbs-up, and the bird gently lifted off, heading north along the shoreline.

The Coral Sea spread out to their right. Shades of azure and turquoise outlined the different depths, small green islands peeking up now and then. The vision reminded Taliya of a strutting peacock tail. Out the left-hand window, a lush swath of land bore witness to the accessibility of water and lower temperatures near the sea. It was nice to be back where things could grow. Something deep in her instincts had felt uncomfortable in the desert of the Outback, knowing it couldn't sustain her.

Reynaldo leaned forward in his seat, "I can't wait to see the reefs. I've never been diving like this before."

Jaguars were potentially even better swimmers than tigers. Taliya had seen videos of full-blooded jaguars attacking crocodiles in the water and winning. Not something she'd ever want to attempt, especially after experiencing what the reptiles were capable of.

Kano said to Carl, "You're gonna have to work hard to keep up with the three of us well-bred swimmers."

"I'm more worried about sharks," he said, eyeing the water out the window.

Reynaldo patted his knee. "The guides know what they're doing. Wouldn't pay to lose one of us."

Carl did not look consoled. Taliya, however, was highly entertained by mental images of Carl doing battle with a shark. And winning, of course.

After a twenty-minute flight, the chopper lowered down on a giant X next to an aquarium on the shoreline. The pilot took off his headgear and turned to them.

"Watch for the blades gettin' out. You're some tall ones, for sure. No need for a haircut t'day."

They all laughed, and Carl gave him a sharp salute. Ducking carefully, the foursome exited the helicopter and headed inside the building's main doors to meet their guide.

There were several humans in line, so they joined the queue. A middle-aged man and woman in front of them were engrossed by their coms, watching footage of the dragons.

"They're so huge!" the woman said, using her fingers to enlarge the image on the screen.

"Makes you wonder what other kinds of crap those labs are messing 'round with that we know nothin' 'bout," the man grumbled.

Taliya grunted a laugh. "You have no idea."

Everyone turned to stare at them—living proof of what the government labs had produced—and the couple both flushed with embarrassment. The woman opened and closed her mouth twice, but nothing came out. Taliya just winked and looked away.

A stocky man with wild white hair and an extensive matching beard came out of a side door, and his face nearly split in two with the smile he aimed at Taliya's group.

"G'day!" he called out and strode over to them. "Name's Henry. I'm gonna be your liaison for the day."

He stuck out a hand to Carl first, then shook with each of them in turn. Taliya didn't sense any agitation or nervousness from the man, so that bode well for a pleasant day.

"I won the lottery. Yes I did!" Henry said, continuing to grin. "Not every day I get to take celebrities on tour."

"We appreciate it." Taliya smiled but kept her fangs hidden. No need to scare the guy, who seemed like a fan.

"My pleasure. One-hundred-percent. Butch'll take you snorkeling, but I'm your man on land."

Taliya suspected Butch was one of the dolphman she was dying to lay eyes on. There were very few images on the interwebs of what he might actually look like.

Carl heaved a dramatic sigh. "Henry, I may be spending more time with you than in the water."

Reynaldo frowned, and Taliya suspected there'd been a discussion last night when the two were alone.

"I sink like a boulder," Carl admitted.

Rey's golden eyes were pleading. "But you're going to try, right?"

"Yeah, I'll try. For you."

"You'll get on okay, I reckon," Henry said with a grin. "If not, Butch won't let you drown."

Kano laughed at the look of horror on Carl's normally composed face. Taliya chuffed at the general. *He wouldn't like needing to be rescued. Not at all!*

Henry started down the nearest hallway, motioning that they were skipping the line. "Let's start out here with some history."

He led them to a massive map on the wall that showed the shoreline and details about the large reef off the coast.

"At one time in the twenty-first century," Henry said, beginning what sounded like a routine tourist speech, "scientists were sure the coral reefs would be bleached and dead. Water temperatures got so high, coral and other animals were literally cooking. Carbon converters and some amazing science saved the day on that. The same kind of genetic research that led to you three outstanding creatures also saved our coral reefs."

Videos played on a media wall that showed plant life, colorful fish, sea turtles, and full-blooded dolphins swimming around the pink, purple, and blue reef structure.

"I won't bore you with all the details," Henry said, "but let's just say that something called CRISPR and genetic splicing brought about sturdier and hardier coral that could withstand what we humans were doing to the planet. Experts seeded the coral and rebuilt this particular reef from scratch with the help of a team of determined indigenous women. Broadcasting sounds from a healthy coral reef brought back many sea creatures. A reef is a whole ecosystem, so all that science led to saving not just the coral but thousands of other species who moved in or were transplanted here over the decades."

Kano sighed. "Something good to come out of all that disgusting genetic science."

Henry looked confused. "It brought a cure for cancer and other horrible diseases—and got us you three as well."

"Very true," Taliya said. Henry only saw the positive side of genetic research, not the pain and trauma she, Kano, and Rey had experienced. Along with thousands of others. *It's a beautiful day. Let him be happy.*

Henry motioned toward a set of bathrooms. "Go on and get changed now, and let's get you out in the sea. Do you have everything you need? Remember, security for the reef says no devices or cameras allowed in the water."

All four nodded and headed into their respective changing rooms. The males had brought swim trunks, but Taliya was going to wear the lightweight top and shorts from yesterday that she had on under her clothes. She loved the feeling of floating in a body of water, though it usually involved skinny-dipping. Excitement for the dive made her skin tingle. After taking off her outer layer of clothing and storing it in a locker with her com, she followed the arrows to an exit that led outside to a bamboo dock area.

For a moment, she just took in the scents and blinked while her eyes adjusted. Several rowboats were lined up on one side of the dock, and a few sailboats dotted across the sea in the distance. Tourists in bathing suits waited next to boats here and there, and most pretended not to stare at her. At least no one was obviously taking pictures or recordings because coms weren't allowed. A few women gasped and covered their mouths, looking past her.

Taking in the sight of the three males joining her on the dock, Taliya couldn't blame them. Kano and Reynaldo were glorious specimens, muscular stature on full display in nothing but their swim trunks, and Carl was perfectly toned, quite a spectacular example of a human male. From a distance, the gawkers probably didn't notice Rey's scars and strips of missing fur. Evidence of how scientific labs treated creations who gave them trouble. Or the pale scar on Carl's chest, along with other healed injuries. Carl's dark skin and Reynaldo's black fur glowed in the bright sunlight.

While Carl and Reynaldo were tall by human standards, her husband was a head taller. Watching him sniff the air and take in the vista of the sea in all his black-and-white glory made Taliya feel all gooshy inside, even after the quality private time they'd enjoyed just hours before. Or maybe because of it.

Kano turned and grinned. "Bonza day for a dive, ya reckon?"

"It is," she agreed with a chuckle at his attempted

accent, enjoying the fresh-yet-salty scent of the air as she sidled up to slip in under his arm. The day was warm for her idea of fall weather—and she knew the water would be warm as well, instead of refreshingly cool—but a constant light breeze made it tolerable for creatures with fur.

Henry trotted across the deck, still in his uniform. Clearly not joining them.

"You look ready to take on the sea." He handed Carl a mask and snorkel. "I've been informed you creatures won't need gear." The questioning look on his face made it clear he was following instructions but not too confident about them.

"I'd appreciate goggles or something," Taliya admitted. "In theory, the saltwater shouldn't bother my eyes, but I'd rather not test that out."

Kano and Reynaldo both nodded their agreement.

"I've done some saltwater swimming," Kano said, "and it does irritate them."

"But we don't need snorkels," Rey said. "Hybrids like us can hold our breath for a long time. And I'm not sure how it would work around our teeth." He grinned, white fangs glistening in the bright sun.

Henry's eyes went wide, but he nodded. "Well, then." He trotted over to where a variety of equipment hung on a peg wall, seemed to consider the masks, which might not work on their nose shape, and removed three diving goggles. "Largest size we've got."

As Carl helped Rey try one on and Taliya and Kano

fussed with theirs, Henry yelled out a greeting toward the water. All four of them turned to where he was focused.

"Oi, Butch's here."

"G'day!" the dolphman called out with a wave of his human-looking arm before he dove to meet them.

Butch swam up to the dock and resurfaced. Similar to most hybrids, his head was shaped like a human, but with a longer nose and mouth, forming a snout. His black eyes were strangely far apart—nearly on the sides of his head. The skin of his whole body had that rubbery-gray look of a dolphin, and a tuft of black hair sat on top of his head. Below the surface, the dolphman wore fitted swim trunks to cover his privates, and long legs that were each like a muscular dolphin tail ended in a flipper-style foot. Taliya decided getting around on land would be tricky but not impossible.

He smiled, revealing tiny spiked teeth. "Welcome to the reef," he said, his voice deeper and richer than Taliya had expected. "Good to meet you! Gonna be some fur in the water today! As I'm sure Henry told you, I'll be your guide during the dive. Would you rather take a boat out or just swim?"

"Boat," Carl said as the other three said, "Swim."

They all chuckled, and Carl puffed out his chest with a grin. "Human man need boat!" he insisted.

"Let me get you a guy for the oars," Butch said.

Carl stopped him. "That's okay. I can handle it."

"I'll bet you can." Butch winked a large black eye. "Snag that boat to your right. The rest of you, dive on in."

While Carl got settled, Kano arced a perfect dive into the sea, leading to some giggles from the women nearby. Rey and Taliya glanced at each other.

Rey grinned. "One, two, three . . ."

They jumped in with a giant splash, curling into cannon-ball form. Carl shouted as the spray rained down on him. Taliya surfaced to tread water, reveling in the weightless feeling, the water warm as a bath.

When Butch turned to lead the way, Taliya spotted a blowhole on the back of his neck and a fin along his spine. They swam or rowed the 400 yards to the reef. The three creatures got their goggles on as tightly as possible, and Carl prepped his snorkel and mask before doing a strange military-style upright jump from the boat while Butch held it steady.

"You can explore and enjoy the area at your leisure," Butch said, treading water in front of them and revealing webbing between each finger. "However, no touching. The coral looks sturdy, but it's easy to damage. And some of the fish and plants will take a chomp if you annoy them."

Taliya tried to imagine a plant that would bite and didn't need more convincing to keep her furry hands to herself.

"My team keeps an eye out for sharks," the dolphman continued, "but you are not gonna be a tempting meal. Your smell might intrigue them, though."

Three more dolphman—two males dressed like Butch

and a female in a full rainbow-colored swimsuit—popped up a few yards away.

"If you need anything," he continued, "just wave your arms or give a holler." He looked at Carl. "You need any training on the snorkel?"

Rey snorted. "General Thompson here used to train grunts for special ops scuba night raids."

"A snorkel is different," Carl said with a smirk, "but I got it."

"Roger that." Butch gave the general another sly wink. "I'll call for a rendezvous in twenty minutes, just to be sure we're keeping track of you. Off you go!"

Taliya glanced over at Kano—who looked weird in his goggles—and grinned, realizing she must look just as odd. All four of them dove down and entered the world of the coral reef.

It looked exactly like the video from the aquarium. Taliya marveled at the variety of colorful fish, who kept their distance but didn't seem bothered. A green eel poked its head out of a hole in the pink coral and regarded them with one eye. She wondered if it had caught their scent. *How does an animal smell underwater?* Scent must be as important to sea animals as it was to land animals . . . and genetic hybrids. Underwater, her nose was sealed up tight.

Kano swam past, and it was funny to watch as he dove and turned, using his tail like a rudder.

The kits would love this, she thought.

Carl and Rey explored on their own, a bit away from

Taliya and Kano. All four had to surface periodically—to breathe and for the creatures to drain and readjust their goggles. A tight seal was impossible to accomplish on a furry face. And poor Carl could only hold his breath so long for a dive below the surface.

There were humans snorkeling around them here and there. One of the women pointed out a school of fascinating purple-and-yellow fish, making sure Taliya saw it and giving a thumbs-up. Several official-looking women in full scuba gear were cleaning green bits off the coral. Maybe something invasive and damaging.

After the first twenty minutes, a sharp whistle carried through the water. Taliya turned in the direction it seemed to come from and spotted Butch. He surfaced, and a whole blast of whistles and sharp noises followed, announcing the check-in.

That blowhole isn't just for looks.

Once Butch had eyes on everyone—humans and creatures—they dove again.

Splashing sounds caught Taliya's attention, and she looked up to see four dolphman racing and leaping out of the water, just like videos she'd seen of wild dolphins. They also seemed to be communicating among themselves with squeaks and whistles. It reminded her of Rey and his panthran language, as well as the new communication skills the dragons seemed to have developed.

After about an hour, Carl was done. He really did sink like a stone. Not such a problem with a scuba air tank, but he couldn't just easily float at the top and breathe through the snorkel. Butch held the boat steady so he could climb back in, and Carl rowed to shore.

"He didn't want to do this at all," Rey admitted as they treaded water and watched him leave. "But I doubt he's sorry. It's amazing down there."

Taliya nodded and dove to continue exploring.

After another hour, the three creatures agreed it was time to head back. They thanked Butch and the other dolphman. Taliya wondered a hundred things about the hybrid—where they lived, what they ate, how they survived in the human world—but it felt rude to ask. Maybe Henry could fill her in once they'd gotten cleaned up and changed.

The trio started a leisurely swim back to the aquarium. Taliya couldn't think of how to use her connections to help promote and support what the scientists had done and were continuing to work on in the Coral Sea, but she'd figure out something.

"We should document some video here, with the reefs behind us," she suggested to Kano as he backstroked alongside her.

"Excellent idea."

Since this was part of their tour still funded by the zoo, she already planned all kind of photos afterward to post. Waiting until they were done kept the crowds from showing up but would get the aquarium some attention.

When they neared the docks, Taliya spotted Carl watching their approach—fully dressed, hands on his hips, general-on-alert written all over his face. The wind was wrong for a scent, but his body language alarmed her. Henry was pacing the dock, talking animatedly on a communicator.

Kano stopped next to her, followed her gaze, and frowned. "Something's wrong."

The odor of Kano's sudden anxiety overcame the salt-water surrounding them.

"The dragons," Taliya whispered. "I thought they'd be safe at the zoo."

"Could be. But Henry looks concerned too."

She nodded, and her throat clenched. *Who would Henry be talking to about that?*

Reynaldo had continued swimming, not noticing his husband or what was unfolding on the dock. Kano and Taliya freestyled quickly to catch up and arrive when he did. As they climbed the ladder, the sight and smell of Carl twisted Taliya's stomach in knots—panic, frustration, and bloodlust-level rage wafting from him.

"We have to leave. Now." Carl wore an expression she couldn't translate, jaw tight. "I was about to send a dolphman to find you. Your belongings are already in the copter."

"What's going on?" Taliya gasped, trying to catch her breath.

Before Carl could answer, Henry hurried over. "She wants to speak to you."

He handed the com to Taliya. At the sight of President Nakobi's face on the screen, wet hackles spiked from ears to puffed tail. *It's bad. Really bad.*

"Taliya, Kano, oh gods." Padme's voice was muffled, but her face was clear and looked more distraught than Taliya had ever seen. And they'd been through some intense situations together. Behind the president looked like the inside of Air Force One.

"Did something happen to the dragons?" Taliya asked.

"No. No." The crease between Padme's dark eyebrows deepened. She breathed in and out slowly. "There was . . . a situation at your homestead. We're still gathering details, but a private jet is scheduled to bring you straight home."

Fury clenched Padme's jaw. Kano's hand rested on Taliya's back, his claws extended.

Home. A situation? That sounded like presidential diplomatic-speak for an attack on their compound.

The beautiful day around her narrowed into a pinprick of vision, focused on Padme's face.

Taliya's lungs refused to function.

"There's a whole team of security there," Kano said.

They both looked at Carl, tears now brimming in his eyes.

Gods, no.

A security breach would not break Carl. He'd be in control, chewing someone a new asshole.

"Is anyone hurt?" she managed to sputter.

Carl made a horrible noise, like a repressed sob.

Padme frowned. "A team at the hotel is packing your things now. They'll meet you at the airfield with your luggage."

She didn't answer. Why didn't she answer? The innocent faces of each of her kits flashed through her mind. Her breath now rapid pants, she leaned forward, putting her free hand on her knee. Next to her, Kano emitted ragged growls.

"Is anyone *dead?*" Taliya whispered.

"Carl has all the specifics," Padme said, again clearly avoiding the question. "Once you are in a private place, he'll tell you everything we know so far. We should have more details by the time you get on the plane."

Carl was next to Taliya, taking her arm. "Let's go now."

She glanced up at him, and he nodded his head to the right, where several humans were watching them intently. She immediately straightened up and nodded, though tremors vibrated through her body. Whatever horrific thing Carl had to tell them, this was not the place.

"Thank you, Padme," she said. "We're leaving."

She ended the call, vaguely aware of Carl taking the com and putting it in his pocket. Doing her best to behave and breathe normally—knees threatening to take her down—she let him lead her through the doors and into the aquarium, past the giant map and media screen, and out the front to the waiting helicopter. Kano and Rey followed close behind, both reeking of stress and anguish. They all loaded in, buckled up, and the machine lifted off with a lurch. Taliya's eyes met Kano's next to her, worry switching to dread.

As they took to the air, she spotted Henry on the

ground, waving hesitantly. The ambassador-for-her-species part of her mind scolded her for not thanking him and saying a proper goodbye, but he seemed to know what was going on and would understand.

As they leveled off, she glared at Carl across from her. "Talk."

16

Carl shifted in his seat, and Taliya watched the brigadier general struggle to the surface again: unemotional and ready to debrief. Readying to tell them what horrendous event had occurred.

"An hour ago, there was an attack on your compound. It was well-planned and orchestrated. Professionals. In a coordinated effort, the entire security team surrounding the property was shot with tranquilizers. The dogs too, so the attackers knew what was waiting. They came from all sides at once. Around a dozen masked, armored individuals, from what the security cameras recorded before they went offline." He paused and stared down at his clenched hands.

Taliya's body went numb. *Professional attack. Someone came for the girls. While we were off gallivanting around. . . .*

Based on the avoidance of her questions, the kidnapping was successful. She just waited for Carl to admit it. He didn't seem able to.

"Just say it." She inhaled a jagged breath. "They're gone. Aliania and Amrita."

Carl nodded, and a tear dripped off the end of his nose. He sniffled and raised his head to reveal bloodshot eyes. "Yes. They were taken."

Kano erupted with tiger screams, fist pounding the side of the helicopter, the fancy plastic wall denting. The machine tipped and then righted itself, like he'd scared the pilot. Taliya caught his arms before he did serious damage and held him close until he was only making a rumbling noise, his breath shuddering into hisses through bared fangs. Reynaldo sobbed, covering his face with both hands.

She released Kano but found herself frozen, unable to process the reality of it. They had just been celebrating the success of the dragon rescue. Diving a coral reef with dolphman. She felt out-of-body, floating outside of it all as an observer.

Carl cleared his throat. "The president is gathering intel from satellites and other resources right now. By the time we get on the plane, she'll hopefully have a rescue plan."

Taliya didn't have to ask about ransom demands. The kits themselves were worth more than any money even the government would pony up to save them. Aliania, with her pure-white fur. Amrita, maybe the only strawberry tigran in existence. So rare and "valuable." Memories of being tortured years ago—trying to convince her to help mercenaries get their hands on the kits—made Taliya tremble. At least she could be reasonably confident the kidnappers wouldn't hurt the girls.

But Carl still looked uneasy. There was more.

The girls hadn't been alone.

"Just spit it out," she said.

"Luna and Lilly are fine. As is Little Jai. It was so stealthy to begin with, they didn't even know what happened."

Her ears swiveled backward. "But . . . ?"

Carl rolled his shoulders and sighed. "When the assailants left with the kits, they tripped an extra security line at the door. Separate from the rest of the system. Installed for exactly this scenario. It set off an alarm and woke Marla."

Kano moaned. "Is she okay?"

"It seems she rushed outside to . . . She must have surprised them. . . ."

Taliya slapped a hand over her mouth as icy shock ran down her spine.

"Dammit, Carl," Kano said. "What happened?"

"She was in surgery when the president called." The general lowered his head again, and his knuckles turned tan-colored from squeezing so tight.

A sob forced itself from Taliya's throat. Marla had finally begun to move past all the horrors she'd faced during the Gathering. One more gut punch from an indifferent universe. "Was she shot?"

Carl heaved a sigh. "I don't know."

Taliya wanted to scream and then cry and then break a thousand things into millions of pieces. But she doubted any of that would help with the rage and fear building in her core—the utter helplessness, once again, in the face of human greed.

"Do they think she'll survive?" Rey whispered, finally pulling his hands from his face.

Carl shrugged one shoulder in defeat. "Another update to expect on the plane."

Taliya blew out a puff of air, determined to remain calm and focused. "Have they contacted Parth?" *Gods, he's going to blame us. Exactly what he always feared would happen.*

"Of course," Carl said. "I'm sure he's at the medical center already."

He took Taliya's hand. "There's no evidence to suggest this happened because you were away. It may be an opportunity the kidnappers took advantage of, but it was clearly a professionally developed plan that didn't just materialize over the few days you've been here."

She nodded but still felt a ball of guilt in her stomach. Being hysterical or sick about it would have to wait. They needed to get home. Padme would put a rescue plan in place. Doctors would save Marla. It would all be okay.

But Carl still hadn't settled. She couldn't read his scent.

Everyone's accounted for, aren't they? She squeezed his hand. "What else?"

"When the alarm went off . . ." He paused, then cleared his throat. "When the alarm went off, your parents raced out of their house as well." He rubbed a hand across his face and groaned. "Your father had a gun. He got off several rounds before . . ."

Before what?

Kano bent over with a moan and wrapped his hands around the back of his head.

"What're you saying?" Terror burned in her chest.

Carl wiped a tear from his cheek. "It was a clean shot to the heart."

Taliya felt like her own heart exploded. The world around her spun, and she dropped her head between her knees to keep from passing out. "He's *dead?*"

"I'm so sorry."

Kano pounded the side of the helicopter with a fist again and low growls rumbled through him.

"My mother?" Taliya wasn't sure she could handle the answer.

"Maybe they didn't see her, or maybe she didn't pose a threat. Either way, she's unharmed."

Taliya was grateful he didn't say she was *fine* because her mother would not be *fine* for a long time to come. None of them would.

Memories of her peaceful father flashed through her mind. Visions of him playing with his grandkits in the yard. Bits and pieces of her youth. Him working on their log home and explaining how humans lived hundreds of years ago. Always the teacher, even after he was forced to leave the school during the Gathering and join the rebel army to protect his family and his species. That he'd been murdered, surrounded by fear and violence, was an affront to his whole nature.

Taliya mumbled, barely coherent. "All that danger during the war, and he's shot down in his own front yard."

"Valiantly trying to save the kits. Grampa Jai is a hero."

Taliya understood Carl's way of looking at things. Dying in an honorable fight was noble. But she just couldn't. However you spun it, her wonderful father was gone. She pushed that down for now, again feeling like she was watching this all from afar.

"A new security team is in place." Carl took her hands again and pulled her chin up to face him. "We *will* find them, Taliya. Just like I found you. Just like I found Rey. . . . I will find my strawberry sundae Amrita and my little marshmallow Ali." He swallowed and squeezed her fingers, making her claws pop. "There's nowhere on this earth to hide them from Uncle Carl."

The rest of the helicopter flight to the airstrip was spent in stunned silence, broken up periodically by Carl sending and receiving messages but no new information. Taliya knew she had to stay focused, but the frustration of being so far away, ultimately helpless, threatened to bubble up and explode. When they landed, Wolfie was waiting to meet them while their luggage was loaded onto the plane. He ran over and enveloped Taliya in a massive hug before she could say a word.

"I'm so sorry," he whispered. "Anythin' ya need, just let us know." He released her and wiped tears from his dark eyes.

"Thank you for helping get us home quickly."

He nodded toward the luggage. "Everythin's here. I oversaw it all personally."

Releasing her, Wolfie exchanged quick hugs and pats on the back with Rey and Kano, but Carl had headed straight for the plane and was already aboard, probably plotting with the pilot.

"I know it's the least of your worries now," Wolfie said, "but the drags are settlin' in fine. It's all good there. Go home and find your kits."

Taliya nodded numbly—wondering if Wolfie knew the full extent of what had happened—and let herself be led to the plane and up the stairs.

The inside of the private jet was ridiculously fancy, clearly meant for the rich and famous who could afford such luxuries. Decorated in calm browns and beiges, there were eight leather chairs set in pairs along the walls, with a table between each and more leg room than necessary. A small meal galley and a bathroom were in the rear of the plane. All Taliya really cared about was the machine getting them home.

Wolfie turned to the cockpit for a quick word with Carl and the pilot before exiting the plane. Taliya felt there was more she should say to the dingman who'd been so wrapped up in the last days of their lives, but words wouldn't come. She settled into a seat and spotted him out the window, making sure the last of the bags were loaded and safe. The engines fired up, vibrating her seat. Wolfie looked up, spotted her in the window, and gave a wave goodbye. She raised a hand and mouthed "thank you."

Kano sat down next to her while Rey picked a seat across the aisle and stared out the window, shoulders hunched. Each of them had been drugged, captured, and held captive at least once. Avoiding any of those memories wrapping up with images of what might be happening to Aliania and Amrita at that moment was impossible.

Carl joined them and sat next to Rey, immediately putting a hand on his husband's knee. Rey didn't turn from the window, but his shoulders shook as he uttered small whimpering noises. Kano sat like a rock next to Taliya, barely seeming to breathe. Rage and frustration emanated from him in waves.

The pilot—a middle-aged human with a paunchy gut—stepped out of the cockpit. "I'm Captain Jones," he said in an American accent, "and my co-pilot is Captain Frank. We'll be taking shifts during the flight and have you home as quickly as possible, but it'll take around thirteen hours to get you to Sacramento. We'll refuel, meet with a special customs team, then zip you to Arkansas. Because of the rush, we're operating without a flight attendant, but Carl has agreed to serve that function for us."

Taliya glanced at Carl, who made two-finger motions with both hands. "Exits in the front and back. There's a float pad under your seat, in case we crash into the ocean." He gave a wry smile.

"Buckle up," the pilot said before returning to the cockpit.

The chairs were wide and deep, which was helpful for a tigran, and Taliya could see they maneuvered to become beds. She fastened her seatbelt, but sleep seemed impossible.

As the plane revved forward, Carl pulled out his communicator and scrolled through the messages. Taliya realized she hadn't checked hers, wasn't even sure where it was. Clear disposable bags stowed along the wall nearby showed the clothes she'd worn to the aquarium—Carl must have had them—and she realized she was still in her lightweight swimming outfit. Kano and Rey wore nothing but their swim trunks. Her fur was stiff with salt water. She didn't have the energy to care.

Once they were in the air and leveled off, she unbuckled and grabbed her bag, finding her communicator. She handed Kano his from the other bag.

They both had a message in a group chat from her mother sent a few minutes ago.

All is as well as can be expected. The L-twins and Little Jai are back asleep. They didn't witness anything except the sound of the alarm. But Jai knows his sisters have been taken. I haven't told them about Marla or Grampa yet. At least for the L-twins, it may be more than they can understand. I'll tell Little Jai in the morning. I know you're hurrying home, but President Nakobi assures me an investigation is already underway. There's nothing to be done but wait. Love you. See you soon.

Such calm words from a wife who just held her husband as he died while two of her grandkits were kidnapped. Did her mother literally watch as the girls were carried away into the night? Taliya's body clenched at the thought, claws extending and retracting. She hoped her mother was asleep now, but just in case, she typed a response, assuring her they were on the way.

Kano gripped his com in his lap. He hadn't responded, but it wasn't necessary. Taliya reached over, took the device from him before he snapped it in two, and placed it on the small table between their seats. She looked over at Carl, who was reading a new message.

"Word on Marla," he said, "finally. This report says she's out of surgery and expected to survive."

A small blessing in this shit show. Taliya bristled her whiskers, imagining what was going on at the hospital. How fearful and enraged Parth must be for his wife. "So, was she shot?"

Carl frowned and turned to face her and Kano. "No. We don't know exactly how it went down yet, but they suspect she surprised the attackers from behind. Probably hoping to get the drop on them. . . . Her wounds look like blows from fists and gun butts."

Taliya's skin crawled, and her ears turned back flat. "They beat her? So badly she needed *surgery*?"

"If they'd wanted to kill her, they would have. We can be grateful for that. They just left her unconscious. Shreya says Marla was already down by the time she and Grampa Jai made it outside, so it was quick."

Taliya swallowed the lump in her throat but had to ask. "If my father hadn't fired on them . . . ?"

Rey made a choking noise, still resolutely facing out the window.

"Yeah," Carl admitted, "they probably wouldn't have noticed him. Since they didn't just kill the guards or dogs, orders must have been not to. But once he fired . . ."

Tears welled in her eyes and rolled down the black-striped fur of her face.

"If we'd been there," Kano growled, "I'd have shot at them too. Chased after them like Marla. Tried anything to stop it. To get the girls back."

Carl huffed. "Damn straight."

Her father's valor was noble. Taliya understood that. But it still left him dead. She wiped her face and sniffled.

Carl cleared his throat and unclenched his fists. "There's some ale and food in the mini cooler. Your clothes are here from the aquarium. There's a shower in the back," he said flatly. "Take turns getting cleaned up, then we should all try to sleep. We're gonna need it."

Kano stared straight ahead blankly again, maybe the only way he could stay in control. Rey had finally turned to face forward. The grief washed across his majestic face was devastating. As a creature held captive in deplorable conditions for the majority of his life, Taliya could only imagine what was racing through his mind.

She realized it would all crash down eventually, but numbness still clung to her. It all felt unreal. If she let it, the helplessness of the situation could pull her under, so she stuck with numb. For now.

Carl whispered to Rey, and the panthran nodded before unbuckling and grabbing his bag of clothes. The pair moved to the back of the plane. Carl offered soothing words to his mate. Rey said something in panthran, and they embraced before he went into the bathroom.

After some shuffling around and clunking, Carl handed Taliya and Kano each a bottle of ale and a wrapped sandwich—roast beef and Swiss cheese.

"Eat," he said. "It's well past lunch. You'll rest better with a full stomach."

Taliya obeyed, but it was mostly tasteless. Then she took her turn in the bathroom.

It was a weird sensation on a plane in flight—to strip and take a shower, however fancy. At one point, hysterical tears threatened. She let the hot water blast her in the face. A meltdown was tempting but pointless. And she wasn't sure she could rein it back in if she released the fury. Inside a metal tube flying over the ocean was not the place for an out-of-control tigran. Taliya wrestled with her emotions until she breathed normally again. *Save it. Save it for later.*

By the time Kano returned from his shower, Reynaldo and Carl were watching a movie with headsets on. It looked like a silly rom-com. Perfect for distraction. Carl checked his com now and then, but didn't share anything.

"What time is it?" Kano asked as he sat back down, smelling like the fruity shampoo provided on the plane.

"I'm not sure," she admitted. "As we travel through time zones, my com keeps updating. I think it's about midafternoon Brisbane time. Home is fifteen hours behind that."

"Morning will come there soon enough."

And Mother will have to tell Little Jai everything. As much as he and Amrita bothered one another, they also adored each other. He would be terrified for her while trying to mourn his grandfather and worry about Aunty Marla. She sent her mother another text.

> Call if you want when Jai's awake. I don't imagine we are falling asleep anytime soon.

She waited a few minutes, but the text was not marked as seen. Hopefully, that meant they'd all managed to sleep. Her mother's health had not been the same since her time in the POW camp and the brutal declawing done there. All the stress she was facing would hit her hard. Taliya wished the plane would fly faster.

"Want to try watching something?" Kano asked, crinkling up the wrapper from his sandwich and tucking it in the side pocket of his seat. "I can't just sit here stewing."

She picked up the media selection device, and their shared screen lifted from the floor in front of them. Hundreds of options scrolled past. She stopped on one. Kano nodded with a small smile. The fourth Dragonriders of Pern movie began playing, and they both put on their headphones.

Distract me, please, Taliya hoped, expecting to be disappointed.

Taliya managed to sleep a little while. Being part tiger forced the issue. But every time she closed her eyes, her mind wandered disturbing places.

Marla bolting upright at the alarm, discovering the kits gone, grabbing a weapon, running from the house in a panic, only to be savagely beaten and left on the cold ground.

Her father emerging from their house, seeing his grandkits being kidnapped—their fur bright-white in the darkness—raising his gun to fire and being shot down where he stood.

Her mother, sobbing, holding him as he took a last breath.

Hearing the girls screaming as they were dragged away into the night.

The ones Taliya woke herself up from quickly involved Aliania and Amrita being hauled from their beds, handcuffed, stuffed in cages, drugged.

Scenarios where they were on display. Standing on an auction block, trembling and crying while waiting for the highest bidder to claim them.

Aliania being shoved into a room like at the breeding facility, expected to produce pure-white kits. Sometimes Colonel Narlin was there with his leering gaze and cattle prod, inspecting every curve of her innocent daughter.

All of the dreams ended with Taliya jerking awake, fur spiked and heart racing.

In the last hour of the flight, Carl finally read a message that made him smile. Rey was asleep, so he leaned over and whispered with a gleam in his eye, "We found them."

His excitement washed over Taliya. "They're safe?"

"Not yet, but you can be grateful for your political connections. I suspect some secret government satellites were employed."

Knowing where the kidnappers went wasn't the same as her daughters being recovered. "So where are they?"

"I'll play you the message," Carl said, tapping the screen on his device and handing it to her.

Padme's exhausted-looking face appeared on the screen, and she gave a weak smile.

"Finally, we have a solid lead. Some highly skilled tech folks were able to track the vehicles from the compound in Arkansas, through several changes of transports and elaborate efforts to hide their travels. Tricky, but not as good as my team. We know where they ended up. But we're not sure exactly what the facility is. It's well hidden in the Colorado mountains."

"What is it with scumbags and those mountains?" Kano grumbled.

Taliya shook her head. The disgusting breeding facility had been hidden the same way, in an area where humans rarely lived or even bothered exploring.

Padme continued, "Whatever this complex is, it's located east of the Rio Grande National Forest. . . . You know what that means." She grinned.

Taliya gasped and paused the video. "Pull up a map."

Kano tapped some buttons on his com and then cast the images onto the media screen in front of them. He whuffed and fell back in his seat.

"Seriously?" Taliya examined the screen.

"What?" Carl asked, frowning.

Kano moved the image slightly west so the Tigran Conservation Reservation appeared in tan highlighting.

"No shit." Carl whistled through his teeth. "When was the last time you visited your buddies there?"

Kano shrugged one shoulder. "How old are the L-twins?"

Taliya's head raced with the idea that her connections with the uncivilized tigran living wild in the Colorado mountains might be the key to saving her kits.

"We were there in the fall of '76," Kano said, looking annoyed no one had caught his joke. "A year and a half ago."

Taliya's assignment from the government had been to make contact with the "uncivilized" tigran in that area north of Pagosa Springs, who had escaped from labs or just refused to live among humans. Their numbers had been significantly reduced by a raid of Enforcers during the Gathering, but dozens still remained, living off the land and keeping to themselves. Ranchers had accused them of killing livestock, but the investigation revealed the attacks were actually from three full-blooded tigers and a male lion. It was never clear where the four big cats had come from because they'd been held illegally. No one was going to claim them. Or admit why they were running free in the Colorado forest.

She and Kano spent a few weeks living with the wild tigran there—the Nuche Clan—to help establish some borders on their territory. By February of 2177, the government had agreed to the creation of the reservation. Respectful tourists were permitted to hike and climb in the area, but no hunting or farming was allowed beyond what the clan themselves did. Ranchers were forced to cease trying to expand their land into the tigrans' area. Taliya was more proud of that accomplishment than most anything else she'd done as a government employee.

And now the kidnappers had dragged her daughters within a few miles of that territory.

She'd been considering visiting the clan over the summer, now that the L-twins were older. They'd been conceived on the reservation, after all—a fact Aliania had declared "major eewwey." Taliya never followed through on the request to bring the clan some tigran males willing to basically be breeding stock—fresh blood for the females who wished to start families. Regardless, she was confident Severo and Jacy, the alphas of the clan, would offer assistance.

"They'll help," Kano said, clearly running through the same thoughts. "You know they will. Finish Padme's message."

Taliya tapped play again.

"The building is heavily guarded and camouflaged," Padme said, "so even our techs can't determine exactly what's inside. My guess is some kind of facility to keep creatures and animals that are illegal. That would make sense for why it's so protected. And why they'd want your girls there."

A lump caught in Taliya's throat, and Kano growled. But it was actually good news. If it was a collector of some kind, he definitely wouldn't hurt them. They were the prize. Amrita was too young for anything but display. Aliania, however, was technically mature enough . . . Taliya cleared her throat and refused to go there.

Padme said, "Teams are finding out what they can, but we don't want to alert the kidnappers that we know where they've taken the girls. I highly suspect your wild-living friends are our best bet to scope out the complex and gather intel. They might even help us with the final rescue itself. Nothing is as stealthy as a tigran." Padme chuckled. "Except maybe an *uncivilized* one. Let me know if you want to go home and check on your family there first or go straight to Colorado."

Kano hit pause this time. "What do you think?" he asked, blue eyes worried and nose flushed red.

"Everything in my body wants to get home and hug our kits. To comfort my mother and grieve my father. There's only one instinct stronger."

Kano nodded. "Saving our daughters."

"The longer we wait to attack that facility, the more chance they have to move them."

She looked at Carl, and he nodded once sharply. "Shreya will be okay. You know what she'd tell you to do."

Kano pressed play on the recording again.

"I only sent this message to Carl," Padme said, "in case someone is monitoring your devices. His and mine are encrypted. Let me know what you decide." The recording ended.

"Tell her Colorado," Taliya said. She reached to pick up her com, but then hesitated. *Not secure.* "And have her relay a message to Mother."

Carl set about furiously typing a string of texts.

Taliya leaned past the general so she could see Rey, who was now wide awake but staring at the wall in front of him, hands clenched on the armrests. "Once we land in

California," she said, "you two can go home. This isn't what you signed up for."

Rey turned to her with wide golden eyes while Carl lowered his communicator and said, "Fuck that."

"You can imagine we'd just *go home*?" Rey said. "While your kittens are in danger?"

"I would understand if you did," she said, mostly looking at Rey. "What comes next is a lot more dangerous than rescuing the dragons."

Rey made an odd face, like he'd smelled something bad. "If we risked life and limb for the dragons . . ."

The panthran turned back to looking out the window. Carl raised one eyebrow at her and resumed texting.

Guess that's the end of that conversation.

Kano glowered at the map on the media screen and shifted it back to the east, where Padme said the kidnappers' complex lay. He zoomed in on the large area of flat land. "There's the Monte Vista Wildlife Refuge, where those escaped big cats ended up. It's not like this facility is in a totally unpopulated area."

Taliya inspected closer. "Do you see any actual buildings?"

"No. They must have done something to camouflage the roofs."

"I wonder if the clan already knows about it."

"It's outside of their land," Kano said, "but not by much."

Taliya wondered if the facility was already there when she, Kano, and Severo had been hiking that area and planning borders for the reservation. She pursed her whiskers in aggravation. *How long have they been collecting creatures?*

"Hey," Carl said, leaning back their direction. "Marla's awake."

"Thank the gods." A tiny bit of the anxiety in Taliya's chest eased. Marla had recovered from her multiple POW beatings, mostly. The healed fractures in her feet could predict the weather better than the media, and too much walking left her in pain. Taliya hated that her friend had to begin that process again. But at least she was alive.

"The text from medical says the head wound they were most concerned about is okay, no brain bleeding, and they were able to repair the internal damage."

Taliya frowned. "*Internal* damage?"

"Sounds like they did some midriff kicking once she was down," Carl said bluntly. "Hopefully, already unconscious." He paused. "Maybe they left her when your father started shooting."

Kano chuffed. "He might well have saved her."

Taliya smiled as best she could. If the gods had picked her father instead of Marla, she would have to accept it and be grateful they weren't both dead—the other kits killed or taken too. It occurred to her that maybe she should be praying. To some god. At the moment, she couldn't think who that would be.

"Marla sent a note to you two." Carl showed them his device.

Taliya's heart felt like it stopped for a second, and Kano rumbled next to her.

Aunty Marla was the calming influence in their home. Always looking for the bright side, trying to move on from their traumatic past, and aiming for peace among the kits. But that day, she had a clear message.

Kill them. Kill them all.

17

The Sacramento International Airport arrival was at a remote gate, where rich people received special treatment. One customs agent boarded and talked to the pilots while they fueled up. Being a government-hired aircraft, it was a perfunctory check. Captain Frank had instructed the passengers to lower all the blinds, just in case the ground crew got nosy. The enemy might be watching for their plane or any indication they weren't heading to Arkansas, though there was no reason to suspect anyone knew they were even on this specific chartered plane. But secret surveillance satellites went both ways.

It was nine am there, but the same calendar day they'd left Australia thirteen hours ago, which was all confusing. Another three-hour flight to Colorado Springs lay ahead. A helicopter would then deliver them to the uncivilized tigran camp. There were landing spots along the shore of the lake that was once the Vallecito Reservoir. They'd have to select one carefully to arrive in full view—but far enough away not to scare the stripes off the clan. After the cleansing their group experienced during the Gathering, it would need to be abundantly clear the arrival was friendly and not an attack.

While they waited to takeoff again, Taliya and Kano used Carl's device to call home. Several ticks went by before Shreya's exhausted-looking face appeared on the screen.

Taliya struggled to get words out, and tears sprang to her eyes. "Hi, Mama."

"Hello, my kitten." Shreya sat down in front of the screen in their living room at home. "Are you back in the country yet?"

"Yes, and heading to Colorado. I'm so sorry we can't come right to you, but Padme is confident they've found the girls."

"A Marine told me. Don't worry about us right now. Save the girls. That's all that matters. The rest . . . Well, we have our whole lives to deal with that."

Taliya sniffled and took a deep breath. "You've explained everything to Jai?" She almost clarified which one she meant, then her skin tingled icy-cold, realizing that would no longer be necessary.

"Yes. I'm not sure he's fully processing it. We've decided to focus on the girls for now," Shreya said. "He's terribly worried. Feeling bad about every time he was mean to his sisters or teased them."

Kano sighed. "He'll have a chance to beg for forgiveness very soon."

"I'm glad he didn't witness anything," Taliya said.

Shreya frowned and glanced toward the bedrooms. "He's admitted to seeing more than I thought."

Taliya returned the frown. "How much more?"

"He awoke as a man in black armor dragged Amrita from her room. He could hear Aliania's muffled screams in the hallway. Thought it was a nightmare." She hesitated. "He feels guilty. That he didn't wake up quickly enough to realize what was going on and help."

"Oh Jai." Taliya's soul ached for her only son. Normally a furry ball of sass, she couldn't imagine how he was handling such sadness. There was nothing she could do to shelter him from it, like she normally sheltered them all from the world.

"When the alarm went off," Shreya said, "he jumped out of bed and was not too far behind Marla. He yelled what happened, so she raced out the door."

Kano growled and huffed and shifted in his seat, anxiety wafting from him.

"Did he see what happened outside?" Taliya caught her breath. "To Grampa?"

"Apparently not," Shreya said. "Or he doesn't want to admit it. He claims he stopped and hid in the kitchen when he saw them attack Marla. Another thing to feel guilty about. I've assured him he did the right thing. That he had no way to protect her or stop the kidnappers. They would only have hurt him too. Or worse. But, you know." She shrugged one shoulder.

Taliya and Kano both nodded.

"What about the L-twins?" Taliya asked.

Shreya sighed. "They think it was a false alarm. One of the dogs accidentally tripped it. I've told them the girls have gone on a trip for a few days. With Marla and Grampa. It's the easiest, for now."

"Save the truth for later," Kano said. "If they can even understand. Hopefully, the only thing they will need to hear about is Grampa Jai."

"I wish we could be there to support you." Taliya inhaled deeply, trying to keep it together.

The thundering of the L-twins' feet came from the hallway, and both of their orange-and-black striped faces popped up onto the screen. "Mama! Papa!"

"My kittens!" She did her best to look excited. It was reassuring to see them safe and their normal, giggly selves. "Are you being good for Grammy?"

They both scrambled onto Shreya's lap.

"It's fun to not share her with big sisters," Lilly said.

"One knee for each of us," Luna added.

While Taliya was glad they were happy, the reason for all that undivided attention clawed at her insides. And her mother had to pretend nothing was wrong.

"Go on now, you sillies," Shreya said, clearly holding back tears. "Say bye-bye to Mama and Papa so they can finish their work and come home to us."

"Bye-bye!" both girls shouted and then climbed down to toddle off to their room.

The innocence of youth, flashed through Taliya's mind. Followed quickly by, *Ignorance is bliss.*

"Do you want me to wake Jai?" Shreya asked. "I gave him a mild sedative earlier, but it's probably worn off by now."

Taliya shook her head, though Kano looked like he disagreed. Probably wanted to lay eyes on their son as much as she did. "Let him rest. If he sees us, he'll feel the need to dredge it all back up and tell us details. Let it be, for now."

Shreya wiped a declawed hand across her black-striped face. "Okay. Go get my grandkits. Bring them home."

"We won't return without them," Kano said.

Taliya hoped that wasn't too much to promise. "I love you, Mom."

"I love you, my darling kit. And you too, Kano." She smiled with teary eyes, and the call disconnected.

Taliya and Kano sat back in their seats.

"I'm sorry about Jai," Carl said. "Big and little."

Kano chuffed gently at him and put a hand on top of Taliya's. "We'll get through it, just like every other challenge before."

It was a wonderful sentiment but hard to imagine being on the other side of this horror. The plane vibrated as the engine revved up. *Time to go get my kittens.*

WHEN THEY DISEMBARKED IN COLORADO SPRINGS, TALIYA TRIED to associate the specific smells, like pine trees, to her time with the wild tigran, not the breeding facility. It was a beautiful part of the country that "workers of iniquity," as her mother liked to call them, had ruined for her. Kano wrapped an arm around her waist, and they both turned to watch the luggage being unloaded. Again, they were on a private landing strip, far from prying eyes.

A familiar scent caught her attention, and Taliya turned to see massive Samson the ligran unfolding himself from inside a military troops helicopter. At nearly eight feet tall, the tawny creature with intricate liger markings on his face was always a splendid thing to behold. That day, just the sight of him made her feel it would all be okay. He was dressed simply in a brown tunic and slacks, so he wasn't there for business, with four backpacks slung over his arm. The exhausted travelers watched while he sauntered over to join them in the languid pace his huge physique required.

Before anyone got a word out, Samson dropped the backpacks and enveloped Taliya in a hug.

"I'm so sorry," he whispered. "About your father. Marla. About the kits." He kissed her on the top of her head, released her, and gave Kano the same embrace. Carl and Rey exchanged sad head nods with him.

"I brought fresh travel bags," Samson said, "like Carl requested, so you can pack a few things."

Carl took one from him. "We'll have to keep it light, but we may be out there a few days."

"I'm betting it gets cold after dark, now that we're back where it's spring," Kano said, taking a bag for himself.

Samson nodded. "I brought jackets for everyone. And purchased a few warm shirts."

There was a cool breeze across the landing strip. May in Colorado was not the same as May in Arkansas. Taliya wished she'd packed more warm clothes. For the Australia trip, there'd been no reason to.

After going through their suitcases, picking a few useful clothing items to layer up and changing into their boots from the Outback rescue, she hitched the pack over one shoulder and grumbled. All she wanted to do was run to the helicopter and find her daughters. Kano seemed just as antsy. However, this wasn't going to be a five-minute operation. Preparation was wise, but still frustrating.

Taliya glanced at the hanging bags being carried away by a woman in an airline uniform—their fancy clothes from the wedding and what they'd planned to wear to the pterodragon unveiling ceremony.

"We will store it all here in private lockers," Samson said, following her gaze. "One way or another, we will get it back to you when this is over."

Taliya nodded, but all those precious belongings could

be chucked into the sea if it meant getting her kits back unharmed.

The ligran continued, "Someone along the way suggested gifting some supplies to the wild tigran, so there's food and some outstanding knives and other hunting tools they may appreciate on the copter."

Taliya doubted Severo and Jacy needed anything but knew they'd appreciate the intention. She hoped the invasion of their lives could be as limited as possible. Even bringing Carl and Rey along felt like a violation.

"Ready to head out when you are," Samson said, watching the last of their luggage being taken away on a cart.

Carl heaved his pack over one shoulder. "Let's roll."

Samson headed back to the machine, and Taliya noticed he wore heavy-duty hiking boots. It took a moment to process that he was joining them. Samson was enormous and strong, but he was a lawyer. He fought constantly for tigran and their rights, but not in a physical way.

Kano leaned toward her. "Did you think he was going to sit it out while Aliania is in the hands of dangerous men?"

Taliya chuffed and shook her head. Their eldest kit and Samson had a unique bond, far beyond her crush on the ligran. There was also a healthy level of mutual respect. Taliya often wondered if Ali would become a lawyer as well. As long as she could work from the safety of their compound, that was a wonderful plan.

As soon as the five of them were inside the helicopter, the rotors started.

The pilot turned toward them. "I've got the coordinates to set you down at the east end of the lake. Anything changed?"

"No," Carl said. "We want them to know we're coming."

"Roger that," she said, giving Taliya the impression she was military, like the machine they rode in.

It made sense. Padme and her team wouldn't send just anybody right to where the clan lived. It wasn't classified, but it wasn't a detail that was shared freely either.

"Buckle up," the pilot said. "We'll be there in thirty."

Looking around the cabin, Taliya was a little concerned about how much weight it held. Besides the four of them, Samson was like a 500-pound boulder.

"It can hold a dozen burly men," Carl said with a chuckle, catching Taliya's eye. "We're fine."

They lifted off, but to Taliya it felt like the bird struggled a bit. *Probably just my own stress.*

Carl checked his device and then pocketed it. "Nothing new."

"So that means the girls are still in the same place?" Kano asked.

"Yeah. The Marines are keeping their distance for now, but they're definitely on the lookout for movement from all sides. Whatever that place is, it seems to be the final destination."

Taliya's bowels churned, making her wish for a bathroom on the copter. She and Rey were usually the ones being rescued. Not like experience as tenured rescuers was keeping Kano and Carl calm. So much rage and worry emanated from her mate, she just wanted to squeeze him until it stopped.

Samson was busy on his com. She couldn't tell if it related to them or just work stuff he was trying to keep up on. A smirk crept out at the thought of the ligran meeting the clan.

"What?" Kano said, raising one black line of eyebrow.

"I'm trying to picture the scene where Severo and Samson meet."

Kano paused a second and then chuckled. "That's a lot of testosterone in one place. I doubt Severo's ever met a creature bigger than him."

Taliya chuckled too. A welcome bit of humor in the middle of so much anxiety. "Not sure if Samson is taller. We'll have to put them back to back and check."

"You go right ahead and suggest that."

Taliya snorted. "Yeah, nope."

Not much else was said during the short flight. Before long, Taliya saw the wildlife refuge off to the right and then the lake up ahead, with landmarks she recognized from their trip.

"We're coming in from the south," the pilot shouted, "so we don't get near the kidnapper building. And we don't want to startle the forest tigran."

"I'm sure Severo and his clan already know someone's coming," Taliya said. "From the vibrations."

The pilot laughed. "Never try to get the drop on a tigran. Bettin' the wild ones are even sharper."

Taliya didn't disagree. During their stay, Severo had been able to smell a storm coming hours before she'd noticed anything. It made her wonder, once again, how much being "civilized" had let their tiger-related abilities dull. She'd never quite determined if actual genetic alterations between most tigran and those who decided to live wild determined their unique rebellious natures. One visible difference was tongues with papillae, the rough spikes most cats had but most tigran did not. She hadn't shared this suspicion with even Padme. If scientists found out, they be determined to investigate. Nothing good could come from that.

The copter flew around the main camp for the Nuche Clan, stopped at the eastern edge of the lake, hovered for a moment, and then lowered slowly. No tigran immediately emerged from the forest, so Taliya hesitantly opened the door.

"I'm sure they're watching," she shouted to the pilot. "Let me get clear so they can see and smell me."

The pilot nodded and slowed the rotor but didn't turn off the engine. Maybe hedging her bets against needing to make a quick getaway.

Taliya climbed out and ducked until she was clear of the blades, and Kano followed. They both walked a short distance from the machine and took a moment to enjoy the remarkable sight of the ten-thousand-foot-high mountains reflected in the lake—like a painting that belonged in a museum. When they'd been here before, Kano had commented that it smelled like Christmas because of all the pine trees, and that was still true. A tickle in the back of Taliya's mind wanted to strip, jump in for a swim, and try to forget all the worry racing around her body.

"They're close," Kano said, scenting the air and holding his arms out to the side to show he was unarmed.

Taliya suddenly wondered if this would be the same group of tigran they'd met before. Any number of changes could have happened in the last seventeen months.

"Severo?" she called toward the tree line. "Jacy?"

Not a leaf stirred.

Taliya turned and motioned for Carl and Rey to join them. The sight of the extraordinary black panthran might spark enough interest to encourage a few members of the clan to investigate. They'd certainly never seen anything like him. Samson followed as well, and she wasn't sure if that would garner interest or territorial angst.

The group of five wandered farther away from the helicopter along the shoreline. Last she knew, the clan didn't have any laser guns or weapons that could shoot from a distance.

A deep voice, sounding a bit amused, came from the trees. "A dark human and those other two hybrids are not what we had in mind when we asked for willing breeding males."

Taliya smiled. "I'm afraid I'm behind on that agreement, though I'm not sure what a panthran and tigran combination would look like. Might be quite impressive."

"Certainly easier to camouflage than you, pale one."

Kano put his hands on his hips. "Hey, we all work with what the scientists gave us."

"Bare tongues and white fur do not seem like upgrades," Severo said, stepping out of the trees, Jacy right behind him.

If Carl, Rey, or Samson reacted to the fact the wild tigran were both naked, Taliya didn't sense it. Definitely a detail she'd neglected to remind them about. If the assembled males were tempted to "whip it out and compare," she was confident Severo would win. *Eyes high, Taliya. Eyes high.*

"Welcome, friends," Jacy said with a fang-baring grin. "It's good to meet you again." She hesitated, nostrils flaring and smile fading. "But this isn't a casual visit."

Taliya walked toward her, and the two females met in the middle, leaving the males behind—visually sizing each other up, the scent of testosterone heavy in the air. Mostly from Severo, who was faced with eight-foot-tall Samson standing eye-level with him, triggering territorial instinctive reactions. But Taliya didn't sense any danger in it. More the shock she'd expected.

Jacy embraced Taliya and then held her by the arms. They locked eyes.

"You are covered in unfamiliar scents and so much anxiety," Jacy said, pursing her whiskers, then releasing her hold and stepping back. "What has happened?"

"Nothing you need to fear right now. But we desperately need your help. Let me introduce the friends I brought and ask if you'll allow them to stay."

Jacy tipped her head, then stepped back closer to Severo.

"This is Reynaldo," Taliya said, motioning to each of them, "and his husband, General Carl Thompson."

Severo's eyes narrowed at that for a moment, and Taliya hoped it wouldn't be a problem—the same sex or the different species. As a human, they might not accept Carl there at all. She hoped he was prepared to get back on the chopper if they didn't.

"And this is our friend Samson. We've known all three of these males since the refugee camp during the Gathering. I trust each of them. Completely. Samson battled with the legalities of getting your reservation approved."

That shifted something in the stance of both wild tigran.

"You work with the humans in the government as well?" Severo asked.

"Sometimes." Samson stood tall but exuded a diplomatic demeanor. "I am a lawyer, mostly working on cases involving hybrid species and protecting their rights within the laws of our country. Helping to create new laws and protections."

"Then we are grateful to you," Jacy said. She glanced at Severo, and something unspoken passed between them. She looked back at the visitors. "And you are all welcome here."

"Thank you." Taliya whuffed, the first hurdle crossed.

Kano put his hand on her back. "Fill them in while we get supplies from the copter."

Taliya's tail swished as she moved closer to the clan leaders while the others returned to the machine. Severo watched her intently—and was probably considering her scent just as intently too.

"There is something dangerous going on," Jacy said, concern creasing the black markings on her forehead.

"Not like the Gathering," Taliya assured them. "But a new version of the same kind of threat." She sighed, flattening and then consciously raising her ears, forcing calm. "Two of our kits were stolen."

Jacy covered her mouth with both hands, claws extended, and tears burst to her eyes. "No!"

"The ones with the white fur?" Severo asked. "I remember you felt they would never be truly safe."

Taliya nodded. "And I was right."

Jacy shook her head and wiped her cheeks while Severo rumbled almost inaudibly.

"While we were away for a few days," Taliya explained, "our home was attacked. Despite heavy security, both girls were taken, our dear friend Marla was viciously beaten, and . . ." Taliya inhaled deeply, tail thrashing, not having spoken the words out loud yet. "And my father was murdered."

Jacy enveloped her in an embrace, and Severo raged next to them. These tigran had lost so many of their clan at the hands of humans. She knew they would understand. But how much they could or would help was still the question.

Taliya stepped back from Jacy. "The kidnappers were traced to a complex a few dozen miles from here."

Severo look liked he'd been slapped.

Jacy huffed. "We knew there was something bad there."

"You know where I mean?" Taliya asked.

"We do." Severo grumbled deep in his throat. "We don't often go near that border because of the wildlife refuge and so many humans in the area, but recently, we followed a herd of elk that way. The scent of stressed creatures and animals, many weapons and humans, was overwhelming."

"It's not in our territory," Jacy said. "We didn't know what was going on there, so we just stayed clear."

Taliya nodded. "That was wise. Any one of you might be an excellent prize."

Jacy's eyes widened at that thought.

Severo growled. "And you believe this is where your daughters have been taken?" He folded his arms across his chest. "These humans have them?"

"That's what the government team believes. They saw the kidnappers enter with the kits but have not witnessed them leave."

Something sparked in Severo's golden eyes. "Before they come hunting for us and our young, it sounds like a raid is in order."

Taliya smiled at his enthusiasm. "That's where we're

hoping you can help. Scope out the situation and give the military ideas on how to approach without the creatures inside being harmed.”

“I will gather scouts immediately.” Severo shifted his eyes to the males reapproaching with their packs from the helicopter. “Your gigantic lawyer with the strange markings may not be as helpful as the panthran.” He hesitated with suspicious eyes, ears slightly laid back. “You trust the human? I understand he is mated with the panthran, but still.”

“Carl has saved my life more than once. And nearly died in the process. He’s freed thousands of creatures from facilities over the years. There is no human I trust more.”

Severo and Jacy both gave a quick nod, acknowledging her certainty. When the males rejoined them, Rey stepped forward with the bag of supplies Samson had brought as a thank you. Taliya suspected the ligran wanted it to come from Rey so he had an immediate connection with the clan.

“I’m not sure how helpful any of this will be,” Rey said, handing the pack to Jacy, “but we wanted some way to say thank you. Anything you specifically require, we can get later when we have more time.”

“We appreciate the thought,” Jacy said, not opening the bag but smiling kindly.

Behind them, the helicopter lifted, hovered for a moment, and then flew off to the south.

Severo gave a sharp whistle. One by one, members of

the clan stepped out of the trees, where they'd been hiding out of eavesdropping distance.

"Taliya!" a kit shrieked, dropping her mother's hand and rushing forward.

Taliya bent down to receive the enthusiastic hug. Then she leaned back to face the kit. "I'm surprised you remember me."

The kit grinned. "You and your mate are the only outsiders I have ever met."

Taliya suspected the young one was about four. She didn't remember her but was thrilled by the welcome, though it tugged at something deep inside. Fears she needed to set aside while they established a plan of action.

The kit's mother joined them. "Welcome back. I see you've brought friends. But none of your own kits?"

Taliya swallowed past the tightness in her throat. "No. It's complicated."

The wild tigran opened her mouth, probably getting a good whiff of Taliya for the first time and sorting it through the Jacobson's organ on the roof of her mouth.

"You're safe," Taliya assured her. *At least for now.*

She nodded but pulled her kit close.

Carl seemed distracted by his communicator, and Taliya excused herself to see what was going on. He looked up at her and frowned.

"Intelligence reports say a number of private jets—very elite private jets owned by questionable men—have filed plans to land on a small airstrip at the Colorado

Springs Airport tomorrow morning. They suspect this has something to do with the kits." Carl swallowed and cleared his throat. "Maybe just a showing for a price. . . . Maybe buyers."

Taliya's whole body chilled, like all the blood had drained out. Then it returned with a rush she could hear pumping in her ears. She turned back to the group. "We don't have much time."

A slight shift in Severo's stance revealed the proficient predator he ultimately was. He bared his fangs and sent out a rumble that wasn't audible but traveled through the air and ground around them. The rest of the clan responded with growls and hisses.

Jacy flexed her claws. "Then let's go get your kits."

18

Severo led the group over to the campfire meeting area on the shore. At Jacy's command, an older female gathered the kits and escorted them back into the trees. Taliya was grateful because the capture of young ones was not something they needed to hear about. The adults—about fifty of them—settled onto logs and in the sand, though Carl hung back. Severo motioned Taliya to join him at the front, and she stood by his side, nervous and feeling dwarfed by the massive male.

"We are grateful to welcome Taliya and Kano," Severo said, "and the friends they have brought with them."

She tried to nod and smile, searching for faces and markings she recognized, but the clan seemed uneasy. Maybe unsure as to why she was there. Maybe upset about the human in their midst. Prepared to speak, Taliya inhaled deeply but was cut off as Severo continued, getting right to it without formalities.

"Our friends have presented an opportunity for us to thank them for protecting our land and way of life."

She hadn't considered asking for their help as repayment—a way to describe it that made refusal nearly impossible.

"I will allow our friend to provide the details." Severo motioned for her to speak.

Taliya steadied her nerves, forcing her ears to stay forward and her tail to relax. *Get right to it, like he did.* "When we were away from home, humans attacked our heavily guarded compound, beat an aunty so badly she required surgery, murdered my father, and carried off two of our kits."

The reaction from the clan—growls and hisses of rage—washed over her like a physical blow. She plowed ahead.

"Both daughters are unique and considered unimaginably valuable. One is pure white and just turned eight years old. The other is a strawberry tigran. White with pale stripes. Maybe the only one in existence. . . . She's only four."

Her audience whispered amongst themselves, and their fury flared again.

"With my government connections, the kidnappers were traced. We're confident the girls are being held in a camouflaged facility not far from here. Just past your eastern border."

One of the males tiger moaned. "I knew that place smelled dangerous."

"This isn't like the Gathering," Taliya continued. "This is private individuals. But I do wonder if the location of the facility has something to do with being close to your group. A threat for you and your kits as well."

That received more outbursts of rage, ears flattened and hackles raised.

"We believe the kits are unharmed. They're too valuable to be mistreated. But if we don't hurry, they could be sold or moved, and we'd lose track of them." She hesitated. "Lost to us forever."

"Never!" one of the females shouted, leaping up, fangs bared.

Taliya nodded her gratitude. "We have the support of Marines, but they don't want to risk attacking and having the enemy harm the girls or other prisoners we suspect are being held in the building."

Images of the dark underground prison, where she and Kano first met, flashed through her mind. Rey's stories about the horrific lab where he was born and his years with his own kidnappers. Taliya choked back a sob. The reality of it all—being so close and still feeling so helpless—settled in.

"We need . . ." Her whiskers flared with the effort to remain calm. "We need your help."

Severo took the lead, moving on like that help was already assured. "Our first step is for a small team to travel immediately to the area and gather information. I need five runners."

Ten tigran sprang to their feet—half male and half

female—and Taliya's nerves calmed a little. Part of her had feared they wouldn't want to get involved or take on the risk. Their enthusiasm gave her a spark of hope. Severo selected five volunteers who looked young and fleet of foot. The other five he instructed to prepare for joining the full team to travel to the site.

It occurred to Taliya that this was one of the moments tigran were created for. Their heightened sense of sight, smell, and apex-predator stealth made them perfect first-wave soldiers.

"Runners, you leave immediately," Severo said. "We'll bring food and supplies when we join you. Care for what you must in the next two minutes and meet back here."

That small group ran into the trees as Jacy rose and wrapped an arm around Taliya's waist.

"All will be well," she whispered. "Hold on to that."

Taliya nodded and swallowed back her tears. "What can we do to help prepare?" *Get us there faster.*

"It is traditional to share a community meal before setting off on a dangerous journey. Some fresh fish would be useful."

Sitting down to eat wasn't what Taliya had in mind, but Kano slapped Rey on the back. "Let's get to it!"

In seconds, Kano had stripped off his clothes and was running into the water. It took a moment for Rey to catch on, but he stripped and raced after him.

Samson watched them splash into the lake, a con-fused look on his regal face. Taliya wondered if he'd ever skinny-dipped or even fished human-style. With a determined snort, the massive ligran carefully removed his clothes, folded them neatly on a boulder, and strode into the water. Jacy made a rumbling noise in her throat that Taliya interpreted as approval. Especially since she'd been wrong about who would win the manhood-comparison contest. Samson should walk around naked all the time, just to show off.

"You may not have brought the males for breeding," Jacy said, "but they are certainly outstanding specimens."

Taliya laughed, and the knot inside relaxed a bit more.

Two members of the clan carried out heavily stained tables to set along the shoreline, and Carl pulled an assortment of knives from his pack. They eyed his steel blades but didn't comment.

Carl shrugged. "Without claws, I do what I must."

Several clan members chuffed or laughed, seeming to break the tension of having a human among them. Taliya wondered how uncomfortable Carl felt—or if he would suddenly strip and dive into the lake too. At the moment, they were the only two wearing clothing of any kind. She had no immediate plans to change that.

Rey emerged from the lake carrying an enormous fish, which he lugged to the table. Plopping it down, he grabbed a knife from Carl's pile, swiftly stabbing the struggling trout through the brain. Before he ran back to the water, he smacked his impressed husband on the ass. "Gut that sucker!"

"Hoo-ah!" Carl called after him. The general pulled his

shirt over his head, tossed it on top of Samson's clothes, then cleaned the trout in a few seconds.

With an impressed look on his face, a clan member grabbed the prepared fish and started it cooking on a metal grate over the campfire someone had already lit. Taliya was also impressed and reminded that her friend Carl was a seasoned warrior. She wondered what else he'd gutted that quickly and effortlessly over the years.

Carl turned to the water, waiting for the next victim. His dark skin all but glowed in the sun, and at the sight of Rey returning with another fish—rising from the water like a demi-god—he grinned and chuckled. Kano emerged in his own unclad glory with an enormous and vigorously flapping fish clutched to his chest, making her grin as well.

"Our husbands are very useful," she said.

"To say the least."

Carl prepared both fish while Rey and Kano headed back to the water. Samson passed them coming ashore, proudly carrying a decent-sized fish himself.

His tiger DNA must have figured it out.

The smell of fish cooking on the fire made her stomach rumble. That upcoming meal was all that stood between her and the trek to recover her daughters. She glanced around for some way to help, but no one seemed to need assistance.

"Human Carl," Severo called from where he stood with the runners. "Join us for a minute. Bring your communication device."

Carl hesitated, looked at his gore-covered hands, then jogged over to the lake to rinse them before joining the group.

"I'm sure they just want to confirm the plan," Jacy said to Taliya, who realized she was frowning at the group of tigran. "We can help with the packing. You will need food and supplies."

Taliya followed her into the trees, toward the main camp. They met several clan members, who were preparing three large backpacks of dried meats and berries. Taliya found it fascinating what man-made equipment the clan had from trading with the Ute tribe at their southern border, along with the supplies they created from the environment.

"Bena, we need enough for sixteen for three days," Jacy instructed a young female. "In case they have to wait for an opportunity to attack."

Bena glanced at Taliya with wide eyes before looking back at Jacy. "I'd like to go. Help rescue the kits. I was just too nervous to stand up since I'm not a great runner and that's what Severo asked for."

"We appreciate your willingness," Jacy said. "However, this is not the time. Only experienced, skilled hunters."

Bena looked heartbroken but nodded. Taliya said a quick thank you and followed Jacy deeper into the camp. For the next few minutes, she did as she was told and carried baskets of food to the tigran packing for the trip. As they finished, a loud whistle came from the lake area.

"The meal is ready," Jacy said.

Everyone headed back to the beach, carrying the prepared supplies. A solemnness hovered over the scene now as the cooked fish was shared around on wooden plates. Everyone ate in silence. It felt like there was deep symbolism to the shared meal beyond what she could understand about loading up on protein. Adults and kits together, but no one uttering a word. She rinsed her plate in the lake like the clan members and then joined now-clothed Kano, Samson, and Rey where they gathered with Severo and Carl and the five wild tigran joining the raid. All of the loaded backpacks sat at their feet.

"The runners have gone?" she asked.

Severo nodded. "They should arrive at the facility in an hour."

Part of Taliya wanted to scream for Severo to run ahead and get her daughters. Now. He could make it there as quickly as the runners. The team of outsiders was only slowing him down.

"Let's get going," she said, anxiety already racing her heart like a steep climb. "We can make it halfway before sundown."

Carl snorted and typed into his communicator. "Did you think we were *hiking* sixty miles?"

Taliya hadn't considered the details on how far it was. "But the runners . . ."

"They met the bird not far from here," Carl said, "and were delivered already."

Kano tightened the laces on his hiking boots. "The

copter will get us within ten miles of the facility, like the runners. That's more than enough to travel on foot but far enough not to alert them to our presence."

Knowing the males had been making decisions and arrangements without her was annoying, but clearly, it was the right call. The reality of even ten miles of hiking through the forest made her claws flex.

Jacy joined them and eyed the packs. "You should have everything you need."

She caught Taliya's gaze, and the two mothers shared a moment. Jacy grabbed Taliya in a strong hug, and she melted into it.

"Know that we have thought of you often. You are our friend. We hope your daughters are recovered safely."

Jacy released Taliya, and the two exchanged quiet chuffs.

The five clan members loaded themselves up with packs, and Taliya felt guilty.

"I can carry something beyond my own supplies," she offered.

The five wild tigran looked to Severo, and he shook his head. "Rough terrain and heavy packs are not a part of your lives like they are for us. You just worry about your own bag and keeping up."

Carl swung his pack over his shoulder. "Haven't hiked like this in years."

Samson glanced off into the trees—and the mountains—and looked like he regretted his decision to join them. Taliya suspected he'd never done any hiking. It was funny to think of the immense creature as an "indoor cat," more useful for his mind than his physical abilities. He'd unofficially been in charge of so many details of life at the refugee camp, but on this mission, Samson was way out of his element.

The rest of the clan hovered around the edge of the tree line, waiting to see them off as the copter *whop, whop, whopped* back into view. Taliya noticed the kits squirming impatiently, and a bitter pain stabbed her chest.

Severo made a series of sharp hand motions to the clan, and they motioned back at him. Jacy huffed and repeated the same thing. It seemed to be some sort of goodbye and directions for during his absence.

"See you soon," Taliya said to those remaining behind. "And thank you."

Several of them raised a hand in farewell as she turned to follow the team to the helicopter.

⁕

ONCE THE TEAM WAS DROPPED OFF, THE WILD TIGRAN STARTED out at a brutal pace. Taliya struggled to keep up. Kano, Rey, Carl, and Samson fell into line behind her, with Severo bringing up the rear. *Watching our six*, Taliya decided. Attack seemed unlikely. However, she doubted any human would surprise Severo and his team.

They traveled relentlessly and silently, stopping twice to rest—a break Taliya assumed was for her group, not the wild tigran. Carl checked his com several times, but no updates had come in, which was a good thing. Any news would probably be about the girls being moved. Taliya's heart fluttered every time he pulled the com out. It was hard to move until he confirmed there were no changes. Her only distraction was trying not to trip or get whapped in the face with a branch as they moved through the woods.

No one from her group grumbled or complained, but she knew they had to be as fatigued as she was. The wild tigran could certainly have gone faster on their own and would have taken a more direct route, instead of sticking to valleys and well-worn trails. She could smell that Carl was pushing his limit but knew he'd never admit it. Samson surprised her by keeping up and often joining the lead group. Big cat genes meant all the creatures were strong inherently, but Taliya was not used to putting all of that into action beyond chasing her kits around the yard. At least she didn't have to chat along the way and could save her breath. Panting in front of any of them would have been humiliating.

As the sun started to sink below the horizon, Severo made a bird whistle and stopped. Everyone gathered around.

"We are about two miles away now and near the small town of Del Norte," Severo whispered. "Let's wait until it's fully dark before we skirt north of it and make the final approach."

Taliya's skin tingled with anticipation. She wanted to

storm forward, guns blazing. *Patience.* They'd asked Severo's help for a reason.

His team set their packs down, and he turned to Taliya and her group, leaning in close for quiet conversation. His breath smelled like the smoked elk jerky from their last stop.

"This is outside our territory, but we've wandered this way on occasion for fishing along the river and following herds. I can smell the wildlife refuge from here, but not anything from the facility where your kits are, like we could before."

"That's weird, isn't it?" Kano asked.

Severo shrugged one shoulder. "At this distance, a human wouldn't stand out from the nearby town, but I don't get a whiff of any creatures or unusual animals. Not a single one."

Taliya turned to Carl. "But the girls are still there?"

He nodded. "There's no sign of them leaving."

"Maybe they're underground," Kano suggested with a frown, reminding Taliya of waking up in that dank prison cell at the breeding facility.

Rey bared his teeth in a grimace, personal experience with basement cells probably coming to mind. His hackles spiked up the back of his head. Carl smoothed them down and whispered something in panthran to his husband. That prison was where they'd first met, when Rey was freed. Carl surely remembered it too.

Taliya bristled her whiskers. Focusing on an image of

the girls being held somewhere decent because of their value was the only thing keeping her sane at that point.

"We'll know more soon," Severo said. "I'm going to send one of my team ahead to meet with the runners. See what they've discovered."

Taliya exhaled sharply. Answers were what she desperately needed—and what she feared deep in her heart. Her thoughts threatened to swing toward the kits injured, dirty and abused, crying for help, but she shook that off. *Stay positive until you have proof otherwise.*

Kano's hand rested on her back, and he rubbed in small circles—his go-to when he felt her stress. She reached back and squeezed his hand. Before morning, it would hopefully all be over, one way or another. There's no way she was hovering on the edges for days and waiting, no matter what anyone advised.

Severo moved silently away, chatted with his group, then a young female raced off into the trees without a sound. It was an impressive skill. Taliya was pretty sure her civilized group was able to keep from alerting humans of their presence, but they made enough noise for any animal around to get out of the way.

They ate in silence and waited for the sun to set. The runner returned and reported the facility appeared to be shutting down for the night. Very little activity. Certainly not the arrival of any gawkers or buyers. Taliya suspected that wouldn't last long.

When the light grew dim, Carl pulled out his night

goggles. Severo rose and gave a nod. The whole group gathered their packs and followed him through the trees.

19

Taliya took deep breaths to calm herself. They still had two miles to hike. She sensed exhaustion from Samson—though he didn't show it outwardly—and worry from Rey and Carl. Kano seemed to be fighting a desire to grumble in frustration. Soon Severo stopped, and Taliya spotted the runners on the path ahead, bright feline eyes shining in the dark forest. They led the way, veering to the right and up a steep hill.

Severo turned to the group and whispered, "Watch your footing. Do not dislodge rocks or make noise."

Kano glanced up the slope and frowned.

"We'll take it slowly," Taliya whispered.

She and her team crept up the incline, sometimes on all fours to feel for solid footing, doing their best to follow in the path others had taken. They reached the top with only a few minor rock slips. Nothing that would call attention to them.

The others were on their bellies and staying hidden behind a row of bushes, so she did the same and elbow-crawled next to Severo at the edge of a cliff. The facility and its complex of buildings was spread out in the valley below, just visible in the moonlight. One massive structure covered several acres. The metal roof and walls were camouflaged into the landscape, and the only light came from one side. Very faint. Maybe a door. Several similar but more house-sized buildings were scattered around the valley, all dark.

"You were not exaggerating about the size of it," Samson mumbled. "If that is full of rooms, we have quite a search ahead of us."

"They must be doing something to purify the air coming out," one of the runners whispered. "But the echoes and blending of noise from inside makes me suspect it is one open space."

"How many creatures?" Kano asked. "Can you tell?"

"Many. That is the best I can say. And different species."

Carl made an almost feline growl. "Quite the collectors."

"That is good, in a way," Samson said. "The girls will be coveted prizes."

Taliya nodded, but the fur spiked along her spine.

Carl pulled laser guns from his bag. None of the wild tigran had wanted one, and Taliya, Kano, and Rey still had theirs from Australia. "The Marine support team is ready, on all four sides. If we call for it, they'll be here in seconds."

Taliya flexed her claws a few times to release the tension. She knew one thing for certain. She'd have no problem killing any human she found in that building.

"First goal is the girls," Taliya said, "but what about the rest of the creatures?"

"We won't leave anyone behind." Carl added two chargers to his ammo belt with a determined look. "Our job is to get the girls and let the Marines secure the facility."

Samson huffed and looked back at the building. "We will capture and detain any humans. Then the full rescue can be accomplished."

Taliya clenched her jaw and mentally adjusted that to *dismember and kill,* which felt more satisfying. Whoever they found guarding the place was just as guilty as the humans who'd actually attacked her home. Something primal in her DNA wanted them all bloody and lifeless. Wanted retribution. Her ears turned backward instinctively, claws flexed.

That was Marla's demand. Kill them all.

Taliya was happy to oblige.

Severo scented the air with an open mouth. "Rain. We should be inside before it hits. Spring storms are brief but intense."

"Marines haven't mentioned it," Carl said, "but you'd know. How long?"

Severo slow-blinked at the general. "Maybe twenty minutes." Then he shifted to crawl closer to the runners.

Rey moved away from the cliff edge and sat cross-legged on the ground, rubbing the long scar that started behind his ear. From his acrid smell, Taliya could tell he was stressed. As much as she and Kano had been through, his life had been a hundred times worse. That he was mentally stable at all was a miracle.

"You can sit this part out, you know," she whispered, moving closer to him. "There's no need for you to face what's inside that building."

Rey growled. "I wouldn't be here if soldiers hadn't risked their lives to rescue me. More than once. It's right for me to do the same now."

Taliya appreciated that feeling. But she wasn't sure she'd be as willing to risk her hide if her daughters weren't among the captives. Rushing into danger wasn't ever her first impulse, like it was for Carl.

"Maybe you can help secure the outside and not go in," she suggested.

"If that's where the team needs me, that's what I'll do. But I'm not waiting here or hovering at the edges."

His determined golden eyes shone in the darkness, and she chuffed an acknowledgement.

"Besides," he said, "I'm more camouflaged at night than any of you. We may have to rub dirt on Kano."

The white tigran supplied the necessary grumbled response.

Carl chuckled. "That's not a bad idea. You all but glow."

Kano glanced at Severo, and they both smiled. "Not the first time I've heard that," he said. While his clothes covered most of his fur, his head was a big white ball in the darkness.

Carl reached into his weapon bag and pulled out a black ski mask. "Wear this." He tossed it to Kano.

Kano pulled it over his head. Then he turned to Taliya, his bright-blue eyes peeking out of the slits. "I can't hear very well. The bugs' nighttime singing just went quiet."

She snorted. "Better than getting shot in the head because you're an easy target."

"Fine."

The bit of whispered banter helped still her nerves, but in that valley, her kits were being held prisoner. Terrified. It took every ounce of self-control not to storm down the mountain, screaming like a deranged tigran, and slaughter every human in sight.

Kano rumbled at her, probably smelling the rage. "Soon," he whispered.

She added him next to her in the mental image, rampaging together into the facility. But . . . *He's never killed anyone.*

When his wife was murdered and Aliania taken, he'd been restrained, though he'd done serious damage to the Enforcers before they secured him. While he'd been in on Taliya's rescue years ago, he hadn't been required to kill. Something to be grateful for in normal life, but it concerned her now. Not that he wouldn't be capable of it, but that he might have to. As impressive and enormous as Kano was, he was also innately gentle and kind.

Thinking back on the warehouse attic, where she'd killed two Enforcers to protect herself, Taliya understood something deep in her nature had shifted that day. She'd held a human's throat in her jaws—her body weight pinning him down, fangs in the jugular—as he bled out. Blood dripped from her mouth before she did the same to a second Enforcer. All tiger.

That moment was the demise of believing she was a gentle creature. Civilized. Innocence smashed by the Gathering and what she'd done to survive.

Kano had experienced violence and danger, but she hoped whatever they faced that night didn't change him. Didn't alter any of them.

And she hoped they all survived. As much as she'd tried to avoid thinking about the dangers ahead, not everyone walking away was a genuine possibility. As was not successfully saving the girls.

Severo chuffed and caught Taliya's eye. Her skin tingled, every hair on end. It was time. The group of wild tigran were already working their way back down the slope. She and her team joined Severo away from the ledge in the heavier brush.

"The runners will go first," Severo whispered. "Make sure it's as clear outside as we anticipate." He looked to Carl.

"No changes," the general said. "Still getting the go-ahead."

The intelligence report indicated there would probably be only one guard on duty overnight. The facility relied on lots of tech security instead. Marines had brought equipment to help with that, but not knowing the full extent of what they'd face was intimidating. All the rescue team had to work with was a day or so of observations. Carl knew a potential code for the door and where cameras and maybe all of the security alerts were outside. The Marines would block signals to the security cameras, but it was impossible to know if it would affect what might be inside.

Far too much was unknown or potentially misinterpreted with so little intel. And there wasn't much of a plan beyond getting in. Taliya's heart sat like a rock in her chest as she and the others followed Severo back down the incline and into the valley.

By the time they reached the tree line around the main building, the only members left were Severo, Taliya, and the males she'd brought. The ten wild tigran were scattered through the compound, ready to assist and watching for danger. Marines were out there too. She buckled on her ammo belt, loaded in a gun, and stored her pack behind a tree while Kano and Rey did the same. The silence and waiting made Taliya's insides churn. Even the crickets and nighttime insects were quiet, which set her nerves on end. She hoped that didn't alert the guard.

The front of the main building, about thirty yards

away, reminded her of the entrance at the refugee camp—a huge opening with bi-fold metal doors, designed to allow long-range transports and over-sized cages to roll right in. Perfect for a facility full of captured creatures. At least that's what they expected to find. Maybe some illegal animals too. She still couldn't smell what was inside. Couldn't scent out her kits.

The guard outside the main door paced back and forth in the dim redish light of a window. Taliya thought he looked a little bored. Laser guns hung from each hip, but his hands were empty. A waft of cigar smoke blew past, and she struggled not to cough. It stunk of real tobacco, not a vape. A spike of red lit the guard's face before he reached up to remove the plug from his mouth.

With a nod, Severo slipped into the shadows. The guard sauntered to the corner of the far side of the building, out of the light from the door for a moment, then vanished. A grunt and the *pop* of bones snapping. Then silence.

Severo calmly rejoined them from the darkness. "All clear."

It took Taliya a moment to process that he'd just broken the guard's neck. No fuss, no muss. No blood. No scream. She took a deep breath, ears turned backward. A sense of admiration came from Carl as he led the way toward the entrance. Shock emanated from Kano and Samson as they followed. Rey was hard to read. Still highly stressed. Severo waited until Taliya moved past him.

"Humans are quite fragile," he whispered.

"Yes, quite."

Severo's method was merciful and quick. One that would have come in handy in the past. Though she hadn't wanted to kill Narlin quickly. Or mercifully.

At the door, Carl lifted his night goggles and entered the code the Marines had provided. He whispered something into his device, then threw back the bolt and slid one side of the huge sections open. The group slipped through, and he closed it behind them.

The odor of the place finally hit her. Scents from liran, tigran, others that were familiar, and dozens she couldn't place accosted her sensitive nose. Dirt and hay and wood chips, probably from bedding. Metal from cages. Raw beef and chicken from a recent feeding. But the facility smelled clean. No buildup of manure. No disease or infection.

A dim glow from red emergency-exit lighting provided just enough illumination for the team to see. The inside was one enormous open area. Two hundred yards long and another one hundred wide, the high ceiling was equipped with complicated-looking air filtration and ventilation systems—why no one outside was smelling the place anymore.

Laid out in three orderly rows ahead of them were metal-bar cages. From the front, two wide walkways led toward the back of the building, with dozens and dozens of cages lining the center and walls. The scent of many different creatures made it complicated for

Taliya to sort through them, searching for her daughters. There was no movement, like everyone was asleep.

Taliya sensed Rey's heart racing and his breath coming in short, panicked bursts.

"You can wait here and watch the door," she suggested.

Rey shook his head. "No. Let's secure this place and get everyone out."

Severo hissed, and they shut up. He pointed toward closed doors along the wall behind them. Storage rooms, maybe, or offices. Carl raised his weapon and moved toward a door. He inched it open, checked inside, and whispered, "Clear."

A deep male voice came from somewhere close among the cages. "There's a security grid in the aisle."

The whole team froze. Carl pulled out a device and scanned up the row. Several infrared lines appeared, running across from cage to cage.

"See them," Carl said. "Thanks." He moved to check the other doors, with Rey backing him up.

Taliya stepped to her right and spotted an enormous berman—a human/bear hybrid—standing along his cage bars. His dark fur kept him hidden, but the distinctive long snout, massive body, and musky smell were obvious. She nodded in his direction, and he returned it.

"You shouldn't be here," he said. "You'll end up with the rest of us."

"Not a chance," Taliya said. "There's a whole Marine

unit waiting to take over this facility. We're getting you out of here."

"To go where? We can't just live out in the world, like you do."

Kano stepped beside her and pulled off his hood. The berman's dark eyes went wide enough the whites showed in the dim light.

"I remember you," he said. "From the camp."

Taliya whuffed. "Yes, we were there."

She'd met a pregnant female berman and her mate when they were all rescued from the Colorado breeding facility, but the pair lived in a different section at the refugee camp. Kano hadn't been the only white tigran there, but he was one of a handful. Easy to remember.

"Once you're free," Kano said, "we'll worry about where you go next."

"Have you seen white tigran kits, like him?" Taliya asked. "They would have just arrived."

"There was a fuss at the far side of the building yesterday. But creatures come and go a lot." He hesitated. "Your kits, yes?"

Taliya nodded. "They are very valuable."

"I'm sorry you are so cursed."

Taliya swallowed a lump in her throat. *Valuable* was a burden this creature understood as well as them. Human females enjoyed a kink for sex with male berman—some taming and screwing a wild bear fantasy come to life. Mates and young were held as leverage to force the berman to perform. Maybe that's why he was there.

Before she could say more, Severo made a shushing noise again, and she tipped her head in acknowledgement.

Carl and Rey returned. "All clear," the general said, typing on his com. He aimed a device up the aisle. The walkway between cages lit up with red lines for several seconds, then they vanished.

"Hoo-ah," Carl muttered. "Should mean we're clear of that specific bogie, but keep your eyes open."

Taliya hurried to the berman's cage. He stood at the bars with his massive furry hands wrapped around them. She placed her hands on top of his and looked up at his face. "We'll get all the cages open soon. Help is coming."

The berman nodded but looked sad. Defeated. Smelled exhausted.

"Look in the back for your young. That's where the newest arrival was put."

Taliya squeezed his hands and followed the team down the right-side aisle.

They passed cage after dark cage, scents giving a rough idea of who was inside but mostly unfamiliar. A growl came from the right, and Taliya flinched. Yellow eyes glowed and revealed a black-and-white snow leopard, an animal extinct in the wild. *Definitely not just genetic creatures.* She considered reassuring the animal but had no idea how to communicate with it.

"I've spotted two full-blooded white tigers so far," Kano whispered.

"I smell polar bears," Rey said with a frown. "Saw them in a zoo once."

"So mostly exotic animals," Carl said, scanning the ground ahead of them. "But there's the berman. Maybe they're upping their game."

Taliya turned her ears back. "I still can't smell the kits. What if they're not here?"

"We'll save who is," Kano said. "Then go find the girls."

That was charitable, but she had no idea what would be done with the wild animals. *A zoo? Would that be any better?* They couldn't just open those cages and let them all out to run free.

As they reached the end of the first row, Taliya caught a familiar scent. "A crocodile?"

Kano hesitated and then nodded his agreement. "Why would a collector want one of those?"

"Smells like more than one," Rey added. "And saltwater, not fresh."

Taliya huffed. "So weird. Not rare at all, except around here, I guess."

Captives were waking and standing at the bars of their cages. The creatures just stared at her blankly. Didn't utter a sound. Taliya made eye contact with liran and cheeman and even a pair of rooman, who must have been shipped in from Australia. All of the prisoners who could ask for help didn't, which Taliya found unsettling. Their eyes were flat and dull.

Are they drugged?

"Stay calm," she whispered. "We've brought help. We'll be back."

No response beyond stares and scents of sadness, worry, and anxiety.

As the team reached the back of the building, Taliya spotted a Plexiglas enclosure for the polar bears along the farthest wall. It was a complicated menagerie.

Thunder rumbled outside, vibrating the packed-dirt floor under their feet. The storm Severo had predicted. Taliya hoped that didn't complicate things for the Marines. The patter of rain on the metal roof would normally be a peaceful sound, but the staccato of it rattled down her spine. Echoed through the silence of the vast room.

Kano tiger moaned. "This place makes my skin crawl."

"You'd think they'd be excited to see us," Taliya whispered to Carl.

He nodded but didn't answer, eyes alternating between the pathway and his scanning device, checking for more security.

"Have we figured out how to unlock the cages?" Kano asked.

Carl hesitated and glanced at his com. "Outside team's silent." He stared at it for a moment, and his body tensed.

A diminutive puman wrapped her hands around her cage bars and whispered, "Run."

20

Taliya stopped in the aisle, shuffling and animal noises from inside the facility growing louder within the cacophony of rain pummeling the metal roof overhead. She locked eyes with the puman in her cage. "My daughters are here somewhere. We have to find them. Then get you all out."

Samson stepped up to the bars. "Little one, have you seen two white tigran kits? Their young we are looking for?"

The puman skimmed all the way up to his face and nodded with wide greenish-golden eyes. "They're at the end of the row. But you'll never rescue them. It's too late."

Fear flashed through Taliya in a burst. The whole group stopped in front of the cage, Carl typing furiously on his com, trying to connect with the Marines outside.

The puman mewed. "They're waiting for you," she whispered in a panicked breath.

Taliya's body went cold, and Kano whuffed anxiously next to her.

"Marines are off-line," Carl said flatly, putting his device in his pocket. "Starting to feel like a trap."

"That doesn't make any sense," Taliya said, shaking her head. "What would they want with *us*?"

A horrifying realization made her fur puff from nose to tail. A white tigran. A ligran, maybe the only one in existence. A rare black panthran. They were all standing there, waiting to be captured.

"Where's Severo?" Rey said, glancing back down the aisle.

Taliya's whiskers flared. When was the last time she'd laid eyes on the clan leader? Not since they first entered the building.

A bank of overhead lights switched on at the entrance, and the puman skittered back into darkness. Another set flickered on, closer this time.

"Here kitty, kitty." A female voice cooed over a sound system somewhere in the ceiling. "Who's a good kitty, kitty?"

Taliya's lungs refused to function. Like the walls were closing in. Next to her, Reynaldo made a horrible screaming noise. Carl drew his gun, and they all followed his lead.

"Oh please," the woman's voice said, condescension dripping from every word. "Don't bother with that futile nonsense."

Carl looked around for the source. "Fuckin' hell."

Kano stepped closer to Taliya and wrapped his tail around her legs, like that could protect her.

"Put all of your weapons in a pile," the voice ordered over the racket of the rain on the roof. "And move away from little Chica's cage."

Carl gave a nod, and they all dropped their guns in the aisle. Taliya suspected there would be trouble for them, the kits, or some other poor creature if they didn't comply. Snipers could be aimed at their heads right that moment. Whoever was talking clearly had eyes on them somehow.

Samson raised his hands and yelled, "Do you realize how many people know we are here? They are watching this rescue closely. The president is supporting us. Let us leave with the kits we came for. This does not need to get violent."

"But violence is *entertaining*. And so many people watching," the voice agreed. "So many private planes heading for the airport. They're anticipating what I have planned for Taliya."

The group looked to her, and she stared back, wide-eyed. Of all the creatures there, she was the least valuable. Black-and-orange tigran were hardly a rarity.

"Taliya, ambassador for her species," the voice said, condescension turning to anger. "Taliya and her nasty big mouth. Who leads marches in Washington. Who makes trouble wherever she goes."

A memory started to click in the back of Taliya's mind. The voice was familiar, but she couldn't place it. This was sounding like a motive besides collecting creatures. Something highly personal.

The woman chuckled. "Do you know how much certain people will cough up to see you punished? Taliya, the savior of the tigran. They've shelled out a king's ransom to watch you get what you deserve."

Kano made a horrible squeaking noise in his throat. The males shifted—surrounding her, facing out—though there was no one visible to defend against. Thunder rumbled and vibrated the walls around them.

"I didn't expect you to bring so many rare friends," the voice said. "A delightful extra treat. But you, Taliya, are the cherry on top of the revenge sundae. And I know you'll cooperate because . . . well . . ."

A light overhead clicked on, illuminating the space around them.

"Mama? Papa?" Amrita's voice.

Kano spotted the girls before Taliya and rushed to their cage on the left.

"No!" Aliania called out just as her father reached toward the bars.

Kano flew backward through the air like he'd been hit with a bat, smashed into the cage across the aisle, and then landed face down in the dirt. He moaned and rolled to his side. Samson and Carl rushed to help as Taliya stood frozen, staring at her daughters.

"I'll survive," Kano grumbled, dusting himself off. "I barely touched it. Don't get too close."

Rage roiled through every inch of Taliya's being,

making it hard to focus and breathe. She stalked to her kits, who were both in a small cage that looked more like a holding cell than any kind of long-term enclosure. Something out of an old prison movie, with a metal bed and a toilet in the corner. Just inside the steel bars, there was a Plexiglass block, a secondary layer of division. Why they couldn't smell the girls. She could feel the electricity like a forcefield around them.

Aliania stood a few inches from the front of the glass wall, and Amrita clung to her waist. They were both still in their pajamas, but looked clean and unharmed. Taliya forced herself to remain calm. Finding them was no longer the biggest obstacle.

"Stay back," Ali said. "It's wired up."

Her voice sounded off, like it was coming through a sound system as well. Something the woman could control to let them communicate—or not.

Taliya folded her arms across her chest. Too tempting to grab the bars. "Are you okay?"

"Amrita's scared, but we aren't hurt."

My kittens! screamed through her brain, fury rattling her as much as the rain outside was hammering the building. *I'm going to shred that bitch into a thousand pieces.*

Taliya squatted eye level with Amrita. "Nothing wrong with being scared in a terrible place."

Amrita stared at her mother but didn't let go of her sister.

Ali huffed. "They said they weren't going to hurt us. We're too valuable, blah, blah, blah. We knew you'd find us. I'm more pissed off than scared. Especially hearing we were bait for you."

"Seems like that's part of it," Taliya said, standing and looking up the aisle toward the front of the building.

Kano moved next to her, and she confirmed he was unharmed.

"I'm fine. Just pissed off too." He stared at the girls, and Taliya felt the frustration he was trying not to show.

"Was that the truth," Ali asked, "about President Padme?"

"Yes. But our military backup may have been captured." *Or killed.* Severo and the ten wild tigran were possibly still in the mix. "Padme knows we're here, but now she's got a hostage situation on her hands."

"So help will be coming, eventually?"

"Yes. Eventually." Taliya stepped as close to the bars as she dared. "Take Amrita and sit on that metal bed thing. Whatever happens out here, don't let her see."

Aliania's blue eyes looked worried, and her ears laid back. "Yes, Mama," she whispered.

"Do you know who that is on the sound system?" *Who's gone quiet. Probably coming for us now.*

Ali nodded. "Natas—" Her voice caught in her throat. "Natasha Kerkaw."

Every hair on Taliya's body spiked painfully, like she'd grabbed the bars and been electrocuted. Natasha Kerkaw. Psychotic, hybrid-loathing former-President Kerkaw's eldest daughter. She had been one of his advisors, skulking around in the White House even though she didn't have security clearance or any specific job in the administration. When it all collapsed, Natasha had vanished, like her disgraced father.

What she wanted with Taliya, her kits, and their friends would be nothing good.

Lights throughout the building resumed turning on, and the group joined Taliya in front of the cage holding the kits. The stench of rage and frustration wafted from each of them. Even placid Samson. His breath came in short bursts, almost panting. Rey's aroma was riddled with anxiety and fear. They never should have let him come inside.

None of us should have come inside. We should have let the Marines and the wild tigran handle this. The wild tigran who had possibly abandoned them. But she could forgive Severo. He needed to protect his clan.

This wasn't a raid but a well-sprung trap.

"I see you're beginning to understand the situation," Natasha said over the sound system, her voice almost purring now amid the sounds of the violent storm outside. "Just so we're clear. Every time you resist, every time you don't obey, your daughters will be punished."

It was said with such glee, Taliya imagined the woman was eagerly anticipating trouble and being justified in torturing the kits. She choked down the bile rising in her throat.

"Nothing that will leave a *mark,* of course," Natasha continued. "They're going to fund my new life overseas. Buyers with all kinds of plans for them are freaking out and throwing tens of millions at me. But if threatening their unique hides isn't enough motivation, there's an elaborate choice of creatures I can maim and kill. We can start with little Chica, who tried to warn you."

Taliya glanced back at the cage, where the puman was hiding. Natasha didn't need to harm anyone. Taliya would comply. At least to buy time for help to arrive. *How long will that take?* At some point, Padme and her team would figure out something was wrong. She'd send in the proverbial cavalry. *What does Natasha have waiting to stop them?*

Taking several deep breaths, Taliya forced herself to focus and calm down. It had been years since someone threatened her. Held her captive. But each and every memory was quite tangible. She'd never forget the smell of the room where Narlin tried to rape her, threatening her brothers and Kano. The unborn kits she was carrying. Vivid memories of the exact feeling of every stab of the cattle prod and dental probe mercenaries had used to convince her to give up her valuable kits. The same pair of kits who now stood facing her from behind an electrified cage and glass walls.

Why does it keep coming to this? Why won't they just leave us alone?

It usually came down to money and greed. But this felt different.

Revenge. Natasha wants revenge. On me.

Taliya wasn't sure exactly what she'd done to enrage the Kerkaw family—except manage to survive the Gathering. Drimavil Kerkaw and his daughter Natasha might be revolting humans, but they were not dumb. Arrogant, for sure. Definitely avaricious. But not stupid. Didn't waste time and energy. Natasha had an agenda.

"Daddy was mostly successful," the woman said over the speaker, "managed to eliminate thousands of hybrid abominations. Too bad we didn't move faster. Close, but not a complete cleansing."

Gods help us, is her father here? Taliya's skin prickled again.

Kano had his back to her, watching for trouble. She squeezed his hand, and he returned it without turning around before letting go.

Pain radiated through Taliya's chest. An ache that was partly comforting because she knew it was about Kano. Whatever happened to her, he would never stop fighting to free their girls. He would search the ends of the earth.

She stepped out of the protective circle and faced the males. Carl and Rey looked just as determined as she knew her husband was. If Natasha captured Kano or killed him, Carl would continue the search. He would die for the kits. Samson appeared less confident. For the ligran, this was new territory. He was more rare and valuable than the rest of their team. Potentially in as much individual danger as Taliya herself. The realization that she would do anything to protect her family and friends settled in her heart. *Whatever it takes.*

She tipped her head to the ceiling. "So, what're you waiting for?"

"Tell your harem to stand down," Natasha said.

Kano held out his empty hands, and the others followed suit.

"You know what I mean. Step away. Return to the entrance. . . . Leave her *alone*."

Kano's blue eyes met Taliya's golden ones, and he growled.

"Fuck that," Carl muttered.

Taliya shook her head. "Do it. She's just looking for an excuse to hurt someone. Cooperate until help comes."

Carl mumbled a string of obscenities, and Rey hissed. Kano grabbed Taliya in a hug so fierce it hurt. Behind them, she heard Amrita start crying. They broke apart and faced their daughters, who were now sitting on the metal bed, as instructed. Amrita's face was buried in her sister's chest.

"You heard what Mama said," Kano reminded them. "No matter what you hear, don't watch."

Aliania raised her white chin defiantly. "Kill them *all*."

Tears burst to Taliya's eyes at that from her sweet kitten, but Ali knew far more about the world than she should. Her maimed grandmother and favorite aunty were living proof every day of what violence humans were capable of. She was living through proof of it right that moment.

"That's just what Aunty Marla said." Taliya wiped her eyes and flared her whiskers, proud of their bravery.

Then it occurred to her, *There's an ALL to watch out for.* She locked eyes with Ali and discreetly held up three fingers on her chest. Then four. Raised a questioning black line of eyebrow at her eldest.

Ali showed both hands with her fingers splayed. Closed and opened them again. Sighed and cuddled Amrita, like she'd just been stretching.

So, over a dozen who could cause trouble. Taliya wondered if most of those humans were outside, dealing with the Marines. Maybe even Severo and his clan.

"Roger that," Carl said, nodding at Ali. He'd gotten her message too.

"Love you, Uncle Carl."

"Love you too, marshmallow. See ya soon."

Then he turned to leave. Rey hesitantly followed.

"Go," Taliya whispered to her mate, hoping the rain pummeling the roof covered some of what they said. "We need to stall and keep the girls and everyone else here safe."

Kano rumbled in his chest, glanced back at his daughters, then followed Carl and Rey.

"We will do whatever Natasha says until help comes." Samson stepped up to the cage bars and gazed down at Ali. "Then I will kill her for you."

Aliania slow-blinked at her friend, not appearing as shocked as her mother felt. Samson glanced over at Taliya and smiled sadly. He was the most civilized, tranquil creature she'd ever met. But she knew he would keep that promise.

"Not if I kill her first," Taliya whispered, confident one

of them—either her or Natasha—wasn't walking out of the facility that night.

"Let's go, freaks!" Natasha's shout echoed off the metal walls. "I haven't got all night!"

Samson glared at the roof but then followed the other males to the front entrance.

Taliya stood alone in the aisle. Whatever happened next, it was about her.

Only her.

And she intended to keep it that way.

<h1 style="text-align:center">21</h1>

A door slammed off to the left, near the scent of crocodiles in the far corner. Taliya followed the sound to the back aisle, where Natasha sauntered toward her with two heavily armed men. The Kerkaw heir was stocky and tall for a human woman, but still only reached Taliya's chest. Her black hair was pulled in a tight bun, which distracted from the notion she was lauded as beautiful. She wore an Enforcer uniform from the war—black and red and inherently threatening on its own. Her guards had on armor reminiscent of the war as well. All three were rain-speckled but hadn't been out in the torrential spring storm that pummeled the metal roof, wind and thunder periodically sounding like it was taking out the whole forest. They stunk of onions, processed food, and human body odor covered up with chemical deodorant and musky perfume.

"I hope you and your band of misfits don't try

anything foolhardy," Natasha said, stopping two cages away. She smirked. "I heard you whispering about help coming soon. Don't hold your breath. I own this whole area. Anyone with an ounce of power answers to me. Whatever I say happens, happens. To you and every living thing in this building. It will all be over before that feckless cunt of an illegitimate president gets a rescue team in here."

Taliya growled but nodded her understanding. Determination flared in her chest. Getting the girls out before Natasha could sell them was all that mattered. All she could focus on.

"Now, hmmm." The woman popped one hip and set an index finger to her cheek, like a teen prepping for a selfie. "I have to decide exactly which of the scenarios our soon-to-arrive guests will pay the most for. They've had a whole slew of outstanding suggestions."

Taliya forced herself not to respond. No raised hackles or flattened ears, ignoring the tingle in her fingers, the instinctive rush to extend her claws.

Natasha began exaggerated pacing. "Should you face off against a polar bear in a death match? Meh. . . . I suspect you could easily defeat a full-blooded tiger. Boring. So. Many. Options."

Natasha stalked past the cages that ran along the back, peering into them like she was making a selection. "Eeny, meeny, miny . . ."

The thought that she might have to kill an innocent

animal—or a captive creature—made Taliya's stomach roil.

The woman paused and turned to face her. "We could string you up, I suppose. Let the guests take turns stabbing you with a dull knife. Gut you with a spoon or something." She mimed what either of those might look like, glee sparkling in her dark eyes.

Despite her best efforts, Taliya's hackles spiked. She hoped her clothes covered most of it.

"Still, kinda boring." Natasha discarded that idea with a dismissive wave of her hand, revealing long, pointed fingernails painted dark red.

So death is the ultimate plan. Torture and entertainment first. Taliya felt oddly numb. Out-of-body. Heightening what she'd been feeling since she found out about the kidnapping. It was all too surreal. She'd prepared for so many scenarios. But not this.

"Of course," Natasha said, "I saw part of those crocodile videos from your fake vacation. That could be an interesting pairing."

Visceral images from the Crocoseum—the inside of the reptiles' jaws as they stomped forward—flashed through Taliya's mind. Chomping on dead chickens with massive force. Dinosaur-scaled, muscular bodies. Unarmed, she might be able to win, but it would be ugly. And she imagined somehow Natasha would ensure the croc won.

Now that she was in the aisle running parallel to the back of the building, she could see a crocodile cage in the far corner—more like a full zoo exhibit. Five-foot metal fencing surrounded a large pond containing at least three animals bigger than the ones she'd seen in Australia. Maybe a special breed. A ledge hung over the top, for exhibitions or feeding displays.

Natasha chuckled and adopted a bad Aussie accent. "How's a roll with a croc sound?"

Before Taliya could answer, piercing, primal screams came from outside the building—many individual ones, hitting different pitches.

Screams from the front.

Then from the back.

Then both sides, in quick succession.

Not human. More like the furious noise Rey had made earlier.

The shrieks seemed to dart around, one beginning when another ended, creating an unending, nerve-wracking cacophony. Viscerally, instinctively terrifying. Taliya's ears lay flat, the cries running through her.

From the look on her face, it wasn't something Natasha expected. Her two guards leveled their guns, searching for the source, though it was clearly outside. The woman adjusted her surprised expression and focused on Taliya.

"Tricky kitty. Do you have more friends than I expected?"

Taliya shrugged one shoulder, but hope surged through her. *It's a war cry. Severo!* He hadn't abandoned them. And it sounded like his team was alive and well.

The pile of discarded guns lay on the ground up the side aisle. Too far away to grab before a guard shot her, though she'd have cover for a second once she rounded the corner.

The screams grew louder. This time inside, echoing through the building. The eleven wild tigran made it sound like there were hundreds of them. A blast of the scent of petrichor-filled night air and rain hit her from the main door, followed by barking shouts and whoops. Taliya twitched a bit each time. Deep and primitive reactions.

"Tell them to back off!" Natasha charged forward, a laser pistol drawn.

Raising her hands in surrender, Taliya frowned. "They don't answer to me."

Flashes of red reflected off the Plexiglass of the polar bear cage behind her as the *schwep* of multiple guns came from the front of the building. Shouts, grunts, and thuds from physical blows. Taliya could hear and interpret more than the woman, even through the din of the storm that now sounded like it was indoors as well. All of her team were there among the skirmish with whatever guards had been near the entrance.

Rey, adding his panther scream to what had to be the wild tigran.

Carl, cussing and yelling.

Samson, shouting where to watch out for incoming attack.

Kano, in what sounded like hand-to-hand combat.

Continued screams from Severo's clan. Getting closer.

One of the guards grabbed Taliya's arm, and she focused on the woman still pointing a pistol at her head.

"Remember what would happen if you didn't cooperate?" Natasha's face flushed with rage, but her hand trembled.

Taliya sensed the woman's confidence slipping. She hadn't expected to do any of the dirty work herself. Maybe hadn't ever actually fired a gun. Taliya growled, eyes narrowed and ears back.

Natasha turned to the other Enforcer. "Bring me the little one with the pale stripes."

"No!" Taliya struggled with her guard, who calmly placed the tip of his gun on her temple. She tried to still, but the growl/hiss of rage couldn't be controlled. Spit landed on his black shirt. He didn't flinch. Reeked of hatred and anger. Happy to kill her if he was allowed.

"Get that abomination. Now!" Natasha shouted at the second guard.

He looked distracted by the battle noises from the front of the facility but obediently started toward the kits' cage, pulling a key card from his belt. As he rounded the corner to the side aisle, he froze and raised his hands.

Naked and sopping-wet, all eight feet and several hundred pounds of Severo leapt onto him with a warrior scream that made Taliya's ears ring. After a head smack that probably snapped the spine, he buried his fangs into the man's throat. Taliya's own jaws clenched at the squelch as the guard's life oozed onto the dirt floor. The body convulsed twice and went limp.

Severo reared back, more feral-looking than any wild tiger. An orange-and-black nightmare, his wet fur spiked in fury. Blood dripping from his mouth and whiskers, he bared his fangs and growled followed by a hiss that splattered gore in the dirt. An underlying rumble flowed through Taliya. Severo settled his sights on Natasha and sneered.

"Kill him!" Natasha screeched, aiming her gun. Tigran screams from behind made her spin defensively instead of firing.

The Enforcer restraining Taliya hesitated, gawking at his fallen comrade. That was all the opening she required. Sinking her teeth into his wrist, she ripped muscle and sinew with a decisive wrench. Hand and weapon hit the floor.

The guard screamed and crumpled to the ground, blood spraying from the arterial wound, before passing out.

Taliya turned back to the woman, who looked ready to shoot but also mid-panic. All her tidy plans gone to shit. Taliya wiped the blood from her mouth with her arm, leaving a dark smear across her sleeve.

Natasha seemed torn between just shooting her prize and ending things or possibly trying to regain control of the situation. She swung her aim from Taliya to Severo, then back to Taliya. One of them could attack before she got off a second shot.

Severo hissed again, splattering crimson gore at the woman, then extended his tongue in a "stinky face" from hell, revealing the bone-cleaning spikes on his tongue. Taliya scented his anticipation and bloodlust. Opened her mouth and extended her bare tongue to let it fill her senses.

Laser fire flashed down the side aisle, but Taliya couldn't tell who it came from. In the moment that distracted her, Natasha opted to flee.

"He has a key." Taliya pointed to the body the wild tigran still crouched on top of, like a predator guarding his kill. "But careful, you'll need to get the electric grid off first."

Severo nodded and yanked the key card from the body as Taliya grabbed the gun from the dismembered hand and raced after Natasha.

Taking several shots at her fleeing form, Taliya searched for cover, but the woman didn't return fire. She was heading for the exit door past the crocodile exhibit and a clean escape. Before she reached it, a wild tigran burst in, blocking her way. Natasha shrieked—the sight of the enormous, unclothed, fang-bared, rage-filled tigran enough to shock anyone. She veered left, around the side of the fencing. Taliya took a shot, but narrowly missed, frying a black mark on the wall.

The quickest route to intercept was through the exhibit. Steeling her nerve, Taliya rushed the fencing and vaulted over it, landing on the edge of the wide crocodile pond. The surprised reptiles shifted in the water, but she was out over the far side before they could react. That dropped her right in front of Natasha, trapping the woman along the wall with Taliya on one side and the clan tigran on the other.

Natasha aimed her weapon with both hands the second Taliya's feet hit the ground. "Drop it!"

Through the adrenaline rush, Taliya slow-blinked to clear her head. The wild tigran growled and inched forward.

"Take another step and I'll end her," Natasha threatened without turning his way, her alarmingly black eyes glaring at Taliya. "Twitch like you're raising that gun, it's over."

Taliya glanced past the woman to the wild tigran. His golden eyes flared, pupils wide, eager. But if Natasha could keep her back to him and not go into primal panic, Taliya had underestimated her. Continued sounds of fighting and shouts from the front of the building meant neither team was currently in charge. She needed to buy time.

Tossing the gun to the ground, Taliya showed her empty hands.

"I've got this. Go help the team," she said to the tigran. She didn't know the runner's name, but he looked lean and feisty. Excited to kill.

Natasha snorted. "Like there's any way this ends well for you."

Taliya nodded at the young tigran. He reluctantly stepped back, then turned and ran up the left-hand aisle. She focused back on the woman, who looked like she was considering taking a shot at his back.

"It has already ended well," Taliya said calmly, redirecting her attention. "My kits are safe. More help is coming, if not already here."

"So I guess there's no reason to delay. No one arriving to enjoy your humiliation in person. Good thing I already have their payments. Enough to make a clean departure from this shitty country."

Taliya's skin prickled, remembering what Natasha had been planning for her demise. "Things might take a turn. Worth waiting a bit."

"Nope. We're recording all of this. Have to give 'em something. Up there." Natasha motioned with the gun. "Go."

Looking behind her, Taliya found the stairs leading to the crocodile-feeding platform. The idea of being in clear view without easy escape gnawed at her instincts, but maybe it kept her alive a little longer. So she climbed to reach the wide expanse of bamboo decking that hovered directly over the pond. Four large cameras were aimed at the platform, perfect for catching every moment of what came next.

Below, three crocs stared at her from the pond, fully alert after her incursion through their territory. Each was bigger than twenty-foot Boris back at Australia Zoo. Taliya stepped away from the edge and an easy push over the side. Natasha hovered back on the stairs for a moment, probably also realizing how vulnerable a position they were taking.

From that perch, Taliya now had a full view of the battle. Aliania was right, the number of humans Natasha had with her was daunting, though a good portion lay on the ground, covered in laser burns and blood—hopefully dead. Wild tigran darted throughout the building, leaping from cage tops, screaming, avoiding gunfire, and executing Enforcers. Most of that was focused on the massive front door, which stood wide open to the night. Lightning flashed, revealing two wild tigran standing outside on guard in the downpour. The electric charge of it tingled through her claws.

Kano and Samson were tucked down the left-side aisle, using the corner as cover to shoot toward the action in the front.

Severo was unlocking some of the cages, but it looked like he was telling the captives to stay put for now. Out of the line of fire.

The girls' cage was open, but they still huddled on the bed. Outside their door, Carl stood in the aisle, a repeat-laser rifle in each hand—cussing, yelling, and firing at any guard who tried to come near, working his way toward the battle at the entrance.

"Well, that's a cluster fuck." Natasha joined her on the platform.

Taliya didn't turn to face her. "You can just walk away. By the time things settle, be long gone."

With a scoff, Natasha moved closer but kept out of reach. The platform creaked with each step. "Not a chance. Why miss this victory?"

Despite Natasha's optimism, Taliya realized her side was winning.

A guard tried to run past the berman's cage, and the creature reached out, grabbed him by the uniform, and slammed him into the bars repeatedly until the man stopped moving. The berman dropped the body, picked up the gun, and stood ready.

With a panther scream, Chica leapt from her cage onto the back of a guard, burying her fangs in his throat. She might be small, even for a puman, but he couldn't shake her off and ultimately fell to his knees as blood poured down the front of his Enforcer-style uniform.

Through the chaos, Taliya felt a familiar rumble. Kano was staring at her, probably calculating if he could risk a shot. It was nearly 90 yards. Too far. He stealthily maneuvered down the left-side aisle toward them, leaving Samson to defend the corner. Taliya looked away so Natasha wouldn't notice.

Unfortunately, the next thing that caught her eye was her daughters, both gawking at her. Not watching was easier when Mama wasn't up near the ceiling and in easy view. She shook her head slightly, and Aliania covered Amrita's eyes before ducking her own head.

"You could jump," Natasha suggested.

Taliya huffed. "I could. Without getting hurt. Tigran are quite good at things like that. Why scientists made us."

"Then I'd just shoot you."

"Most likely." Taliya bristled her whiskers. "So I won't bother."

Kano was getting close. *Keep her talking.*

"Ah well." Natasha sighed dramatically, waving the gun. "I wasn't counting on those forest freaks. The government should really catch some for study. Quite remarkable."

Taliya wanted nothing more than to put an end to the woman's ranting. Maybe that's what Natasha was trying for. *See me react and rage before she burns a hole in my face.* Taliya refused. Just stared across the building to where two polar bears were now awake and pacing along the side of their pool.

"What I really—" Natasha began but then screamed at flashes of red light and *schweps* of a gun, followed by her hitting the decking.

Whipping around, Taliya realized Kano had fired. In a second, she was on top of the woman, pinning her down face-to-face. From the scent of blood, at least one of the shots had found a mark, just not enough to end the vile woman.

They rolled and wrestled for the gun, Taliya biting at the woman's shoulders, unable to get the right angle for a solid jugular bite. Images of old movies flashed through Taliya's mind—where the good guy and bad guy fight for the gun and one of them ends up shot in the gut. Rolling and raising her knees, she heaved the woman across the platform, where Natasha sprawled and lost hold of the gun. It clattered to the ground below. From somewhere nearby, Kano whooped a cheer.

As she tried to crawl for the staircase, Taliya grabbed Natasha's leg but was surprised by the slash of a switchblade across her arm—a backup the woman must have had hidden somewhere. Letting go, Taliya fell back, grateful she'd only received a glancing blow. The woman bellowed in rage and lunged at her, managing to stab her in the thigh but losing the weapon in the process.

Taliya screamed at the flash of pain, pulled out the knife, and threw it off the platform. Blood seeped from the wound. Undaunted and fast for a human, Natasha leapt to her feet—screeching, raising her hands like her talon nails were claws and could actually inflict more damage. She attacked Taliya, who easily grabbed her, rolling so they were on the edge of the platform with the tigran on top.

"Enough," Taliya hissed, pinning Natasha's arms with her legs.

Weapons gone, it was over, no matter how much the woman writhed, struggled, cussed, and screamed about locking the nasty kitty in a cage where she belonged. Killing her and sending Taliya to hell, where atrocities belonged. The tigran sensed Natasha's heartbeat, the artery now one bite away, its rhythm throbbing through her fangs. She could already taste the satisfaction of ending the woman.

But Taliya hesitated. What if the girls were watching? Witnessing Mama rip out a person's throat. But there was no way she was trusting human justice through the legal system. It ended now.

She heaved Natasha until the woman's head was forced off the platform, hanging over the edge. Blood dripped off the side from her shoulder wounds. *Plink. Plink.* Into the water.

"You can't have me," Taliya growled, her face inches from the woman's. "You can't have my kits." She hauled Natasha more, so her shoulders were over the edge too. "You can't have *any* of us."

Natasha grinned like she was going to respond with some revolting last words before being dumped off the platform, but her eyes went wide when Taliya spotted movement below and leaned to the right.

For the tigran, every motion slowed, her predator DNA focused and aware.

A crocodile jumped straight up from the pond and snapped his dinosaur jaws around Natasha's head. The rows of thick teeth crunched through the woman's skull like a sledgehammer bursting a melon, spraying blood and gore, wrenching head from body as the croc fell back into the pond with his prize. Taliya hissed and shoved the remains of the carcass off the platform.

While the splashing of death rolls came from below, she shouted, "Crocs can jump, you inhuman piece of shit!"

Natasha Kerkaw was past being able to appreciate her fatal error, somewhere under the writhing bodies of three armored reptiles.

Endorphins rushed through Taliya, bringing the world

back up to speed. Crouching on the platform, she realized there were no more bursts of red from laser fire. The building was eerily quiet. She pulled off her top-layer long-sleeved shirt and tied it around her leg wound. It hurt like hell, but the bleeding was minor. Then she surveyed the damage below.

Samson stood near the girls' cage with Severo, but the kits were still inside, staring up at her again. She hoped they'd missed Natasha's death. Wild tigran stalked the aisles, stopping to talk with prisoners and leading them toward the front of the building.

Kano thundered up the stairs to the platform and grabbed her in a crushing embrace. He had a small wound on one arm but was okay. Assured she wasn't badly hurt —most of the blood on her was the guard's or Natasha's —he looked for the girls and sighed in relief. They were now in the aisle. Samson held Amrita on one hip, and Aliania stood tucked under his other arm.

"It's done," Kano said. "We won." He raised a fist and shouted, "Hoo-ah!"

But there was no answer.

Taliya rested her head on his shoulder and let exhaustion wash over her. Since the moment they'd heard about the kidnapping back in Australia, she hadn't relaxed. Fear and tension had hovered, even when she'd managed to sleep. The hiking, the stress, the battle—it all caught up with her and left her wanting to collapse on the platform. Maybe go to sleep there.

But first, she needed to put hands on her kittens. Feel for herself that they were safe and secure.

An animal scream split the air.

Unearthly keening followed, waves of high and low pitches echoing, filling the building, making it hard to even breathe.

It wasn't the kits.

"No!" Aliania struggled to leave Samson and run up the aisle. "No! No! No!" A scream and a growl/hiss of rage spewed out as she tried to escape. Samson, his expression unreadable, held the kit back—a strong arm wrapped around her middle as her feet kicked at the air. Amrita, in the other arm, buried her face in his chest.

Severo stood down the aisle from them, hands on his head but with a look of dismay, not surrender.

The front doors to the building were still open, rain and fresh air flowing in from the darkness. Thunder rumbled, but it was met by that unearthly wail. This time, Taliya found the source. Where all the creatures were heading.

Reynaldo panther screamed again, a primal cry of rage and grief. He sat on the ground in the aisle, Carl's bloody, limp body sprawled across his lap.

22

Taliya flinched at each volley from the antique rifles. Seven soldiers in dress uniforms fired in unison once, twice, three times in the honorary 21-gun salute for General Carl Thompson. Reynaldo stood between her and Kano, wearing the suit from his wedding two weeks earlier, his hands clasped in theirs. He released them when "Taps" was played to place his palm over his heart. Beyond the scent of grief only another creature would notice, Rey was stoic. Rangers stood at attention around their group, as honor guard and genuine security guards.

The American flag that covered the coffin was ceremoniously folded thirteen times, forming a triangle, ending with Carl's old comrade Dan, who'd been with him through many rescues and had helped free Taliya's family from the breeding facility. The soldier who'd done the folding saluted the flag Dan held at waist level for three seconds before turning and stiffly walking away. Dan tucked three spent cartridges from the salute into the flag.

One for duty. Another for honor. The last for sacrifice.

Since Carl had no living family, President Padme Nakobi accepted the flag as commander in chief. Dan said something Taliya couldn't hear and saluted. The president paused for a moment, checking to be sure every media camera was on her, then strode around the burial site directly to Rey.

"I am so sorry, just devastated, honestly, over your loss," she said loudly enough for all to hear, "but your husband's sacrifice saved many lives."

President Nakobi handed the folded flag to the panthran, and he held it in front of him, chest heaving. Padme hadn't warned them about this part. Maybe she'd decided in the moment. To publicly acknowledge the marriage, even if it wasn't legal in the U.S.

The president then stood with them as hundreds of humans and a handful of creatures departed, passing by the coffin to pay their respects. A few mourners acknowledged Rey with a nod or quick condolence. Most didn't. When the crowd thinned, Padme shook Rey's hand and headed out to do something presidential while the troops and important people who'd attended got back to their lives.

Dan and Kallie the liran were last. He stood for a solid minute, whispering thoughts to the casket. Carl wasn't inside. He'd been cremated. Padme had insisted the pomp and ceremony of a full military funeral at

Arlington National Cemetery was important, so they'd gone along with the parade and public hours of acknowledging his service to their country. Taliya's family had planned a private ceremony at the compound in Arkansas that afternoon to scatter his ashes.

Before leaving, Dan approached Rey, hand extended. Rey shook it but stared at the ground.

"Thank you . . ." Dan cleared his throat. "Thank you for loving my friend."

Rey met his gaze, and Dan, tears staining his cheeks, pulled Rey in for a hug.

The creaking of the casket being lowered into the grave made them all turn.

"Blaze of glory," Dan whispered. "How he always wanted to go out." He looked back at Rey. "He saved your life in his last moments. Carl would have *zero* regrets about that."

From what Severo had witnessed, this was true. Carl had jumped into the line of fire from the last Enforcer standing to save Rey, taking the hit himself instead and killing the guard in the process. Died to save his mate. But no one had discussed it so openly yet.

Rey collapsed onto the chair behind him and covered his face with his hands, clutching the flag to his chest. Taliya and Kano shifted to be sure he was blocked from any determined paparazzi.

Dan wiped his cheeks with a sleeve as Kallie stepped up and hugged Taliya. Their frantic escape from men at the Colorado facility—led by Carl and Dan—only lasted a few minutes, but it had formed a unique bond.

"I'm happy your kits are safe," Kallie whispered. "And all the others too. But Carl . . ."

Taliya leaned back to meet her eyes. "I know. One brave rescue too many."

⁕

WHEN THE BLACK SEDAN RETURNED THEM TO THE COMPOUND after the flight home from D.C. on a private plane, Aliania was standing on the porch. Canine guards Cairo and Elektra sat at attention on either side of her. Taliya wasn't sure if Ali had been stubbornly waiting there the whole time or had seen their arrival on the security monitors. Dressed in a white tunic and slacks the same color as her fur, their beautiful daughter scowled with arms folded across her chest. She'd relax once they scattered Carl's ashes and conducted a ceremony it was safe for her to attend. At least Taliya hoped so. A massive weight of guilt seemed to simmer under all of the rage Ali did not attempt to keep to herself. If beloved Uncle Carl hadn't fought to save her, he'd still be alive—guilt Taliya could empathize with.

Kano didn't wait for the driver to open his door and was headed toward Aliania the moment the car stopped. Taliya and Rey exited quietly. He still hugged the flag to his chest like it could fill the emotional void there.

Aliania allowed her father to embrace her, then broke

away and headed into the house with the dogs trailing behind, as if someone had ordered them to guard her. Maybe they had. Through the open door, the rest of the kits peered out, all dressed in white in Hindu tradition. Ready for what came next. Taliya had hoped there'd be a short rest before starting Carl's ceremony, but Ali was clearly ready to start immediately.

Taliya adjusted her dressy black sari with gold embroidery, wondering if she should change now that the public event was done. Seemed like more effort than she had energy for. She could imagine Carl saying, "Fuck that. Just get it done." A smile slipped out, but she inhaled and pursed her whiskers to cover it.

Shreya stepped from her home across the lawn, followed by Tuscan, Tyler, and Parth, who pushed his wife Marla in a hovering recovery chair. Evidence of the attack had left her face odd shades of yellow and purple, but she was well enough to leave the hospital. Fresh guilt flashed hot through Taliya's chest.

The sedan pulled away, and Taliya suspected the security detail on the compound would keep an eye on it until it was off the property. The constant military presence was a new normal for their lives. Kerkaw himself was still out there somewhere—and probably self-righteously pissed off about his daughter's violent death. Captured on video and secretively shared widely. Kerkaw sending mercenaries to slaughter Taliya's family for revenge wasn't out of the question.

Aliania emerged from the house carrying the box of

Carl's ashes, tears wetting the unstriped fur on her cheeks. Jai and Amrita followed, the dogs flanking them. Luna and Lilly came next, holding hands and frowning. Taliya hurried over to help as they navigated the stairs down from the porch. The L-twins smelled annoyed, probably wondering why everyone was sad and weepy again.

She doubted they'd understood the miserable ceremony in the forest a week ago, scattering their grandfather's ashes. Just that morning, Luna had asked when Grampa Jai was coming home, making Taliya's heart ache. Death was too final a thing for them to comprehend.

Ali stopped in front of her mother, glower still in place. "Samson didn't come? Didn't attend the fancy ceremony?"

"Padme agreed he shouldn't. Too much attention is dangerous, same as you." Taliya let go of the L-twins, who ran to their grammy and Aunty Marla, climbing up in her chair with her. "He's gone to pick up Bena. When they both arrive next week, he can pay his respects."

Something that might equate to jealousy flashed across Aliania's face. Another issue to deal with eventually because Taliya anticipated Bena—the wild tigran who'd wanted to join them in the raid—could be planning more than a brief visit to the human world.

After the facility had been secured by the Marines and the government, Taliya, Kano, Samson, and Rey returned to camp with the uncivilized tigran. Rey spent the day mostly alone, mourning. The clan conducted a bereavement ceremony based on rituals learned from the Nuche/ Ute Indians. They'd lost three clan members in the battle, their bodies buried in the forest with the dozens culled by Enforcers during the Gathering. Aliania and Amrita seemed to be comforted by the opportunity to wail, scream in rage, cry, and openly share their grief. But Rey remained silent as he tried to process not only the loss of his husband but the shock of his shattered future.

Before a helicopter picked the group up, Bena expressed interest in joining them. Joining Samson. The ligran agreed to return for her in a few weeks, once he'd arranged for all of the rescued creatures and animals to be settled into new, safe homes. He'd left her a communication device, and Taliya could feel the uncivilized tigran's excitement about the technology.

While Severo expressed concerns over Bena being too young and unprepared for the world, Taliya assured him that Samson would see to her safety. She also explained the concept of trying out a different life, like rumspringa in the Amish tradition. Something her father had taught her about from human history, though it was still part of that community's practices.

Taliya inhaled deeply, letting more thoughts of her father run through her memories. Grampa Jai's flat stone marker rested under the huge black hickory tree where they'd scattered his ashes. Now they would do the same for Carl, establishing a tradition Taliya expected would continue.

Rey led the group to the spot he'd selected for Carl—

the tallest, strongest tree on the property. Another black hickory twenty yards away from Grampa Jai's. Tuscan and Tyler had placed the stone marker at dawn, taking their own private moment to honor the man who'd rescued them from the Colorado facility when they were still kits. Who'd drunk ale with them when they were older. Who'd teased them about girlfriends and played media games with them over the web late into the night. The man who genuinely felt like their uncle.

Aliania traded Rey the box of ashes for the flag, which she then hugged to her own chest. He stood silently for a minute, staring at the memorial plaque at the base of the tree.

"We all knew you would die for us," Rey choked out, golden gaze lifted into the branches. "But you seemed immortal. Too extraordinary to ever die. I never believed . . . I never considered it might actually happen. Thank you for all the times you saved us. All the *ways* you saved us. . . . Saved me."

He opened the lid and moved around the tree, tipping the box to dust Carl's ashes over the grass. Then they all stood quietly, alone with their own thoughts. Ali's chest shuddered as she gasped past a sob. Amrita and Jai held hands and stared at the ground. Over the two weeks since Carl's death, they'd cried and shared stories and said all there was to say. He hadn't been religious, so there was no point in Bible verses. Shreya murmured "Om shanti om" three times.

At Grampa Jai's memorial, she'd reminded them that

Hindu beliefs involved reincarnation. The soul is indestructible and never dies. It was a lovely idea, but Taliya would rather have both men still standing beside them in this world. Though it made her ponder what each of them might return as. Her father would be a graceful deer or butterfly. Something peaceful. Carl had always been jealous of not being a hybrid with heightened abilities in his DNA. Imagining him as a black-maned lion, protecting a pride on the African plains, made her smile and chuff.

Kano glanced her way, and she shook her head. "Tell you later."

She stared at the marker as pain radiated through every inch of her skin, tingling across the new scar on her thigh.

Carl Thurgood Thompson
Beloved Husband, Protector, and Friend
March 2131 - May 2178
"I'd die a thousand times over
to assure every creature can live safe and free."

Rey had provided the quote, something Carl told him many times. Why he'd been risking his life for that cause since early 2172.

Glancing over at Rey, a different scenario played in Taliya's mind. One where they were all gathered to celebrate the couple's surprise wedding, like they'd planned. Letting that image linger was too depressing.

The panthran turned toward the house. The others

followed, Aliania trailing at the end, still clutching the flag. So much sadness, it felt like a heaviness hung over the compound. Taliya suspected each of them would wander back to both trees and markers over the next few weeks.

All of them except Rey.

The black panthran was leaving in three days, returning to Australia to work at the zoo with the dragons. Robbie had been ecstatic to have Rey join the team, though "gutted" about the reason why. With no legal standing in America, the panthran needed to vacate the military lodgings he'd shared with Carl, though Padme had assured him there was no rush. Rey had already packed, sorted, donated, and shipped personal items ahead to the zoo before coming to stay with Taliya's family until he departed for good. He would have a nice home right on the zoo grounds, like the Irwin family did. It was bittersweet, but Taliya expected life with the dragons and other animals, as well as the creatures working at the zoo, would be not only distracting but healing. Rey would also be in a place more accepting of genetic creations and their rights.

Taliya hoped the president's open support of mixed-species marriage began changes in American laws. It was a tricky subject, as they'd learned during the wedding vows in Australia—how to allow for mixed families, like Marla's parents, without risking the safety of hybrids who might become victims of fetishes and collectors. Taliya was grateful that was Samson's problem, not hers.

When they returned from the forest, food was waiting in the kitchen at the main house, like an old-school wake—sandwiches, meat pies, a roast beef and a ham, spicy-smelling chicken, homemade rolls, and the veggie samosas that were traditionally a part of offering comfort to those grieving. Tuscan and Tyler lifted warming lids and served up plates.

"Mom, great gods." Taliya wrapped an arm around Shreya's waist. "Were you up all night cooking?"

Shreya shrugged and waved her away. "I couldn't sleep anyhow. What we don't eat now will keep us all fed for the next few days."

Or weeks, Taliya thought.

Worry over how little rest her mother was getting made her ears flatten. Shreya had admitted sleep was illusive without her husband by her side in bed. Taliya was about to comment on all of that when Luna and Lilly thundered down the hall to their room, giggling and probably planning mischief. Amrita met her mother's eyes and nodded, following them to limit the damage. One-year-old kits didn't allow much space for wallowing.

Kano wrapped an arm around Taliya's waist, and she rested her head on his chest. He would need to leave for work in a few days. The first hurricane of the season was set to make landfall in the south at Category 6, and all tigran with rescue or rebuilding skills were expected to help in the aftermath.

She'd have to find good tutors for the kits because

there wasn't a chance in Naraka they were going back to public school. Maybe ever.

Rey would leave soon. Next week, Samson and Bena would arrive to visit.

Life would move on. Getting back to a more normal routine might be healing in itself.

One by one, they each changed into everyday clothes. Leftovers were stored away, the dishes washed, and they gathered on the porch. Daylight was growing dim, so Kano and Jai started a fire in the pit. From the Adirondack chairs, the group watched the flames dance while Cairo and Elektra scanned the woods for signs of danger. Marines were out there somewhere, guarding as intently.

Luna and Lilly both curled up on Marla's lap in her hover chair. One of the gray tabby cats who called the property home wandered onto the porch and settled under Amrita's seat. Normally, she'd have persistently coaxed it onto her lap, but she ignored it. Aliania stared off into the trees, Carl's flag on the small table next to her chair. No more glower or tears, but the miasma of grief still enveloped her.

Parth brought Tuscan's guitar and quietly played songs Taliya recognized from their time in the refugee camp. So many memories of evenings like this—but filled with joy and gratitude for their freedom and futures ahead. Futures that mostly came true.

Her twin brothers returned from their house and settled near the fire. Shreya finally emerged from the kitchen and sat next to her daughter. The air around them felt calm but full of remorse. All those years of happiness regained on this property after the Gathering had been smashed in a few days. Taliya wondered if she'd ever truly feel safe again—for herself or her family. It was hard to envision what came next.

The rooster crowed and hens clucked unsettled noises, maybe reacting to the music in the dark. The dogs glanced toward the coops but didn't seem concerned. In the morning, there'd be eggs to gather and chores to do, but it all felt untethered to reality at that moment.

Rey leaned forward with his elbows on his knees, staring at the flames. "Do you remember the 'Walk On' song'?"

Parth nodded. "We used to holler that one out."

"Maybe no yelling tonight," Rey said with a sad smile, "but I'd love to hear it."

After the first few notes, Taliya thought back on the night, just two weeks ago, when they'd flown dragons through the sky while Carl and Rey sang the same tune. At the camp, they'd belted it after many ales and tried hitting the highest notes as loudly as possible. Tonight was different.

Parth and Rey began singing, and the tigran slipped into deep harmonies. It wasn't long, so Parth began again, giving them all a chance to not only enjoy the melody but ponder the words. Consider what it meant to walk on through life's storms, when your dreams are tossed and blown. When everything feels destroyed beyond recognition.

Maybe that's all any of us can do. Walk on and on and on. Just keep walking, chin held high.

Shreya reached over and took Taliya's hand. She gently squeezed the maimed fingers and met her mother's eyes. There were tears there, but also resignation and a bit of peace. Since that Thanksgiving night years ago—when Shreya packed up her three kits and sent them into hiding, maybe to never see them again—they'd learned how to walk on and rebuild and adapt to life's storms. It could be done again, though dread about what other battles might lie ahead sat heavy in Taliya's chest.

As the second round of the song ended, Rey glanced at each creature present and whispered, "We never walk alone."

No one there was going to face the future alone. Even though Rey was leaving, he would be joining new friends like Jaxon and Wolfie and be in his element with the beloved dragons to train and care for. Taliya was confident he could recover from this horror, just like he'd moved on from so many others.

Aliania huffed and got up, stomping into the house. Taliya moved to follow, but Shreya shook her head and held her daughter's hand.

"Let her be. Give her time."

Amrita watched her sister go but didn't follow either. When Taliya met Amrita's eyes, the lost innocence there made her tail puff. Humans had broken her kit's spirit. Now her job was to attempt to restore it.

Kano and Jai gave up fussing with the fire and came to

join the group. Jai climbed up in the Adirondack with his grandmother, and Kano settled on the deck next to his wife's feet, resting an arm over her leg. Parth moved on to another tune, something more upbeat and not fodder for moroseness.

"Can we get a bunny?" Lilly asked.

Kano chuckled deep in his chest, and Taliya glanced over at the L-twins in Marla's lap.

"Would you like that?" Marla asked, wrapping her arm tighter around Lilly.

Luna reached up, rested a small hand on Aunty Marla's bruised face, and then nodded. "A black one, with long fur."

"A bunny or two sounds *delicious*," Tyler said, glancing at his brother with a gleam in his eye.

Tuscan took the bait. "Mmmm. With cream sauce?"

"No!" Luna and Lilly squealed, earning a laugh from the adults.

Parth stopped playing, thought for a second, and began a plucky rendition of "Little Bunny Foo-Foo." Luna and Lilly joined in.

Amrita frowned and pulled her knees to her chest, but Taliya sang too as Shreya made the required bopping motions with Jai.

This is how walking on happens, Taliya realized. Life keeps going, and you follow where it leads. One step at a time.

23

OCTOBER 2178

When the private plane rolled to a stop on the tarmac in Brisbane, several transports from Australia Zoo, a dozen police vehicles, and Wolfie in his khaki uniform were waiting. The flight attendant opened the door, and familiar smells drifted through the cabin. Taliya inhaled and sorted the aromas on the warm air. They'd left a country preparing for fall festivals like Halloween and landed on a continent where summer was just beginning.

"Can't smell the beach," Lilly grumbled, already unbuckled and tugging her backpack from under the seat.

Kano leaned over to help. "You can see the water from our hotel window. It's just not right here at the airport."

"I'm gonna swim with the dolphman," Jai said to his father. "You promised."

"None of us are going to miss that," Bena assured him,

pulling her case from the overhead storage. "And diving the reef. It looks amazing."

Bena turned too quickly in the aisle and lost her balance, bracing on Samson's chest, then placing a protective hand on her belly and the new life growing there. He caught her by the shoulders and planted a kiss atop her head. Bena reached up and ran her fingers through his short tawny mane, which he'd let grow out instead of trimming it back to seem less threatening.

"We are here for a week," Samson said with a chuckle. "No need to rush."

Stairs were rolled to the door, and Wolfie climbed up to greet them from the front of the plane. "Welcome!"

"G'day!" Kano called from the back of the aisle, earning a whuff of delight from the dingman.

All five kits froze, staring at Wolfie and scenting him out. He met each of their gazes with a canine smile. Taliya refrained from saying something like, "My, what big ears you have," imagining that racing through their minds. *Wait till they meet the rooman.*

Wolfie rested his gaze on Aliania and Amrita, still sitting in seats near him. "Well, I certainly know who you two are. Welcome to the Land Down Under."

The girls mumbled a greeting with wide eyes. Even after seeing him on video and hearing his accent, like they all had before the trip, the real thing was remarkable. Both kits stared at his feet, which Taliya couldn't see but assumed were bare, revealing long, nonretractable claws poking out from the tan fur.

"Hello, Wolfie," Marla said, extending a hand. "We've heard so much about you."

The dingman took it, noticed the declawed fingers, and clasped it in both furry hands. "And I about you, Aunty Marla. You must be Parth."

The two males exchanged a handshake, then turned to the rest of the family.

"I'm Jai," the kit said, stepping forward and presenting his hand for a greeting as well. "I want to try fairy floss. I do *not* want to feed the crocodiles. But I *do* want to ride a dragon."

Wolfie laughed. "Sounds like a solid plan." He leaned down toward the L-twins. "And look at you, adorable little kittens."

"This is Luna," Taliya said, "and this is Lilly." The kits gawked up at him from their spot in the aisle, but he didn't seem bothered. "My brothers, Tuscan and Tyler, are in the back there."

The twins hooted and waved from where they stood at the tail of the plane.

"And this is my mother, Shreya."

Wolfie met her eyes for a moment and gave a small head tip that seemed to acknowledge not only her but her loss five months earlier. Then he smiled at the group again. "The zoo is abuzz, and we're all super-stoked for the Dragoceum grand opening. Rey's waitin' for ya at his house in the village for lunch."

"Is it *lunch* time?" Tuscan said. "Feels like the middle of the night, except for the sun."

Tyler grabbed his luggage. "I could eat."

"Well," Wolfie said, "let's get to it."

As they all gathered carry-ons and deplaned, Kano leaned toward Taliya. "I thought Rey was meeting us."

"That's what he said." She shrugged. "Maybe seeing us all again on his home field is easier."

Communication with Rey had been sporadic since he'd arrived on the Sunshine Coast. At first, Taliya wrote it off to all of the adjustments he must be going through and the demands of establishing new routines with the dragons—not to mention a 15-hour time difference. Once he'd invited them to participate in the grand opening, they'd chatted more. Mostly about the dragons. Definitely not about anything sad or complicated.

Heading down the stairs out of the plane, Taliya stuck to the middle of the group, keeping the L-twins between her and Kano in case they got daring. All of the vehicles and police waiting on the tarmac were off-putting, but it was the only way to travel with Aliania and Amrita. Something Taliya never thought she'd do.

For most of their lives, Taliya had managed to keep the girls hidden from the world on the compound or in their small-town community, but Natasha Kerkaw was too big a name to die without publicity. In the news coverage that followed, the girls' unique faces had been plastered throughout the media for weeks. Every detail spilled and discussed by talking heads around the world. There was no going back to anonymity.

When Ali suspected she was going to be left behind

for the visit—or that the trip might not happen at all because her parents refused to leave her again—she was blunt in her threats to find her own way to Australia. She was going to be there for Uncle Rey-Rey if she had to run away and fly commercial. The indomitable personality of their eldest kit was a bonus when recovering from trauma but made keeping her safe feel impossible.

As she got older, it was going to be problematic to keep Aliania locked down on the compound. Teaching her to navigate the human world would have to happen eventually. With all the promotion around the grand opening, Taliya couldn't imagine anyone attempting a kidnapping. They felt reasonably safe.

Amrita, on the other hand, had made it clear she wanted nothing to do with humans or their world, ever. If she never left the compound again, it was fine with her. Since the kidnapping, she'd stuck close to the house, rarely even venturing into the yard alone. Just the idea of a trip to the local market—previously one of her favorite things—brought on panicked panting. One of the dogs trailed her constantly, sensing the fear, and nightmares were frequent. Over the last few weeks, they'd engaged professional therapeutic help for the kit because that anxiety wasn't healthy, even if it made keeping her cloistered easier.

Amrita only agreed to the Australia trip when assured she never had to interact with anyone she didn't want to. Having the entire family there seemed to ease her fears. But as they stepped onto the tarmac, Taliya noticed the kit eyeing all of the human police officers and drivers, clutching her father's hand in a death grip.

The group loaded into the transports while humans in zoo uniforms gathered the rest of the luggage from the plane. Fourteen creatures in a foreign country for a week meant a lot of baggage—literally and figuratively. Then they were whisked off to the zoo to meet Rey before settling into the hotel where they'd stayed before, though Taliya suspected the rooms would be less impressive this time. It all seemed like a substantial expense for the zoo, but the new dragon show promised to bring in major revenue. Getting that promotion started with a bang was important.

Locals had anticipated their arrival, and the streets were lined with humans as they drove along. The L-twins were fascinated with how fascinated Australians were with their family. Sitting between their parents in the back of the transport, they struggled to see out the windows and giggled. Aliania and Amrita, in seats facing them, remained reserved and mostly stared at the floor. Taliya chuffed at them, and the girls met her eyes. Ali chuffed back and then stared at her hands in her lap, but the strawberry kit just sat wide-eyed, the scent of anxiety wafting from her.

"We'll be at the zoo and Rey's house soon," Taliya assured her. "People get very excited when I show up places. But the glass is tinted, so they can't see us."

She was about to suggest looking out the window at all the posters welcoming them, but one with ABOMINA-

TIONS WILL BURN IN HELL!!! stopped her short. There were always a few of those. Taliya felt a low rumble from Kano, so he must have seen it too.

"Remember," Taliya told the kits, "anyone of you who wants to stay back at Rey's house during the big grand opening can do that. If you don't like the crowds, you can watch the videos instead."

Amrita nodded, sniffled, and stared at the floor again, but the L-twins only bounced and giggled more.

"Dra-gons. Dra-gons. Dra-gons," Lilly chanted, immediately joined by Luna with a clap on each syllable. Kano added his deep voice, "Dra-gons. Dra-gons. Dra-gons!"

Taliya chuckled. For her family, the dragons were a thrilling novelty. For her, they were old friends. Rey had shown them pictures of the upgraded enclosures for the animals and the Dragoceum, but Taliya was excited to see it all in person. See Bunny again.

As the transports drew closer to the zoo, she spotted several billboards and banners announcing the grand opening of the Dragoceum. The animals had been on exhibit for a few months, but seeing them fly and perform was something new and exciting. Most of the advertisements included her headshot and the cover of her memoir: *Accidental Ambassador*. She'd be offering a book signing at the event—a celebrity to draw the crowds.

Once the convoy reached Australia Zoo property, most of the police escort stopped at the gates. Security was already tight, so only two remained with them. A team of six armed dingman waved them through the same back entrance they'd used for the wedding. Memories made Taliya's chest tighten. Kano reached over the twins and rubbed her neck. She patted his hand with a sigh.

I'm gonna have to control my emotions because that's not what Rey needs.

The panthran had gotten months to relive his time there with Carl, process the memories of their wedding, and begin to move forward. For Taliya, it all felt like yesterday. But she refused to drag the scent of grief into their reunion.

After weaving through roads behind the scenes of zoo exhibits, the transports pulled onto the campus where some human employees and most of the creatures working there lived. It was like a tiny village, with a grocery store, a medical building, a post office, two restaurants along with the main commissary, a library, a bank, a small schoolhouse, and dozens of modest bamboo homes. Rey had mentioned that he never needed to leave the zoo property if he didn't want to, and now she understood why. It was designed with that purpose.

Aliania gasped at two rooman talking near the road, who waved as the transports rolled past. Amrita waved back like she was in a trance. Again, seeing photos didn't do the creatures justice.

"Did you see their tails?" Luna whispered. Lilly nodded with pursed whiskers. "And their feet."

Reynaldo stepped out of his home as the vehicles came to a stop in front of it. He wore a khaki zoo uniform, sandals, and a huge grin.

Taliya hesitated in the transport while the others clambered out and greeted the panthran with hugs and fang-filled smiles. Her first thought was that he looked wonderful and healthy. His house was smaller than the others around, but maybe those held families or groups. Rey had requested to live alone. Feline hybrids were rare in Australia, and she worried that made him feel isolated. Her ears lay back at the idea that being with them again would stir up unhappy memories.

Kano glanced back at her still in the vehicle, and she realized her absence was about to become obvious. Rey was kneeling down and talking to the L-twins, but in a moment he would look for her. Shreya headed back toward the transport, maybe to see if something was wrong.

Something's definitely wrong. Carl isn't here. Rey's going to think about that when he sees me. Remember it's all my fault.

It took every ounce of will Taliya could muster to step out onto the lawn. Shreya met her and rested a hand on her back as they joined the group. Rey spotted them and grinned.

"Finally, another dragon wrangler!"

That made everyone laugh, and Taliya shook off the guilt and sadness threatening to ruin the day. Rey jogged forward and caught her up in an embrace, her breath hitching as he lifted her off the ground.

"So happy you're here," he whispered.

"Me too."

"I can't imagine doing this without you."

He set her down, and she sniffled back tears that were mostly happy but also not. Rey flared his whiskers.

"We are celebrating *victory* this week." He put his dark hands on either side of Taliya's face. "We rescued the dragons. We rescued the kits. Now we celebrate. Show the world we *won*."

He rested his forehead against hers, and Taliya struggled not to say, *But at what cost?* Leaning back again, their golden eyes met. She took his hands in hers. "Celebrating the victories," she agreed.

A perky blonde female approached from the street. It was easy to imagine the woman in a peppy cheerleading uniform. She put on a good face, but reeked of anxiety. The group of feline-predator creatures on the lawn was logically daunting for someone half their size. Her eyes went wide at the sight of all eight feet tall, five hundred pounds of Samson, and Reynaldo chuckled.

"Friends," the panthran said, "this is Wendy, our village coordinator."

Wendy gave a little wave and did her best to smile. "Welcome to Irwinville. We're all thrilled you can be here for the grand opening."

Taliya considered offering a handshake, but she didn't want to frighten the tiny thing any further. "We're thrilled to be here," she said instead, returning a smile but keeping her teeth hidden.

"Lunch is ready for you at the commissary," Wendy said, looking down at the kits. Maybe they were less threatening. "You probably want some tucker after the long flight."

The L-twins gawked at her like they'd never seen a human in real life, which wasn't far from true.

"Thanks," Rey said. "We'll be there shortly."

Wendy gave a nod and scooted over to the transport drivers, probably offering them a meal while they waited to take the group to the hotel.

Aliania huffed. "Poor thing. I think we scared her."

"She's not much bigger than me," Jai said.

Bena whuffed through her nose. "I have yet to meet a human I could not snap in two like a twig."

Everyone stared at her for a second, and Rey snorted a laugh.

"You should keep that thought to yourself," Taliya said. "Even if it's true."

"Let's see your house," Marla said, slipping her arm through Rey's.

They led the way up the steps to the front porch. Samson whispered something to Bena about not reminding humans how vulnerable they are. It upsets them. She apologized. One of many "civilized" things Bena needed to learn. At least she'd agreed to wear clothes on the trip. Taliya suspected the wild tigran only did that when absolutely required.

Rey gave them a quick tour of the bamboo house. One bedroom with a single creature-sized bed, a small kitchen, and a main room with some seating and a media wall. All the basics, but nothing else. No photos in frames. No homey touches. The folded flag from Carl's military funeral was displayed in a glass-front triangle-shaped case on the dresser in the bedroom. Taliya wondered if he'd like a framed photo of their wedding to sit next to it, or if that would be upsetting.

"I don't use the kitchen much," Rey admitted. "Meals are provided at the commissary three times a day for all employees. That's easier."

The L-twins sprawled out on the blue sofa, giggling, and Shreya reminded them to behave.

Rey looked down at the twins with a gaze that seemed filled with longing and sent a wave of remorse through Taliya.

How will a family ever work for him now? Can a single male creature adopt? There were always orphans or kits needing homes, but she had no idea how any of it worked.

"Didn't that girl mention lunch?" Tuscan said.

Rey looked up and blinked, then smiled. "Yeah, why don't we head that way. Then I'll take you to the dragons."

Mention of the animals made Luna, Lilly, and Jai cheer. Samson led the group out. Taliya noticed they'd drawn attention from the neighbors, but it all felt friendly. They were expected guests. As they walked to lunch, several villagers—rooman and dingman—waved or called out a greeting. It was an interesting community, with only a few humans here and there. The atmosphere reminded Taliya of the refugee camp, but without the uneasiness of an unknown future.

In the commissary, a buffet had been set up for them,

though it was clearly between normal mealtimes because no one else was there. Plates of individual meat pies, barbequed chicken, roasted lamb with vegetables, a white fish in sauce that smelled wonderful, and a pavlova for dessert were served up.

Taliya found herself sitting at the opposite end of the long table from Reynaldo, who was flanked by Amrita and Aliania. Observing him, she was grateful to see joy and lightness as he chatted with the girls. Eventually, he spotted her watching, paused, and slow-blinked. She responded in kind and tried not to stare anymore. Her attention shifted to the L-twins, who were devouring everything put in front of them like they'd never seen food before. Taliya hoped that wasn't a comment on her own cooking.

"Did you know that, Mama?"

Taliya turned to Amrita. "Know what?"

The strawberry kit sighed, like mothers were so exasperating. "About Nimmy and the panthran joining the dragon program."

Taliya looked to Reynaldo, who smiled and winked.

"We've kept that part secret from the public," he said, "to protect their travels. And as a nice surprise for you."

Nimmy, another of the original dragon wranglers, being asked to help was something she'd suggested, but Taliya had never considered where the panthran from Rey's group had ended up. Or that they might come to Australia. "That's wonderful!"

"Nimmy was living at the refugee camp," Rey said.

"She packed up her family, and they're all coming here, along with five panthran from the facility where I was born. Caring for the animals is a huge job, and we need the extra help."

Taliya whuffed. "Nimmy has *a family*?"

"A mate and three kits."

Taliya let the news settle into her tired brain. Logically, Nimmy had a family now, years after their refugee days. Panthran coming too was incredible. "When will they arrive?"

"Sometime tonight," Rey said. "Their flight was delayed by a big hurricane in the Pacific."

Parth nodded. "We flew far off normal course to avoid it."

"Will they be at the hotel too?" Shreya asked.

"No," Rey said, "they already have homes waiting here in the village."

A voice echoed in the mostly empty commissary. "Why're ya wastin' time chowin' down?"

"Jaxon!" Kano jumped up to greet the rooman who'd been their guide during the last zoo visit. They embraced with some back slapping, then Jaxon hop/walked to the table. Kano introduced him, and everyone waved or said hello. The kits all gawked without shame, like only the young can get away with. Shreya took this as a signal to end the meal, stood up, and began gathering plates.

"No need for that," Jaxon said. "Crew'll clear up. You lot have an appointment to visit the *draaagons*." He dragged out the last word with a gleam in his eye at the L-twins. They giggled and nodded vehemently. "Well, let's get to it."

The group grabbed last bites and left the table.

Jai raced over to the rooman and stared at Jaxon's middle. "Do you have a pouch?"

Taliya gasped and put a hand on his head. "Sorry."

"No worries." Jaxon bent over to be eye level with Jai. "Boy roos don't ever have pouches. Just the mamas."

"Remember I told you about Quinn and her little Mia?" Taliya said. "From when we rescued the dragons?"

Jai nodded and started to respond, but before he could ask something else a bit too personal, Taliya said, "Let's head to the zoo."

"And get fairy floss," Jai said with a determined flick of his tail.

Jaxon laughed. "Sounds good, my man. Fairy floss for everyone."

24

Outside the commissary, a zoo tram was waiting for them. Taliya wasn't sure exactly where they were on the property, but she was glad they didn't have to walk. All the prep and the long flight were catching up with her. Plus, the open-air tram would be a great way to enjoy the sights.

She fell into step next to Aliania at the end of the line. The girl had kept to herself over the last few months. Not as outwardly filled with rage now, but silent and with-drawn. So far, the trip—which she'd demanded to go on—had been no different. Was she upset about Samson and Bena? Feeling guilty about Carl? It was challenging to keep up with her moods. At eight, Ali was comparable to a teenage human. Taliya had gotten used to the fact this daughter was now as tall as her, but the rest was hard to negotiate.

"You've been awfully quiet," Taliya said tentatively, worried she'd set off an explosion.

Ali looked around and inhaled deeply. "I love it here. Just the smells. All the other creatures. Love it."

That wasn't the answer she'd expected at all. "You do?"

"This village. All the creatures together, with a buffer from the human world. It feels safe. I can totally imagine living here."

Panic fluttered in Taliya's chest, but she breathed through it. The time was coming when Aliania would need to plan for her future. To leave the "nest" of their lair. But across the ocean was not what she had in mind for her eldest.

The group loaded in the tram, and Jaxon hopped up next to the human driver. "Once 'round the park, Jeeves!"

The driver gave a smile and a nod. "Everyone stay seated and keep your bits in the vehicle. Here we go."

The tram elevated, hovering a few inches off the ground, then glided forward along the recycled plastic road through the village. There were more houses, with rooman of all ages outside, and a security building with several dingman sitting on a bench out front. Three of them were female dingman, the first Taliya had seen. They were smaller and daintier than the males but otherwise the same. All of the dingman sat nearly on top of each other, like a pile of puppies, and one was scratching behind his tall ear. Their canine DNA hovered very near the surface.

Then the tram whooshed through private gates into the zoo itself. There would be time for a full tour later, but the tram buzzed them by several exhibits. The kits were wide-eyed at giraffes and hippos and all the animals they'd never seen in real life before. Ali didn't even attempt to play it teen-cool but gushed *ooos* and *aaahs* and snapped photos with her com. After about thirty minutes, the tram stopped at a fairy floss stand.

"Jai, what color for you?" Jaxon asked, hopping out of the tram.

"Orange," Jai called out.

The L-twins shouted that they wanted blue. Ali and Amrita didn't make a request, but Jaxon brought them pink balls of fluff anyhow. Marla grabbed a taste of the pink and puckered her cheeks at the sweetness. Samson and Bena accepted samples of the orange from Jai, but both looked horrified at the taste. Taliya wondered if Bena had ever had candy or straight sugar like that. Most creatures didn't have a liking for it. The L-twins played with theirs more than they ate it, ending up with blue goo in their orange fur.

It was hard to tell how Jai really felt about the fairy floss. He'd made such a fuss over wanting some but seemed disappointed. And unwilling to admit it or let it show, eating the whole thing quickly and resolutely. Taliya hoped it didn't make him sick.

Jaxon passed out wet wipes for the sticky fur and hands, then gathered up the leftovers and trash before climbing back in. "Next stop, the pterodragon exhibit."

That announcement was met with cheers, and the tram whooshed along again.

Taliya smelled the animals before she saw them. That musty scent from their feathers. Her heart raced. Kano, sitting behind her, rested a hand on her shoulder. More than anyone, he knew how much Bunny meant to her.

The tram pulled up in front of the enclosure where the dragons had been first released. Bunny and Polly were settled in the grass, dozing. Between them, two smaller pterodragons—miniature replicas of their mothers—were preening but then stopped to inspect the strange visitors.

Taliya's heart felt like it was going to beat right out of her chest. She knew about the chicks hatching. Rey had shown her images. Most of their conversations over the last few months involved the dragons. But seeing them for herself . . . It was exhilarating.

The tram lowered. "Okay," the driver said. "Safe to disembark and check out the main attraction."

"Wow," Aliania said. "I forgot how big they are."

Kano chuckled. "You were just a tiny kit last time you saw them."

Samson and Bena moved to the edge of the fencing, and the others joined them.

"You flew on one of those?" Bena asked Samson.

He nodded with a wistful smile. "Just once. It was amazing."

Taliya hung back, taking a moment for herself. The dragons looked content and well cared-for, but she'd expected nothing less.

Bunny lifted her head and scented the air. "KAAAH!" Wings spread, she rose and stomped in place, much to the delight of her rapt audience. That woke Polly, but she stayed in place and simply glanced around to see what the fuss was about.

Bunny hop/walked in her bird-like way to the edge of the enclosure. Looking over the heads of everyone else, she squawked, "Taah-yaa!! Kaaah! Kaaah! Taah-yaa!"

Tears burst into Taliya's eyes as the group turned toward her in shock.

"Well," Rey said, "that answers one question."

"Mama, she said *your name*." Amrita glanced back and forth between Bunny and Taliya.

The L-twins chanted and clapped their little hands. "Taah-yaa! Taah-yaa! Taah-yaa!"

"Hi, Bun-Bun." Taliya nodded and sniffled.

The dragon flapped and stirred up the dust around her. "Taah-yaa! Taah-yaa!"

Taliya jogged forward, climbed over the safety barrier, and moved around to the side of the Plexiglass, putting her hands flat on the netting of the exhibit. Bunny lowered her head and pressed her beak into them.

"Taah-yaaaaaa," she rumbled deep in her chest, followed by a string of cooing sounds.

Taliya looked back at the group. "Guess she's not mad about all that stealing her egg and stuffing her in a cage stuff."

Rey joined her over the barrier but motioned for the kits to stay put when they tried to join him. "During the rescue, we were shocked when Bunny seemed to be saying Taliya's name," he said to the group. "Pegasus sometimes makes a noise that sounds like my name, but it's hard to be sure."

"She's obviously saying 'Taliya'," Marla said. "No doubt."

"And that answers my concern about having you ride her," Rey said, turning to his fellow dragon wrangler.

Taliya's tail thrashed. "Ride her? When?"

"The zoo mucky-mucks really want you to fly her during the grand opening exhibition." Rey grinned. "One more thing to draw the crowds."

"Like a black panthran isn't interesting enough?"

"The more, the merrier."

Taliya glanced at Kano, who tipped his head with a knowing smirk. "Why not?" she said, chuckling. The attention might even sell a few more of her books. Not like sales were a big problem. Humans were obsessed with her.

Bunny raised her head and *kaahed* at the chicks. They *kaahed* in response with odd little voices that made everyone laugh.

"Which is which?" Jai asked.

Rey considered for a moment. "The one on the right is Pearl. And the other is Constance."

"Constance is an odd name for an animal," Parth said, looking back at the dragonets.

Rey shrugged. "Naming them was a fundraiser. Highest two donations got to pick. Constance is the formal name of Connie, the woman who runs the zoo, like her family has for hundreds of years."

"We met her," Kano said, "after the rescue. It's an excellent choice."

"I'm sure Robbie agrees," Taliya said. "I'm surprised we haven't seen him yet."

Rey glanced down the path, like Robbie might suddenly appear. "I'm sure he's whizzing around on his minibike somewhere. Probably fussing with details for the event. We have a rehearsal at six, once the zoo closes."

Jai piped up, hands on his hips. "Where are the other two dragons? The big boys."

"They live in a separate exhibit for now." Rey looked to Taliya and pursed his whiskers, like she should explain.

"The zoo isn't ready for dozens of little pterodragons," she said, moving over to where Jai stood on the correct side of the safety barrier. "If you keep the mamas and papas together, that means more baby dragons."

Ali rolled her eyes, and Amrita giggled, flaring her whiskers. "Oo-ooo."

Jai huffed. "Lots of baby dragons sounds like a good idea to me."

"We'll get there," Rey said. "And be able to send them to other zoos."

Taliya pondered the idea of the dragons becoming just one more captive animal in the world. Assuming the kidnappers hadn't been actively breeding them and selling the offspring. Maybe there were already dozens of pterodragons out there somewhere. Their future, as a species, would be interesting to watch unfold from the sidelines.

Bunny settled back down in her well-worn spot, but she kept her green eyes on Taliya. Polly and the dragonets had lost interest in the visitors and were preening each other. Being gawked at was a routine part of their day.

Rey motioned toward where zoo guests were being kept back by staff members to allow their group private time with the dragons. Jaxon chatted with them energetically, probably about being sure to come later in the week for the Dragoceum opening.

"Let's move on," Rey said, "so the traffic flow can come through. Lots of interest with the celebrations tomorrow. You'll get your fill of dragons before you head home."

Marla chuckled. "I'm sure our crew is catching some interest as well."

"But of course," Rey said with a grin.

Taliya climbed back over the safety barrier, hoping she hadn't given any humans ideas about doing that too. There were dozens of security cameras, just in case.

The tram carried them around to where the two male dragons, Coconut and Pegasus, were on exhibit. They lounged on rocks, looking majestic and content, but neither did more than open an eye and sniff the air at the tram's occupants. If they remembered Kano and Taliya from the night of the rescue, they didn't react.

As the group stood along the fencing, Marla slipped up beside Taliya and leaned her head on her friend's shoulder.

"Imagine," Marla said. "What if I hadn't come racing back to the house that day to drag you off to see the crazy new arrivals that looked like dragons?"

"Little did you know how wrapped up in them I'd become."

"You could have had a calmer life, relatively speaking." Marla lifted her head and looked over at the family. "We certainly wouldn't be here now. Be a part of any of this."

Sunlight caught the glints of gold in her friend's eyes. That first telltale sign revealing Marla wasn't as human as she looked. "If my parents hadn't sent me into hiding with you, imagine that."

"That's a whole lifetime ago." Marla spread out her hands, inspecting her cropped fingers. "But the Gathering would have come for me anyhow. It was all a little less traumatic, having a friend and your family to recover with."

Taliya wrapped an arm around Marla's shoulder. "You are part of our family *forever*."

Rey joined them as he checked a schedule on his com. "Let's get you all to the hotel so you can settle in and have a rest."

The L-twins looked sleepy, already being carried by Kano and Samson. Taliya attempted the time-difference math to determine if they needed a nap or more. "I'm not sure, but I think it's way past our normal bedtime, though we did nap on the plane."

"Not everyone has to come back tonight," Reynaldo said, "but you'll need to join us for a rehearsal." His eyes met hers, and she sensed there was a plea there for something more.

"You want me here to practice at six," Taliya confirmed. "But maybe for dinner too?"

"That'd be nice." Rey smiled, gave a nod, then left to herd the group back onto the tram. "Who wants to check out the hotel and smell the sea?" he called out.

Even the adults seemed happy to move that direction. But Aliania hung back and stared at the dragons. Taliya recognized a familiar longing there, one she could understand better than anyone.

"You should bring her with you tonight," Marla suggested, ever the attentive aunty. "Something about her is sparking, being here."

Taliya nodded and sighed. *It most definitely is.*

<hr>

TALIYA AND ALIANIA GRABBED QUICK POWER NAPS BEFORE THEY left everyone else sound asleep at the hotel to return to the zoo for dinner with Rey and rehearsal for the grand opening exhibition.

A small transport from the zoo—escorted by three police vehicles—dropped them at Rey's house. He'd picked up dinner from the commissary so they could visit in private. Sitting at the small table in his kitchen, the three creatures chatted about the dragons and caring for them.

"The plan," Rey said, spearing a hunk of rare steak with his fork, "was for us to put them through their paces and then have me ride Pegasus to show off. Now, you can ride Bunny too." He chewed for a moment. "I'd hoped to have all four set with riders, but Faria and Karma aren't interested in coming to Australia."

Taliya nodded, and a thought popped out before she really considered it. "What if Ali rides Bunny instead?"

Aliania dropped her fork with a clatter and stared at her mother. "Me?"

It should have been a shocking idea, but calm surety settled in Taliya's heart. The whole scenario unfolded in her mind. "Nimmy will be here. I expect Pegasus will let her ride."

"Okay." Rey nodded but looked concerned.

"You're planning maneuvers the dragons know. They won't require much guidance."

Reynaldo and Aliania looked at each other and then back at Taliya. She could hear the kit's heart racing.

"Coconut should be agreeable to me riding him again," Taliya continued. "You can ride Polly, and Ali can ride Bunny."

Aliania picked her fork up, looked like she was going to comment, then stabbed a piece of chicken and chewed instead. She was always hard to read, but Taliya could smell the excitement wafting from her, regardless of the neutral expression on the girl's face.

Rey tipped his head thoughtfully. "If you're sure, we can try it tonight. All four drags in the air with creatures riding would certainly make for a great show."

"I won't fall off." Ali set her fork down and lowered her hands to her lap, blue eyes flashing and crossing a bit. "I've heard enough about Bunny over the years to know she won't give me trouble. You teach me what to do. I can do it."

The tip of Taliya's tail flicked as she absorbed what she'd put into motion, but it felt right. If Ali was intrigued by this world, let her be a part of it, at least for a while.

"I've been practicing on all of them," Rey said. "Drills we did hundreds of times in camp. You'll catch on quickly."

Rey's communicator beeped, and he smiled at the message. "Nimmy's here and getting her family settled at the house. She'll meet us at the Dragoceum in thirty minutes." He looked at Ali. "Then we'll give the plan a try."

The girl all but vibrated with anticipation, tail whipping and whiskers flared. She gobbled up the rest of her dinner, and Taliya laughed, reminding her eldest that choking would put a damper on her chance to ride Bunny. That increased the chewing a little.

Rey didn't mention the other panthran, who should have been on the same flight as Nimmy and her family.

Maybe that was something little Wendy was handling. But it lessened Taliya's hope there were true friends Rey was excited to see in that group.

⸻ ❖ ⸻

THE DRAGOCEUM WAS IN A NEWER PART OF THE ZOO, NEXT TO the dragons' enclosures. Taliya had seen videos of the show arena, but the immensity of it in person was overwhelming—four times the size of the Crocoseum, where she'd performed and fed the reptiles. Raised seating formed an oval around a center section, like a sporting stadium with a retractable roof. It was astounding that all of this had been built in a few months. Kano was going to be mightily impressed. As he often said of work projects, "Where there's pots of money and a will, there's a way."

"The overall setup is the same as the Crocoseum," Rey said as they walked through the building and gawked. "But we needed a roof, just in case. Crocs can't fly."

"Thank the gods for that," Taliya said with a laugh, though her skin tingled with a distinct memory of how high they could jump. "It's twice as big as what we had back at the refugee camp."

Rey nodded proudly at the facility. "We used that size as a model."

The scents of the place—concrete and metal and the underlying mustiness of dragon feathers—stirred up happy memories. There was a slight echo with the ten thousand seats empty, but she could imagine it filled with guests, some kind of hologram show or appearances from other animals warming up the audience for the dragons' display. She glanced from the surroundings to the flooring that smelled more like recycled plastic than the cushioning protection they'd used in the dragon building at camp.

"No mulch on the ground," Rey said, noticing her focus, "because it made too much dust, but the surface is like an acrobatic floor, in case of falls."

Ali hopped and bounced into the air like she was on a trampoline, higher each time. "This. Is. Amazing!"

"And much more practical," Taliya said. "I went home every day covered in that dust."

"I remember the smell of it," Ali said, pouncing into the air with a giggle, rocking the floor under them.

Rey jumped a few times himself then smiled at Taliya, trying to keep her balance as the ground shifted under her. "The zoo is really committed to having the dragons and their offspring long-term," he said. "A show like this will bring in the extra funds to feed and care for them."

"And those new enclosures, getting ready for the dragonets," Ali said, lightly stepping on the flooring to test it. "You can tell they have plans for the future."

Taliya slow-blinked at her daughter, wondering if those plans would include the pure-white kit. What would Kano think of that possibility? *I should have asked him about letting her ride Bunny.* If he was upset, it would be at his wife, not Ali. But she suspected he wouldn't be. Or about having her perform in the show. Struggling to hide Aliania wasn't the solution to her safety. Her existence wasn't a secret anymore. Out in the world—as a public figure—might well make her more secure.

Rey led Taliya and Ali down a tunnel that ran backstage and through an Employees Only door. Massive cages and a long, gray concrete hallway connected to the backs of the dragon exhibits. Rey blew a whistle, and *kaahs* from outside echoed around them.

"That's their signal to come in for the night." Rey headed toward the first cage as Bunny hopped in from her exhibit.

"Taah-yaa!" she greeted them, head bobbing and wings spread.

"Hello again, Bun-Bun."

The dragon came right over to the bars, which were designed far enough apart for feet and beaks to stick through. Probably for medical checks. Taliya reached in, scratching Bunny's favorite spot behind her ears, and the animal clucked happily.

"Do you remember Ali?" Taliya said, taking her daughter's hand and pulling her close. "A-li?"

Bunny shifted her gaze from Taliya to Aliania, giving the girl several long sniffs, then resting her beak against Ali's chest. "Ya-yi," Bunny mumbled into the fur.

Ali rubbed behind Bunny's ears and cooed to her, earning a rumble of appreciation from the dragon. Rey silently pumped both fists in the air at the easy acceptance. A flush of happiness and jealousy filled Taliya, making her hackles rise. She shook it off. This was an outcome to be thrilled by, and anything else was just nonsense.

"She's a natural," Rey called back as he jogged down the hallway to greet the other dragons, who were obediently returning to their night cages. "Give her dinner, Ali, and you'll seal the deal."

Aliania grabbed the waiting bucket of nuts and berries, opened the hatch next to the trough, and poured it in. "Chow time, Bunny-Bun." The dragon squawked and went right for it. "Good girl. Get all fueled up before we fly."

Taliya chuckled. "I thought you'd be more nervous."

"I don't remember a lot about the camp," Ali said, watching Bunny eat, "but I remember flying. It's vivid, with smells and all, like it happened yesterday." She smiled at her mother. "Not scared at all."

"Taliya," Rey called, "come feed Coconut and see how he reacts."

Leaving Ali with Bunny, Taliya grabbed another bucket. Coconut watched her cautiously until the food was poured into his trough. While he ate, she reminded him about escaping over the Outback together. "Think we can do some flying again tonight?"

Coconut didn't answer, but she hadn't expected him to.

Suddenly, Pegasus spread his wings. "Kaaah! Kaaah! Kaaah!" Sticking his beak through the bars, he called out and sniffed loudly.

"There's my boy." Nimmy came into sight from the other end of the tunnel.

Any question that Pegasus would remember his former dragon wrangler was answered by excited screams as he flapped and leaped around. When Nimmy reached his cage, he stuck every body part through he could. The tigran rubbed his face.

"Who's a good boy?" she chortled. "Pegasus is my good boy."

Taliya thought it sounded more like she was talking to a dog than a dragon, but each of them had their own bond with the animals. Nimmy looked over at the three of them and smiled. "Guess he'll be okay with me riding him again."

"I should say so." Taliya headed her way, and the two shared a quick embrace. They hadn't been in touch since Taliya and Kano left the camp. It definitely spiked some odd feelings, seeing Nimmy again. She sensed the same from the other tigran.

"I hope you had a good flight," Rey said, approaching and shaking hands with Nimmy. "Everything at the house as it should be?"

"All good," Nimmy said. "Ready to do what we need here tonight while the family unpacks a bit. And probably falls asleep. I'll get to that later."

Taliya and Rey nodded their understanding. Sleep was good, but dragons were better.

"We're planning to ride all four of them tonight," Rey said.

"All four?" Nimmy glanced past them at Aliania, who still stood with Bunny. "Hello, there. I remember you. But you were just a kit back then." She lowered her voice. "I heard about her and the others on the news."

"It was hard to avoid," Taliya said. Then quickly changed the subject. "Ali's going to ride Bunny."

Nimmy's eyes went wide, but she shrugged. "Alrighty, then."

Three human zoo employees entered the vast hallway.

"Looks like it's time." Rey motioned for the three to join them. "We have help getting the drags ready, so let's see how practice goes."

Rey filled Nimmy in on the new plan while the keepers helped get all four animals in their riggings. The cages were for keeping the dragons secure rather than any needed protection for the staff, like a wild animal would require. Aliania listened attentively and worked with Bunny while Taliya took the opportunity to reunite with Coconut, who seemed content to have her in his space. The two dragonets watched from their separate cage, peeking their heads through the bars and making little *kaahs*, clicks, and chirps now and then. It would be a while before they could join the fun.

Once the dragons were prepped, Rey led the way through the tunnel and back out into the Dragoceum. The animals spread their wings, flapped a bit, and bounced on the elastic flooring, probably excited. Rey motioned for everyone to stand back before shouting, "Go!"

All four dragons said "Go!" in response and, with a running start, took to the air.

"Wow!" Aliania spun and grinned as they swooped and dove and played above her. "Just like I remember."

"Go! Go! Go!" Nimmy called, jumping on the flooring so she bounced high.

Taliya laughed at the pure joy around her. After a few minutes, Rey called the animals back to the ground, where they pranced and preened their wings.

"I've worked with them on some flight patterns to put on a show." Rey explained the basics of how it would work, and it sounded like what they used to do back at camp. Easy, but impressive for the crowd below.

"Are you sure about riding?" Taliya asked Ali. "It's okay if the reality of it is too much. You understand what you'd need to do?"

Aliania looked like she might explode. Her nose flushed red, and she struggled to keep her eyes from crossing. "I'm positive!"

Rey blew his whistle three times. Immediately, the dragons calmed down and lined up in front of them.

"That's new," Taliya said with a chuckle.

Rey beamed up at the foursome. "They are so smart. I can't wait to get past this event and really see what they can learn." He turned to the group. "Are we ready?"

Getting a thumbs-up from the keepers and agreement from the tigran, Rey headed for Polly. The rigging had a mesh ladder to reach the saddle. Taliya waited until Ali was mostly to the top before climbing aboard Coconut.

The dragons fussed as they got used to the riders and the ladder bits were tucked in, but Taliya noticed Bunny seemed calm. Aliania looked comfortable in the saddle—a massive grin all but splitting her face in two. Nevertheless, her mother still worried.

"Mama," Ali said, looking over at her from atop Bunny, "you're going to make them nervous. Remember, they can sense your feelings."

Taliya nodded, took a deep breath, and blew it out, humored by the lecture but knowing it was correct.

Rey urged Polly out from the line and turned to face them. "Pegasus is used to leading."

"Of course he is. My man," Nimmy said with pride in the alpha dragon as she patted his flank. Pegasus flared his neck feathers and made a noise that sounded like human laughter.

"You remember the routine?"

Nimmy shifted in the saddle and took a tight hold on the riggings. "Absolutely."

"All right, then. Call it." Rey secured his own grip.

Taliya wrapped the straps around her wrists and watched Ali do the same. "Bunny knows what to do. Just hang on."

Ali nodded and giggled, like she might cry with happiness.

"Go!" Nimmy shouted, giving Pegasus a signal with her legs as well.

"Go!" Pegasus called back and ran for a take-off.

Each of them followed in turn, Rey and Polly next, then Coconut, with Bunny bringing up the rear.

That first thrill of hitting the sky still took Taliya's breath away. Coming around a turn, she glanced back at Ali, safe in the saddle—laughing, not a bit scared. Pegasus began flying the pattern, and the other dragons followed. Coconut barely needed guidance. They rose and dove and wove together around the Dragoceum. Bunny glided past her, and Taliya heard Ali hooting.

When that set was done, Rey motioned to continue in a crisscross pattern around the arena. "That went fantastic!" he called out.

Taliya wasn't sure yet what the whole program looked like for the grand opening, but she was glad to be able to do her part. To support the dragons at the zoo. To support Rey.

"I'm never leaving!" Aliania stretched her arms to the sides as she swooped past.

Taliya wanted to tell her to be careful, to hang on, but Bunny flew calmly. Instead, she focused on appreciating the moment—the familiar smell of the dragons and the sounds of excited riders coming and going as they swooped around each other in the air.

On Ali's next pass, Taliya inhaled deeply, opening her mouth to take it all in. The scent of her daughter was different than it had been for months. Like she was a tiny kit again, without a care in the world.

Aliania was happy. That felt like a miracle.

Reynaldo whooshed by, and Taliya caught the same scent from him.

Rey was happy. Another miracle to celebrate. Her friend had found a new home, work he loved, and a safe life.

Contentment flowed through her, tingling in her whiskers with a sense of peace she'd feared would never occur again.

Taliya patted Coconut's shoulder, stretched out her arms, closed her eyes, and soared.

EPILOGUE
FIVE YEARS LATER, AUGUST 2183

Aliania adjusted the tunic of her khaki uniform, leaned forward in the riggings to give Bunny's shoulder a pat, then sat back and scanned the line of year-old hatchlings—all alertly waiting for direction. She chirped in imitation of dragon-speak for *get ready*. The dragonets responded with their own chirps, telling her they were ready and waiting.

"Run the routine," Reynaldo called from the middle row of the Dragoceum, where he was observing the training with his husband, Mateo, and five of their motley gang of offspring adopted over the last four years.

Mateo rolled up the sleeves of his uniform, revealing black jaguar rosettes on his tawny fur, and picked up the youngest kit, a tigran. "Pay attention to Auntie Ali. This is her last practice before the whole family arrives to judge her."

Aliania glared at him, then rolled her eyes. "No pressure or anything."

With a full-throated laugh, Mateo bounced the kit and sing-songed, "Auntie Ali is nerrr-vous."

Ali flicked an ear at them, jingling the new triple-pierce of small golden hoops that her mama was definitely going to have opinions about.

"You've got this," Rey said, wrapping his arm around the waist of an older dingman cub who was almost as tall as him now. "Just run through the routine one more time."

Ali knew the seven dragonets were prepared. She'd spent her whole summer vacation—which was winter there—at Australia Zoo training them. Her chest ached at the reminder that her family would arrive in the morning to celebrate her success . . . and escort her back to Arkansas. At thirteen, she couldn't move to the zoo on her own just yet.

But it was only a matter of time. Maybe two years. Her parents still needed convincing. This performance would be a chance to prove herself. Prove that Australia Zoo was where she belonged.

Inhaling and letting out a whoosh of breath, she focused her gaze on the dragonets and squeezed her legs to get Bunny's attention.

"Kaah! Kaah! Kaah!" the dragon called out, lifting her head so it echoed around them.

The dragonets returned the call in their higher-pitched voices, making Aliania smile.

"Go!" she shouted and pointed toward the ceiling of the Dragoceum.

The panthran and their kits cheered as the sky filled with the beating wings of the newest generation of brilliantly white pterodragons.

All under Aliania's command.

AUTHOR NOTES

Once again, piles of gratitude go out to my critique group, Ozark Mountain Guild (OMG), for offering suggestions and guidance on this novel. Over the four years it came and went from my active writing pile, they saw every page, and the story is richer and better for it. Thank you also to my early readers: Shannon Iwanski and Jennifer McMurrain. Sorry I made you ugly cry before bed, Jennifer (but not really!). And special gratitude to Helen Thornton-Gussy at editCo for providing an "authenticity" read and avoiding cringe in the Aussie sections. I'm so grateful you chatted with me at WriterCon as a fellow editor. Once I heard that accent, I knew you could help.

A few notes on this story.

It felt right to add some animals to Taliya's homestead, but they would have to be useful ones. Cats for keeping down the rodent population. Bee hives are mentioned in the novellas, and I assume they are still doing their thing. Chickens for eating and providing eggs. And dogs for part of the protective detail. Of course, it would need to be a specific breed for that job and carefully named. Cairo is the Belgian Malinois who was part of the

SEAL team that got Osama bin Laden in 2011, and Elektra of *Daredevil* fame just seemed cool.

Jovita Idar is inspiration for the name of Jovita the puman. She was an American journalist, as well as a political and civil rights worker who championed the cause of Mexican American immigrants. I imagine creatures sometimes select names for their offspring from inspiring humans, or the scientists creating them do it, so I loved that tie to South America, where Jovita the puman's human DNA would originate.

Severo and Jacy's names were selected from the history of the Ute/Nuche Indians. It seemed logical that the uncivilized tigran who traded with the Ute Nation would adopt names from that source and people they met over the years. Severo was a chief of the Capote band of the Utes and traveled to Washington at one point to negotiate a treaty. By the 1890s, he held a position as a tribal policeman. A monument at Ute Park in Ignacio, Colorado, includes a bronze plaque honoring Chief Severo for his contributions to the tribe. The name Jacy in Native American tradition means "moon" and represents gentleness, wisdom, and guardianship. You can read more about that Nuche Clan of wild tigran and Taliya's adventures with them in *The Tigran Novellas: 2176*.

Selecting Thurgood for Carl's middle name is along the same lines, after Thurgood Marshall, an Associate Justice of the Supreme Court of the United States. A callout to his family celebrating their Black heritage and a civil rights icon. But Taliya imagining Carl as a lion with a dark-black mane has nothing to do with his heritage. In the world of lions, the darker the mane, the more macho the lion. Yes, Scar should be a leader instead of Mufasa. So Taliya is imagining Carl as the machoest of studly lions in his next life.

Sorry I had to kill Carl. And Grampa Jai. In science fiction, as in real life, victory rarely comes without sacrifice.

The idea for including the Indigenous Women of the Great Barrier Reef came from an article in *People* magazine (December 19, 2022), which included all the Earthshot winners—a contest run by William, His Royal Highness, the Prince of Wales. It said this group was planning to expand their network of female rangers, tasked with protecting the Queensland reef. I could only imagine what that would look like in 150 years.

And yes, Robbie Powell is supposed to be a direct descendant of Bindi Irwin, whose husband is Chandler Powell, and named after Robert Irwin. If you've never seen videos of the Crocoseum at Australia Zoo, YouTube and other places are full of them. It's fascinating. And yes, crocs can genuinely jump out of the water to the tips of their tails. It's actually considered "vertical swimming" because they use their tails to elevate. It defies gravity and is quite terrifying. Here's a link to the Crocoseum information from the zoo itself: https://australiazoo.com.au/expe riences/habitats/the-world-famous-crocoseum/

And finally, if you are not familiar with the musical *Carousel* and the song I reference, here's one clip you can watch. https://youtu.be/1izigJX1pxI I imagine it had meaning to the creatures in the refugee camp but took on a whole new importance to Rey as he mourned his husband.

I hope you enjoyed this next chapter in the tigran saga. And have read the novellas that take place in the three years between the end of the first book and the epilogue. I have notes for the next story in the series but no plans for how that might unfold. If you're a fan of the Tigran Chronicles, tell your friends and post reviews. That's the perfect encouragement to get an author moving forward on the next installment. Thank you for reading!

AT THE CORNER
—OF—
Magnetic
and Main
Meg Welch Dendler
#1 BEST-SELLING, AWARD-WINNING AUTHOR

ABOUT THE AUTHOR

Meg Welch Dendler has considered herself a writer since she won a picture book contest in fifth grade and entertained her classmates with ongoing sequels for the rest of the year. Beginning serious work as a freelancer in the 1990s while teaching elementary and middle school, Meg has more than one hundred articles in print, including interviews with Kirk Douglas, Sylvester Stallone, and Dwayne "The Rock" Johnson. She has won contests with her short stories and poetry, along with multiple awards for her best-selling "Cats in the Mirror" alien rescue cat children's book series. *Bianca: The Brave Frail and Delicate Princess* was named Best Juvenile Book of 2018 by the Oklahoma Writers' Federation, and *Snickerdoodle's Shenanigans* earned the same honor in 2024.

Visit her at www.megdendler.com for more information about upcoming books and events and all of Meg's social media links.